MW01413892

LIVELY STONES

The Evolution of the Congregational Church of Boothbay Harbor, Maine, from Its Origins in 1766 to 2016

written by
JOHN F. BAUMAN, ROBERT W. DENT,
SARAH M. FOULGER, AND CHIP GRIFFIN

edited by
DOREEN C. DUN

LIVELY STONES
The Evolution of the Congregational Church of Boothbay Harbor, Maine, from Its Origins in 1766 to 2016

Copyright ©2015 Congregational Church of Boothbay Harbor

ISBN: 978-1-940244-48-8

All rights reserved. Except for brief quotations used in reviews and critical articles, no part of this book may be used or reproduced in any form or by any means, electronic or mechanical, including photocopying, recording, or by an information storage and retrieval system, without permission from the publisher.

For photo credits see Illustration Credits, pp. 391 & 392.

Designed and produced by
Maine Authors Publishing
Rockland, Maine
www.maineauthorspublishing.com

Printed in the United States of America

*To the glory of God,
the author and inspirer of all lively stones.*

The Congregational Church of Boothbay Harbor, UCC

CONTENTS

List of Settled Pastors: 1766–2016 viii

Introduction 3

Chapter 1
The Presbyterian Founding: 1729–1766 13

Chapter 2
The First Settled Pastor in Boothbay: 1766–1779 33

Chapter 3
Struggling to Survive: 1779–1798 63

Chapter 4
Becoming Congregational and Losing Control: 1798–1830 89

Chapter 5
Shadows and Countershadows: 1830–1848 125

Chapter 6
Age of Prosperity and Sorrow: 1848–1870 145

Chapter 7
The Rise of Tourism and Industry: 1870–1892 175

Chapter 8
Charting the Course: 1892–1919 191

Chapter 9
Tough Times and Good Times: 1919–1941 223

Chapter 10
The Church at War and Peace: 1941–1965 265

Chapter 11
The Church in an Age of Turmoil: 1965–1986 297

Chapter 12
Faith for the Future: 1986–2003 325

Chapter 13
Celebrating the Past, Claiming the Present,
and Preparing for the Future: 2003–2016 355

Illustration Credits 391

Acknowledgments 393

Endnotes 395

Index 455

SETTLED PASTORS

The Boothbay Presbyterian Church, 1766–1798
Rev. John Murray, 1766–1779
Rev. Elijah Kellogg, 1785–1787
Rev. Jonathan Gould, 1789–1792
Rev. Pelatiah Chapin, 1795–1796

The Congregational Church of Boothbay, 1798–1848
Rev. John Sawyer, 1798–1805
Rev. Jabez Pond Fisher, 1807–1816
Rev. Isaac Weston, 1817–1830
Rev. Charles Lewis Cook, 1830–1832
Rev. Thomas Bellowes, 1832–1833
Rev. Joseph Washburn Sessions, 1833
Rev. Nathaniel Chapman, 1833–1834
Rev. Henry Merrill, 1835
Rev. David Quimby Cushman, 1836–1843
Rev. William Tobey, 1844–1847
*Rev. Samuel Lamson Gould, 1848–1851
*Rev. Jonathan Adams, 1852–1861
*Rev. Horace Toothaker, 1861–1864

The Second Congregational Church, also known as the South Parish Church, 1848–1929
Rev. George Gannett, 1847–1850
Rev. Joseph Smith, 1850–1852
Rev. John Kendall Deering, 1852–1853
Rev. Edmund Burt, 1854–1855
Rev. John Forbush, 1856–1857
Rev. Jonathan Edwards Adams, 1858–1859
Rev. John Johnson Bulfinch, 1859–1862
Rev. William Leavitt, 1862–1864
Rev. Leander S. Coan, 1865–1867
Rev. Andrew Jackson Smith, 1868–1872
Rev. Ezra Barker Pike, 1873–1877
Rev. Richard William Jenkins, 1878–1883
Rev. Lewis Darenydd Evans, 1884–1889
Rev. Arthur G. Pettingill, 1892

SETTLED PASTORS

Rev. M.O. Patton, 1893–1895
Rev. Donald McCormick, 1895–1902
Rev. George H. Hull, 1902–1906
Rev. W. Stanley Post, 1910–1915
Rev. Walter P. Bradford, 1919–1922
Rev. Dr. Peter MacQueen, 1924
Rev. George H. Woodward, 1924
Rev. William G. Kirschbaum, Jr., 1925–1928

The Congregational Church of Boothbay Harbor, 1929–1961
Rev. Louis Lincoln Harris, 1929–1930
Rev. Elton K. Bassett, 1930–1936
Rev. Kenneth Vernon Gray, 1937–1944
Rev. Aubrey Hastings, 1944–1945
Rev. Ernest Whitnall, 1945–1948
Rev. Dr. William James Campbell, 1948–1949
Rev. George Gledhill, 1949–1953
Rev. Edward Manning, 1954–1955
Rev. Ivan Welty, 1956–1965

The Congregational Church of Boothbay Harbor, United Church of Christ, 1961–present
Rev. Richard B. Balmforth, 1965–1970
Rev. Bruce A. Riegel, 1971–1972
Rev. Charles S. Hartman, 1972–1978
Rev. Karl Phillippi, 1979–1981
Rev. Joseph David Stinson, 1982–1992
Rev. Peter Baldwin Panagore, 1993–2003
Rev. Dr. Sarah M. Foulger, 2003–present

*Revs. Gould, Adams, and Toothaker, 1848–1864, served both the Congregational Church of Boothbay, known after 1848 as the First Congregational Church, and the Second Congregational Church. The following eight clergymen, Revs. Gannett to Leavitt, 1847–1864, served the Second Congregational Church only.

LIVELY STONES

INTRODUCTION

Since 1798 the Congregational Church of Boothbay, Maine—relocated to Boothbay Harbor in 1848—has been guided by its covenant, which pledged the congregation to "build up of lively stones, a spiritual house, growing into a holy temple." Like the nation and the world over the past 250 years, 1766 to 2016, what is today the Congregational Church of Boothbay Harbor, United Church of Christ, has experienced enormous change. This history explores that change, enshrining in particular the role of human actors in the long historical drama, those "lively stones" who undergird the religious institution's long growth and development, those people who firmed the church's foundation out of wood, out of stone, and out of faith.

The "lively stones" theme that continues to inspire the people of this Congregational church in 2016 emerges chapter by chapter in descriptions of people whose faith, whose fortitude and wisdom enable the church not only to survive, but ultimately over 250 years to prosper. Herein are the stories of the McCobbs, Aulds, Beaths, Fullertons, Reeds, Kennistons, Murrays, and other Scots-Irish Presbyterians who in the 1730s and 1740s carved the town of Boothbay out of the rocky Maine soil that was then part of the Province of Massachusetts. In this early history, the Reverend John Murray looms as a famed Presbyterian preacher and patriot. Later, the Reverend John Sawyer in 1798 transformed Boothbay's struggling Presbyterian kirk into a Congregational church, then left Boothbay ultimately to found Bangor Theological Seminary. The church's Rev. David Cushman led revivals in the revivalist

1830s, evangelistic *tours de force* in New England that helped fuel the antislavery and abolitionist movement leading to the nation's Civil War, where fifty-one parishioners, including Charles McCobb, fought, and many, like McCobb, died. After the Civil War, in the 1870s, Welsh-born Rev. Richard William Jenkins grew church membership and enlarged the church physically and spiritually, as did the Reverend Charles Hartman in the 1970s, and the Reverend Dr. Sarah Foulger in the twenty-first century.

But, those "lively stones" and their church never existed in a vacuum. All were part of a much larger social, economic, physical, and spiritual sphere. The church exists within the framework of a community. Indeed, its mission, its growth, its very survival is contingent upon and intertwined with the fortunes of the community, the region, and, finally, the nation. Some small churches can become cathedrals, as happened in such places as New York, Boston, Chicago, and Philadelphia. Or, given the unforeseen circumstances of urbanization, they can become restaurants, as in the cases of Pittsburgh, Pennsylvania, or Portland, Maine. Or they can be demolished!

The Boothbay center meetinghouse, dedicated as a Presbyterian church in 1766 and led by the Reverend John Murray, was used for town meetings and Presbyterian church services until 1798, when the church became Congregational. In around 1846, the meetinghouse was moved to East Boothbay, where it became, first, part of Benjamin Reed's shipyard and later part of the Goudy & Stevens yard. It was torn down in 1943. The Congregational Church of Boothbay, built on the same site at the center around 1846 or 1847, was remodeled into a schoolhouse in 1913 and abandoned in the 1970s when local schools were consolidated. It was burned down by an arsonist in the 1980s. The church's former Boothbay center site, adjacent to the town's Civil War monument, ultimately became the location of a war memorial and park.

The Second Congregational Church, or South Parish Church, built in 1848 in its present location in Boothbay Harbor, was enlarged in 1881, and again in 1954. It became part of the United Church of Christ in 1961 and was enlarged again in 1991, at which time it was moved back thirty-five feet from the verge of Townsend Avenue. It was enlarged again in 2015. However, the church never attained the size or status of the majestic edifice that is New York's Riverside Church, pastored in the mid-twentieth century by the Reverend Harry Emerson Fosdick, a summer resident of Mouse Island and a regular summer preacher at the Boothbay Harbor Congregational church. Nevertheless, the Boothbay Harbor church, with its gleaming white façade and towering steeple, welcomes all who visit Boothbay Harbor; and its "lively stones" for over two centuries have been leaders in the Boothbay region. The Harbor church's growth and mission remained steady, always shaped by the larger Boothbay region's ebbs and flows, and by national and worldwide forces and fortunes.

That had been true 250 years ago, when those hardy original Scots-Irish settlers from Northern Ireland carved out the community of Townsend two miles inland of the deep, spacious, and commercially valuable harbor. Chip Griffin's first four chapters of this volume focus largely on the extraordinary pastorate of John Murray; the fledgling community of Townsend, now Boothbay; together with Southport and the Boothbay Harbor settlement. As Chip explains, the region endured as a subsistence farming community with a nascent, but soon to be thriving Harbor-based maritime economy, built upon shipbuilding, fishing the Grand Banks, and on coastal commerce, especially with the West Indies and the Carolinas. In the 1790s, despite the sagging fortunes of the little Presbyterian church bereft of a settled pastor, Boothbay's maritime economy grew; although, like Wiscasset and Portland, between 1807 and 1820, it suffered from the Napoleonic wars and the embargoes imposed by Presidents Thomas Jefferson and James Madison.

The region resurged after 1820. The Harbor, not Boothbay center, emerged as the main focus of economic activity and by the 1840s was the center of the town's social and spiritual life as well. The new "South Parish Church" arose in 1848 and the Harbor became the center of initially Federalist, later Whig and antislavery politics, in contrast to its Lincoln County hinterland, where Jeffersonian Republicanism and, later, Jacksonian politics and revivalist Free Will Baptists and Methodism ruled. In fact, in the 1840s the Boothbay center Congregational church steadily lost membership, not only to the Harbor's South Congregational church but also to the Baptists and Methodists. After the Civil War, in which fifty-one members of the South Parish Church fought (and a number died), Boothbay Harbor's fishing and shipbuilding economy survived; but, as Sarah Foulger explains in Chapter 7, in the 1870s the town's maritime economy was increasingly buttressed by an influx of summer visitors and other tourists drawn by the beauty and charm of the New England town with its harbor and white-steepled Congregational church.

Served in the nineteenth and twentieth centuries (indeed, until the 1960s) by an extensive railroad network (the Maine Central, Boston and Maine, and Grand Trunk, among others) and by steamship lines, towns like Bath, Boothbay Harbor, and Rockland preserved their fishing, shipbuilding, ice, and limestone economies. However, Maine towns, despite the growth of textile, paper, and shoemaking industrialism in places like Lewiston, Bangor, Saco, and Skowhegan, never experienced the urban industrialization that grew places such as Boston, Providence, Manchester, Worcester, Chicago, Philadelphia, and other urban industrial centers. Instead, during the first half of the twentieth century, Maine marketed and nurtured the image of "Vacationland." During World War I, World War II, and Korea, region shipyards, firms like Samples, Hodgdon Brothers, and Goudy & Stevens, won sizable government contracts for large, wood-hulled minesweepers; but as Chapter 10 makes clear, by 1965 it was lobsters, twenty-one-foot sailboats, yachts, tugboats, plus tourism that sustained the towns and the Boothbay Harbor church, not urban-style manufacturing. Thus, on a positive note, the Boothbay region escaped the trauma of de-industrialization that after 1960 gripped Baltimore, Boston, Philadelphia, and other large cities that in the nineteenth and early twentieth centuries had witnessed the large-scale influx of foreign-born immigrants and African-American migrants from the South.

All of these forces impacted the nation, Maine, and Boothbay Harbor, particularly population trends. Originally the Maine District of Massachusetts until it became a state in 1820, Maine had historically been the home of the Abenakis and other Native Americans. During the eighteenth century, the Boothbay region witnessed European settlement by groups like the Scots-Irish, and then, following the American Revolution, by veterans of that struggle holding tenuous titles to land held by wealthy, Massachusetts-based "Great Proprietors." After 1820, however, population growth in Maine slowed considerably. Both early industrialism arising in Pennsylvania, New York, Connecticut, Rhode Island, and New Hampshire and the promise of almost free land available in the trans-Appalachian West lured settlers away from still-rural Maine. In 1849 gold appeared in California, and in 1862 the Homestead Act enticed homesteaders with the prospect of 162 acres of free land in the West. Maine youth found greener pastures elsewhere. Other than a sizable immigration of potato-famine Irish into Portland, Bangor, and a few other Maine towns, and of French-Canadians in Lewiston, Saco, and other textile centers, population growth in Maine stagnated.

Thus, churches like Boothbay Harbor's Congregational church remained small, yet relatively stable. Throughout the nineteenth and early twentieth centuries when a disproportionately large number of its ministers had similar credentials from Bowdoin College and Bangor Theological Seminary, many of the church's clergy were youthful. During the early nineteenth century, influenced by the Second Great Awakening (1790–1840), many also shared enthusiasm for the message of revivalism propounded by such great American preachers as Henry Ward Beecher, Charles Grandisson Finney, and Horace Bushnell. And, befitting an ethnically homogenous seaside community with its roots in the British Empire, over time a significant number of pastors hailed from the British Isles, including Richard William Jenkins (1878–1883) from Wales, Lewis Darrenydd Evans (1878–1883) also from Wales, the Reverend Dr. Peter MacQueen (1923–1924) from Scotland, the Reverend Ernest Whitnall (1945–1948) from Southwold, England, and lastly the Reverend Richard B. Balmforth (1965–1970) from London.

As the Reverend Dr. Sarah Foulger relates in Chapter 5, this history of the Congregational Church of Boothbay Harbor contains shadows as well as light. History does not unfold prophetically, in linear form, as the "City on a Hill" beholding a manifest destiny of endless progress toward foreordained perfection, a continuum linking one triumphant ministry to the next. There is joy, there is despair; there is light, there is darkness. From its Presbyterian beginnings, the church has hosted in its pulpit several notable, history-making pastors, including its first settled pastor John Murray and summer guest preacher Harry Emerson Fosdick. And, because of the Harbor church's idyllic location, during the summer months, additional nationally distinguished ministers have preached in its sanctuary, including Dr. Wallace Robbins, President of Meadville Theological Seminary, and Rev. James Lenhart of the Plymouth Congregational Church of Des Moines, Iowa.

But the church has also endured dark periods such as the long era after the American Revolution and the departure of John Murray, when, as a Presbyterian church where the distant Boston presbytery proved ineffective, it spent a decade without a settled pastor (1779–1789). Likewise, during the 1830s, troubled by the legacy of the Cook scandal (discussed by Sarah Foulger in Chapter 5), successive pastors served no more than a year or two. Similarly, after World War II and again in the late 1960s and early 1970s, the church suffered short and troublesome pastorates. In the late twentieth century, one of the longest, darkest periods ensued when embezzlement thrust the church to the edge of the abyss. Yet, whether borne through sunlit, blossoming meadowlands or through the darkest, deepest valley, sustained by its "lively stones," the Harbor church pushed onward and emerged triumphant, supported by its mission and its faith. It regained members over time and made its meetinghouse more spacious, more inclusive, and more welcoming.

This history of the Congregational Church of Boothbay Harbor contains thirteen chapters, which, as implied by the preceding discussion, are organized chronologically and attempt to cast our church's history within the larger context, not only of local and national events, but also within a framework of changing spiritual and theological trends. These include the First and Second Great Awakenings, pre-Civil War revivalism, the emergence in the 1870s of the optimistic theology of the Reverend Walter Rauschenbusch and the Social Gospel, twentieth century modernism, the clash between modernism and fundamentalism, which involved Harry Emerson Fosdick, and finally, the rise of evangelical sects in the late twentieth and early twenty-first centuries and the loss of membership in many urban and suburban "mainline" Protestant churches such as Episcopalian, Lutheran, Methodist, Presbyterian, and, yes, the United Church of Christ.

The first four chapters, written by lawyer and local historian Chip Griffin, tell the story from the beginnings of our church amidst the seventeenth century Scottish Reformation led by John Knox and the brutal oppression of the Scots-Irish, through the early settlement of Townsend (now Boothbay, Boothbay Harbor, and Southport) and the founding of the Boothbay Presbyterian Church. Chip carries the story through the Murray pastorate, the American Revolution, and the church's struggles of the 1780s and 1790s, ending with the transformation of a Presbyterian polity into a Congregational one. He concludes with the revivalism of the Second Great Awakening, the efforts of Boothbay and the church to cope with the trauma of the Napoleonic Wars, and the dire effects on the region's infant maritime economy of Jefferson's and Madison's embargo and of the War of 1812.

Chapters 5, 6, and 7, by the Reverend Dr. Sarah Foulger, current pastor of the Boothbay Harbor Congregational church, carry this history from the 1830s to 1892, a period of over sixty-years that includes discussion not only of the impact of early nineteenth century voluntarism on Boothbay and the nation, the rise of the temperance movement, the Seneca Falls women's rights movement, Mormonism, and the Millerites, but also the rise of antislavery and abolitionism. In a reputedly heavy-drinking region, where fish and lumber sold in the West Indies brought many barrels of "demon rum" into Boothbay, alcoholism and temperance played an important role in the history of our church, as did the antislavery and abolition movement, which led to the Civil War and to great loss of life in the Boothbay region.

While industrialism arose early in New England, it exploded after the Civil War, producing in the Boothbay area a few fish oil factories and shrimp-processing plants, but more importantly, beginning in the 1870s as a popular reaction to pell-mell urban industrialism, the impetus for tourism in the imagined simpler, less frenetic world of northern New England. Tourism complemented the region's shipbuilding, lobstering, and struggling ground-fishing economy. The Reverend Robert (Bob) Dent, a retired Presbyterian minister, carries the church's story from the turbulent depression year of 1892 through World War I, the roaring 1920s, the Great Depression (1929–1940), to the eve of World War II. His chapters 8 and 9 are rich in the history of the theological debates that raged during this period, the social gospel, Billy Graham, Billy Sunday, and the rise of fundamentalism. His chapters include the emergence of theological modernism, the theological innovations of Soren Kierkegaard, Harry Emerson Fosdick, Paul Tillich, and Reinhold Niebuhr, the latter two theologians deeply influenced by the horrors of World War I and the rise of Nazism in Germany. As in all the thirteen chapters of the book, Bob Dent profiles the pastors and the pastorates that marked the era, the role of women in the church, church organizations, church polity, and the interior and exterior physical changes that occurred during that time in the church's history.

The next three chapters (10, 11, and 12) by historian John F. Bauman, explore the church at war, 1942–1945, and the postwar years, 1946–2003, years that witnessed Boothbay Harbor and East Boothbay becoming wartime shipbuilding centers and, after the Korean conflict, casting their lot firmly with tourism. The Reverend Kenneth Gray safely guided the church through World War II and the hardships caused by blackouts, rationing, and shift work schedules. However, following World War II the church experienced a period of relative instability until strong leadership was restored under the ministries of the Reverend Charles Hartman, who had been the pastor of a large urban church near Pittsburgh, Pennsylvania, followed by the Reverend David Stinson. Stinson also launched a major building program called "Faith for the Future," a project that, alas, remained unfinished when he ended his long ministry in Boothbay Harbor. In the wake of "Faith for the Future," during the 1990s, the church faced an embezzlement scandal and financial tribulations that darkened the history of the church as it approached the millennial year 2000. Bob Dent's final chapter (13) brings the story of the once Presbyterian kirk down to the present, a bright and a glorious new day and era in the history of the 250-year-old church.

Through wars, battles over liquor, economic depressions, weak pastorates and strong, the untimely deaths of ministers, and wrenching perfidy, the church found in its covenant spiritual nourishment, a shining beacon girding the faithful and guiding the church steadfastly toward the future. What follows is the history of that journey.

—JOHN F. BAUMAN

CHAPTER 1

THE PRESBYTERIAN FOUNDING: 1729–1766
by Chip Griffin

First Effective Settlement, 1729–1730

Culture and history matter in the development of community. "[R]eal community [is a] community of memory, one that does not forget its past…Communities of memory that tie us to the past also turn us toward the future as communities of hope." In fact, "[t]radition is a lifeline to hope." This "usable history [consists of] stories told for the purpose of strengthening community by deepening its spiritual practices and renewing its vision of social justice."[1]

The Doctrine of First Effective Settlement[2] speaks to the lasting legacy of the special, Scots-Irish Presbyterian microculture on the Boothbay peninsula within the dominant Puritan culture in northern New England. The doctrine asserts that a band, however small, of settlers who establish a self-perpetuating society in an empty territory can create the dominant culture for centuries, regardless of far larger numbers of later arrivals.[3] The Midcoast Maine culture, especially in the Boothbay and Bristol peninsulas, was founded by Scots-Irish Presbyterians who established the peninsula's dominant and distinctive culture, which tends to be highly egalitarian and libertarian, in contrast to the Northeast's dominant Puritan culture, which tends to be highly hierarchical and communitarian.

No area of New England was so strongly Scots-Irish Presbyterian as the area between the Kennebec and Penobscot rivers.[4] This was the opinion of Alexander Blaikie, in 1881, in his *History of Presbyterianism in New England*. And the heaviest concentration of Scots-Irish Presbyterians in the Midcoast region was found on the Boothbay and Bristol peninsulas.

The Boothbay region wilderness was permanently settled in 1729 and in the 1730s by Scots-Irish Presbyterians, who were Calvinists from Northern Ireland, where their ancestors had ventured from Scotland a century earlier.[5] Beginning around 1605, King James I of England had planted Presbyterians from the Scottish lowlands bordering England into Catholic Northern Ireland, the first massive "plantation" of settlers anywhere in the world.[6] The Scots-Irish had a uniquely libertarian spirit of freedom and were often violent in their restlessness against institutional restraint. This very special concept of liberty was far removed from the ordered liberty of the New England Puritans, the reciprocal liberty of the Delaware Valley Quakers, and the hierarchical liberty of the Virginian Anglicans.[7] This Scots-Irish heritage remains influential in the region today through their staunchly held belief in liberty, freedom, and equality and, regrettably, through the dark tendency of many Scots-Irish toward alcoholism, domestic abuse, and excessive violence.[8]

Many parents and grandparents of Boothbay's original frontier settlers fought and defended their family, kin, and adopted homeland in 1689 in Londonderry in Northern Ireland, during the infamous 103-day siege, which followed other oppressions and wars that had forged the Scots-Irish into a fierce fighting force. Among those who defended Londonderry against the French and Irish Catholic forces in the service of the deposed English king, James II, were such familiar Boothbay names as Clark, Montgomery, Beath, Boyd, Kennedy, McFarland, Wylie, Reed, Blair, McCobb, Fullerton, and Murray.[9] They rallied to the cry, "No surrender!"[10]

Elizabeth F. Reed, Boothbay Harbor's leading historian in the mid-twentieth century and descendent of Walter Beath and other

Boothbay founders, preserved the family's oral history. According to Reed, Walter Beath's father, who fought for over three months on the walls of Londonderry, gave nine-year-old Walter a club with instructions to kill the rats when they came out of the rat hole, so that the Beath family could eat rat soup to avoid starvation and so retain and pass along their Presbyterian religion and culture.[11] The Scots-Irish became one of the most formidable fighting forces in the world and the most recruited frontier fighters in America. They still comprise an extraordinarily high percentage of America's military warriors to this day.[12]

Like Presbyterian churches across the American colonial frontier, the Scots-Irish could not obtain settled pastors due to requirements for Presbyterian ministers to be highly educated in Scottish universities and because many unchurched areas, including Maine territories, were considered to be wild and uncivilized. This educational requirement[13] existed in Scotland and England until 1746, when the College of New Jersey, later Princeton University, was founded by Scottish Presbyterians. This was the first true Presbyterian institution of higher learning in the American colonies, and it provided some much needed Presbyterian ministers, especially to the southern colonies.[14]

As in the Puritan culture of East Anglia, mostly middle class merchant families from the urban London area dominated Boston and environs with an emphasis on building towns and cities and a focus on education and Calvinistic religion in the new frontier.[15] The Scots-Irish culture of Northern Ireland, with its pronounced egalitarian and libertarian ethos, similarly dominated the Boothbay and Bristol peninsulas, as it did later along the Appalachians. The American frontier experience shaped the cultures of these eighteenth-century Puritans, Scots-Irish, and others who arrived in America. Living on the frontier, including in the Boothbay region, forced the Scots-Irish immigrants to switch from raising sheep to pigs, to settle as individuals great distances away from the watchful eyes of neighbors, and, most significantly, to base their informal social class system on personal character, on feats of strength such as wrestling matches, gander pulling, and on raucous wedding celebrations where all the community was invited. The ever-changing frontier lines forced constant movement of the Scots-Irish and eroded family emphasis and social ranking systems. In short, the mobility of the Scots-Irish, coupled with their egalitarian ways, swept away the rigid foundations of the class system. Although some social distinctions remained among the Scots-Irish, by 1800 the tradition of inherited social distinctions had largely disappeared; and individual achievement trumped family heritage. Community status now rested on one's own strength of will, self-control, and inward determination.[16]

Moreover, the Scots-Irish exuded an intense concern for equality of esteem amidst extreme inequalities of condition. Colonial contemporaries complained about the Scots-Irish traits of undue familiarity, lack of deference, and refusal to obey orders from officers. In the back country, Scots-Irish, rich and poor, dealt with each other more or less as social equals, honoring the verity of such Scots-Irish egalitarian proverbs as, "The rain don't know broadcloth from jeans," "no man can help his birth," and "any fool can make money."[17]

Until August 4, 1718, not many Scots-Irish had arrived in New England, and only a few had landed in Midcoast Maine. However, from the mid-seventeenth century onward, the major port of entry within the northern colonies and the magnet for most Scots-Irish was Boston, where an incredible surge of Scots-Irish arrived.[18] On that date, five shiploads of Scots-Irish landed with about 120 families in Boston Harbor. This event was sparked by the Reverend Robert Holmes, who had visited New England a year or so earlier and returned to Ireland with a very favorable account. Holmes, his father, and three other Presbyterian ministers, James McGregor, William Cornwell, and William Boyd, recruited over 217 persons to New England. Nine of them were ministers, three were graduates of a Scottish university, and all but seven were able to sign their names rather than making marks for their signatures, a quite remarkable rate of literacy in the colonial period.

Rev. James McGregor, in his sermon upon leaving Northern Ireland, stated four reasons for emigrating: "to avoid oppression and cruel bondage, to shun persecution and designed ruin, to withdraw from the communion of idolaters, [and] to have an opportunity of worshipping God according to the dictates of conscience and the rules of his inspired word."[19] Scots-Irish were pushed out of Northern Ireland for economic reasons due to a new law prohibiting export of Irish wool to England, for religious reasons due to the enforced payment of tithes to Anglican churches, and due to the recent expiration of long-term leases in Ulster plantations. They were pulled to America by the first opportunity of multitudes in human history to attain cheap, good land in what were then the least taxed territories on earth.[20]

These Northern Irish Presbyterians were "warned out" of Boston by Cotton Mather and his Puritans, who called them "a parcel of Irish."[21] Many historians have pointed out the antipathy of the Puritans, who desired the Scots-Irish mainly for their fighting prowess out in the wilderness to protect Boston, which had become one of the largest cities in America almost a century after its founding in 1630. For example, historian Alexander Blaikie remarked that these Scots-Irish were not favorably received by the Bostonians, but were "pelted," not with "rotten potatoes on leaving the wharf, for there were none in New England until they then brought them, but with other missiles." He added, "They were Irish and not English," and they were Presbyterians and not Puritans, whom he described as a sect that "had hitherto dwelt so nearly alone, under the union of the government of the colony with their peculiar ecclesiastical regimen, which had taken its rise in New England." Consequently, they [the Scots-Irish] generally went to the interior, to the wilderness, and less cultivated parts of the country."[22]

Sixteen emigrant families left Boston and went to Casco Bay in late autumn of 1718 to found a settlement. They suffered throughout the cold winter, most aboard the ship that had brought them. A majority explored to the eastward but ultimately relocated westward to Haverhill, Massachusetts and then to Nutfield, later named Londonderry, in New Hampshire.[23] At the time, Boston was ordered "to be secured against passengers lately arrived from Ireland." This "warning out" continued in the spring of 1719, when Robert Holmes and his wife and William Holmes and his children were ordered to depart. In June and July 1719, several newer Scots-Irish immigrants were similarly warned out of Boston.[24] A few hardy souls did travel eastward, founding Cork and Somerset on the east and west sides of the Kennebec River, respectively, around 1718, until the Indians burned them out from Merrymeeting Bay south to and including Brunswick, on the Androscoggin River. Some settled in Georgetown, and a few of these landed in Townsend in 1729.[25]

Although the Scots-Irish migration to America started as a trickle, it reached a magnitude of more than a quarter million people. This was truly a mass migration on a scale altogether different from the preceding migrations of Puritans to New England and of Anglicans to Virginia. And the rhythm differed, in that it was not a single migration but rather wavelike movements during most of the eighteenth century.[26] The Scots-Irish migration, which crested in 1729, comprised the largest movement of any group from the British Isles to British North America in the eighteenth century.[27]

Settlement of Townsend, now Boothbay

Colonel David Dunbar, a Scots-Irish Presbyterian and native of Ireland, actively recruited and led groups of Scot-Irish Presbyterians in 1729 and 1730 to settle in the Maine territory. Dunbar, Surveyor of the King's Woods in America, promoted his position as protector of the royal masts to temporarily control the entire Province of "Sagadahock" (sic), a frontier area between the Kennebec and St. Croix rivers in what was then considered eastern Maine.[28] Dunbar settled his Scots-Irish families in Sagadahock Province after he had first obtained a royal instruction and proclamation and then secured the goodwill and cooperation of Richard Philipps, Governor of Nova Scotia. Dunbar planted his Scots-Irish brethren in three townships that lay between the Sheepscot and Muscongus rivers: Townsend, formerly known as Winnegance (the area between the Sheepscot and Damariscotta rivers),[29] now Boothbay; Harrington, the southern and greatest part of today's Bristol and South Bristol; and Walpole, the upper part of Bristol now known as Nobleboro. Dunbar himself laid out the city plan for Pemaquid.

This Midcoast Maine area had been disputed territory for almost a century, and such disputes multiplied over the next two centuries. Dunbar gave shaky assurances of title from the outset, handing out feudal types of leasehold indentures rather than the emerging fee-for-land ownership as in most of mercantile New England. Inflated with successes, Dunbar promised each of the new emigrants one hundred acres of land and one year's provisions. Trying to obscure Massachusetts' jurisdictional rights, Dunbar procured not only the king's instructions and proclamation but also a royal order to Governor Philipps of Nova Scotia for taking possession of this territory, along with thirty men and an officer to man the fort at Pemaquid, then called Fort Frederick. A century later in 1832, historian William Williamson noted, "The descendants of settlers introduced into Townshend by Rogers and McCobb under Dunbar form, at the present time, most of the inhabitants of Boothbay."[30]

By 1732, the Puritans succeeded in evicting Dunbar, but the Scots-Irish settlers of Townsend and Bristol retained possession of the disputed land that Dunbar had conveyed to his countrymen in Boothbay, Bristol, and Nobleboro. Those land disputes would simmer and erupt for another century.[31] The Boothbay Scots-Irish settlers and their progeny clung tenaciously and successfully to their land against overwhelming odds. As historian Gordon Kershaw remarked, "Their opposition to [Boston-based Puritan] Kennebec Company schemes proved out of all proportion to their size."[32]

There were few settlements along the Maine frontier east of the Kennebec River and fewer Presbyterian churches in the early 1700s, the region having experienced five devastating Indian wars between 1676 and 1749, when the final war concluded with the

Treaty of Falmouth.[33] Increasingly, these wars had become part of English and French efforts to dominate colonization of New England and all of North America. The fledgling Townsend settlement on the Boothbay peninsula was nearly decimated several times into the 1740s by Indian attacks during winters.[34] The Townsend area had always been a wilderness frontier, thinly settled, battered by Indian wars—indeed, wretched and precarious. The few Scots-Irish settlers were scattered along the harbors and rivers, the highways of their era.[35]

Just after the signing of the Treaty of Falmouth in 1749, Samuel Ball and Obadiah Albee almost triggered another war in Wiscasset. They became the most wanted men along the eastern American coast when they surprised and murdered an Indian chief, who had just signed the peace treaty. They also seriously wounded two other Indian leaders camped out around a fire with their wives. Ball and Albee got away scot free and lived the rest of their lives for many decades until their deaths as old men on the Boothbay peninsula, protected by its Scots-Irish settlers.[36]

The Presbyterian Background

While the beliefs and works of John Calvin (1509–1564) were fundamental to the development of both the Congregational and the Presbyterian churches, the term "Calvinism" today connotes not so much his theology of predestination and individual justification by faith as the extreme strictness with which he governed in Geneva and the ruthlessness with which parishioners who deviated from his authority were punished. In Scotland, influenced by Calvin's theology and church organization, John Knox (1514–1572) became the founder of Scottish Presbyterianism.

As Martin Luther (1483–1546) was the unrivaled leader of the German Reformation, John Knox single-handedly led the Scottish Reformation, which he launched in 1559 following the Beggars Summons, a revolutionary manifesto pinned to the doors of Roman Catholic institutions in Scotland demanding the departure of all friars. Knox, a dour, passionate, devout, and remorseless reformer, was also humorless, and by modern standards, narrow and bigoted. He was a prolific writer and a preacher of truly terrifying power. Knox was a man of heroic will and tireless energy, often uncompromising, dogmatic, and driven. Son of a small farmer, John Knox made it to the top of the church hierarchy, known then and now as the Scottish Kirk, by his ability and tenacity. He imposed on Scottish society new rules, such as no working, no dancing, and no playing of the pipes on the Calvinistic Sabbath, and banned gambling, card playing and theater. He also required approval of the minister before anyone moved out of the parish. The right of communion belonged to everyone, the Bible was no longer a closed book but was open for everyone, and church rafters rang with the singing of psalms and Gospel recitations. The congregation was the center of church organization, electing their board of elders and choosing their minister.[37] As St. Peter was the rock of early Jerusalem Christianity, John Knox was the rock of Scottish Presbyterianism.

In recognition of the growth of several "nonconformist" Protestant churches, the English Parliament in 1644 called for an assembly of all reformed churches to develop a unified statement of faith. Nonconformist church leaders conducted meetings for four years in Westminster Abbey, and in 1648 issued the Westminster Confession of Faith, which became the standard, particularly for Presbyterians. The Westminster Confession of Faith clearly separated the nonconforming churches from the Church of England, which became the only lawful church in England in 1662. The Confession had the effect of loosely linking the Puritans and later Congregationalists, Presbyterians, and Baptists as Nonconformists. As summarized more than 120 years later by Boothbay's first settled minister, Rev. John Murray, "[B]efore the end of the year 1648, a general synod of all the churches unanimously agreed on the Westminster confession of faith, as the public declaration of their own principles...with the reformed churches of Scotland, France, Bohemia, Holland, Geneva, and Switzerland."[38]

In New England's seventeenth century Puritan theocracy,

Scots-Irish Presbyterians were essentially powerless. In 1643–1644, a new Puritan assembly in New England, the General Court, took the first administrative action against Presbyterians, who had set up Presbyterian government under the authority of the English Parliament's call for the Westminster Abbey assembly. Ongoing persecution and dominance by the Boston Puritan government was a significant factor in increasing emigration by Scots-Irish Presbyterians warned out of Boston to the Maine frontier, where Presbyterians could worship, live more freely, and serve as a bulwark to protect the urban Bostonians from the Indian menace. In reality, though much closer to Presbyterians than most other denominations of Protestantism, Puritans denied even Presbyterians communion in Puritan New England's churches.[39]

The First Great Awakening

Amidst, or perhaps because of, the apocalyptic Indian wars that raged in New England, there arose in the 1730s and 1740s a great spiritual awakening. American revival meetings, derived from John Knox's large field meetings and prayer societies in Scotland, forged a link between Scottish Presbyterians and the intense Protestant revivalism of the Great Awakening in New England. Led by Jonathan Edwards (1703–1758), New England's most brilliant theologian and a reforming minister in Northampton, Massachusetts, "Scottish Presbyterians were front and center in the movement from the start."[40] Edwards preached that the past had passed, and the future was alive with possibilities for celebrating the glory of God and the coming of Christ's kingdom, which, he argued, would begin in America. Any Protestant, regardless of denomination, could be touched by God's grace, and all of the righteous would join together to form a single Christian commonwealth. Righteousness, not birth or status, determined one's place in the coming kingdom of God. According to historian Arthur Herman, this was "a revivalist message that echoed the themes of Scottish Calvinism since Knox's day."[41] The Great Awakening transformed the culture of colonial America, touching its inhabitants with the spark of promised redemption and daring them to challenge orthodox assumptions and institutions. It helped set the stage for the American Revolution.[42] Indeed, it could be argued that the Great Awakening was the original dynamic of the continental move for independence.

Jonathan Edwards, more than any other religious leader of this period, wrestled with, wrote about, and preached a sophisticated defense of the Awakening and the role of emotion in religious life. He argued that deep emotion was essential to genuine religion and that it is required in order to alter one's life. Faith rested on knowledge, but moved beyond understanding to will and heart. A change of heart, more than a change of mind, would lead to deep feeling, new direction, and a transformed life. The Awakening involved reshaping not only theology, but also liturgy. Edwards succeeded in joining Puritan and Presbyterian theology to evangelical piety and practice, creating "a forceful blend that long shaped the religious and intellectual life of New England."[43]

The 1740 revivalist tour of the Englishman George Whitefield (1714–1770) ignited the Great Awakening in Protestant congregations all along America's eastern seaboard.[44] Whitefield may even have ventured as far as Maine in his travels. Certainly some of Boothbay's founders traveled to Boston or other places to hear Whitefield preach.[45] The Old South Presbyterian Church in Newburyport, Massachusetts was built for Whitefield, who is buried in it. According to the Newburyport church website, he arrived in Newburyport in September 1740.[46] Boothbay region historian Francis Greene reported in 1906 that back in 1800 Boothbay people believed that George Whitefield, "that renowned and shining light of Methodism, preached in the 1740s to the early Townsend settlers," and this, opined Greene, "is not improbable."[47] Whitefield later parted ways with the Methodists over the doctrine of predestination. In 1807, the western half of Balltown, Maine, still "overwhelmingly Calvinist Baptist in religion and Jeffersonian in politics," was incorporated as Whitefield in honor of the great preacher and evangelist. Two years later the eastern half of Balltown became Jefferson. This nomenclature was anathema to the state of Massachusetts, of which Maine was still a part, as the views of both Whitefield and Thomas Jefferson were deplored in that Federalist state.[48]

While the Great Awakening committed many New Englanders and other colonists to a more earnest spiritual life, it also divided their churches into two "armies," as noted by Jonathan Edwards. These two camps were the New Lights, who favored the revivals, and the Old Lights, who opposed them. Whitefield challenged the standing order and doubted the zeal of the clergy and of noisy and critical itinerants who preached where they were not invited and left in their wake angry ministers and divided towns. This spelled doom to the Puritan, later called Congregational, monopoly in most of New England, as other churches began to form. Many New Light churches first separated from the town's control and morphed into Baptist and later Methodist denominations.[49]

Early Presbyterian Churches in Maine

Presbyterian churches in Maine were scarce, and by the end of the eighteenth century, they were nearly extinct. One reason was the dominant Puritan and then Congregational churches throughout New England with similar Calvinist leanings. Another was the rigorous educational requirement for Presbyterian ministers that made it difficult to find, let alone attract, qualified ministers to frontier areas. As a result, church loyalties were quickly transferring to churches with fewer educational requirements, such as Methodists and Baptists, who often had more lively and popular meetings outdoors as well as in barns and churches near the end of the 1700s and early 1800s, when Puritan church governance and control were crumbling.[50] Beginning in 1734, Presbyterian churches were originally gathered in Maine in Georgetown (1734-65), Newcastle (1754-76), Brunswick (1747-69), Boothbay (1766-98), Bristol (1767-96), Topsham (1771-78), Warren, Gray, Canaan, and Turner.[51]

According to Presbyterian historian Alexander Blaikie, during these early colonial times, "no part of New England was so strongly Presbyterian as was the country lying between the Kennebec and Penobscot rivers, yet, to effect settlements of this church order was difficult, owing to the tenacity or obstinacy of the Congregationalists in the different parishes. They seldom became Presbyterians, while others frequently united with them."[52]

Between 1729 and about 1758, the region between Brunswick and Pemaquid was served by five Presbyterian ministers, all of whom probably preached from time to time in Boothbay. They were:

Rev. Robert Rutherford—1729-c. 1734
The Reverend Rutherford preached chiefly at Pemaquid in Bristol for four or five years, from 1729, at the behest of Colonel David Dunbar,[53] and occasionally in Nobleboro and Townsend.[54] He hailed from Northern Ireland and was a staunch Presbyterian minister. He came to Pemaquid at the call of fellow Scots-Irish colonizer, Colonel David Dunbar. Rutherford may have been regularly appointed and paid by the government[55] (and probably gave his name to Rutherford Island in South Bristol). He moved to Brunswick, where he became the settled minister of the First Parish Church from 1737 until 1742.[56] He then preached in Georgetown for a short time and probably returned to Pemaquid. Rutherford was known for his respectable literary attainments and pious ministry. He remained a warm friend of Colonel Dunbar, and after Dunbar's death and the remarriage of his widow to Thomas Henderson of St. George, Rutherford moved with his family to St. George, where he died in 1756 at the age of 68. He was buried at the fort at St. George in Cushing. The family left seven daughters and numerous descendants.[57]

Rev. William McClanethan—1734-c. 1739
(a/k/a McClanathan, Macclanaghan, and McClenahan)
The Reverend McClanethan preached in Georgetown and vicinity from 1734 through at least the late 1730s, with a failed two-year stint in Cape Elizabeth, where his temperament was such and the Congregationalists there so opposed his ministry that "he stirred

up a controversy which ended in his dismission[sic]," according to a journal of the Reverend Thomas Smith of Falmouth.[58] He encountered splintered towns fractured along Congregational and Presbyterian lines in both Georgetown and Cape Elizabeth.[59] By 1741, McClanethan left the Province of Maine and became the settled minister in Blandford, Massachusetts, formerly known as New Glasgow.[60]

Rev. Robert Dunlap—c. 1736
The Reverend Dunlap, a zealous Presbyterian preacher born in Ulster in 1715, preached at Boothbay. He had survived a shipwreck en route to America in 1736 on the Isle of Sable, where 96 of the 200 passengers perished. In Boston, Dunlap joined the Presbytery, soon moved on to Dracut, Massachusetts and then to Nobleboro. Later he resided briefly at Townsend, Newcastle, and then Brunswick. After a probationary period, Brunswick voted to settle him as their minister, and he preached separately to both Puritans and Presbyterians, who shared and fought over most church issues in Brunswick for thirteen years, until he was dismissed, in 1760, after difficulties had arisen over his salary. Robert Dunlap, known for his vehement and persuasive style of preaching, had met and modeled himself after the most famous of the Great Awakening preachers, George Whitefield. Dunlap resided in Brunswick until his death, a week before the Declaration of Independence, at the age of 61.[61]

Rev. Daniel Mitchell—c. 1747
The Reverend Mitchell, from Northern Ireland, was licensed to preach the gospel as a probationer for the ministry, and on August 11, 1747, he was appointed to supply in Georgetown and Sheepscot and "also [was given] a discretionary power to go to any other places there (In Maine) as he should judge safe." On November 11, 1747, Mitchell was appointed to supply until March in Wiscasset, Souhegan [probably Skowhegan], and Litchfield.[62] Presumably, he preached in Townsend, or the Townsend settlers sailed up to Wiscasset or across to Georgetown for Presbyterian worship.

Rev. Alexander Boyd—c. 1748

The Reverend Boyd was perhaps a son of the Reverend William Boyd, one of the original four ministers in the five ships that sailed from Northern Ireland to Boston in 1718. Alexander Boyd had studied theology at Glasgow University, subscribed to the Westminster Standards appointed by the Scottish Kirk in 1647,[63] and was licensed in 1748 to supply at Georgetown for three months, with discretionary power to go to "Wiscasset and Sheepscote, as he may judge it to be safe."[64] Boyd came to Georgetown, but could not harmonize the conflicting and roughly equal numbers of Congregationalists and Presbyterians there, so he went to Newcastle, where he was ordained at the Sheepscot church, with the understanding that his pastorate did not extend to the Damariscotta side of town.

Rev. Boyd occasionally preached in Townsend, was said to be eloquent, and attracted congregations in the barns, houses, and other places where he preached. But he was ultimately unsuccessful in his calling and bred dissension, perhaps partly due to his blemished reputation brought about by an irregular marriage before he left Scotland and desertion of his wife when he came to America.[65] Rev. Boyd suffered until his death that personal problem that plagued him with the Londonderry Presbytery, which reached and exerted some control over many Presbyterian churches from New Hampshire into the Maine frontier. In October 1748, he "acknowledged his irregular marriage with Mary Buchan, confessed his sorrow for the offence he had thereby given, and declared his resolution to adhere to her as his wife." Boyd was later minister in Newcastle from 1754 to 1758, but he also suffered from the divisions of Newcastle's Presbyterian majority from its Congregational minority. He returned to Georgetown in 1752, only to find that the people there had left Presbyterianism.[66]

Rev. John Murray—1766-1779

The Reverend Murray was Townsend's first settled minister, founding pastor, and the most renowned and remarkable Presbyterian preacher in northern New England. He preached in Boothbay from July 28, 1766 until 1779 and then in Newburyport from 1780 until his death in 1793, at the age of 51. A full account of his life and ministry is found in Chapter 2 of this book.

Almost forty years after the founding of the first permanent settlement in what is now the Boothbay region, a local community leader wrote eloquently of the spiritual struggles endured without a settled religious leader from Townsend's settlement in 1729 until the Reverend John Murray's appointment in 1766. The words are probably those of John Beath, who was a Townsend founder, in 1749 an Indian captive,[67] town of Boothbay negotiator, and Boothbay church and governmental leader and secretary.

> The inhabitants of this town having long been harassed and distressed by the natural difficulties of settling a new country without any considerable resources of wealth, and more especially by the frequent wars with the Savages on the border by which the settlement was repeatedly broken up, and the whole place laid waste; had hardly recovered strength enough for the settling of the gospel amongst them and therefore had long been languishing under the heavy affliction of silent Sabbaths; various transient preachers 'tis true they from time to time had opportunity to hear both here and in the neighborhood… [N]o hope remained of any settlement of the gospel here; and the people dispirited by long and fruitless attempts sat down in an inactive despondency; but in the midst of this gloomy prospect their minds were relieved by the arrival of Mr. John Murray.[68]

Acquisition of Land and Buildings for the Early Boothbay Church

Townsend's first murderer, Edmund Brown atoned before his execution, thereby setting the stage for a future parsonage. Brown and his father-in-law, David Bryant, the only known early Townsend settlers not of Scots-Irish descent, had come from Sudbury, Massachusetts and were of English stock.[69] On August 22, 1739, after a drunken afternoon and night with his father-in-law and two companions, a sudden brawl developed between Brown and Bryant. Brown swung his ax into Bryant's head, killing his father-in-law instantly in front of two witnesses.[70] As penance and knowing he would be executed within a month of the murder, Edmund Brown donated his real estate at and near Lobster Cove to Townsend's first settled minister.[71]

Brown's deed, dated in 1739 in the presence of neighbors John and James McFarland but not recorded until 1770, granted "to the first settled minister that shall be obtained in the aforesaid Townsend...by estimation fifty acres," bounded by Lobster Cove, land of John McFarland and Samuel McCobb, together with Brown's rights to Reed's Meadow, probably pasturage held in common with others for "the said minister of the gospel."[72] John Beath, perhaps Boothbay's leading citizen and clerk, probably laid the groundwork, or paperwork, that confirmed Edmund Brown's last wishes while in Brown's "house in company with a number of his neighbours, expecting soon the arrival of an officer to apprehend him," as attested by William Miller in 1739. Miller's deposition was recorded over thirty years later, in 1771, to clarify record title for the parsonage.[73] At Boothbay's second town meeting, on April 12, 1765 (the very first town meeting having been held less than two months earlier on February 27), recorded only two votes, one of which was for the approval and acceptance by the town that "the lott of land left by Edmond Brown, deceased, to the first Settled Minister is to remain to that purpose in Boothbay."[74]

In the summer of 1768, three decades after the execution of the deed, three years after the town's acceptance of the deed, and a year after the arrival of Boothbay's first settled pastor, the parsonage was built by John Leishman on the Mount Pisgah land, a high point of land west of Lobster Cove Road and Lobster Cove, donated by Edmund Brown, when Brown had been about to meet his maker.[75] The "parsonage, where Reverend John Murray lived, on Pisgah,...was considered in those days of rude abodes an imposing structure."[76]

The first Boothbay meetinghouse, both Presbyterian church and town meeting hall, was raised on September 27, 1765, built by Boothbay builder Samuel Adams, practically complete upon the arrival of Rev. John Murray in 1766, and formally dedicated July 28, 1766, a mere ten days after Murray's suspension from the Presbytery of Philadelphia and just a month prior to his return to Boothbay. The meetinghouse was located at the current site of Boothbay's memorial park north of the Civil War monument, toward the north end of the ancient Boothbay Common of eleven acres, much larger than the current Common of about two acres located in the middle of the ancient Common. A settled minister and meetinghouse were essential for the newly incorporated town of Boothbay two years earlier, in 1764.[77]

John Beath built the first session house, which was also located at the north end of the Common, just west of the church. Habitable by 1768, the session house was used by the elders of the church Session, who heard and decided church and town disputes. It still stands as the Nicholas Knight House today. In 1770, David Reed sold one hundred acres of land under and near the session house to Rev. John Murray, probably as payment in lieu of money for his ministry. In 1779, about when Rev. Murray was to leave for Newburyport for his final ministry, John Beath, then and for many years clerk of the church Session, sold the building he had built jointly to Murray and the elders and deacons of the church, perhaps also to compensate Rev. Murray for salary still owed for his ministry. Soon after Murray left that year, his cousin, also named John Murray, moved into the session house and operated it as an inn for many years. Rev. Murray, at his death, included a will provision forgiving cousin John Murray all debts owed to himself.[78]

The first parsonage at Pisgah, where Rev. John Murray and his family would reside, harked back to the murder of 1739. In 1770, fearing that the deed could be questioned, William Moore, one of the witnesses to Brown's murder of Bryant in 1739 and a ruling elder of the new church, testified under oath and signed a deposition supporting the real estate title for the newly built parsonage and separate field. John Beath, who had drafted and witnessed the Brown deed in 1739, also a ruling elder of the new church, signed a deposition in 1772 to bolster the title to the parsonage land, among other motivations. The church soon deeded the parsonage and adjacent land to Rev. Murray. This parsonage was two miles, a healthy walk, from the meetinghouse at Boothbay Center.[79] This 1768 Pisgah parsonage, like the Presbyterian church, was in decay by 1796, when a new parsonage was built at the north side of the Boothbay Common, and the 1768 Pisgah parsonage ruins soon moldered[80] into the earth.[81] [82]

CHAPTER 2

THE FIRST SETTLED PASTOR IN BOOTHBAY: 1766–1779
by Chip Griffin

The Reverend John Murray's Early Career: 1764–1766

John Murray was the founding minister and first settled pastor of one of the last of the eighteenth-century Presbyterian churches founded north of Newburyport, Massachusetts in the Maine wilderness. Like Scotland's Kirk founder John Knox, Murray was a charismatic leader, daring diplomat, fierce fighter for his causes, and famous in his own time and place. He lived only into his early 50s. Unlike John Knox, John Murray was personally popular and a spellbinding preacher.

Rev. Murray quickly became the leading Presbyterian minister in eighteenth century New England and "the most prominent resident preacher in New England for years."[83] He was born in County Antrim, Northern Ireland, on May 22, 1742.[84] An unusually precocious student, he graduated with high honors from the University of Edinburgh at a very young age. He commenced ministry at age eighteen. At twenty-one, in 1763, this young Scots-Irish minister sailed to New York and then to the thirty-year-old frontier settlement of Townsend, later Boothbay, where his uncle and aunt, Andrew and Sarah Reed, had lured him to be their minister. On December 22, 1763, the Townsend inhabitants unanimously voted to call Mr. Murray to be their pastor, and five residents obligated themselves to pay him an annual salary of five pounds sterling.

Before he would consider being its settled minister, however, Murray required that Townsend become incorporated as a town. On January 31, 1764, twenty-eight Townsend men signed a petition to the royal Massachusetts governor to incorporate Townsend as a town, reasoning that incorporation was needed because "we have a desire of settling the gospel among us" and adding that they had seventy-five men able to pay the poll tax. The 1771 valuation had listed Townsend's population at 150 men.[85] John Beath traveled to Boston to advocate for the incorporation of Townsend with the Massachusetts General Court.[86] Two other Townsend founders and leaders, Andrew McFarland and Andrew Reed, traveled as commissioners to the Presbyterian synod of New York and Philadelphia, then the two largest cities in America, to negotiate the appointment of Murray to Townsend.[87] The wilderness hamlet of Townsend was competing hard against America's two largest cities for this amazingly gifted Presbyterian minister.

Murray, as he departed from Townsend in early 1764, had told the settlers he was headed back to Ireland to resolve some difficulties.[88] He added that there was little prospect of ever returning to America and certainly not in less than one year. According to John Beath, Murray, while waiting for his ship to sail out of New York for Ireland, was stopped by a call for settlement in the Presbyterian Church of New York City.[89] The Second Presbyterian Church of New York reported to the Synod that they had received candidate Murray under their care. Mr. Murray declined accepting this call."[90]

The Presbytery of Philadelphia, on May 8, 1764, encouraged the Second Presbyterian Church of Philadelphia to call John Murray to that church.[91] Prior to August 1764, the Second Presbyterian Congregation in Philadelphia voted to call Murray as its pastor, but held the call in readiness while Murray was under the care of the New York Presbytery. By October 1764, it was clear that "Mr. Murray did not choose to take the Call from Philadelphia under consideration without further Time to deliberate," and so Philadelphia presented Murray with a second call on October 25, 1764.[92]

Murray accepted the church's call and preached in Philadelphia during the last part of 1764 and early 1765.

Rev. Murray later told his Boothbay brethren that he had assumed that his promise to return to Boothbay was null and void since he never did return to Ireland and because he had heard nothing further from Boothbay. Further, he had "been solicited by ministers and people to the southward," leading him to accept the Philadelphia call. In truth, many letters had been sent from Boothbay, including a letter dated February 7, 1765 and signed by most of Boothbay's inhabitants. In the same period, Murray had frequently written to Boothbay to update them about his affairs, but had received no responses. Meanwhile, the Philadelphia Presbytery hurried through his ordination and installation.[93]

The Boothbay settlers and probably John Murray came to believe that the Philadelphia Presbytery had held his mail, as revealed in Boothbay's later session minutes, quite probably penned by church secretary John Beath: "On the very next day after he had expressed his acceptance of their call; all of which appears from his own minutes; on the following week he received several of our letters which we suspect were carefully secreted until the Church there should have his [settle]ment secured, particularly one dated February 25, 1765 signed by most of the inhabitants of this place," confirming that Boothbay had been successfully incorporated, had voted to build a meetinghouse, had employed the workmen, had purchased the materials, and had hastened all preparations for his settlement.[94]

In May 1765, John Murray and the Philadelphia Presbytery held a series of critical meetings. On May 13, Murray preached a sermon and then requested a private meeting regarding his call to Second Presbyterian, admitting he "could not see it clear to be his duty to accept of the call, non [sic] altogether to give it up & therefore referred it to the Committee to attempt to remove his difficulties & determine the affair for him." The Presbytery requested his sermon and his exegesis of John 17:3 ["And this is eternal life, that they may know you, the only true God, and Jesus Christ whom you have sent."] The Presbytery also requested Murray's concurrence in an important Calvinist concept, that subjective certainty is the essence of saving faith. The next day John Murray accepted Philadelphia's call, but the Presbytery deferred action. On May 25, the Presbytery encouraged a "spirit of candor and forbearance," indicating some grumbling and dissent in the Second Presbyterian Church and cleared the way for acceptance of Murray's call. On May 27, after Murray produced his diploma from the University of Edinburgh and certificates of licensure from two Northern Ireland presbyteries, the Philadelphia Presbytery unanimously approved him for ordination at Second Presbyterian Church. On May 28, 1765 the Presbytery proceeded with the ordination and installation of John Murray. However, on August 29 it recommended that Murray travel to England and Ireland to defend himself and to bring all of his papers from the Presbytery with him. The Presbytery held another meeting on October 31, to which John Murray arrived late, having just sailed back from New England. The Presbytery committed to arrange for supply for the church since Murray needed to sail to England and Ireland to confront his accusers and charges against him that impugned his integrity and his pastoral credentials.

On December 18, the Presbytery presumed that John Murray was en route to England and Ireland to face a charge against him and hoped that he would return with a verdict of innocence. The Presbytery indicated that the congregation and Presbytery had great affection for him and were willing to assist and wait for him. The Presbytery declared loyalty to John Murray, although with some doubts about him: "There does not appear sufficient reasons for Mr. Murray's liberation from his present pastoral charge."[95] John Murray had surpassed a much older, famous, and experienced predecessor, Gilbert Tennent,[96] during Murray's brief stay in Philadelphia: "During his short pastorate in Philadelphia, there had been many conversions under his labors, and more additions to the Church than during the whole time of Tennent's ministry."[97] Gilbert Tennent had a co-revivalist, his brother William, who founded in Bucks County, Pennsylvania a log college that was later moved to Princeton, New Jersey. On the site of this log college was later founded a high school, called William Tennent High School, the first major teaching assignment of co-author and professional historian John (Jack) Bauman.

However, on January 31, 1766, John Murray sent a letter from Boston to the Presbytery at Philadelphia, and so by then they knew he had not departed for Ireland and England to face the charges against him.[98] In early February, Murray wrote another letter from Boston to his Boothbay family and friends, informing them that he had left Philadelphia and sued for dismissal from the Philadelphia Presbytery, that he was in Boston and on his way to Ireland on necessary business, that the purpose of the letter was to no longer keep Boothbay in suspense, that he would not return to Boothbay, and that the prospect of his return to America was dim due to his present state of ill health. As soon as Boothbay received Murray's letter, they called a meeting of the selectmen, who hastily dispatched an expedition to Boston comprising Andrew Reed (selectman) and Andrew McFarland (town clerk), who, along with John Beath, had signed the responsive letter of March 6, 1766 that offered Murray 120 pounds annually, one third more than the 90 pounds offered in 1763. Salary did not seem to be a negotiating point, as Murray "never had any hand" in his salary; in fact, a year later, in May 1767, at Rev. Murray's written suggestion for an abatement to relieve the struggling settlers, the town at its May meeting reduced his annual salary to 100 pounds, still 20 times the amount of Boothbay's 1763 pledge to Murray of 5 pounds sterling annually.[99]

A week later, on March 13, the two Andrews met with a very ill John Murray, who was in no condition to return to Boothbay and who pointed out he was not liberated from his former charge in Philadelphia, had no power anyway to accept Boothbay's call, and did not believe he would live much longer. Just in case, however, he proposed certain queries and received answers, all in writing, from Andrew Reed and Andrew McFarland. They assured Murray that the town vote was legal; worship and governance were to be

Presbyterian; Murray could wear a Geneva gown in public ministrations; they could not guarantee Dr. Watts's "Psalms and Hymns" in public worship; and there was no dissent against these votes of the town. Commissioners Reed and McFarland then sent a letter to the synod of New York and Philadelphia, which was to meet in New York in May 1766, imploring it to honor Boothbay's former call to Rev. Murray and informing it that Boothbay did again "renew their former call and are determined to prosecute it before every judicatory of the Church until it is issued in his transportation to us;...and that the whole town of Boothbay unanimously concur herein."[100]

Less than a month after he met with the Boothbay commissioners, on April 9 or 10, 1766, Murray sent another letter to the Philadelphia Presbytery requesting liberation from his charge at Second Presbyterian Church citing health reasons. The Presbytery discussed and deferred the request on May 24. Later in May or early June, Andrew McFarland and Andrew Reed arrived in Philadelphia to personally and repeatedly request Murray's release. The Presbytery was reluctant to release Murray from his successful pastorate in Philadelphia despite rumors against his character and questions about his credentials.[101] Finally, the Philadelphia Presbytery suspended John Murray on June 18, 1766 and dismissed him almost a year later, on April 9, 1767.[102]

The Reverend John Murray

The Reverend John Murray in Boothbay: 1766–1779

After much discussion and multiple negotiations, in July, 1766, John Murray was free and well enough to travel to the District of Maine, where he soon became the first settled minister of the Boothbay Presbyterian Church. Murray first disclosed some irregularities concerning his ministerial certificate obtained in England.

The irregularities related to unethical conduct of some Northern Ireland friends in expediting Murray's credentials when he was around twenty years old. Murray's memoirs fully disclosed all the history of his education and degrees, his licensure to preach, certain difficulties with some ministers in Ireland, and his remorse for attempting to support the error of his Irish friends and authors regarding aspects of his documentation. He also disclosed some censures in public prints, read all the minutes of the New York and Philadelphia Presbytery regarding him, and begged pardon of God and man. When the Reverend Murray asked for support at his first Boothbay town meeting, it was unanimously granted. The Boothbay residents affirmed in that first meeting that they had no problems with any such formalities.[103] Although the Boothbay settlers did not care about such faraway Presbytery credentials, these were taken much more seriously in Philadelphia, later raised again when Murray was transferred to, and preached the rest of his life in, Newburyport, literally made him deathly sick at times, and conceivably hastened his death, at age 51 in 1793.[104]

Meanwhile, in 1764, John Beath and others had negotiated with the Massachusetts General Court in Boston and had succeeded in getting the Town of Boothbay incorporated in the next few months. However, a mystery remains as to how, in 1764, when the town incorporated, the Massachusetts General Court bestowed the name Boothbay for the frontier settlement known since the early 1730s as Townsend. It had been clear, particularly to John Beath, that the town could not be named Townsend because for many years a town in Massachusetts already had that name. In fact, Walter Beath, John Beath's father, had left County Derry in Ulster and arrived with his wife and older son, John, in Boston in 1718, when Walter Beath soon purchased real estate and lived in Lancaster and then Lunenburg, a town adjacent to Townsend, Massachusetts. Then, in 1731 or 1732, when John Beath was about twenty-one, Walter Beath moved his family from their home near Townsend, Massachusetts to live next to their Fullerton relatives in what was then Townsend and then became Boothbay in the Province of Maine.[105] Barbara Rumsey, the Boothbay region's leading local historian, leans toward the belief that Boothbay may be an appellation for Beathbay. Some Northern Ireland scholars have indicated the possibility that the Scots-Irish pronunciation of "beath" and "booth" may have been similar during colonial times.[106] As previously noted, John Beath was a leading citizen of this area and a former Indian captive. The Beaths had owned much of the business district for over thirty years, and John Beath was instrumental in getting the town incorporated, the church settled, and the town name obtained.[107] Although spellings often varied during colonial times, John Beath was particularly gifted in his writing abilities, and so there remains some question as to whether or not "Boothbay" was in honor of his father or of his family, or perhaps slightly disguised for modesty. Further, Scots-Irish, unlike English, far less frequently named towns or other places after individuals, particularly themselves.[108] On the other hand, one wonders if the Beaths also brought the name Townsend when they arrived around 1731, in recognition of the adjoining town named Townsend in Massachusetts, which they had just left.

Despite the lack of any prior settled minister in Boothbay up to 1766, the Reverend John Murray formed probably the largest church in Maine. He was one of only a handful of settled ministers east of Woolwich, in the eastern frontier of the District of Maine. An eloquent orator, Rev. Murray was also an uncommonly active and faithful pastor. His tireless and zealous visiting reached not only all areas of the Boothbay region but all over the Midcoast, including Pownalborough, Sheepscot, Walpole, Harrington, Bristol, and Belfast. His lodgings were frequently crowded and conversations animated, often until three in the morning. His evangelical revivals brought in many new church members. Multitudes who saw and heard him preach the gospel, often for two to three hours at a time, compared him favorably with the great evangelical revivalist, George Whitefield, the renowned English evangelist in America during the First Great Awakening of the 1730s and 1740s.[109]

The smaller reawakening in Lincoln County, which appeared

in the winter or early spring of 1767, was almost entirely inspired by John Murray,.[110] William Williamson (1779–1846), Maine's second governor, one of its first congressmen, and renowned Maine historian, lived just after this remarkable reawakening period in Bangor, Maine. In 1832 he discerned, "Rev. John Murray, a native of Ireland, was a burning light to this people, for 15 years (sic) prior to 1779, when he removed to Newburyport—a minister whose piety was as incense both at the fireside and the altar."[111] Murray's diary extracts "show the vital, energetic character of the man and his deep solicitude for others. His powers did not end in his oratory, but he was an active, faithful pastor in every sense."[112]

In the late 1760s, the Brunswick church reached a tentative and tenuous compromise whereby the Reverend John Miller would occasionally switch pulpits with Boothbay's new and youthful Presbyterian pastor, John Murray. When Rev. Murray, then in his mid-twenties, rose up to preach on Elijah in the Brunswick pulpit, he was interrupted by the staunch, esteemed, and antagonistic Congregationalist, Judge Aaron Hinckley, who was no admirer of Scots-Irish Presbyterians. Rev. Murray had just finished reading the lesson of Elijah under the juniper tree. Judge Hinckley arose from his pew onto the broad aisle of his church, and condescendingly asked Murray if he knew in whose presence he stood. Murray answered completely and accurately that he was aware that he was in the presence of one of the judges of the Inferior Court of Common Pleas. Aiming to rattle the young minister, Judge Hinckley queried: "I say unto you, as the Lord God of Hosts said unto Elijah: 'What does thou here,' John Murray?" Rev. Murray immediately responded by quoting from memory Elijah's answer, "I have been very jealous for the Lord God of Hosts; for the children of Israel have forsaken thy covenant, thrown down thine altars, and slain thy prophets with the sword." Murray discarded his prepared sermon and extemporaneously preached a lengthy sermon on the Elijah text unkindly invoked by Aaron Hinckley. Murray succeeded in sprinkling some severe and sarcastic remarks and ended any further questions.[113]

The Reverend John Murray had free lodging from the outset. His aunt, Jean Murray, born in Antrim in 1698, had married Andrew Reed, and they arrived at Townsend in 1730, among the first wave of founding settlers. Around 1764, Rev. John Murray's father, Robert, and another John Murray, who was a nephew of Robert and a cousin to Rev. John Murray, had departed Northern Ireland and probably arrived at Boothbay in the early 1760s. Cousin John Murray was married to Anna Montgomery, presumably by Rev. Murray, at Captain Andrew and Jean Reed's home on January 22, 1767. He soon became a leading town figure, along with Andrew Reed and the Reverend John Murray.[114]

In 1767, two years before he died, Boothbay resident John Reed signed his will, asserting:

> First of all I commit my Soul unto God thro' the hands of my only Advocate, the Lord Jesus Christ, on whose perfect righteousness alone I depend for Justification, thro that everlasting Covenant of Grace which I desire to the embracing as the only plan of my redemption, and my body to the dust to be interred, with decent Christian burial at the discretion of my Executors: hoping to receive the same again at the resurrection of the Just.

Reed appointed "my trusty friends, the Revd John Murray, Mr. Robert Murray, and Mr. David Reed all of Boothbay to be the Executors…and Guardians of my beloved Wife and all my Children." Reed directed his executors "to take care that all my children be educated in the fear of God, in the Protestant reformed Religion, agreeable to the Westminster Confession of Faith and Catechisms, according to their Circumstances in life, at the expense of my Estate."[115] Religion, faith, and education were central to John Reed and to many of his contemporaries, often spelled out in their wills; and the Reverend Murray, particularly during this 1767 reawakening, was a popular choice for many tasks, including that of executor and guardian for John Reed, who owned land adjacent to Murray.[116]

On April 13, 1777, more than a decade after the construction and dedication of the meetinghouse/church, this Presbyterian community held its first celebration of the Lord's supper. The earliest officers were both elders and deacons, similar to the Congregational church's trustees and deacons today.

As early as September 1768, the Newburyport Presbyterian Church was pressing for John Murray to preach in that town. Newburyport also requested that Boothbay join the Presbytery of Boston. Boothbay refused both overtures.[117] Again, in February 1769, Newburyport requested six to eight "Sabbath supplies" of Murray to their congregation beginning in April. The Boothbay Session, comprising elders and deacons elected by the membership, with John Murray present but silent on the subject, quickly and unanimously rejected Newburyport again, as they had "maturely considered, we cannot but suspect some formed design of removing him from us entirely," reasoning in part that "the Summer is the principal season in which multitudes can attend…public worship here." Interestingly, Boothbay's Session, probably referring to slanders about John Murray in the Boston press and to tensions with Philadelphia a decade earlier, praised Newburyport's Presbyterian support of Murray:

> "[As] the patrons and friends of oppressed truth in the worst of times, who have nobly struggled in the cause of Good at Newbury for many years thro' a continual torrent of opposition and persecution, and in the year 1760 [sic] dared to stand up tho' almost alone and espouse the cause of a persecuted stranger whom the Pastors of Boston and Philadelphia had conspired to destroy whilst all the country stood silently by."[118]

In 1776 John Murray wrote the Massachusetts General Court and voiced the land title concerns of Boothbay's townspeople. In doing so, he was echoing the depositions of four of Townsend's founders and leading men four years earlier. The Reverend Murray, like the four founders, described the promises made and broken by Dunbar in 1729 and 1730, assuring good title to the land they had settled. Murray described how after the Indian wars, Boothbay's settlers "have been attacked by several persons claiming the property of their lands under various pretexts." Murray went on to chronicle how "the settlers have been constantly harassed and many so terrified as to purchase their own farms at different times and from three or four different and opposite claimants." Murray added, "Others still continue to disturb them in like manner." Fearing the exodus of townspeople, the town of Boothbay, in 1769, 1777, and 1787, agreed to pay for legal defense costs of townspeople against outside claimants.[119]

Boothbay Presbyterian Church
Sessional Records: 1767–1778

The sessional records of the Congregational Church of Boothbay Harbor are a treasure trove of facts and feelings that open the doors for us to peek into and catch glimpses of life in and outside the church almost 250 years ago. During these colonial years, the church was the town government as well as the church government, as there was little separation of church and state. During this period, Boothbay settlers were also ruled from Boston by the Massachusetts General Court, the legislature, the Boston governors and the Boston-based court system. In 1760, Lincoln County was incorporated, and the county seat was Pownalborough, now Dresden. Perhaps most important, except for the events from 1766 to September 1767, the Boothbay church session records were recorded contemporaneously, and even the first-year records were written only one year later, before September 27, 1767, "brought in and read and this Session declares it to be a true and faithful history of fact from the first steps to the settlement of the Church down to this day; which we attest with our hand" by the deacons, elders, and pastor.[120] It appears that John Beath (1710–1798), the very literate clerk of Session, was the author. The Sessional Records of Boothbay, discovered by Boothbay Harbor historian Francis B. Greene in 1902 and delivered by Greene to Elizabeth Freeman

Reed in 1930, are now in many hands, including the Congregational Church of Boothbay Harbor website.[121] Somewhat mysteriously, these detailed sessional records, which reveal the wonders and warts of our community and our church, ended abruptly. Except for lists of church communicants, baptisms, and marriages, the sessional records stop on March 23, 1770, amidst a very notable lawsuit brought by Boothbay's McCobb clan, who were pressing serious charges against cousin John Murray and very possibly against the Reverend John Murray himself.

Many session meetings took place at the homes of some of the church leaders, deacons or elders and increasingly later at the "Session house," where the Nicholas Knight House is today. Murray attended most session meetings and served as moderator. Many session meetings were spent in prayer, fasting, singing, and spiritual conferences.

The Session's first meeting, held on September 20, 1767, was organizational. Article 1 made the close-knit relationship of church and state quite clear, just nine years before the American Revolution: "That the town of Boothbay shall be deemed to be under the ecclesiastical constitution of Presbyterians as to worship, ordinance, discipline and government."[122]

The Presbyterian Second Book of Discipline empowered ministers with doctrine, elders with discipline, and deacons with distribution and care of ecclesiastical goods.[123] At the outset, on September 20, 1767, the four ruling elders were William Moore (witness to Boothbay's first murder in 1739[124]), Robert Murray (father of the Reverend John Murray[125]), John Beath (a Townsend founder and leader in incorporating Boothbay), and Nehemiah Herrenden (a petitioner in at least three court cases and a payer of poll tax in a log home of two residents). Deacons were Israel Davis, Samuel Adams, and Ephraim McFarland.[126] Three years later, on February 7, 1770, the Session queried about the absence of Deacon Ephraim McFarland from so many session meetings, but decided not to censure him since "circumstances and business by sea has made his absence unavoidable…; therefore the Session judge that his name need not be continued in our minutes until he returns to answer it."[127] However, the session minutes only continued one more month, into March 1770 and abruptly ended, with the rest of the manuscript missing.[128]

John Murray immediately "began a course of pastoral visitations, in which he went to all the inhabitants, at their houses, and conversed with every one, old and young, separately, and one by one, concerning the states of their souls and the great work of salvation that was necessary that all should experience in order to their final welfare." He entered in his book his remarks, the name of every person, and the state in which he found them. He concluded every visit with prayer.

Next, in 1766, Murray set up a Monday evening society for prayer, which rotated to every house, where three or four heads of families went to pray. Soon these prayer society meetings became so crowded with young and old of both sexes that Murray turned them into evening lectures, where he spent more time expounding the scriptures than focusing on prayers. He maintained that format for many years.[129]

Around the same time, Murray established a Wednesday lecture series, held in turn in several quarters of the town. Those in attendance were separated into three groups: children under fourteen, unmarried persons, and heads of families. The meetings consisted of public catechizing, where each group answered Rev. Murray's questions concerning matters of religious doctrine.[130]

In the winter of 1767, Rev. Murray was concerned about the warmth and distance of the meetinghouse (just north of today's Boothbay Common area) from most dwellings. He raised funds, purchased a large iron stove in Boston, and returned with it and all its furniture in the beginning of winter. The meetinghouse, boarded, shingled, and heated by the wood stove, enabled all people to "sit with some comfort even in the coldest weather."[131] However, by November 1768, the discouraged church leaders ceased further work in finishing the session house until spring, but appointed Deacon Robert Murray "to take care that the brick for the chimney be secured & hauled to the place in the Winter."[132] Sessional records show that deacons Robert Murray and John Beath bought and hauled shingles to the session house in October 1779 for repairs.[133]

By the spring of 1767, eleven men and twenty women applied to be members of the new Boothbay church. Soon, an additional seven men and thirteen women had joined.[134] Women would forever outnumber men in the Boothbay Presbyterian and later the Congregational church.

Throughout the winter of 1767, a reawakening occurred in Boothbay. Maine historian Louis Hatch observed, "John Murray… had a remarkable ministry at Boothbay from 1767 to 1780 (sic). The first great revival in the history of the State attended his abundant labors, and his journal is a devotional book of the first order."[135] The session minutes reveal that "a very unusual seriousness and solemnity appeared amongst the generality of the people here, accompanied with an insatiable desire after the word, and several persons awakened to an anxious concern for their souls." Nothing remarkable happened publicly "until the sacrament; then there were such symptoms of the powerful and special presence of God of grace as every one might discern and we can never enough be thankful for; it was a solemn, sweet and glorious season."

This period of awakening in Boothbay quickly catapulted the Reverend John Murray to his two-week "Gospel errand" at Squam, Free Town, Pownalborough, Sheepscut Head, Walpole, and Harrington. Each day Murray preached, "some were awakened; many souls old and young were pricked to the heart, many obliged to cry out, in their distress, some were clearly brought out into the light of the gospel." This period of awakening, like all such eras, "was very joyful to all who had ever tasted any thing of religion—very alarming to the secure—and greatly confirmed the convictions of such as had been awakened; religion became the conversation of all companies; the voice of opposition was struck dead; upon almost every occasion of public worship, which as then more frequent than usual, the congregation was drowned in tears." The pastor's lodgings were "daily crowded with poor wounded souls," finding "sweet employment day and night, sometimes till three o'clock in the morning, often till midnight." Indeed, "great companies would retire to the woods to sing hymns of praise," and "it seemed as if heaven was come down to dwell on earth."

During that spring and summer of 1767, the awakening seemed most pronounced in young people. At one church service in the western end of town, over thirty men and women cried out after the blessing was pronounced in church. Pastor Murray was called to visit numerous neighboring places and visited several times in Pemaquid, Muscongus, Broad Cove, Walpole, and Harrington. In Broad Cove (now Waldoboro), the crowds were particularly large, and in Bristol, Murray helped them organize a Presbyterian church and ordain its elders.[136] In October 1767, an astounding 220 communicants participated in a communion service, with "several persons being remarkably awakened & many comforted in a surprising manner" with tokens of divine presence and great power shown in the solemn and general affection that were present throughout the service.[137]

Women dominated the numbers of Boothbay's church, but men ruled. Women outnumbered men in Boothbay's colonial Presbyterian church, except for the April 1767 list of new members and the May and October 1770 lists of communicants. And yet only thirty-three men, one-fifth of the 150 men listed in the 1771 valuation, joined the church.[138] Moreover, only men held the church leadership positions of deacons, elders, and pastor.[139] More men congregants were censured (Benjamin Thomas, Hezekiah Herrinden, William Reed, and Samuel Wheeler), while only half that number of women congregants were censured (Mary Thomas and Jane Reed). No women congregants received the lighter sentence of suspension, while two men congregants were suspended: William McCobb and Israel Davis.[140] As chronicled below, women more than men were charged with adultery and fornication, were roughly equal with men on charges of intoxication, and suffered more severe penalties.

Baptismal notations from 1766 to 1778 in the session records reveal that most baptisms occurred in 1767, John Murray's first full year, when sixty-six individuals were baptized, and in 1770, when around eighty were baptized. Far fewer baptisms occurred during the tumultuous Revolutionary War years. Baptismal congregants or their parents came from the following locations: Pleasant Cove, Sheepscot, Hopkins, Walpole, Carletons, Oven Mouth, Pemaquid, Harrington, Muscongus, Broad Cove (now Waldoboro), Salt Marsh Cove, Damariscove, Georgetown, St. George, Patterson, Hylers, Robinson, Head of Tide, Newcastle, Meduncook, Copeland, Kirkpatrick, Fox Islands, Pownalborough, Whitefield, Topsham, Hallowell, Gurnett, Gouldboro, Eastern Bay, Western Bay, Frenchman's Bay, Union River, Deer Island, Winterport, Winslow's Port Harbor, Damariscotty, Edgecomb, Salem, and Pisgah.[141] In addition, sessional records included marriages, which also help develop an interesting portrait of the Boothbay region. A notable name in the records was that of Faithful Singer, who married Susannah Knight, on April 8, 1768.

Much session business, beginning in October 1767, had to deal with cases of drunkenness, fornication, and other social sins. For example, a case of drunkenness was lodged by Samuel Kelly, Sr., against Benjamin Thomas. However, procedurally, the complaint was lodged with the church too late for compliance with the necessary "gospel steps" of due process, and so the Session directed deacons Davis and McFarland to "immediately call Mr. Thomas aside and converse with him faithfully on this matter." They were to try to resolve it informally and, if not, to be "at liberty to refuse him communion until the case come to a full hearing before us." The church leaders quickly satisfied themselves after conferring with Mr. Thomas, but Mr. Kelly continued to plague the session meetings with ongoing complaints, with the apparent aim "to destroy the character of Mr. Thomas." Although Samuel Kelly, not a member of the church, had not taken one "gospel step" to help address the problem with Benjamin Thomas, the Session decided that they needed to hear this heinous case, which was utterly denied by Thomas, although he was known by all his acquaintances to have "labored" with his drinking problem for years.

Due to the death of Thomas's daughter, trial was delayed until March 9, 1768. Despite much compassion shown, a decision was reached that Thomas was unfit for communion. Surprisingly, at the conclusion of the session decree, Benjamin Thomas admitted his drinking problem, asserted that he had taken liquors as medicine for his illness, begged forgiveness of the Lord and of the church, and was willing to submit to any decision of the Session. Just as surprisingly, the Session reversed its decision and received Benjamin Thomas back into the church.[142] The last word occurred at the meeting of September 26, 1769, after Benjamin and Mary Thomas and their family moved out of the region, with the Session "solemnly warning the said persons to take heed to themselves in the land where they now dwell as those who must give an account in the day when the secrets of all hearts shall be laid open."[143] This pronouncement appears to have been more for those left behind than for the Thomas family, which had already flown the coop.

A similar drunkenness complaint was brought against Martha Reed, a church member. The church moderator, presumably the Reverend John Murray, directed her "to abstain," from drinking alcoholic beverages, from church attendance, or from communion, which shall remain unclear until a hearing could be held. Martha Reed, while the moderator was speaking, appeared before the Session, freely confessed her sin, professed her sorrow, humiliation, and abhorrence of the crime, and begged whatever censure except being "debarred." The Session gladly accepted her acknowledgment, directed her to stand and be publicly rebuked before the session, and dismissed her to her former standing.[144]

Another intoxication complaint, lodged by Eunice Decker against Samuel and Elizabeth Pierce, husband and wife, was due to excessive liquor consumed on September 15, 1768. The Pierces refused to appear, and the Session could do nothing. On April 21, 1769 it requested that the deacons meet with Mr. Decker to resolve this informally and, if not, to issue citations again for both Mr.

Decker and Eunice Decker to appear.[145] Finally, on August 1, after two deacons went to the Pierce house at Ebenecook and listened to the testimony of the Pierces, Mrs. Decker and her witness, Captain Jonathan Ingraham, the deacons found the intoxication charge false, based on "groundless suspicions," and secured the confession of Mrs. Decker of "her error in suspecting and debating so publicly the scandal now in agitation." Mr. and Mrs. Pierce forgave the injury and "peace and reconciliation between them appeared."[146]

A decade later, in November 1778, a different Decker, Margaret, who was a member of the church, wrote a letter that contained "many sentences of slander against the Session, the Boothbay church, and the whole Presbyterian Communion, occasioned by this Session having refused occasional communion to her father, a member of some other Church, on account of various charges of adultery tabled before us against him." The Session judged that the letter required the Session's written "answer of admonition and rebuke" against Margaret Decker, who had "acted unbecoming her profession."[147]

The first fornication case, in October 1767, was one raised by Sarah Bowers, an applicant from Bristol to the Boothbay church, after she had prematurely taken part in communion. She submitted herself to the censure of the Session, sincerely repenting of not only this communion misstep but also of fornication years earlier with a man now her husband. She made a public appearance in the congregation, where she was rebuked and admonished publicly. Pastor Murray declared that God had already forgiven her sin and that it was not the prerogative of a pastor to forgive anyway. He concluded with an exhortation to her and also to the congregation, especially to parents and youth of both sexes, followed by a prayer and dismissal. An interesting side note is that the Boothbay elders were having great difficulties policing who could or could not take communion since they could not distinguish among the many persons from neighboring towns.[148] The church failed to rebuke Sarah Bowers' husband, either because he may not have been a member of this church or because he was male.

Another fornication case was lodged against Jane Reed, a former member of the church at Portglenone in Ireland and under scandal for fornication with William McFarland. She was rebuked for that sin in March 1768, when she repented. For some reason, she was hauled back to the Session in August for a second repentance "before the congregation to conclude her probation and have the said scandal wiped away." No such rebuke of William McFarland was made, but he does not appear to have been a member of the church.[149] Actually, neither was Jane Reed, who joined the church as a member only in September 1768.[150]

Jane Reed faced another fornication charge on September 26, 1769, when moderator Rev. Murray informed the session that he had found "certain evil reports" about her including "a suspicion of fornication with Robert Hogg, a tradesman who has lately resided in this town." Due to the desire that "the Church may be kept clear of all scandals, the Session judge it necessary to inquire into the grounds of said rumors without delay." Rev. Murray had already examined both Jane Reed and Robert Hogg and all witnesses one by one in her presence. Both Reed and Hogg were waiting outside the session door to appear and keep their liberty through the oath of purgation, or purification, to "clean-wash" themselves if they could prove themselves innocent. However, because Hogg was a transient and not a member of any church, the Session could not summon him for trial nor censure him if found guilty. As for Jane Reed, the Session decided that although prior allegations proved false and the present accusations could not be proven, some of her behavior required the Session to suspend her from enjoyment of special church privileges until "evidences of a penitent and holy conversation [with God or the church leaders] shall have removed all grounds of these suspicions."[151] Hardly innocent until proven guilty.

Yet another fornication case arose in April 1769 concerning a church member, the wife of Hezekiah Herrinden, who recently "has been delivered of child." Since she was not Herrinden's wife until January 4, 1769, "said child could not have been begotten in lawful wedlock." A church member was designated to confront Herrinden, who neither denied nor acknowledged he was the father. The Session considered this "scandal," declared Herrinden guilty until properly cleared through "ecclesiastical process," and "to prevent the scandal from falling on this church, and to show their abhorrence of fornication & all uncleanness," judged Hezekiah Herrinden unfit for communion and debarred from church membership.[152]

In November 1769, James Kennedy and his wife Phoebe had been "on tryals since the Spring and having received a first and second rebuke before this Session for the crime of fornication are ordered to appear before us on the morning of the next Lord's Day that they may be admitted to make known the evidence of their repentance..." Having complied with sessional orders and submitted to examinations, James Kennedy was allowed admission to make his public profession of religion. The Session also permitted the baby and Phoebe to be baptized.[153] A month later, Phoebe Kennedy again appeared and was "examined and exhorted before this Session," then "made public profession of religion," and "was received solemnly and baptized after the manner of adults."[154]

In December 1769, Susannah Dey applied to the Session, acknowledging her "sin of fornication in order to clear the way for her taking the requisite steps to have her children baptized." However, "this Session having heard that her husband strenuously opposes it, and that our granting this request is likely to produce bad effects in the family, judge it our duty to defer the matter till we can see." The sessional records do not contain any further information on this fornication and baptism dispute; however the extant, monthly minutes of the session ended in March 1770.[155]

The Reverend Murray, at the February 2, 1767 session meeting, was concerned about some recent "transactions in a distant corner of the town," constituting "glaring cases" and was also concerned about the "remissness of the civil officers who neglect to the law observed." Rev. Murray, the deacons, and the elders all agreed, a year later, on March 1, 1768, on a set of articles to establish a society for the reformation of manners in Boothbay, with the plan to be distributed throughout the four church districts in Boothbay.[156]

In perhaps an example of just such a glaring case, in the same month, the Session found David and Mrs. Reed and Mr. and Mrs. Wiley guilty of renting rooms to people in from the sea who were living in adultery, with the resulting scandal and bad example for others. The Reeds and Wileys admitted the facts, but denied that they could do anything about passengers and guests, who were not accountable to them so long as they paid their accommodations. Further, they could not restrain them in the use of a public cabin or house. The Session found them "guilty of giving aids and encouragement as well as connivance to the sin they commit," with aggravated circumstances being that they were forewarned of these adulterous activities. Finally, the Session ruled that "the keeping of a public tavern is no excuse for keeping a bad house." The Session ruled the Reeds and Wileys "be publicly rebuked at our Bar, and suspended until repentance." Instead the defendants readily announced their guilt and their sense of sinfulness.[157]

Deacon Samuel Adams and either Rev. Murray or his father, Deacon Robert Murray, reported visiting during January 1768 all the families in their district. The visits were gladly received by all, and many unbaptized adults and families expressed earnest desire to receive baptism. The Session stood ready to "admit all in whom there is a visibility of Christianity." [158]

The Session, in December 1768, grappled with marriage regulations and rationalized that because marriage is not merely "an ordinance of the state, but an institution of the Almighty Creator, it properly belongs to the Church and not to the State to settle whatever pertains to the celebration of it." New rules included the need for "a Gospel Minister lawfully authorized, if such a gospel minister may be obtained" to solemnize marriages and publication of "their banns" for their marital purpose in the public congregation for "three several days" by the session clerk or another person appointed by the Session. In addition, the performing minister "shall receive a gratuity of six shillings lawful money from the parties concerned," and the town clerk for every bann so asked shall be paid by the parties at the time one shilling and four-pence for recording and certifying to same.[159]

The Session also gave relief to the poor, as in March 1769, when the church gave the widowed Mrs. Joseph Farnham one bushel of Indian meal, one bushel of potatoes, and 12 pounds of beef for herself and her family.[160]

Earthquakes shook the region in November 1769. On November 7, the Session met at the session house, but then adjourned to the meetinghouse to attend public worship. This was "a day set apart in this town for public fasting and humiliation under the late awful signs of divine anger manifested in repeated shocks of Earthquake, to deprecate deserved judgments and implore a gracious revival of religion in the world especially in this place."[161]

Earthquakes caused by human activities were also erupting in Boothbay's community and its church during these early years. Church deacons continued to visit community members in each of the four districts they had assigned to themselves. Ruling Elder and Clerk John Beath reported to the Session in January 1770 that he had "performed his official visitations of the families in his bounds and finds them in general improving in peace and desires after divine things;" and, substituting for William Moore in another town district, reported that "family worship is set up in some families that used to neglect it" and found "knowledge improved, especially in youth." However, other church leaders Ruling Elder, Robert Murray, and Deacon Samuel Adams found that "little improvement appears and family religion awfully neglected in the other two districts of Boothbay."[162]

There may have been some hints of a baptismal crack in the relationship between Rev. John Murray and the Session leaders in March 1771.

> The "Session judge that it shall be accounted disorderly for the Minister to baptize within our bounds, without an act of the Session expressly allowing that privilege to the present

candidate, or at least the presence and consent of some of its members, and as there has arisen some inconveniences from baptizing at lectures in the several quarters of the town on account of the absence of the officers of the Church; and as there is a place of public worship in the town to which every person may conveniently repair for gospel ordinances, therefore this Session judge, that no baptisms may for the future be regularly administered in the town except at that place—and Ordered that a copy of this Minute be read by the Clerk on the Sabbath after the public worship is ended."[163]

Was this baptismal dispute directly or indirectly related to a dispute between the Reverend Murray and the McCobb clan that was simmering or perhaps erupting? Or was this a separate tension only between the church leaders and the minister that came to a head when the McCobb dispute against at least Rev. Murray's cousin John Murray erupted again?

In September 1769, a mysterious fray had erupted between cousin John Murray and perhaps Rev. John Murray on one side and, on the other side, the McCobb clan, which included Samuel McCobb and three of his sons, William, John, and James, and their future brothers-in-law, John and James Auld, who had married Samuel's daughters Mary and Frances, respectively in 1770 and 1772.[164] All but James McCobb appear to have been members of the Boothbay church.[165]

No formal complaint had yet been lodged, as "no formal complaint having been before this Session, relative to that unhappy fray—the near approach of the Lord's Supper will not allow time to try the said parties as yet." The church elders rationalized "this SESSION to testify their abhorrence of such practices, to warn all others against the indulgence of such sinful practices, so provoking to God & dishonoring the christian name, and to keep this Church clear of the scandal of this offence." The Session, in September 1769, surprisingly and quickly, before any formal charges were made, suspended the McCobbs and John Auld from taking sacraments until "said offence be wiped away according to the rules of Christ's house."[166] Two months later, in November 1769, the session read the detailed minutes on the McCobb versus Murray case and "are sorry to find that the parties therein mentioned have as yet, notwithstanding their promise, taken no steps to end the difference between them." Indeed, as the session records would later record, the parties had a physical fight of some sort in August or September 1769. Church leaders Elder Herrinden and Deacon Adams were directed by the Session to admonish them, try to "bring it to a close," and report back. Herrinden reported to the Session in February 1770 that "the debate is now under arbitration."[167]

But the feud continued to boil and simmer. These same six disputants, back on August 15, 1769, had "an unchristian quarrel which proceeded to blows." Thus, the "Session considering that they have foreborne them for very long, and that no reconciliation as yet has taken place between them, ORDERED that they all [possibly including their minister who usually served also as the session moderator] be cited with their witnesses to appear before us on Monday the 12th inst. At ten o'clock in order for tryal."

On March 12, 1770, the Session was led by substitute moderator Sloan, an elder of the Church of Bristol, indicating that Rev. Murray was also implicated. Four of the six parties appeared: Samuel and John McCobb, John Auld and probably cousin and not Rev. John Murray, although the minutes only refer to "John Murray." William and James McCobb were the only absent parties. Each attending party was heard, testified, and then examined first by the opposing party and then by the moderator and each member of the Session. The substance was recorded by Clerk John Beath, who then read it publicly. It was affirmed and signed by the "respective relaters" and was retained in the minutes, until hidden and later lost or destroyed. On March 23, 1770, the minutes of the last Session were read and two additional witnesses, Andrew McFarland and Andrew Reed, clearly ready to testify on behalf of John Murray, were sworn as witnesses, examined, signed their depositions, and withdrew.[168] Andrew McFarland, very successful and part of the foremost family "from a society point of view," had been born in 1725, and thus was 45 years of age, son of founder John McFarland, and frequently away from his wife and eight children (eventually to be eleven), at sea in the West Indies and other parts. Tellingly, his youngest son at the time was John Murray McFarland, born September 26, 1767[169] and baptized during Boothbay's reawakening by the Reverend Murray on October 10, 1767[170]. Andrew Reed, uncle of Rev. John Murray, Townsend founder, and ancestor of the largest Boothbay family, had been born in Antrim in 1698 and so was 72 years old when he testified.[171]

What a coincidence that not one more word of the session minutes was retained after March 23, 1770! The only other remnants of session records were the dry lists of communicants, baptisms, and marriages from 1767 to 1780. Was someone protecting the Reverend John Murray? The very literate and capable clerk, John Beath, lived another two decades until 1798, and so it wasn't for lack of a scrupulous scribe. Indeed, Beath recorded the trial, read it out loud publicly, and received the witnesses' affirmations. Beath added, probably later in the last pages of the sessional minutes, that all this trial testimony "is still kept *in retentis*," which means evidence taken to be laid aside until the proper time arrives for adducing it.[172] Did that adducing time ever arrive? We will probably never know the substance and details of this dispute, but we will see in Chapter 4 that this significant feud was not resolved until twenty-eight years later, when it became front and center in the very first act of the new Congregational church.

John Murray During the American Revolution

The Reverend John Murray leaped into politics as Boothbay's representative to the Revolutionary Congress in Massachusetts around 1775. He was the diplomat who saved Boothbay from British bombardment and burning in 1777 and similarly saved Wiscasset from the same fate a year later. Murray shipped out in 1779 with the Continental Army to Castine, a loyalist stronghold, where the patriots were defeated. Subsequently, the American general sent Murray to Boston as his emissary to report the defeat and to plead for aid to the poor in the District of Maine. Following the Revolution, in 1783, while in Newburyport, Murray was at the forefront of agrarian land reform, when he delivered a radical address and published a famous pamphlet in his attempt to continue the American Revolution.[173]

John Murray was a leading patriot from the outset. In March 1775, Boothbay's annual town meeting chose him to attend the Provincial Congress in Concord, New Hampshire in May.[174] The Boothbay and Bristol peninsulas were the most revolutionary of the coastal towns.[175] Scots-Irish on those peninsulas and throughout America had always been fanatically anti-British,[176] and they were regarded as the best fighting men in America.[177]

Murray's role in saving Boothbay in 1777 from bombardment was a tremendous diplomatic achievement. The British had just bombed and burned Portland to the ground. The British commander, Sir George Collier, sailed the *H.M.S. Rainbow* into Boothbay during the summer of 1777 and spent three weeks anchored in Townsend (now Boothbay) Harbor. He requested free passage to the shore to fill the water casks of the *Rainbow* and those of another British ship, the *Hope*. Boothbay's Committee of Safety, remembering what had recently happened to Portland, reluctantly gave permission for taking the water.

The Boothbay militia had just captured Thomas Goldthwaite, an American Tory, and they also had imprisoned some British officers and men from the *Hope*. All of them were marched through Boothbay toward Boston as prisoners of war. Some of the British officers, who had just come ashore for water, saw them and demanded the release of the British men. Boothbay's militia, fearing the worst, released all but the American Tory, Goldthwaite. Next, Sir George Collier weighed anchor, brought *H.M.S. Rainbow* into the inner harbor, sent a flag of truce ashore, and demanded instant release of Goldthwaite, who had greatly aided the British at Penobscot. Collier threatened destruction of Boothbay if the Tory were not returned in a half hour. The Boothbay militia returned the terrified Goldthwaite to the *Rainbow*, where he reported to the British officers that he had no doubt that he would have been hanged by the American rebels.

After again receiving permission from the Boothbay residents, the *Rainbow* sent its longboat ashore with empty water casks to be filled at the same watering place. Ashore just a few minutes, a number of armed Boothbay Scots-Irish hotheads came down, seized the longboat, and took the master and eight British as prisoners. Sir George Collier ordered a flat-bottomed boat that contained fifty marines and some officers in addition to the rowers to fetch the imprisoned men, and the British carried out those orders without the loss of a single man. The armed Boothbay men were taken completely by surprise as they had never seen a flat-bottomed boat before, and they gazed in astonishment as they saw eighteen oars in motion, not a single man in sight, and only the cannon in the bow. Commodore Collier, moored in Boothbay's harbor and aware of Rev. John Murray's widely respected reputation, negotiated directly and only with Rev. Murray, who was the only Boothbay inhabitant allowed to dine and negotiate with him aboard the *Rainbow* under another flag of truce in late August and early September 1777. The toughness and negotiating skills of Rev. Murray are evident in the compromise he and Collier worked out. Captain Paul Reed of Boothbay, who was present, later wrote of Rev. Murray's eloquence, earnestness, and dignity in negotiating with the British; and "he was superior in personal knowledge to any other man that ever walked God's footstool." Paul Reed added that the British "officers were greatly surprised to see such a specimen of dignity coming from the coast of Maine." Boothbay was spared from destruction.[178]

The Massachusetts General Court recognized Boothbay's strategic significance, responded to the town's request for help with the delivery of several cannons, but issued only a paper authorization to raise fifty men to serve as a garrison. Not only were recruits impossible to find, but Boothbay selectmen found the military stores more like bait than a deterrent to the enemy. So Boothbay people saved the cannons and themselves by hiding the cannons deep in the woods, out of the reach of the marauding enemy and of use to nobody. Rev. Murray bitterly complained to the Massachusetts General Court that although "the Eastern Country may seem neglected by the General Court, it appears to be considered of no small importance to the enemy of America," and Murray added that Boothbay's "inhabitants suppose themselves entitled to the protection of Government in common with other parts of the State."[179]

By 1779, the British had concluded that Murray was such a valuable aid to the American cause that they offered a price of 500 pounds (about $3,000 today) for his capture.[180] Murray's descendant and twentieth-century historian, Elizabeth Reed, noted that this price on his head, among other things, resulted in Murray's acceptance of a call to the Old South Parish Presbyterian Church in safer, more prosperous, and larger Newburyport, where he started preaching in 1779 and was formally accepted as their settled minister until his death in 1793.[181] Murray, however, during the remainder of his life and down to today has powerfully and profoundly influenced Boothbay, Maine's Midcoast, and much of northern New England. Without Murray, perhaps no pastor would have been found in 1764, thus delaying the town's incorporation. Boothbay's population and businesses would have been even more impoverished and less significant, and the British probably would have burned Boothbay to the ground, as they did Falmouth, now Portland, during the American Revolution. Further, the Boothbay church would not have had its remarkable revivalist reawakening and its most memorable and famous church leader. The Reverend John Murray's light continues to illuminate living stones, spiritual cornerstones, and worldly wonders in many lives 250 years later.

CHAPTER 3

STRUGGLING TO SURVIVE: 1779–1798
by Chip Griffin

Introduction

With the loss of their charismatic John Murray to Newburyport in 1779, Boothbay's Presbyterian church struggled without leadership from the pulpit and mostly without any regular minister. When the church had a minister, he was generally in Boothbay for only a week or so at a time. The few ministers called to Boothbay were young and lasted only a year or two before the town would refuse to continue their employment or until the ministers found something better elsewhere. Church attendance at weekly meetings dwindled to forty or fewer, even when there was a regular minister, according to the diary of the Reverend Jonathan Gould, who served for just over two years from late 1789 to early 1792. The extant sessional minutes ended abruptly in March 1779 with the departure of John Murray. The Boothbay Presbyterian Church struggled to survive without any Presbyterian support during this period. Sometime after the Reverend Gould's departure in 1792 the church collapsed. It was resurrected as a Congregational church in 1798.

Rev. John Murray in Newburyport, Massachusetts—1779–1793

The Reverend John Murray started preaching at the Second Presbyterian Church of Newburyport in 1779, but was not appointed as its settled minister until June 4, 1781. While the church had for a decade pressed the Presbytery to transfer Murray from Boothbay, a few Newburyport church members strenuously opposed his settlement there at least in part due to the controversies twenty years earlier surrounding his credentials from Northern Ireland.[182] The "Presbytery to the Eastward," which included Boothbay, had over many years given multiple reasons regarding its selection of Murray for Newburyport, Massachusetts, including the fact that Newburyport was the largest Presbyterian church in New England and had "not less than ten times the number of hearers he can preach to at Boothbay." The Presbytery at a meeting in Cape Elizabeth on June 14, 1780 finally required and enjoined the Newburyport congregation to receive and acknowledge John Murray as their settled pastor.[183]

Despite some undercurrents in Newburyport, John Murray continued to evoke his power as a preacher, drew large audiences, and held them in fixed attention throughout his discourses, which were often over two hours in length. Murray "was said to have been slightly pompous, but dignified in presence, courteous, sincerely kind, and by his people enthusiastically loved."[184] Alexander Blaikie, Presbyterian historian of New England, remarked about Boothbay's loss of Murray precisely a century later, in 1881:

> This was a day of desolation for the congregation at Boothbay. They had for nearly fourteen years hung with devotion on his lips; in seasons of vast and imminent danger they had shared with him perils of which he was extensively both the cause and the occasion; and now they were by the demands of Divine Providence and the authority of their own Presbytery bereft of him for whom for some six years they had with heroic fortitude contended against judicious and able commissioners from other churches.[185]

Boothbay parishioners on August 11, 1784, sent a letter to the Presbytery "requesting a supply" of ministers. They did "not appear to have received any of a permanent character, and they eventually in the subsequent eight years in common with all Presbyterianism in Maine, fell asleep in the oblivious embrace of surrounding and assimilating Congregationalism."[186]

On May 19, 1780, months after Murray's departure, Boothbay along with most of New England experienced literally a dark day. The tremendous burning of trees and slash, caused by massive clearing of land for farms and homes as well as for the lucrative lumber trade, resulted in an infamous "dark day," when a vast cloud of smoke combined with thick cloud cover plunged northern New England into nearly total darkness.[187] Three years later, Rev. Murray described the alarm and surprise:

> About a week after the surrender of the capital city of the southern colonies, the inhabitants of New-England were alarmed with an unusual darkness that hung over their states, from ten o'clock in the forenoon till midnight; the minds of the people were greatly agitated, and various essays were published to pass it off as a phenomenon easily accounted for in a natural way; but, however, it might be produced by the operation of natural causes, it would be an impious neglect of divine Providence, to ascribe it to a concurrence of incidents that was merely fortuitous; it was a fact that soon became notorious enough, that, whilst darkness covered the face of the states to the southward, and the defeat and dispersion of our troops at Cambden [Camden, New Jersey]...A cloud of deeper darkness did, at that instant, hang over New England; and menace a storm more violent and ruinous than ever fell in that quarter.

At that very time Benedict Arnold, described by Murray as "that American Judas," who had command of West Point, attempted to bargain away the fort with the British for silver and gold. However, both this dark day in New England and the Revolution's darkest plot came to naught.[188]

John Murray became an even more renowned minister in Newburyport until his death in 1792. But a dark cloud continued for his lifetime to threaten Murray. For example, in 1791, the neighboring Londonderry, New Hampshire Presbytery charged its delegate, Mr. Annan, "to make inquiry respecting the affairs of the Rev. John Murray at the Presbytery of Philadelphia," over a quarter century earlier.[189]

Murray, however, rose above the darkness and illuminated many political, social, and economic ills. For example, in 1783, in Newburyport, Murray helped lead agrarian land reform, when he delivered a radical address and published a famous pamphlet in his attempt to prolong the American Revolution's goals of equality and liberty.[190] Murray did occasionally return to Boothbay, where his relations, his people, his real estate, and perhaps his heart remained.

Lack of Church Governance in Boothbay: 1779–1784
By 1779, during some of the darkest hours of the Revolutionary War, when Boothbay's coasting trade, which was their chief employment, was in ruins, Boothbay patriots, many of them church members,[191] risked and gave their lives in the war. They served in Boothbay, where British vessels frequented; in the Penobscot battle, where many Tories had relocated from the westward and defeated the patriots; and far from home, further south.[192] Francis Greene concluded that "Boothbay was unusually free from the Tory element. Her record for genuine patriotism is unsurpassed, and besides a soldiery that was brave and faithful she had leaders whose influence and reputations extended beyond her geographical limits," both on and off the battlefields and ships.[193] Boothbay's legendary lack of loyalists was reconfirmed by Murray's contemporary, Jacob Bailey, the fleeing loyalist and Anglican minister in Pownalborough, now Dresden, in 1779, when he completed a list of several known loyalists in the Lincoln County area. Not one was from Boothbay.

Boothbay, never prosperous since its founding in 1729, became even more impoverished near the end of and following the American Revolution. War, heavy taxes, and the exodus of many able-bodied men deepened the region's poverty. Boothbay fishermen and traders, with their families comprising much of the population, were away at war or without work because of wartime interference with trade and every other means of support such as farming, fishing, and lumbering. Taxes increased, currency was worthless, and Boothbay's spiritual, religious, and political leader, John Murray, had departed. Murray had been instrumental in securing some help for Boothbay, as when, on April 3, 1776, he petitioned the Massachusetts General Court and noted that Boothbay's inhabitants "have in general lived altogether by their trade at sea, this being now, and for many months past, entirely cut off, all these vessels are hauled up, useless and decaying." The Massachusetts General Court acted in part and responded by quieting titles for the Boothbay settlers and assuring their possession of their lands against conflicting claims, especially from the Boston-based Great Proprietors. Murray was a recognized and effective leader throughout New England.[194]

The church rapidly declined following John Murray's removal to Newburyport. No religious revival recurred following Murray's charismatic leadership in the late 1760s, and no revival would recur in Boothbay for the rest of the eighteenth century, despite other religious revivals, such as the 1791–1792 awakening in Walnut Hill and in the larger North Yarmouth area under the evangelical sermons of longtime Congregational pastor, Tristram Gilman.[195] No Lord's supper in Boothbay was administered in the years following Murray's departure in 1779. The church remained Presbyterian and had been the most easterly Presbyterian church in the rapidly receding eastern frontier. However, the Boothbay Presbyterian Church was no longer affiliated with the Presbytery of the Eastward since it had become simply an independent Presbyterian church with virtually no outside church support.[196] Contemporaries of this period, such as Isaac Weston, who later ministered to Boothbay from 1817–1829, reminisced and observed, "[H]ow disastrous was the effect of the revolutionary war upon the state of morals and religion, throughout the country."[197]

Francis Greene observed, just over a century later, "It is evident that only occasional preaching was had for some time after 1780," in post-Revolutionary Boothbay. The church no longer had a parsonage, as the Reverend John Murray owned the old parsonage, which previously had been granted to him because the town could not meet its commitments for his salary. In 1783, the church Session appointed a committee to employ a minister only during the summer for as much as 100 pounds in salary. A Mr. Merrill may have been employed, as inferred from the 1785 annual meeting that terminated Merrill's appointment upon any terms previously agreed by the committee. Next, a Rev. Williams was employed for six months.[198]

Rev. Elijah Kellogg—1785-1787
Probably during this period, the Reverend Elijah Kellogg, who had been studying divinity under Rev. Murray in Newburyport, moved to Boothbay to preach, most likely at the request of Murray.[199] Kellogg was ordained in 1787 at the Second Parish (Orthodox Congregational) Church of Portland.[200][201] He later married Eunice McLellan, who was the granddaughter of Hugh and Elizabeth McLellan, hardy Scots-Irish settlers in the early 1700s, who, after brief stops in Boston, York, Wells, and Falmouth (now Portland), settled in the Narragansett frontier of what is now Gorham in 1738-1739, as the second settled family in that western area. Elijah and Eunice had a son in 1813, also named Elijah, who became a renowned minister and prolific writer of twenty-nine books sold nationally. Elijah Kellogg, Sr., had served as a musician in the Revolutionary army, graduated from college, developed a strong intellectual and moral character, and brought these gifts to Boothbay during this early post-Revolutionary period. Kellogg was fondly remembered by the old folks in Boothbay a generation later "as a man of great vivacity and buoyancy of spirits."[202]

A Presbyterian minister was needed, one who had many skills. A typical Presbyterian service during colonial times began at 9:00 or 10:00 a.m. and continued for two to three hours in a simple, unadorned building with pews rented by the worshippers. High above the parishioners were the gowned, bewigged minister and just below him in a lower pulpit. the song leader. The song leader slowly sang a line, with the congregation slowing singing it back; only psalms were sung, and organs were not allowed, being the "devil's band." The minister led morning prayers of about twenty minutes with the congregation standing. Next, the minister continued with an exposition of the scripture chosen for the sermon, a lecture of about thirty minutes. After another psalm, the sermon of an hour or more began, when the minister would take a text, deduce from it a doctrine, then expound that doctrine point by point with many subheadings, and apply the doctrine to each listener's life, all preferably by memory. Then followed a collection for the poor. Next was a brief, fifteen-minute lunch intermission, followed by another two-hour service with prayers, lecture, and sermon in the afternoon. The high point of the year was the celebration of the Lord's supper, prohibiting the altar of the mass and instead using a table, around which the faithful shared the bread and wine.[203]

Presbyterian pastors were well educated, generally graduates of the College of New Jersey, formed in 1746 by Presbyterian forces sympathetic to the Great Awakening, and later known as Princeton University. Princeton's first president was the Scottish-born and educated John Witherspoon (1723–1794), the only minister who signed the Declaration of Independence.[204]

Rev. Jonathan Gould—1789-1792

Jonathan Gould, born around 1762,[205] grew up in Massachusetts and entered Brown University, probably at the age of twenty, when the college reopened after suspension of all college exercises during most of the American Revolution, from 1776 until 1782. Gould graduated from Brown in 1786, when he took part in Brown's commencement "discussion on the question whether it would have been better if America had remained dependent on Great Britain."[206] Boothbay's Scots-Irish fighters would not have entertained any debate on the issue of separation from England.

Boothbay's Presbyterians had only substitute pastors for almost a decade between 1779 and 1789. Although Boothbay's inhabitants were sliding toward Congregationalism due to the lack of Presbyterian support in a sea of New England Congregationalism, they remained strongly Calvinistic and "suspicious of this timid young minister's theology and dogma." Boothbay's Presbyterians were well aware that Jonathan Gould had graduated from Brown, well known for its Baptist leanings, and they were suspicious of Gould throughout his tenure in Boothbay.[207] In 1789, the church engaged the unordained Jonathan Gould, who had occasionally preached in Boothbay, to serve for one year, at a fee of 78 pounds with no board provided. The church voted, on March 14, 1791, not to settle or employ Gould any longer due to doctrinal objections, not any moral fault, although he continued to preach in Boothbay for another year. He was ordained elsewhere, two years later.[208]

Just as Jonathan Gould seemed to have little chance of longevity and success in Boothbay, he had little success and longevity in his life, as he left Boothbay after two years when the church and the town refused to retain him. The Reverend Gould was called by the Standish Congregational Parish in 1792, but only three years later he wasted away and died of consumption, at the age of 33.[209] Rev. Jonathan Gould, whose background was English Puritanical rather than Scots-Irish Presbyterian, would have been a mere footnote in this church history, except for his journal entries for all of 1790 through early 1792, illuminating for us glimmers of everyday life in the Boothbay church and throughout and near the Boothbay peninsula during the immediate post-Revolutionary era.

Gould's detailed diary was written in several volumes, but only two survive, including parts of 1790, all of 1791, and January through March of 1792, while young Gould in his twenties ministered in Boothbay. Boothbay historian Elizabeth Reed had access to his 1790 diary, and her handwritten copies of his notes and some typed summaries are extant and preserved in the Boothbay Region Historical Society. Gould's penmanship was horrible and nearly incomprehensible in most places. Elizabeth Reed was more charitable, noting his diaries were "written in a penmanship that is almost shorthand."[210] But thanks to young Jonathan Gould's chronicling of everyday events and Elizabeth Reed's deciphering of some of his scribbles, many of Gould's snapshots of Boothbay's church and peninsular community bring into sharper focus some of the daily details of work, play, joys, and sorrows of many Boothbay inhabitants 225 years ago. Many of these everyday church and life experiences resonate with us today.

Friday, January 1, 1790, was a remarkably warm day with most snow disappearing because of New Year's Eve rain. Gould "read all day in Doddridge's lectures," a ten-volume set on philosophy and divinity written by the English nonconformist theologian, Philip Doddridge (1702–1751).[211] That night for extra income Reverend Gould "kept school" for the church children, including singing. He boarded with Esquire McCobb, whose home was in downtown Boothbay Harbor just below the former Hotel Fullerton, now the Boothbay Harbor Post Office,. Gould often walked roughly two miles north to Boothbay center for his work at the church. He frequently visited parishioners. Sometimes he rode Esquire McCobb's horse and later bought his own.[212]

The next day Gould traveled to "court today. Many here drinking and at night an affray, etc." Court was usually at the Pownalborough Courthouse in what is now Dresden, the oldest court building in Maine and the first and only one in Lincoln County, from 1760 to 1794. The three-story, hipped-roof, Georgian building was designed by renowned architect and Great Proprietor Gershom Flagg. There was a famous tavern on the first floor and a courthouse on the second floor, frequented by all types of people, including, from time to time, young lawyer and future president, John Adams. [212a]

On January 11, 1790, Gould "read all day in ye great J-M-rrys terrible publication and kept singing school at night." Gould was probably no fan of the great Reverend John Murray, his famous predecessor. On a Saturday in September, young Reverend Gould did not even "know whether I shall preach tomorrow or not. Can't find out whether Mr. Murray is in town or not. Sunday: Mr. Murray did not come to church. Many people at meeting expecting Mr. Murray got disappointed." Among them, Gould specifically named the Reverend Murray's cousin, John Murray, Mr. Montgomery, William Reed, and Ebenezer Fullerton, who "went up to hear him." The long shadow of Rev. Murray haunted Jonathan Gould during his brief ministry in Boothbay a full decade after Murray's departure.[213]

Thanks to the Boothbay Region Historical Society, we have three of Jonathan Gould's original sermons, the first delivered to the Boothbay church on Sunday, January 16, 1790. His sermon dwelled on mortality: "As our fields are furrowed with ye wren holes of years they may be enveloped in ye Mantle of Death." Gould added presciently, at least for him, opportunities "to improve ye little time we have…By a blast of ye winds they have sought an early grave." Gould concluded his typical, thirty-six-page, two-hour sermon: To improve ye time which remains considering they know not who stands next of ye bills of Mortality—And may we all so live as to wash our Dis[s]olution with Joy—Amen."[214]

On the evening of Monday, January 25, 1790, Gould "tried to have a wedding at Col. Reed's but Justice McCobb would not." Court officials, not ministers, controlled colonial weddings.

Gould, with some humor, remarked in his diary about April Fool's Day, on April 1, 1790: "The day the cuckoos generally first arrive in England—ye bird is so foolish it has no exclusive nest. Whence men whose wives are unfaithful are called cuckolds having no exclusive bed."

Gould's second extant sermon, delivered to the Boothbay church on April 9, 1790, focused on faith, grace, and salvation. Near the end of the two-hour sermon Gould declared that these Biblical themes "are brought into ye Liberty and Freedom of ye Gospel,"[215] possibly invoking these liberty and freedom themes of the recent American Revolution or pandering to these identical Scots-Irish credos.

A constant theme of Gould's was his inadequacy as a pastor.

On June 1, 1790, he remarked, "Finished another sermon—I will be hanged if I am not ashamed of it…[Deacons] J. Beath and Mr. Briar ran out of the meetinghouse," perhaps fed up with Gould. Another Sunday in 1790, "I was most consummately stupid."[216] On January 1, 1791, while trying to write a sermon for the first Sabbath of the year, "It is not so good as I intended it or am I so good as I ought to be…exceedingly feel discouraged about the meeting tomorrow." The next day, Sunday, January 3, 1791, Gould "found it not so bad as I expected…had upwards of 40 hearers" listen to him preach a New Year's sermon from Proverbs 27. Gould was very earnest, as exemplified by his plea in his private diary the previous Saturday, "Make me useful in thy vineyard and beneficial to my fellow man."

In late July 1790, a Monday, Gould recorded, "Skipper Briar came in in ye morning in ye Esq.'s schooner—Linekin lies dead—a Court met here—Mr. Boyd got mad."[217] Linekin was of English descent, and this Boothbay family never were members of the Boothbay Presbyterian Church. The Linekins, starting with Benjamin, who arrived around 1750, throughout the second half of the eighteenth century and well into the nineteenth century squabbled, fought, and litigated with Boothbay's Scots-Irish Montgomery clan, led by Robert Montgomery, who had arrived in Townsend with his wife Sarah in 1730.[218] On April 8, 1755, Robert and Sarah Montgomery and other Scots-Irish Boothbay residents pulled down and carted away the dwelling house and contents of Joseph Linekin, who promptly sued and lost. Clark Linekin testified that Sarah Montgomery ran after Joseph Linekin "with a stick or broomstaff in her hand." Sarah Montgomery, in her deposition, stated she had shoved some of the house boards and ordered her sons to do much of the work, and supervised putting some logs in the doorway to keep the hogs out, possibly a veiled insult aimed at the Linekins. A jury of their peers found the Montgomerys not guilty.[219] In 1777, Clark Linekin was arrested under a warrant issued by Boothbay's Scots-Irish town and church leader William McCobb, who accused Linekin of trading with the British during wartime. Linekin petitioned the Massachusetts General Court and claimed he was simply trying to supply fish off Fisherman's Island to his starving Linekin Neck family.[220] This Linekin-Montgomery bitter feud centered on family honor, justice, property rights, and revenge and was echoed a century later by the more famous feud of 1863–1891 between the West Virginia Hatfields, primarily of English ancestry, against the Kentucky McCoys, whose roots were primarily Irish and Scottish.[221] Perhaps the Boothbay Linekins and Montgomerys will become the local metonym for extended interfamily feuds.

On an early Tuesday morning in August 1790, young Gould exclaimed, "Went fishing with Mr. Sawyer and a Mr. Stevens in ye forenoon. I catched one fish—ye first salt water fish I ever catched. Stayed all night with Mr. Sawyer." Two days later, the Reverend Gould ventured to Southport and performed two weddings:

> Set out with Esq. McCobb, rod (sic) to David Reed's, procured a boat, went out to Cape Newagen Island to old Mr. Thompson's. There ye Esq. had an invitation to two weddings—old Mr. Nelson's and at Mr. Emerson's. He went and made peace between Hamilton & Decker—then to Mr. Nelson's, sat awhile & married them then set out and walked to Mrs. Pierce's and soon married Mr. Emery."

After staying awhile and drinking tea, it was almost sunset before they left the last wedding on Southport that day.

On Sunday, August 15, 1790, Rev. Gould noted his challenges in dealing with hot-headed Scots-Irish: I believe I have maded (sic) some of them—started some of their Calvinistic blood."[222] Gould clearly recognized the cultural clash between his English-Puritan background and these Scot-Irish Calvinists.

A day or two later, with Deacon Beath riding Gould's horse and the Reverend Gould walking, they traveled to and spent the night at Mr. Montgomery's, presumably at Montgomery's Tavern at Montgomery's Mills, later Hodgdon's Mills in what is now the village of East Boothbay. Gould reported their time together as "quite sociable," but he added insecurely and perhaps accurately, "only they could find some faults."

On August 19 he visited with the failing Mrs. Boyd and prayed with her twice, while "they held a town meeting to give me a call. They chose a committee—to examine me led by J. Murray [Reverend Murray's cousin], Montgomery, and others." The next day, a Friday, Gould socialized with Mr. Beath, Miss Anna Smith, Esquire and Lady McCobb, rode over to Mr. Sawyer's, and dined also with Mr. Cook and Dr. Barber, then went out fishing and came back with two or three fish that went into a common chowder. They dined and then left at sunset.

At or near Pownalborough Courthouse, in September or October 1790, Rev. Gould witnessed a botched execution of a convicted murderer, Mr. Hadlock, "a bad maneuver ye knot slipped and he came down ye first time—bought 4 of his speeches…Mr. McLane preached. Baptist Flagg prayed at ye gallows." So a Scots-Irish Presbyterian preached the sermon, a Baptist minister prayed with Hadlock during his last minutes, and a Presbyterian pastor with Baptist and Congregational leanings watched and chronicled this botched and extended hanging. Two years earlier, another murderer, John O'Neil, had just been hanged for his bloody murder by thrusting an ax or iron bar into the head of his roommate Michael Cleary in their shared rooms at Pemaquid Falls. The gallows stood, according to tradition, in a field northeast of the courthouse and was visible from the river, where many arrived by boat to witness the hanging.[223] Boothbay had not experienced a murder on the peninsula since 1739, when Edmund Brown murdered his father-in-law David Bryant, and would not experience its second murder until 1888, almost 150 years after the first, when young Llewellyn Quimby killed his former employer, the renowned and revered eighty-one year-old William Kenniston.[224] Well over a century later, his Kenniston Hill Inn building on December 14, 2014 was moved across Country Club Road, and Kenniston's ghost may still haunt us today.

Gould often met and traded with Esquire McCobb and frequently traveled with him to court. On August 30, 1790, Gould reported, "Esquire McCobb set out for Wiscasset in his arbitration." Two days later "Esq. and Murray had ye trial neither of them got anything." The following day, "Esq. McCobb returned from his court something scandalized also mortified." The Wiscasset court was just being formed in the 1780s and 1790s, first meeting at the Wiscasset meetinghouse and at the Whittier Tavern, both at Wiscasset Point. The Hon. Jonathan Bowman sometimes held his probate court sessions in the tavern, and Judge Thwing of Woolwich and Squire Davis of Edgecomb occasionally heard cases there before the first courthouse was constructed at its present Wiscasset site a few years later.[225]

In September 1790, Boothbay held a town meeting, which "had nothing but altercations" according to the Reverend Gould, who stayed away at Mr. Skidmore's house. The town meeting "finally agreed to hire [Gould] for an additional three months. "Had Col. Jones from Bristol to assist in my opposite party." Colonel William Jones was either the Boothbay town meeting moderator or leader for the opponents of Rev. Gould. A native of Northern Ireland, Jones was sixty-six in 1790, had been a fierce Indian fighter outside the Pemaquid fort, a leading Revolutionary War patriot who secured the release of two Yankee ships and assured the safe passage of the British warship in Wiscasset, a church elder who often quarreled with his ministers, and a recent representative of the Midcoast area at the United States Constitutional Convention.[226]

A month later, in October 1790, Deacon Leishman was involved in a dispute, perhaps over Gould's tenure. "But my answer in the affirmative to stay another quarter. Received a dollar from Jeremiah Beath for his singing instruction, quite unexpected." Leishman, who sat up in the gallery of the church, rose during one of Gould's sermons, and contradicted Gould on a statement he had just uttered. Gould confided in his diary, "Deacon Leishman contradicted me with the greatest apparent temper. All heard, some were mad, some laughed, some were scared. I kept on preaching, minding not what he said." Elizabeth Reed, who has done the best work to date in trying to decipher Gould's almost inscrutable handwriting, observed 150 years later, "This young minister worried constantly over the criticisms leveled at him," as when he was criticized for a sailing outing and later recorded in his diary, "Made a blunder, wherefore I wish that I had not gone sailing. I am very sorry indeed." As Reed succinctly quipped, in 1948, "He is not the first nor the last clergyman to receive criticism from this parish."[227]

Jonathan Gould traveled to his family home in Dedham, where his uncle and family resided and where he happened upon the sudden death of his young nephew: "a child lay dead at sunset." He then rode home to his father's house, visited many places, including Providence, perhaps visiting Brown College and inquiring of any job opportunities. Gould also on behalf of Boothbay's Captain Reed picked up a written deposition from Dr. Taylor for some court purposes of the captain's. Gould purchased a surtout, a man's long, close-fitting overcoat, was introduced to Miss Faulkner or Foster, and nervously preached on Sunday at Mr. Ward's: "Ye amiable Miss Foster was at meeting. I had rather preach before a Dr. of Divinity than this amiable girl." Gould went to Esq. Foster's house, bid to "ye amiable girl a slight farewell," took his horse to his father's, revisited his uncle, made several other stops, picked up newspapers for Esq. McCobb, and then connected in Boston with the Boothbay ship of Captain Mitchell Campbell. After stays due to bad weather at Cape Ann and Salem, where many knew some of the Boothbay townspeople, they arrived in Townsend Harbor. Captain Campbell refused to take any remuneration for the Reverend Gould's passage, after a ten-day voyage from Boston.

A day or so after landing, the Reverend Gould "went to meeting. Most of Esquire's [McCobb's] family went but only about 20 persons at meeting had but one excuse etc." The following day, Gould "wore my new surtout like a fool and wet it. Monday Pat Herrin came down and cut me out a pair of breeches and took home an old coat to mend."[228]

Rev. Gould learned on Monday, January 7, 1791 that "old Mr.

McCobb," whom he had visited frequently, "departed this life. I have set about a funeral sermon." The next day, Captain Reed and Rev. Gould "broke paths this day for the funeral," probably clearing snow for their travel by horse, as it was "a terrible day." On January 10, Gould delivered his funeral sermon based on Second Corinthians, Chapter 4, but Gould reported, "Very few people; however, we made out with tolerable decency to carry ye old gentleman and bury him."

On January 5, 1791, Gould spent a good part of the day in "bad walking" paying pastoral visits, and then "drank wine and dined till night." On Tuesday, January 11, Gould was "determined to get to Wiscasset" and set out on foot until he arrived at the ferry across the Sheepscot River, where he "Never was more tired—went to May Linckams, drank tea and came back." On January 15, Gould "stopped at Patrick Herrin's for my breeches," which Herrin had mended. No mention was ever made again of the surtout.

Gould frequently worried about his pay and finances, as on January 2, 1791, when he "preached but one sermon—and do not know what they will say about my making up ye time for not preaching two sermons." He frequently borrowed money, as when he received six shillings from Esquire McCobb on January 12, 1791. He also borrowed Mr. Hood's pitch pipe on January 15, presumably for his singing school.

The Reverend Gould often visited with church members during afternoons and, perhaps more often, evenings. For example, on Tuesday, January 4, 1791, he "rose late and read some in the afternoon and went and paid a visit to Mr Sargent's there ye greater part of ye evening." The next day he rose late and read a little, then "went on foot up to Jno [Jonathan] Emmons paid a visit bad walking returned in ye evening—drank wine and dined till night."

Jonathan Gould chronicled "ye fate of winter coasting" when he noted on Monday night, February 14, 1791: "Old Capt. [Paul] Reed arrived having had his vessel founder at sea with his crew, at least two of whom were his sons, and both were frozen badly." The next day, after meeting with the selectmen about his pay, Gould visited and drank tea with Captain Reed and noted the old captain was having a bad time. Saturday, February 19, "ye old Capt's toes cut off and one foot [and] toes of his sons." Son David Reed's foot was cut off Sunday, February 20.

On September 15, 1791, Rev. Gould preached a funeral sermon of "young Mr. Gove." The next day, Gould hurried to Edgecomb, traveled partly by Esquire Sylvester's boat, and walked to the house and preached "my old sermon from Psalm 10, verse 12." Gould whimpered, "Don't know how I made out—poorly tho. Randal ye Baptist minister there—I did not know it till I had done. Considerable many people there." Randal was the Baptist preacher who had prayed at the Pownalborough gallows during the hanging Gould had witnessed. The Baptists would not receive Boothbay town approval for a formal church for another decade. The following Sunday, September 19, Gould preached, but noted, "Randal was in town. A considerable number to hear him." Clearly, Baptists were a source of concern and were making inroads among Congregationalists throughout New England and even among Presbyterians in Boothbay.

Gould left Boothbay shortly after March 1792. He returned from his new Congregational church in Standish for a day or two in Wiscasset, on June 24, 1793, when he delivered a forty-three-page sermon entitled "Christ the Master Builder" to the Wiscasset Masonic Order. Gould pointed out that the enemies within are usually more lethal than the enemies without: "So with the institution of Masonry—it has suffered more apiece tenfold more from unworthy members...[than] from all its avowed enemies." The enemies may be more likely from within, as perhaps Gould experienced when his Boothbay parishioners tested him for over two years and then forced him out a year prior to this sermon in Wiscasset.

Rev. Pelatiah Chapin—1795-1796
There was no regular preaching from 1792 until 1795, when Rev. Pelatiah Chapin was engaged for one year, at four dollars per week, with board for himself and his horse.[229] The Reverend Chapin

(1746–1837) had written some evangelical poetry in 1794, a year before coming to Boothbay, and he later wrote and published theological tracts on renouncing paedo-baptism, the baptism of infants, and also a "dialogue among the tombs."[230]

The church remained Presbyterian, but there was no active Presbytery in Maine, and so Boothbay's church had become independent, no longer affiliated with the Presbytery of the Eastward, as it had been under the forceful leadership of John Murray.[231]

How Boothbay's Scots-Irish Culture Extended the Principles of the American Revolution

Rev. John Murray's Legacy

In 1783, in Newburyport, John Murray, former settled minister at Boothbay, according to Pulitzer Prize winning historian Alan Taylor, was at the forefront of agrarian land reform, when, as mentioned previously, he delivered a radical address and published a famous pamphlet in his attempt to continue that aspect of the American Revolution.[232] Following Murray's two years of sickness and then his death, in 1791 at the age of only fifty, the agrarianism of John Murray and others was promoted through the heritage of resistance, often armed resistance, in some inland frontier towns, such as Balltown (now Whitefield and Jefferson) and in the coastal towns of Boothbay and Bristol.[233]

Alan Taylor, in his *Liberty Men and Great Proprietors*, graphically portrayed these post-Revolutionary, agrarian uprisings in the District of Maine. Boothbay and Bristol led the coastal towns' uprisings; and the backcountry towns, such as Jefferson and Liberty, learned from Boothbay's Scots-Irish predecessors to challenge proprietary claims and to justify violent resistance. For example, Benjamin Tibbetts, born and raised in the Dover section of north Boothbay, on September 5, 1815, led a dozen Liberty settlers, who blackened their faces, disguised themselves as Indians, armed themselves with guns, bayonets, and swords, and confronted a leading Great Proprietor, Joseph H. Pierce, Jr., by bursting into his room, destroying evidence, and threatening to kill him until Pierce took an oath to lower the price demanded from them for their settled land. In essence, Boothbay was known for training terrorists there and elsewhere in the decades following the American Revolution, to extend the Revolution to agrarian land reform and procure titles for long-term settlers against the deed and title claims of more conservative and powerful, Boston-based "Great Proprietors." Midcoast area settlers became leaders in post-Revolutionary resistance and as promoters of ongoing revolutions.[234]

Significantly, when Balltown, the stronghold of the resistance, divided and incorporated as two towns in 1807 and 1809, the inhabitants were overwhelmingly Jeffersonian (agrarian and anti-federalist) in their politics and Calvinist Baptist in their religion. These Balltown settlers chose the name of Jefferson, after the popular, anti-federalist president, for their eastern half, and Whitefield, after the most popular evangelist, Methodist George Whitefield, for their western half.[235] Both Thomas Jefferson and George Whitefield were reviled in Federalist and Puritan Massachusetts. George Whitefield, sparkplug of the Great Awakening, had come from Britain to those parts to spread the gospel decades earlier, and had threatened Puritan Massachusetts' hegemony.

John Murray kept in contact with Boothbay, because of not only his strong pastoral relations and friends, but also his extensive family and property connections. Murray, in the 1760s, had married Susannah Lithgow of Phippsburg, whose family members lived in the Boothbay region. Until 1780, he still had his Aunt Sarah Murray Reed, widow of Andrew Reed, and their clans in Boothbay, including Rev. Murray's cousin, John Murray. The Reverend Murray owned considerable property in Boothbay at and around Mt. Pisgah and in other areas of town, perhaps some from his wife's inheritance but most from the land paid to Rev. Murray in lieu of money and at less value than he was owed. Susanna had given birth to three of their six children in Boothbay. In her *Colonial Boothbay*, local historian Barbara Rumsey has extensively researched the era through such sources as Daniel Herrin's deposition of February 16, 1794 and her own deed research in the Lincoln County Registry of Deeds. She determined that the Reverend John Murray owned quite extensive holdings around Boothbay besides Pisgah, including the Newagen area in 1789, Reed's Meadow (present-day Penny Lake), which may be part of the 100 acres he acquired from David Reed near the meetinghouse in 1770, and the session house at Boothbay center. Rev. Murray acquired thirteen deed transfers in the region by 1788 and owned 250 acres in 1789. Murray also sued the town and other debtors after he went to Newburyport in an effort to collect money owed him. The Reverend Murray's cousin John Murray lived in Boothbay after Rev. Murray moved to Newburyport. Cousin John Murray, for example, soon after Rev. Murray's death, sued Ebenezer Fullerton in the Lincoln County Court of Common Pleas in September 1793, for Fullerton's taking of hay from land that was "his as a tenant of the heirs of Rev. John Murray." Susannah Murray, widow of Rev. Murray, remained in Newburyport and was one of only seven women who filed lawsuits in the Lincoln County Court of Common Pleas in the eighteenth century. She sued Boothbay men twice, out of a total of 204 legal cases involving Boothbay plaintiffs and defendants between 1761 and 1800.[236]

During a particularly gloomy period of the American Revolution, Newburyport was called upon to furnish a full company of officers and men for military service. After days of laboring in vain to fill this company, the officers asked Rev. Murray to address the regiment under arms. Murray delivered an address so spirited and animated that his audience was spellbound, tears flowed from many eyes, and in two hours following his oration the military company was filled with fighting men.[237] The charismatic Reverend John Murray had accomplished in two hours what many officers could not do over many days.

Rev. Murray presented and published a sermon on November 4, 1779, *Nehemiah, or The Struggle for Liberty Never in Vain, When Managed with Virtue and Persistence*. John Murray proclaimed, "The cause of liberty is the cause of God: reason, truth, justice, [and] religion mutually support and are supported by it."[238]

He observed that civil and religious liberties must exist and argued that "religious reformations must generally open the door for the removal of civil difficulties."[239] Rev. Murray welcomed opposition: "Religion, like the palm tree, grows by being pressed. Opposition has helped, but never hurt the truth."[240] Murray warned of "a gross depravity of the heart when religious services of this nature lose their solemnity by becoming ordinary and familiar...[T]his I consider as one of the most gloomy symptoms of the times."[241] Murray lifted up his Scots-Irish egalitarian ethos as his very first proposition: "All men are by nature alike—the faculties, powers, and passions are each substantially the same: to the full exercise of these, and to the enjoyments thence resulting, they are equally entitled." He emphasized that "their entrance into society is on the footing of perfect equality."[242] Murray, ahead of his times, extended this equality to slaves and warned that nations supporting slavery "ought to be considered in a state of war against all mankind," and extended this to the new state constitutions, warning that the slavery "leaven will soon corrupt the whole lump."[243] Murray presciently warned that "prosperity frequently becomes a poison in disguise," because "nations, as well as individuals, are generally intoxicated by it."[244] He warned against oppression and its consequences: "Equally unnatural is the spirit of oppression that is become the epidemic disease of the times—and equally pernicious are its effects," such as "the groans of the poor who, in the midst of plenty, are left to perish."[245] Murray was not just blaming England, he was a prophet in his own time and remains so in our own era, over two centuries later.

Perhaps John Murray's most notable and radical foray into politics took place on the occasion of the public thanksgiving for peace in Newburyport on December 11, 1783, just months after the close of the American Revolution. Murray was a leader in northern New England, where many desired to continue the American Revolution toward a more egalitarian land ownership of the Maine frontier. Murray's discourse, published in 1784, was entitled, *Jerubbaal, or Tyranny's Grove Destroyed, and the Altar of Liberty Fin-*

ished," during what Murray calculated as the 162nd anniversary of New England's thanksgivings in America.[246] Ingratitude "is a crime which, worse than witchcraft in itself, is not less fascinating to its slaves." Murray lifted up liberty:

> Liberty thus improved becomes the mother of learning—the nurse of sciences and of arts—the great patroness of commerce—the best support of navigation and of agriculture—the friendly guardian of military virtues, as well as of those that are social—the best promoter of population and civil grandeur, and the faithful handmaid to true religion.[247]

Murray warned of tyranny:

> When Agrarian Laws cannot be obtained; or must pass unexecuted—when individuals are permitted to purchase or possess such enormous tracts of land as may gradually work them up to an influence, dangerous to the liberty of the state—when commerce, which ought to be open and extensive as the ocean which laces our shores, is…swallowed up in the narrow gulf of partial monopolies—when real estates are publicly known and permitted to be sold, or conveyed to known enemies of the country's peace…when the people at large become inured to the opinion that the business of the state is too mysterious for them to look into, and so shall have forgotten the important duty of watching their rulers.[248]

These issues of agrarian reform, monopolistic control, and vigilance over our leaders remain central in our national debates almost 250 years later.

This *Jerubaal* sermon was considered a wonderful performance at the time. More important, historian Alan Taylor, recently singled out "the Reverend John Murray of Newburyport, the popular evangelical Presbyterian who led New England's largest congregation [of over two thousand in Newburyport] and who had preached in Boothbay on the Lincoln County coast during the 1770s." The Reverend Murray's call for agrarian reform was part of an effort to extend the American Revolution for a more egalitarian distribution of frontier land, which Murray declared was essential to the new Republic's survival. During the late 1770s and early 1780s, just prior to or at the time of Murray's ground-breaking sermon and published pamphlet, some of the more radical Whigs in Massachusetts sought "agrarian laws" to confiscate large landholdings for redistribution to the landless. A proposed 1779 draft for the Massachusetts state constitution would have required the General Court to confiscate all landholdings, many owned by loyalists in exile, in excess of one thousand acres to provide farms for the landless, thereby preserving an egalitarian distribution of land in all generations. Despite the fact that many of the Great Proprietors had been loyalists during the Revolution, their money and prestige finally found favor from the Massachusetts legislators. The proposed constitutional changes were narrowly defeated, and the American Revolution and agrarian reform movement ground to a halt in most areas, although not in Midcoast Maine.[249]

Bath-Kol: A Voice From the Wilderness, written by John Murray in 1783, was a 360-page book, not a sermon, to "support the sinking truths of God against some of the principal errors raging at this time." It is vintage Murray as prophet. In his opening paragraph, on behalf of his Presbytery, which included Boothbay, Murray railed against "the present low state of vital religion in this country, the great and general declension in the practice of piety and virtue; the alarming progress of vice and immorality of every kind, and the growing defection from the pure doctrines of grace as they are laid down in the scriptures." And, as taught by leading Protestants, he lifted up "the most honored instruments of the blessed reformation from popery."[250] Murray decried, "Scarce any book is less improved, understood or believed, at this day, than the Bible."[251] He objected to "the enormities of extravagance and sensuality," and he pointed to "the vanity of fickle and whimsical fashions" and objected to "frolics, balls, and gaming-tables" and "all their concomitant passions." He objected to intemperance and stated that "intoxication that degrades human nature below the brutal herd, is becoming sadly common among us men: It seems to carry some whole families down to its gulf together, and like certain hereditary distempers appears to be handed down as an unhappy inheritance from father to son…and is begun to ravage and destroy even the gentler sex too!"[252]

He also objected to the new scandal of courtship by bundling with man and woman in the same bed, as well as the increased crimes of prenuptial fornication and also adultery, which were too often ignored.[253] Murray clearly declared his core principles: one true and living God, the necessity of divine revelation leading to bliss, the Bible as the whole of divine revelation, and the doctrine and practice in accord with the 1646 Westminster Confession of Faith.[254]

John Murray had preached at Newburyport for not quite twelve years, but he was severely limited due to declining health during his last two years. His service in Newburyport was about the same length of time as he had ministered to Boothbay. His last days and nights were spent in devotion.[255] One Newburyport admirer exclaimed, "In the very place of Whitefield's ashes, Murray rekindled Whitefield's fires."[256] Pastor James Miltimore, who delivered Murray's funeral sermon, asserted: "The beloved, the Reverend John Murray, the tender husband, the faithful father, the benevolent friend, the tried patriot, the improved scholar, the real Christian, and the able Divine is now no more." Murray had "natural genius," was "affable and easy in his manners," "affable and obliging to his friends, and accessible to all," while also being serious and not austere, cheerful, and devoted without superstition or [excessive] enthusiasm. " Murray had "fixedness of principle" without being dogmatic or easily shaken. He had truly distinguished talents for instructing young ministers and for ministering to his parishioners. He never exhibited envy. Murray had seen and recognized his own imperfections and had his enemies, but "when he was reviled he reviled not again." Murray's words in his last illness included the need "to live to some good purpose…for His service and honor."[257] His contemporaries recognized his remarkable rekindling of Whitefield's fires in so many of them; perhaps they also had an inkling that Murray's sparks would continue to light those who would follow for the next 250 years.

Descendant and Boothbay historian Elizabeth Reed noted that the Reverend John Murray's last visit to Boothbay had been about a year prior to his death when, ill with dropsy, or edema, he delivered a funeral sermon at the home of Captain John Reed for Miss Nancy Flood, a beautiful, young lady who had drowned. He noted, knowing his life was ending as well, "I must preach my own funeral sermon."[258] Rev. John Murray had accomplished a great deal in his half-century of life and less than thirty years in America. The last Presbytery met in Maine in 1791, and religiously the Maine frontier had become a "vast howling wilderness."[259] By August 1796, three years after Murray's death, there were only ten settled Presbyterian ministers in New England, and "the descendants of these persecuted Irish brethren" had lost almost all chances to continue or renew their Presbyterian churches.[260]

Upon Murray's death, his 1786 codicil expressly provided for the newer notion of treating children more equally: "[I]t is my will that no distinction should be ever made among my children on account of primogeniture; but that on the contrary the most perfect equality should be observed in dividing to them, including both sons and daughters, their portions of inheritance." Consistent with his advocacy against primogeniture, he treated his sons and daughters as equally as possible while avoiding forced sales of his real estate holdings. His codicil provided first to his daughter Catharina both his farmhouse at or near the Boothbay meetinghouse, his island in Sheepscot River, and the lot in Reed's Meadow located between Lobster Cove and Boothbay center, probably all acquired in lieu of cash and for far less than Boothbay had owed him for his ministry there and substantially less than he could have earned elsewhere, as exemplified by previous offers from New York City and Philadelphia, then the largest cities in North America. He devised to his son Robert all his lands in Belfast, Maine, including all his right in Little Green Island in Penobscot Bay, perhaps for his ministering in Scots-Irish Belfast. Murray next left equally to his daughter Susannah and his son William all his half interest in Washington County land received by him and General William Lithgow by a deed from the Commonwealth of Massachusetts, probably for his excellent service during the Revolutionary War. Rev. Murray also left to his cousin John Murray "in token of love and in full for his diligent and faithful care of my tracts in Boothbay and his other services done or attempted for me," all sums due to Murray on a bond or contract related to a partnership when cousin John Murray began to live at the meetinghouse, as well as a full release of all Rev. Murray's estate claims related to his cousin's use of Murray's property.[261] He was protecting not only his cousin but also his children from future litigation.

The Reverend John Murray was Boothbay's shining star of the Enlightenment, during the peak of its impact, from the 1600s to the mid–1800s, during "one of the most creative eras in Western history, rivaling the golden ages of Periclean Athens, Augustan Rome, and Renaissance Italy."[262] Paramount among the host of intellectual, political, economic, cultural, and other intertwined forces, was the role of leadership that mobilized—and was spurred by—enlightened and engaged followers.[263] Although John Murray had not lived in Boothbay much after 1779, he had visited often and retained friends, property, and relatives in Boothbay. His legendary legacy dwarfed most of those who followed and has endured. His principles of liberty, equality, freedom, compassion, and devotion remain embedded in Boothbay's fertile culture today.

CHAPTER 4

BECOMING CONGREGATIONAL AND LOSING CONTROL: 1798–1830
by Chip Griffin

This new era was one of great growth for Boothbay's new Congregational church, for Boothbay's population, and for Boothbay's commerce. During this thirty-two-year period, the Boothbay Congregational Church, and, even more, Boothbay's newly formed Baptist and Methodist churches, participated in the Second Great Awakening's revivalism. Boothbay's residents shared in the rising tide of trade and manufacturing locally and globally. Boothbay and Maine suffered and grew through the first American civil war, termed by Alan Taylor as "The Civil War of 1812," known locally and distastefully as "Mr. Madison's War," which included the borderland fighting in the frontier area between Montreal and Detroit, a contest between the United States and Britain over the division of the North American continent into two nations, and a stalemate between the United States and Britain over Canada.

Eight years later Maine was instrumental in averting civil war through the powerful Missouri Compromise of 1820, fashioned by the "Great Compromiser," Henry Clay. Under the compromise, northern and antislavery Maine finally separated from Massachusetts and joined southern and slave state Missouri as America's new states, balancing the slave and farming South against the free and manufacturing North, and delaying America's momentous Civil War for forty years. Boothbay's Presbyterians, always Jeffersonian and revolutionary in their spirit and actions, became more conservative as most Scots-Irish Presbyterians reluctantly morphed into Puritan Congregationalists, and as most Boothbay Congregational Church members and voters switched parties from Jeffersonian Republicans to Hamiltonian Federalists.

Long-tenured Ministers and Increased Membership
After Boothbay accepted the seemingly inevitable decline of Presbyterianism in the region and shifted to Congregationalism in late 1798, Boothbay and the young nation experienced turbulent times during the next thirty-two years. Meanwhile the new Congregational church enjoyed a relatively pacific period, when they not only attracted three ministers, but also retained all of them for lengthy tenures. This was a remarkable turnaround from the paucity and short stays of all Presbyterian and any other ministers, excepting the Reverend John Murray, since Townsend's settlement in 1729.

Rev. "Father" John Sawyer—1798–1805
The Reverend John Sawyer first visited Boothbay in October 1797 after receiving a letter from town moderator and town treasurer William McCobb and selectman and deacon John Leishman,[264] who comprised a committee to seek a minister. Boothbay's town meeting unanimously called Rev. Sawyer on November 6, 1797, and Boothbay's withering Presbyterian church called John Sawyer two weeks later, on November 21, 1797.[265] Church and state were still inextricably intertwined, with both church and town votes needed until statewide disestablishment of the Congregational Church in 1834.[266] Rev. Sawyer gave a conditional acceptance to the calls of the town and church, preached solely in Boothbay much of that fall and winter, and returned home to Oxford, New Hampshire. Sawyer moved with his family in March 1798 to Boothbay's new parsonage, built in 1796, probably as its first occupants. He pastored in Boothbay for almost eight years, the longest tenure since the thirteen-year tenure of the Reverend John Murray, who had resided at the Pisgah parsonage.[267] Local historian Barbara Rum-

sey noted in 2014 that this new parsonage, the first at the north end of the Boothbay Common, across from the present location of the Civil War monument, remained into 2015, though with many additions and at least one move to the south end of the Boothbay Common. It became the Center Café until its sale in late 2014.

Upon arrival with his family, Rev. Sawyer found Boothbay's peninsula to be a metaphorical field "all grown over with thorns, and the stone walls thereof broken down." Rev. Isaac Weston, writing in 1856, after serving an even longer tenure of twelve years as Boothbay's minister, observed that Rev. Sawyer "was one equal to the attempt, at least, however he may have succeeded." Weston described Sawyer as being around forty, with extensive experience of "labors in another part of the vineyard, with a physical constitution, vigorous and healthy in a very high degree, and just in the meridian strength of life." Weston heard nothing but "honorable and kind" remarks about John Sawyer, who was "faithful to their spiritual interests, and preached sound and wholesome doctrines." Weston added that the "state of society at Boothbay" needed reform, which was but only partially completed when Weston arrived in Boothbay in 1817.[268]

Rev. Sawyer preached from March into September 1798 to a Presbyterian church that had become "disordered, having been many years without a pastor." The church had "no presbytery in these parts with which a church might unite." So "a number of the members of the Presbyterian church," led by William McCobb on September 15, 1798, "requested the assistance of the Lincoln Association," a Congregational organization for Lincoln County Congregational churches then and now. The association convened on September 19, 1798 at the church meetinghouse toward the north end of the Boothbay Common. The next day a tiny group of eight congregants, almost all of Scots-Irish descent, faced the inevitable, were examined, and then signed the Congregational Articles of Faith and also a Covenant. So the Boothbay Congregational Church on September 20, 1798 was organized out of the remains of the old Presbyterian church, and John Sawyer was installed as pastor. The eight members of the Boothbay Presbyterian Church, soon to be Congregational, were: John Beath,[269] John Leishman, Samuel Montgomery, William McCobb, John McCobb, Rachel McCobb, Mary Knight, and Mary McCobb.[270] All except Mary Knight and perhaps John Leishman, were of Scots-Irish descent.[271] The old Presbyterian church had been founded only thirty-two years earlier, but seemed a relic of a bygone era because of enormous political revolutions, economic industrialization, and social migrations of vast proportions. In reality, a few of these signers were founding members of both the old and the new church. For example, John Beath, born in Northern Ireland in 1710, had been a leading citizen of Townsend, later Boothbay, since around 1731 or 1732, its town clerk, church session clerk, and dominant leader since 1766. He died on December 9, 1798, at the age of 88, just over two months after having participated in the founding of the Boothbay Congregational Church.[272]

These original Congregational founders boldly declared in their thoughtful and treasured 1798 Covenant, "We will make it our business as far as in us lies, to build up of lively, and *only lively stones* [emphasis added], a spiritual-house, growing into an holy temple in the Lord." The Covenant's "lively stones" theme preceded by 216 years the Congregational Church of Boothbay Harbor's 2014 capital campaign theme of "living stones," a biblical reference to 1 Peter 2:5. The 1798 Covenant concluded: "[A]lso, to abstain from all profaneness, chambering [i.e., adultery or fornication],[273] and wantonness—pesting, tattling, and backbiting—and all practices which do not tend to promote godliness."[274]

Rev. Sawyer, a month later and after a day of fasting and prayer was installed on October 21, 1798 as minister for the new Congregational church "to the pastoral charge of the church and town of Boothbay," since both the town and church were still required in all of Puritan Massachusetts to approve the only church in the town. The third required approval was that of the Congregational Council, represented by a delegation of the Congregational churches of Georgetown, Hallowell, Bath, Newcastle, and Bristol. At this meeting, the council read and approved the Boothbay church's new articles of faith and covenant, "and the church was acknowledged a church of Christ." Further, eighteen residents asked to be accepted into the church, but "after careful examination" only half, were "received by the church into full communion" that day[275]

Rev. Sawyer championed women and, on May 2, 1805, advocated that women should be church committee members. Sawyer proposed calling a council to lay before them the difficulties facing the church, including "the doings of this church in refusing to the sisters the privilege of being present at the examination of candidates for admission into the church." After two postponements the church met on May 16, 1805 and voted against Rev. Sawyer on his proposal to allow women to be present when candidates applied for church membership. Church minutes of June 25, 1814 reveal the church's choice of "sister Mary McCobb to take care of Church's linen" and thanked sister Jane Leishman for her care of the church linen, gratis, in the past and her desire to be free from the care of the linen in the future. Church men praised church women for cleaning church linens, but prohibited them from church decision-making or even from being present and influencing such decision-making.

Rev. Sawyer served for nearly eight years, but always on the condition that he could resign at any time and give his reasons, which he eventually did, including citing the high extent of liquor traffic in town and the lack of sympathy in his church with his efforts for a better state of affairs. Sawyer preached his farewell sermon as pastor in October 1805.[276] On December 7, the brethren of the church, fearing:

> the great evil and disadvantage which we just labor under if destitute of a pastor—although ministerial relation between our pastor and this people is at an end, and although he should remove out of this town, we unanimously desire and request him to continue in his pastoral relation to us, and administer to this church the special ordinances of the gospel, until some

further circumstances may make it expedient that the pastoral relation should be dissolved.

This split divided the church, as several members refused to attend, and the church on February 17, 1806 voted that because such members "show an unchristian spirit and are obstinate," and because the church had "taken sufficient pains with them," the church suspended Deacon John Leishman, John McCobb, Rachel McCobb, and Jane Montgomery from taking communion. Sawyer preached once more at Boothbay on June 8, 1806. No church minutes exist from July of that year until October 1808.

Boothbay lost a superlative pastor, who could have continued to improve the church and its peninsula. Instead, Sawyer moved on admirably to uplift Penobscot County as a missionary and to help imagine, create, and lead for over forty years the Bangor Theological Seminary. Indeed, Boothbay's "Rev. John Sawyer, who by some is held to be the first to have suggested the founding of the Seminary, and who was a member of the Board of Trustees from 1814 to 1858," was honored by an oil portrait of "Father" John Sawyer gracing a wall of the Bangor Theological Seminary. Sawyer thrived until his death in Garland at the age of 102.[277] Boothbay's loss was the state's gain.

Rev. Jabez Pond Fisher—1807–1816

Upon the demission of Rev. Sawyer, a town meeting vote in 1807 directed Dr. Daniel Rose, a prominent Boothbay physician from 1795–1823, soon to be a captain during the Civil War at Boothbay's Fort Island, local leader, town clerk, and best known today for his creation of the 1815 map of Boothbay[278] to engage the Reverend Jabez Pond Fisher to preach one year. Fisher, however, remained almost nine years, until 1816, when the town granted him his requested demission after postponing action at its November 10, 1815 town meeting in its second warrant article. Fisher probably lived in the ten year-old parsonage at Boothbay center.[279] Rev. Fisher also served part time during 1815 and 1816 at the Edgecomb Congregational Church, organized in 1801, three years after Boothbay's Congregational formation.[280] The Reverend Isaac Weston, Fisher's immediate successor, later described Rev. Fisher as "a man of no ordinary powers of intellect, sound in faith and an able preacher, although somewhat eccentric in his habits, which could not fail in a measure, to diminish his usefulness."[281] The reader is left to guess the nature of the eccentricities that hampered Rev. Fisher's service in Boothbay.

In 1809, Rev. Jabez Pond Fisher, two years after he started preaching in Boothbay, married Fannie Auld, daughter of James and Frances Auld.[282] The church minutes of May 17, 1812 state that Rev. Fisher's son David and the Reverend's wife Fannie were baptized. On October 24, 1813, Jabez and Fannie Fisher's son William was baptized. On January 21, 1816, daughter Francis was baptized. Rev. Fisher's brother, Charles Fisher, arrived in Boothbay Harbor in 1810, lived on Pisgah, set up his medical practice, married Jennett Fullerton in 1811, and had four children and many descendants, although Dr. Fisher died after only eight years in Boothbay, in 1818.

On October 9, 1816, the Reverend Fisher "asked to be freed from his pastoral charge, in consequence of his support having failed, during the term of a year and about eight months past, and of other trials." The town next extended a call to Rev. Jonathan Adams, a Boothbay native who had already settled in Woolwich. He declined,[283] but wrote a letter to the church that recommended the Reverend Isaac Weston to the Boothbay Congregational Church.

Rev. Isaac Weston—1817-1830

Fisher's successor, the Reverend Isaac Weston, successfully served Boothbay for thirteen years.[284] Weston moved into and lived at the Boothbay center parsonage.[285] He was second in ministerial stature and tenure only to the great John Murray. Weston gave pleasing sermons, exhibited good pastoral abilities, and was popular with congregants and with other Boothbay residents alike. He preached for the first time in Boothbay on Sunday, September 21, 1817 and continued to preach throughout that fall and winter. The church extended Weston a unanimous call on March 9, 1818 to settle with them in the gospel ministry, and his ordination took place on June 10, 1818.

The Reverend Weston succeeded brilliantly in bringing in new members, especially on September 16, 1818, when fourteen new members were admitted and one deferred. The latter was Huldah Wheeler, "there being some difficulty on the minds of the church respecting her." She was postponed again after she appeared at a church meeting at the schoolhouse on November 6, 1818 because of "the brethren being dissatisfied with her religious character." Weston baptized twenty-three children on July 5, 1818 and twelve more on July 19. After three more children were baptized on July 26, Boothbay boasted thirty-eight children baptized in July 1818. Five more children were baptized on August 30. On September 6, 1818, fourteen adults were baptized. Rev. Weston and Boothbay's Congregationalists were on a roll.

Elizabeth Reed noted that on July 4, 1819 Deacon Ebenezer Fullerton's funeral was at his own home at the Harbor. Ebenezer was a patriot who had served in several capacities away from and in Boothbay during the Revolution. Throughout the early 1800s more and more Congregational church meetings were occurring at Boothbay Harbor, away from the center church, and many had already taken place at the Fullerton home well before Ebenezer died.[286]

Also on July 4, 1819, Lewis Thorp, a boy, was admitted to the church. He had just painstakingly created a beautiful backgammon board when he listened to the minister's preaching on the wickedness of playing games. Upon young Thorp's return home from church, he placed his new backgammon board in the fireplace and sorrowfully watched his work go up in flames.[287]

On May 29, 1825, a Sunday, the church voted to send Rev. Weston and one delegate, Brother David Kenniston, to Alna to attend a meeting on June 8 for the purpose of forming a conference of churches for Lincoln County. David Kenniston was the son of a Scottish father of the same name, married Sarah, daughter of Jeremiah Beath, and after she died married widow Betsey Day, daughter of David Reed. Kenniston was a leading member of the Congregational church and particularly admired. He had a warm friendship with the Reverend Weston.

On March 15, 1829, Lord's Day, the church celebrated the Lord's Supper, and then Rev. Weston preached his farewell sermon, with the civil contract between minister and people dissolved by mutual consent, although the pastoral relation had not yet been dissolved. On February 9, 1830, the church still refused to dismiss the Reverend Isaac Weston, even though Weston had asked for his dismissal. Perhaps the Boothbay church had premonitions of worse times to come.

Eventually, Weston went on to Cumberland, where he pastored effectively and wrote at least five publications of importance, including *A History of the Congregational Church and Society in Cumberland, Maine*.[288] In 1856, Weston wrote an article about the Boothbay church to commemorate its ninetieth year, noting the poor state of affairs in the town and in the church, mostly because of excessive liquor consumption. Temperance reform, he observed, had been only partial in 1817, when Weston commenced his own ministry in Boothbay; and even then "the interests of religion suffered much from this cause, until the temperance reform commenced among them in good earnest" between 1831 and 1836. Gradually "the reformatory process has wrought wonders," Weston wrote, "and we believe that but few places equally exposed to temptation now give evidence of a more sober and well-ordered community." Almost fifty years after he began his pastorate in Boothbay, Weston returned to deliver a centennial observance of the church in 1866.[289]

By 1830, when Weston left the Boothbay church at Boothbay center, many midweek Congregational church services were already being held at the house of Deacon Ebenezer Fullerton, now the Boothbay Harbor Post Office site in the Harbor. Indeed, the Boothbay Congregational Church had been gradually bleeding membership for years, not only to the Harbor, but also to local Baptist and Methodist churches.[290]

Boothbay Church and Community Life Comes Alive to Us through the "Lively Stones" Lifted Up in Church Records

Clan disputes must have simmered for decades. For example, the troubles involving possibly the Reverend John Murray and certainly his cousin John Murray on one side and the McCobb clan on the other, described in detail in chapter 2 may have been the reason John Beath suddenly stopped writing, or at least stopped keeping open church minutes in and after March 1770, after doing so in scrupulous detail from September 20, 1767 to March 13, 1770. It was the only instance of covering up public church and town proceedings in colonial Boothbay. All subsequent minutes up to 1798 were lost or suppressed, other than those of March 23, 1770, which summarily mentioned the reading of the minutes of the March 12 depositions of Andrew Reed and Andrew McFarland, which testimony was quashed *in retentis*.

Just over thirty years later, on November 14, 1798, the very first act of the new Boothbay Congregational Church was to address the "difficulties [that] had long subsisted between William McCobb, Esq. and Mr. John Murray, Rev. John Murray's cousin. The ministers of area churches, on September 20, 1798, listened to the ongoing difficulties. William McCobb and John Murray agreed to abide by their decision, and "the difficulties were settled Nov. 14, 1798," with no more details or explanations. Perhaps the disputes were indeed settled, as church records after 1798 were replete with issues, but none resurfaced between McCobb and Murray. Perhaps John Murray had moved out of the area because nothing remains about him after 1798. His first wife, Ann, had died in 1777, and he married Elizabeth Chapin of Ipswich in 1779. At least two of his sons were adopted by Ann Murray's brother Samuel Montgomery and stayed in Boothbay.[291]

The first new case before the Session, on May 22, 1799, involved Margery Reed, one of the nine who were not immediately accepted on November 14, 1798 into the Boothbay Congregational Church. Margery's husband, Captain Paul Reed, had accused his wife, who agreed it was not suitable for her to join the church "till he had restored her character, and good name." William McCobb and John Leishman visited with Captain Reed, "who voluntarily and in a feeling manner acknowledged that he had very wrongfully slandered his wife." The next day, on May 23, the Session met at the parsonage, prayed, and then "carefully examined Margery Reed, as to doctrinal and experiential knowledge of religion," and "being well satisfied, received her" along with Elizabeth Carlisle and Margaret Beath (mother of Margery Reed and wife of John Beath)[292] into full communion.

That same day, Mary Wiley, who also had been one of those not immediately accepted into the church the previous October 31, continued to be rebuffed by the Congregational leaders because of "her dealings with Rev. Jonathan Sawyer." Similarly, on June 25, 1799, the church met, with the Reverend Ezekiel Emerson moderating the meeting, reexamined the case of Mary Wiley, and suspended receiving her into full communion. That same date, the Session examined David Decker, who desired to join the church, but rebuffed him due to unsatisfactory doctrinal knowledge and religious experience. On June 29, 1799, the church readily admitted to membership Colonel Andrew Reed, who lived in his father's homestead just west of the Mill Cove dam, son of Andrew Reed, the founder of the largest family ever in Boothbay.[293] The church celebrated the next day, June 30, 1799, the sacrament of the Lord's Supper for the first time since becoming Congregational. It was the first such celebration in about twenty years in Boothbay.

The church, on August 24, 1799, met by appointment and following prayer, to consider but reject the request of Jeremiah Beath into their Christian fellowship because of unfavorable circumstances. Jeremiah was the youngest son of Jeremiah Beath, brother of John Beath. The elder Jeremiah died only four years later, in 1803, while the younger Jeremiah (1770–1835) endured "the unfavorable circumstances" detailed below and lived on his father's homestead on the Beath Road.[294]

Following several other acceptances and delays of candidates into membership, on August 28, 1802, the Session voted that any future members stand forth in church assembly and publicly assent to the articles of faith and covenant to be read to them in public. These "lively stones" read frequently in open session their Articles and Covenant, which they took very seriously, and required all new lively stones to publicly read and covenant at church services. So all church members remained well versed in the importance of lively stones in the work of the church.

Disputes could be resolved in public at church. For example, Mary Sargent, possibly the wife of Benjamin Sargent and living at or near the Harbor,[295] had some misunderstandings, reconciled, and made public declarations of her reconciliation on Lord's Day in church on August 29, 1802. Mary Sargent, three years later, on November 27, 1805, "became obstinate and refused to attend the trial upon an unclear complaint and spoke disrespectfully of the church." On December 7, 1805, the church heard the complaint against Mary Sargent, examined witnesses, and voted unanimously that the mysterious complaint was amply supported by the evidence. The church chastened Mary Sargent, as revealed in this astounding judgment and judgmental attitude of the church community:

> [Mary Sargent] came under church censure; and…came to an untimely end before any further was done by the church and was buried 31st of Dec. 1805. May the Lord make it a solemn warning to all who condemn the authority of Christ in his church—the very sin for which she was censured was the means of her death.

The church lost some members to other churches. For example, the church, on June 17, 1800, "voted that Mary Tubbs have liberty to remove her particular church relations from this, to the church in Edgecomb; and that the pastor give her a certificate."

The first evidence that the church met in Boothbay Harbor instead of at Boothbay center was on December 8, 1802 at 2:00 p.m., when "the church met by appointment at the schoolhouse at the harbor." They met again, on May 8, 1804, "at the Schoolhouse, at the home district." This was probably the Fullerton House, since the town in 1804 had seven school districts, and this schoolhouse was for children from Wall Point near Lobster Cove to Campbell's Cove, now West Harbor Pond.[296]

The church voted, on December 8, 1802, to receive Sarah Reed into the church and conversed concerning a required confession from Mr. Ingraham and Elizabeth Wiley for their fault and proposed the pastor see them. On May 27, 1803 the church voted that John Ingraham and Elizabeth Wiley publicly confess on Lord's Day, May 29 in the church their sins of fornication. They did publicly confess, and the church readily baptized John Ingraham and also his children, Margaret McKown, John, and Dolly, a servant maid. Another fornication admission happened on Lord's Day November 17, 1811, when Rachel Fuller, wife of John Fuller, publicly acknowledged her guilt of the sin of fornication and asked forgiveness of God and his people. On February 6, 1815, the church met at the parsonage house and voted that Elizabeth Wylie, "a sister, make public confession in the broad aisle of her fault, viz. fornication."

On April 17, 1815, over ten years after his 1803 fornication infractions, John Ingraham appeared on charges made by Nicholas T. Knight at the parsonage house and admitted to adultery, elopement, living with a single female after elopement, and lying; but he denied the charge of adultery during several years previous. The church suspended him for one year. A year later, on May 27, 1816, the church meeting at Brother Nicholas Tab Knight's house unanimously refused to restore John Ingraham "without more satisfactory marks of repentance." This may have been the result of another adultery complaint that same day against Dolly Harrington, who was immediately suspended until the next meeting. Local historian Elizabeth Reed remarked, "John Ingraham was always a fruitful source of gossip at their deliberations."

There were some mysterious church difficulties, on July 5, 1803, resulting from an "evil report against Rebekah Sawyer; "voted that the church meet at the Meeting-house with neighboring ministers Ezekiel Emerson and Kiah Bailey to come and assist us in our difficulties. Concluded with prayer." On July 12, after opening prayer, despite that "the difficulties appeared to originate from mistake and prejudice in some in the church and from falsehood and ill-will in some out of the church," Pastor Sawyer "was very unexpectedly and unreasonably opposed in laying matters of difficulty before the council," and they dissolved the meeting. On September 30, following some intervening church meetings, the church agreed upon a method to settle "the present disorders in the church" by a meeting on October 18, which was adjourned to November 2 and then to November 17, with the only revelation being the complaints of William McCobb, John Leishman, and Mary Daws against Rebekah Sawyer, all church members. The minutes referenced a murky November 17, 1803, result "on file."

By April 24, 1804, the church wrestled with "some circumstances of our members going after the free-will Baptists." The Congregationalists chose William McCobb and Pastor Sawyer "to visit and confer with Benjamin Kelley, Jr., relative to his going to the free-will Baptist, and renouncing fellowship with this church." On May 8, 1804, the church met at the Harbor schoolhouse, probably not a plus for retaining "Brother Kelley," who lived in his family's homestead at Pleasant Cove.[297] He attended the meeting and told that he was "dissatisfied with some doctrinal sentiments made by the Pastor." Nevertheless, on June 9, 1804, Benjamin Kelley, Jr., requested to be restored to the Congregational church, and the church voted to receive him after his making public confession at the next Lord's Day. He did so, renouncing his "undue and hasty conduct...to go to the Freewill Baptists." Over seven years later, on November 9, 1811, the Boothbay Congregational Church excommunicated Benjamin Kelley, Jr., who "has been guilty of railing against the church of Christ in Boothbay, and of wickedly forsaking the church, its order and worship."

Years later, on December 27, 1826, Mrs. Rachel Fuller, a daughter of James and Frances Auld, wife of John Fuller, and a member of the Congregational church who had fifteen years earlier been convicted of fornication, could not agree on the church's views on infant baptism and baptism by sprinkling. So she and her husband had left the Congregational church years earlier and joined the Freewill Baptists, were baptized by immersion, and the church never did excommunicate them. John and Rachel Fuller, who lived north of the center,[298] had fifteen children, and so the Boothbay Congregational Church lost a very large family to the Baptists.

Alcohol remained the looming crisis in the church minutes. On May 8, 1804, William McCobb, a prominent and wealthy citizen who held more and varied positions of public trust in Boothbay than anyone else up to at least 1905,[299] having served as Boothbay's representative to the General Court of Massachusetts for thirteen years between 1785 and 1811, as treasurer of Boothbay for nineteen years between 1775 and 1798, and as one of three selectmen for eighteen years between 1773 and 1812,[300] was questioned by the church leaders about retailing ardent spirits contrary to Maine laws. McCobb conceded to his retailing of liquor and justified himself. After he left, one church leader objected to voting on this issue because of insufficient evidence, and the church postponed this decision. On May 22, 1804, Pastor Sawyer read Maine statutes pertaining to the regulation of licensed houses. Rev. Sawyer then pointedly asked the church leaders, "Are these good laws?" with each church leader responding in the affirmative. Similarly, all agreed with his second question, "Ought the violation of these laws to be considered offensive?" Since Squire McCobb was not present, they postponed any decision again. On May 29, the date of the following meeting, Squire McCobb was in Boston as a member of the General Court, which was the state legislature. Rev. Sawyer asked the church council to take up the trial for William McCobb's violating Maine law by selling liquor, and the church declined to proceed by votes on August 17, September 7, September 28, and October 5, 1804, the latter date after testimony against McCobb was given by Rev. Sawyer, John Emerson, and John McClintock.

Finally, on October 12, 1804, the church voted amazingly that Squire William McCobb had not violated Maine law in retailing and allowing drinking of ardent spirits in his store! Rev. Sawyer at the next church meeting, over four months later, on February 27, 1805, inquired of the church as to whether they were of the same mind. The church voted affirmatively and agreed that their vote, but not the numbers for and against, should be made public. Rev. Sawyer warned the church members that they would be seen in a very unfavorable light, but the church did not budge from its approval to let McCobb sell his liquor. During the following meeting, over two months later, on May 2, 1805, Rev. Sawyer again expressed his dissatisfaction with the church on the McCobb issue and further "that they had justified evil in such a manner that he could not walk with them, or hold them in fellowship, unless something could be done to relieve his mind." The church dithered and postponed another vote on May 2, May 9, and finally rebuffed their pastor again on May 16, when they voted against Pastor Sawyer's suggestion that an outside council of ministers and delegates from sister churches convene on these church difficulties. Unlike the Reverend Jonathan Gould, who clearly had been intimidated by his landlord and creditor Squire McCobb, Rev. Sawyer had the guts to stand up alone against William McCobb time and time again.

Jeremiah Beath continued his long struggle with alcohol addiction and "made a public satisfaction for his having drunken to drunkenness." This was almost certainly the reason he was not immediately admitted when the Congregational church began, or when he had applied but was not received into the church on October 31, 1798. Almost a year later, on August 24, 1799, Jeremiah Beath again requested church membership but was again rebuffed because the church was "not satisfied that circumstances were favorable to his admittance into the church." By 1818, Jeremiah Beath was a member of the church, but on June 14, 1818, the church voted that he "should not partake with them at the Lord's Table at the present time." This was because, as became clear on June 29, 1818, Jeremiah had "drunk of ardent spirits to excess" at multiple places, including at Mr. Kenniston's, at Colonel Auld's house at Bristol, and on board Captain Benjamin Pinkham's vessel. The church found Jeremiah Beath guilty and appointed three church leaders "if possible to bring him to a proper temper." Finally, after several more meetings dealing with Jeremiah Beath's intoxication issues, on December 4, 1818, the pastor admonished him, and the church excommunicated Jeremiah Beath. He was, however, reinstated in 1831 after the usual reformation, abstinence, and public apologies. Perhaps Jeremiah's defense could have been that he had fourteen children.[301] Jeremiah died four years later, in 1835, without any further recorded incidents.

In June and July 1819, several intoxication cases arose for church members, including John Brier, Benjamin Pinkham, William Kennedy, and Nicholas Knight; most stayed with the church as long as they publicly confessed and apologized for their public intoxication. However, Nicholas T. Knight, a man of influence and property, including the Nicholas Knight House still standing at Boothbay center, where John Murray had settled,[302] was excommunicated on April 6, 1826, for his ongoing alcohol problems, and he was present and asked for prayers. In April 1831, after agreeing to avoid ardent spirits and publicly apologizing in church, Knight was brought back into the church. Deacon Leishman, guilty of multiple instances of abusive language to others including to Rev. Weston and of being absent from church services for three years, was excommunicated, on March 5, 1824. As Elizabeth Reed quipped, "At one time or another they pretty nearly all sat in judgment of one another and very cheerfully excommunicated each other."

On December 21, 1809, Mary McCallar confessed at the church meetinghouse to her transgression of the seventh commandment by stealing. Elizabeth Lowell, formerly Elizabeth Decker, who had grown up at Decker's Cove in Southport and married James Lowell of Alna, was suspended at age thirty-one[303] from church for one year after being found guilty of violating the seventh commandment. Mary Bennett, formerly Mary Matthews, one of five children of William (caulker by land and mate and captain by sea) and Lydia Matthews of Spruce Point,[304] was excommunicated on March 27, 1826, for a violation of the seventh commandment as well as for being absent from communion and church meetings for several years. On April 29, 1829, yet another woman, twenty-two year-old Abigail Decker, a sister in the church and daughter of Ebenezer and Sally Ball Decker,[305] was accused of violating the seventh commandment. The church delegated to David Kenniston and Deacon Thorpe the duty of conversing with Abigail Decker.[306]

Losing Members to New Baptist and Methodist Churches
The Freewill Baptist Society, later the Freewill Baptist Church, arising amidst the revivalism of the Second Great Awakening, attracted Calvinist communicants, notably Congregationalists, formerly known as Puritans, and also Scots-Irish Presbyterians. The Baptists were not a national entity until 1814.[307] Freewill Baptists emphasized human free will for salvation by grace that was available to all who would accept it rather than the Calvinist doctrine of predestination.[308] Freewill Baptist minister, Elder Benjamin Randall, without school training, preached what the Bible said to him and evangelized to and converted many, ranging from New Hampshire to the Boothbay peninsula, and many Freewill Baptist churches were organized.[309] Randall preached to and baptized Boothbay converts as early as 1790. At least twice, in 1798 and 1804, Boothbay Baptist inhabitants petitioned the Massachusetts General Court for incorporation and freedom from the Congregational yoke of taxation, but the Massachusetts Court, mostly Congregational, refused each time.[310] The separation of the Baptist Society from the Boothbay Congregational Church had drawn away nearly all of the Back River congregants and a greater part of those former church members north of the center.[311] Boothbay Baptists initially met weekly in local fellowship groups in homes, schools, and barns. A quarterly meeting was established in Woolwich in 1783 and later joined with Edgecomb.[312] Boothbay, in 1806, recognizing the trends, voluntarily exempted the Baptist Society from the ministerial tax previously due to the Boothbay Congregational Church.[313]

In 1809, the Massachusetts General Court approved the incorporation of the Baptist Society of Boothbay, which held its first meeting on February 1, 1810 at the schoolhouse on Back River, but no regular organization as a church occurred until November 18, 1826,[314] when the Edgecomb Baptists were organized.[315] There had been twenty-six incorporators, all men, as women were not yet counted as members. Seven of the incorporators, comprising more than one quarter, were the Lewises, who had been one of the first families to embrace the freewill Baptist faith and organize the church. The Lewises hailed primarily from North Boothbay, in the Back River, Knickerbocker, and Dover areas.[316]

Minutes existed for the July 1, 1816, Baptist meeting at the Back River schoolhouse, known as Schoolhouse #2 by the town. These 1816 minutes contained the first use of "freewill" in its name, the Freewill Baptist Society.[317] Finally, in 1830, the Freewill Baptist Society secured permission from the Boothbay town meeting to build a church on the Common.[318] This Baptist center of gravity north of the Boothbay Town Common toward Edgecomb, together with the growing trade and commerce in Boothbay Harbor, may have hastened Congregational meetings in the Harbor and the church's eventual relocation less than forty years later from Boothbay center to Boothbay Harbor. Perhaps also there was a cultural chasm between wealthier merchants in Boothbay Harbor and poorer farmers north of Boothbay Center.

Meanwhile, only the Methodists had a foothold on Southport, known as Cape Newagen Island from when Christopher Levett encountered Native Americans and English fishermen on its southern tip in 1623,[319] until it incorporated as Townsend in 1842.[320] Boothbay, in 1807, as it had a year earlier for the Baptists in Boothbay, allowed Southport to use half of its ministerial tax for the schoolhouse on the north side, with the other half designated for the schoolhouse at West Southport.[321] Methodism was the only doctrine preached on Southport, which was the center of Methodism on the Boothbay peninsula during this era.[322] The Methodist monopoly on Southport continued until the last century when, in

1906, All Saints by the Sea was consecrated as a summer Episcopal church on Pig Cove, on Southport's eastern shore.[323] Southport had five regular and several itinerant Methodist preachers in 1807. After 1808 Southport's Methodist church prospered. The Reverend Elliott B. Fletcher, who commenced his ministry in the region in 1829, led a tremendous revival reminiscent of the Reverend John Murray's revival some sixty-three years earlier. Fletcher attracted many Methodist converts, and by December 1830 a new church had been erected.[324] Elliott Fletcher was soon preaching also in East Boothbay, holding meetings in the East Boothbay kitchens, shops, and barns around Hodgdon Mills and Linekin. In 1836, the Methodist Church was built just north of the bridge at the mill in East Boothbay village.[325]

Baptists and Methodists split off from Congregational churches all over Massachusetts, including in its frontier in Maine, during the early 1800s. Maine churches split from the Puritans' Congregational churches for reasons of theology, governance, and even for prolonging the American Revolution to obtain a more equitable division of wilderness land on this Maine frontier. This was the struggle of landless farmers against the Great Proprietors. In Massachusetts it was Shay's Rebellion and in Pennsylvania the Whiskey Rebellion. Congregationalism was viewed as the religion of the aristocratic oppressor. Tensions probably developed between the farmers in Dover and in other parts north of Boothbay center and the merchants of Boothbay Harbor. These gulfs may have widened after 1798 between the newly formed Boothbay Congregational Church and the newer Baptist and Methodist churches, particularly in a Scots-Irish culture dominated by Congregationalists with their Puritanical and Massachusetts roots—and stigma. Boothbay Congregationalists were more prosperous, more Federalist politically, and more concentrated in the Harbor. These Congregationalists were thus more separated religiously, politically, and even physically from their northern neighbors, who were mostly Baptists and Methodists, Jeffersonian, and struggling farmers.

Boothbay in thirty-two years had changed dramatically from 1798, when in the words of Alan Taylor, "only along the Lincoln County coast around Pemaquid—where proprietary claims were most overlapping and proprietary generosity was least evident— did front-country towns participate in the resistance."[326] By 1830, Boothbay had become predominantly Congregationalist and Federalist, favoring stability over revolution. The Congregationalists' political, economic, and social dominance was shifting south to the Harbor, leaving the area north of the center to the more revivalist Baptists and Methodists, who had Jeffersonian Republican leanings, presaging and harboring a formal split of the town six decades later.

Second Great Awakening, 1790s–1840s

In the immediate aftermath of the American Revolution, Boothbay's Rev. Murray, who according to Maine historian Louis Hatch "had a remarkable ministry at Boothbay from 1767 to 1780" and led "the first great revival in the history of the State,"[327] decried in his 1783 *Bath Kol* treatise the post-Revolutionary decline of religious sentiment in practice and in spirit. This period when the U.S. Constitution was created in 1787 was "the high tide of the 18th century secularism," and by the 1790s in both Britain and the United States this secular "tide began to ebb and the religious spirit to flood back," launching the Second Great Awakening.[328] From the perspective of many, such as the Reverend John Murray and the last remnants of the Maine Presbytery in 1791, because of religious neglect the Province had "become, religiously, not unlike a 'waste howling wilderness.'"[329] Clearly, many desperately desired a religious revival.

The Second Great Awakening commenced in the 1790s and was essentially a frontier affair led by traveling evangelists, who often sparked huge camp meetings, starting at Cane Ridge, near Lexington, Kentucky, in 1801, whipping participants into frenzies of worship. Rev. Lyman Beecher, a leading Presbyterian luminary nationally and father of Harriet Beecher Stowe of *Uncle Tom's Cabin* fame, believed this revivalist spirit was essential to the creation of a rapidly growing nation based on a free market in land and driven by a strong current of materialistic individualism. Lyman preached that only religious belief and practice could provide spiritual leavening and that only community spirit could civilize this "thrusting people."[330]

The distinguishing feature of religion in America in the late 1790s and the early decades of the 1800s was this second but different kind of Great Awakening, one distinguished by "volunteerism," religious fervor unprovoked by the state and undirected by any supreme ecclesiastical authority. Volunteerism represented an energy and self-reliance that took the form of volunteer religious associations of men and women who preached the Gospel, attacked vice, and relieved suffering humanity.[331] This movement of voluntary associations, strong and flexible enough to meet challenges and address social and intellectual changes, came to be called the "benevolent empire" of the Second Great Awakening.[332]

Volunteerism triggered the American Bible Society, in 1816, when thousands of adherents inexpensively distributed the scriptures throughout the world; the American Sunday School Union, in 1824, formed to defeat or diminish all ignorance or faithlessness; and the American Tract Society, in 1817, which printed and widely distributed ten-page tracts for one penny each to instruct and spread good morals and sound religion. Congregationalists still controlled Dartmouth College in 1819, when attorney Daniel Webster represented Dartmouth and won a U.S. Supreme Court decision that upheld the right of the religious and private trustees to continue their control of the college without a takeover by the state of New Hampshire. This landmark decision affirmed the sanctity of contracts and triggered the founding of many church-based colleges throughout the country.[333]

Finally, like the First Great Awakening, this Second Great Awakening rode the waves of revivalism in cities and hamlets throughout the expanding United States. These revivals stressed the importance of the individual response to Christian proclamations, and they renewed and enlarged church membership through active persuasion and recruitment for church fellowship.[334]

There is little indication, however, that the Second Great Awakening reached the frontier town of Boothbay in the late 1700s or even had much traction in Boothbay in the early 1800s in the newly formed Congregational church. Mired in poverty and almost churchless, the Boothbay Congregationalists probably did not participate much in the early part of this Second Great Awakening. The revivals that were happening in Boothbay were primarily among Baptists and Methodists.

The number of Boothbay Baptists during this period up to 1830 probably exceeded that of many other towns in Maine, while at the same time Boothbay Methodists lagged behind other Maine towns. Baptists had established a Maine foothold in 1768 and by 1820 boasted 9,373 members. Methodists entered the Province of Maine in 1793 and by 1820 boasted 6,192 members, roughly two-thirds the number of Baptists.

Congregationalists, the established Puritan church in 1630, had remained dominant in Maine, which contained a population of roughly 200,000, until the State disestablished Congregationalism in 1834. In 1821, there were 131 Congregational churches in Maine, although almost half of them had no pastors. There was not one Presbyterian church left in Maine in 1820.[335] Boothbay mirrored the ongoing plurality of Congregationalists amidst a rising tide of others, particularly Methodists and Baptists. Thomas Jefferson, in 1818, poked fun at John Adams when Jefferson wrote and rejoiced about disestablishment trends to his old nemesis and friend that "this den of priesthood is at length broken up, and that a protestant popedom is no longer to disgrace American history and character."[336]

And, as British-based world historian Paul Johnson perceived, "The Second Great Awakening, with its huge intensification of religious passion, sounded the death-knell of American slavery just as the First Awakening had sounded the death-knell of British colonialism."[337]

The War of 1812:
Mr. Madison's War and America's First Civil War

Unlike the Revolutionary War, the War of 1812 was highly unpopular in the coastal trading town of Boothbay. Many throughout the country and in Boothbay pejoratively dubbed the conflict "Mr. Madison's War." Five years earlier, in 1807, President Thomas Jefferson, in response to British and French seizure of American shipping during the Napoleonic War, proposed and Congress passed the Embargo Act, forbidding any vessel to set out from the United States for any foreign port. By 1808 the act had crippled Boothbay and most New England shipping. Secession from the United States was openly discussed in New England, the region most extensively engaged in shipping and hardest hit by the law. Boothbay's special town meeting, called August 22, 1807, demanded suspension of the embargo. Church member and leading Boothbay citizen William McCobb formed a town committee and petitioned the federal government, but to no avail.[338]

After 1801 and increasingly in the years leading up to 1812, the dominant Republican Party of Jefferson and Madison challenged the British maritime policies as a threat to American sovereignty. The minority Federalist Party of Adams sympathized with Britain's global struggle against Napoleon I's rising French empire and despised the Jeffersonian Republicans as demagogues pandering to the common people by weakening the national government. By1812, the Republicans believed the Federalists in New England were conspiring with the British to break up the union and accused Loyalists in Canada of covertly assisting Indian attacks on frontier settlements. By invading Canada and defeating the British, the Republicans hoped to unite and save the Republic. Instead, however, the War of 1812 alienated the Federalists, who preferred to smuggle with the British rather than to fight them.[339] Smuggling had become a way of life in Boothbay and in most coastal Massachusetts towns. Jefferson had underestimated American reliance on overseas trade. His1807 embargo through 1808 withered the seaport economy and idled thousands of people dependent on coastal trade.[340] While Jeffersonians denounced smuggling as treason, Federalists favored smuggling before and during the "Civil War of 1812."[341]

Boothbay's seacoast community similarly preferred smuggling to war. Smuggling had been for years a profitable and risky pastime for Boothbay owners and mariners. The *Favorite*, a newly constructed topsail schooner based in Boothbay and partly owned by Boothbay Congregationalist founder John McCobb, sailed early in 1798 with a crew of four Boothbay men out of McFarland's Wharf, loaded with lumber and fish for the West Indies. The *Favorite* landed in March at Barbados, where it sold its cargo and purchased sugar and rum valued at several thousand dollars. Soon after sailing out of Barbados, a French privateer took the *Favorite* and its cargo as prize, sailed it to Puerto Rico, and illegally condemned the ship and cargo. A claim for indemnity was filed in 1798, and the owners finally won the lawsuit and were awarded over $7,000 twenty-six years later, in 1824.[342]

The *Townsend*, built in Newcastle, named after and located in Boothbay, was owned by three local men, including Congregationalist founder William McCobb. The French captured the *Townsend*, loaded with Boothbay codfish, boards, shingles, and staves, in the Leeward Islands, with the result that the sloop was condemned and the cargo confiscated. The litigation lasted over a century, resulting in $5,600 awarded to the owners' successors in 1908.[343]

Maine and American shipping, previously hampered by the French, soon suffered from the needs of the English during the Napoleonic wars, when the English patrolled the seas with its 5,000 vessels in need of crews. The Crown resorted to press gangs, who searched vessels from Halifax to the West Indies. In 1803, Captain Nathaniel Knight's schooner *Harriet* of Boothbay, while lying at anchor off St. Kitts, was boarded by an officer of an English man-of-war, who found Joseph Emerson of Boothbay without protection papers and impressed him on the spot. A year later, the *Harriet* returned to St. Kitts. Joseph Emerson one night quietly went down on the bobstay and into the water, swam ashore, saw and successfully hid from a searching party while suffering mostly from thirst, and remained hidden for four days until the British cruiser sailed. Emerson befriended a slave who provided sustenance and at the waterfront found an American brig about to depart to Portsmouth, New Hampshire. Emerson successfully escaped, and returned to Boothbay.[344] Two years later, Joseph Emerson married Betsey Boyd, daughter of Congregationalist Catherine Boyd, and the young couple soon settled in Edgecomb.[345] British impressment of American sailors was one of the causes of the War of 1812, which in turn fueled hatred and bitterness toward England along the Maine coast for many generations until World War I.[346]

President Jefferson's embargo of December 1807, designed to protect American shipping from French decrees and British orders and to protect American neutrality, resulted in evasion of the embargo; but soon "shipping fell away, and vessels lay idle and rotting at the wharves in Boothbay and Wiscasset." Massachusetts, including the District of Maine, boasted exports in 1807 valued in excess of $40 million. They fell to almost nothing in 1809. Protest meetings were held in all principal seaport towns in Maine, and Boothbay's celebration of the Fourth in July 1808 included many speakers railing against the unpopular embargo, including John McClintock, who offered the toast: "The Embargo, O, may our freedom sing!" The next year, after the January enforcement act passed, Boothbay offered a resolution that the embargo was "contrary to the constitution and extremely oppressive on the sea coast of the District of Maine." Incredibly, Boothbay and other towns in February 1809 also voted to organize a "Committee of Safety," reminiscent of those organized shortly before the Revolutionary War thirty-five years earlier. Instead, the next month, public opinion, lax enforcement, and the end of Jefferson's term combined to repeal the Jeffersonian Embargo, to the relief of the Federalists and of all people in Boothbay.[347]

Jeffersonian Boothbay during the immediate aftermath of the American Revolution had turned Federalist by the Civil War of 1812.[348] Boothbay received news of the actual declaration of war in June 1812 via an "express" horseman who arrived in Wiscasset. Boothbay had little enthusiasm as the seaboard inhabitants knew war would be detrimental to their fishing, coasting, and West Indies trade that formed Boothbay's livelihood.[349] Immediately after war was declared, Boothbay called another special town meeting, held on July 7, 1812. The town voted to petition President Madison for protection of the defenseless town against England. Boothbay's petitioners noted, "Townsend Harbor is one of the best on the whole coast of the United States of America; one of the most easy of access…and in times of peace it affords a shelter for numerous coasters against tempestuous weather."[350] The town directed the treasurer to procure sufficient quantities of bullet molds and established strategic defensive positions at McFarland's Point near Campbell's Cove, now West Harbor Pond, and at West Harbor.[351] As Alan Taylor observed about America generally, "Among rural people…personal relationships mattered more than abstract allegiance to nationalism."[352]

In March 1813, the British Liverpool packet, sloop of war *Rattler*, and tender *Bream* of six guns cruised between the islands of Monhegan and Seguin, captured a number of coasters, and permitted their crews to land on Damariscove Island. Boothbay's William Maxwell Reed wrote a riveting story in the *Boston Patriot* a week later about his giving chase and learning of the *Rattler* about to rendezvous at Townsend Harbor that night. He reported that "some of our coasters are taken daily."[353]

Henry Wadsworth Longfellow helped enshrine in lore the naval battle of the *Boxer* and the *Enterprise*.[354] Early on Sunday morning, September 5, 1813, the American *Enterprise* sailed into Monhegan Harbor and discovered the British *Boxer* silently at anchor. The maneuvering and first shots started around 8:30 in the morning, and the two ships tacked and maneuvered for position until 2:30 in the afternoon. The Reverend Jabez Pond Fisher detected the sound of battle that Sunday inside the Congregational church at Boothbay center. He paused in his sermon, and after a brief word or two as to what he suspected was happening, dismissed his congregation. His parishioners rushed up nearby Kenniston Hill, which then presented a good panorama of the combat. After viewing the battle amidst smoke that the breeze cleared often, they waited anxiously after the firing finally ceased. They quickly recognized victory when they saw the vessels headed westward to Portland rather than eastward to British Halifax.[355]

Another close call for Boothbay came in 1814, indeed the only instance of any loss of life within the town limits during the War of 1812, as related years later by Captain George Reed, in 1812 a boy of seventeen in the garrison service. A British war vessel exchanged several shots with the defenses at McFarland's Point. The British ship then ceased firing, tacked, and sailed out of the harbor and around Spruce Point into Linekin Bay. A boy, the son of John Grover, standing in front of his house on the bay, discharged his musket at the British vessel, which returned fire. The British shot struck young Grover in the head. The Harbor troops had hurried from the McFarland garrison toward Linekin Bay and had almost reached the Grover residence when they heard the fired shots. Moments later they found the Grover boy lying dead with brains and blood spattered on the walls of his house.[356]

Many Boothbay Congregational church men were listed among the more than eighty Boothbay men in the muster rolls for the War of 1812. Multiple Alleys, Aulds, Bryers, McCobbs, McFarlands, Montgomerys, Pinkhams, Shermans, and Wylies, for example, are listed,[357] The war, nevertheless, remained unpopular for them and for most of Boothbay, definitely disrupting their lifeblood of trade, and seemingly meaningless and mistaken from the outset.

Joseph McCobb and Jacob Auld, two young cousins in their early thirties in 1812, were lieutenant and ensign, respectively, in Captain William Reed's Company of Foot during the War of 1812.[358] A decade earlier, at nineteen and twenty, they had formed a general merchandising business, McCobb and Auld, which lasted for decades, dealing in groceries, hardware, lumber, dry goods, and ship chandlery. It was close to the north end of the current footbridge in Boothbay Harbor, near the By-Way's recent bowling alley. They married within a year of each other, Jacob Auld to Sarah Reed in 1806 and Joseph McCobb to his partner's sister, Margaret Auld, the following year. In 1807, they established their homes in the Brick House, built by William McCobb, Joseph's uncle, not themselves as has been recounted elsewhere. The Aulds moved into the northern half and the McCobbs into the southern half.[359] Sarah Auld is listed as a member of the Boothbay Congregational church, joining on June 18, 1818. Boothbay had in the previous twenty-five years likely increased in size, from 761 voters (757 whites and four blacks) in 1785[360] to 1,583 inhabitants (808 men and 775 women) in 1810.[361] Boothbay's voter lists dwarfed Bath's and Wiscasset's, being on the coast and not up the rivers. A federal study on America's fisheries observed that it was "Booth Bay where the bulk of the catch was landed to be cured for market."[362] Boothbay's coasters and traders, like Auld and McCobb, were exchanging goods, news, and ideas with international coasters, as when the *Portland Gazette* spotted the sloop *Patty* entering Boothbay in 1810, "nineteen days from Antigua."[363]

John Murray McFarland, born in 1767 during the Reverend John Murray's revivalism, was another member, along with his wife, Margaret (daughter of Paul Reed and Margery Beath Reed) of Boothbay's Presbyterian and Congregational churches. John McFarland served as Boothbay's first postmaster for many years, town treasurer for thirty-two years, and was one of the principal men in Boothbay.[364] He owned several vessels engaged in the West Indian trade, shipping dry fish and handling products of the islands before, during, and after the War of 1812.[365]

From the beginnings of Boothbay, most commercial activity was started in what is now Boothbay Harbor, such as the Reed mill erected around 1749 at Mill Cove by Andrew Reed. John Beath built a mill at the head of Campbell Cove near McCobb's Hill in the 1750s, and another mill was built by Samuel Adams on Adams Pond. Shipbuilding was concentrated in Boothbay Harbor, but also in East Boothbay in the early 1800s. Related stores were also concentrated in Boothbay Harbor and to a lesser extent in East Boothbay and in other places such as Southport, as related by Francis Greene and inferred from John Gould's diary.[366]

On February 11, 1815, the British sloop of war *Favorite*, possibly the same ship owned by Congregationalist founder John McCobb and seized and condemned by the British in 1798 in Barbados, forty days out of London, brought good tidings of peace to New York. Portland learned the good news forty-seven hours later and Boothbay probably an additional hour or so after. Since shipping lay idle in Maine's harbors, including in Boothbay's, this news was hailed with joy.[367]

In 1815, at the war's conclusion, the world war also ended with the Battle of Waterloo, after which a great flood of immigrants compounded already high American birth rates. Of supreme importance, the Louisiana Purchase of 1803 had opened up a treasure trove of land. Andrew Jackson had led the destruction of Indian power, and the world's demographic revolution exploded, particularly in Europe and even more in America. In Europe alone, population soared between 1750 and 1900 from 150 million to over 400 million, resulting in huge net outflows of immigration all over the world, but above all to the United States.[368] In just twenty years, between 1810 and 1830, the U.S. population soared threefold and included internal migration, particularly of New England settlers leaving scarce land and Old South inhabitants fleeing exhausted land.[369]

This was an era of staggering freedom of movement, when an Englishman without any documentation or luggage could pay just ten pounds at a Liverpool shipping counter, hop aboard, sail to and come ashore in New York without anyone asking him his business, and vanish into American society. If the Englishman had no money, he could sail for free to Canada and bum rides on coastal boats to Maine, Massachusetts, and New York ports, with no control and no resentment.[370] The land-purchase system, starting in 1796, when one could purchase land on credit for two dollars an acre was the single most benevolent act of the U.S. government in its entire history, according to historian Paul Johnson. In the years following 1815, more people acquired freehold land at bargain prices in the United States than had occurred anywhere at any other time in the history of the world.[371] This was truly an incredible era in the United States generally and in Boothbay particularly.

But the clash of freedom versus slavery and commerce versus agrarianism grew more threatening. As Thomas Jefferson wrote a friend in 1820, "This momentous question, like a firebell in the night, awakened and filled me with terror. I considered it at once as the knell of the Union…It is hushed indeed for the moment, but this is a reprieve only, not a final sentence."[372]

Marginalization and Influence of Boothbay Women
Analysis of rural business ledgers during the last decade before the American Revolution points to a narrowing of the gap between male and female earnings, unlike the evidence from urban seaport communities in New England. In those communities, urban women's gains declined as a cash economy gradually replaced the traditional barter economy.[373] Boothbay women during this period were likely more involved and closer to economic and social, though not political, equality with their male counterparts than in many other places in post-Revolutionary America. Boothbay women's relative parity with men, as compared to more urban areas, may be due in part to their Scots-Irish culture of more equality between the sexes, such as work roles not being as sharply divided by gender as in other English cultures. Women worked alongside men in clearing forests, breaking ground, farming fields, and slaughtering animals. Sarah Montgomery, the wife of Robert Montgomery, chronicled in the prior chapter when she led with her husband Robert the removal of the Linekin house from what she perceived as Montgomery land, epitomized the relative parity of Boothbay's Scots-Irish men and women. On the other hand, Scots-Irish men and women had exceptionally differentiated roles in manners, speech, dress, decorum, and status, often with extreme male domination and female dependence.[374]

Women in New England seaport cities, by the early 1800s, were less independent and autonomous than their rural counterparts, yet enjoyed more autonomy than in the 1600s and 1700s, during the founding years of Boston, Salem, Newport, and Portsmouth.[375] Historian Elaine Forman Crane notes that:

> Puritanism was egalitarian to the extent that God's plan for salvation favored neither men nor women. In the unsettled founding decades, outspoken women actively participated on church committees, judged their fellow church members, joined or withdrew from churches as their consciences dictated, and contributed to the decision-making process. God-fearing women greatly outnumbered men as the colonial period advanced, and their numerical ascendancy paralleled a dwindling role in the formulation of church policy. Even Baptist and Quaker women enjoyed fewer privileges by the turn of the nineteenth century.

Particularly urban women, early on, actively engaged in a wide array of mercantile pursuits. When the first English emigrants sailed for the New England colonies, English common law permitted unmarried women to buy and sell both real estate and personal property, enter into contracts, conduct business, and devolve property through wills.[376] Women's mercantile activity diminished between 1630 and 1800, as the urban New England economy became inseparably intertwined with long-distance trade, as a consumer-conscious middle class emerged, and as a cash economy replaced the traditional barter system.[377]

Early colonial American women and men could avoid paper trails and the legal restraints imposed, at least in theory, in the New England frontier. As the legal system took on the characteristics of its English parent, women were increasingly restrained by its dictates. Puritan criminal law was even harsher than its English counterpart on women for adultery, which was a capital offense in Massachusetts.[378]

Spinning provided a meager income for so many women that up until the nineteenth century the terms, "unmarried woman" and "spinster" became synonymous.[379] Colonial Americans grew flax and exported flaxseed, which could have supported a thriving linen industry. However, to protect English economic monopolies, England also exported sizable quantities of linen cloth. Only small amounts of linsey-woolsey, a flax-wool combination, were allowed to be locally produced for domestic consumption.[380]

Charitable institutions, formerly run by women in Europe, had been secularized during the Reformation. In colonial New England, almshouses and poorhouses were generally under the control of men, who oversaw mostly poor women therein.[381]

Remarkable consensus exists concerning the extraordinary influence of religion in virtually every aspect of New England life. Women were deeply involved in the process of church building from the moment they signed the church covenant. Yet our perceptions of women's role in religious institutions are shaped more by ministerial sermons and pamphlets written by men than by an examination of the internal organization and operation of the churches. Numerically, women dominated the church, not only in Boothbay but also throughout New England, forming nearly seventy percent of the rank and file of the churches where men wielded ultimate authority.[382] As Elaine Forman Crane put it, "Consciously or unconsciously, ministers and elders managed to retain minority control of churches whose vast majority was female."[383] Boothbay's Presbyterian church and its successor Congregational church certainly reflected this in its all-male composition of clergy and elders amidst women-dominated congregants. All Presbyterian sessional and later Congregational church records reflect the overwhelming majority of women among church members from 1767 to 1830. Women, comprising the vast majority of Boothbay's Congregational church, may explain the earlier exodus for the Baptist church in the early 1800s. Baptists throughout New England were generally more willing to extend a share of church governance to women, although only the Quakers approached equality.[384] However, the Boothbay Baptist Church allowed no women members until two decades later, in 1826.[385]

Despite and perhaps because of the feminization of New England churches, men, who were the sole church officers and town officials, defined disorderly conduct and the rules by which women were determined immoral. New England women were disproportionately charged with fornication and excessive drinking. This was true not only in Boothbay during colonial times and early post-Revolutionary times,[386] but also throughout most of New England, even in the seventeenth century during the Salem witch trials.[387] The Boothbay Presbyterian Church's sessional records reflect this disproportionate prosecution of women for acts of fornication: seven women (Martha Reed, Eunice Decker, Sarah Bowers, Jane Reed (twice), Herrinden's wife, Phoebe Kennedy, and Susan Dey), as contrasted with only one man, James Kennedy, Phoebe Kennedy's husband.

Only three intoxication cases appear in the sessional records of 1767 to 1778, although alcohol was probably a common contributor to other sessional cases. The most notable intoxication case was against Benjamin Thomas over many months. Another intoxication case was made by Eunice Decker against Samuel and Elizabeth Pierce of Southport, but the male elders found that this was based on only groundless suspicion, Mrs. Decker confessed her error, and the Pierces forgave the injury and reconciled with Mrs. Decker. Another complaint was brought to the Session against Martha Reed, who frankly confessed her sin, professed her sorrow and great humiliation and prayed that she would not be debarred from the church. The Session required her to stand and be publicly rebuked, and she was dismissed from her former standing. The Congregational church records during this period from 1798 until 1830, as chronicled above, shows this same pattern of prosecuting women far more than men for intoxication, adultery, and fornication. Particularly,

> in a community where many men earned their living at sea, women could count on those wages only periodically and at

erratic intervals. Independent, unmarried women were, paradoxically, in the most precarious financial situation, usually eking out a living in the needs trades (tailoring, sewing, spinning, knitting, and weaving) or as landladies or shopkeepers. Such economic fragility undermined the day-to-day operation of the churches.[388]

Disproportionately few women owned pews or parts of pews. When they did they often couldn't make the stipulated pew payments. Husbands usually held title to their wives' pews, even when husbands never saw the insides of churches.[389] Despite male dominance as church leaders, women appear to have had significant influence in church membership, though not in executive committees during the first half century of the Boothbay church. However, women's power and influence in governance matters declined as the power of the church waned and that of the all-male state became ascendant.[390] This male dominance was mirrored in Boothbay in 1814, when ruling men voted against Rev. Sawyer's proposal to simply allow church women to be present when men were discussing and deciding prospective member applicants. Men also refused, in 1805, their minister's request to allow women to simply watch their men decide alcohol issues.

Although women often navigated around the shoals of male dominance quite successfully throughout the colonial and post-Revolutionary period, they suffered a decline in economic standing, a growing public invisibility, and a heightened reliance on male decision-making in New England seaport cities and possibly in Boothbay's seaport and farming community during the late eighteenth and nineteenth centuries.[391]

Prophetic Warnings in 1828
The Trustees of Phillips Academy in Andover, Massachusetts, on February 1, 1828, prepared young men for the ministry and warned "not to encourage worthy men in preaching prematurely," to help ensure "the purity and respectability of our Ministry." They

advocated at least a three-year course of theological study, "a period scarcely sufficient for acquiring that fund of knowledge which is necessary for a Minister of the Gospel." They concluded,

> We respectfully request Ministers especially, in their individual and collective capacities, to adopt such measures as they may deem proper for guarding against the evil of young men being urged forward, or permitted to appear, as public preachers, who have not been examined and approved for that purpose by some regular Ecclesiastical body.

This cautionary letter contained a handwritten note at the top, "For the moderator of Lincoln Conference, Maine."[392] Unfortunately, Boothbay paid no heed to historical patterns and ignored cautions from their wider church leadership in 1830.

Like the legendary John Murray's extraordinary ministry in Boothbay, Weston's astounding success in Boothbay was followed by dismal failures of church and pastoral leadership. This failure will be readily apparent through the extraordinary story of the Reverend Charles Cook that is brilliantly assembled and related in the next chapter.[393]

CHAPTER 5

SHADOWS AND COUNTERSHADOWS: 1830–1848
by Sarah M. Foulger

Introduction

In 1830, Andrew Jackson was the President, the first U.S. railroad station opened in Baltimore, the Book of Mormon was published, and American readers were enthralled with authors such as Edgar Allen Poe and Nathaniel Hawthorne. The population in the United States was expanding dramatically, the 1830 census indicating a growth of thirty-three percent during the previous ten years. The Oregon Trail held a steady stream of pioneers and hopes of settlements on the West Coast. Although loudly protested by the American Missionary Society, a mission and advocacy organization supported by most Congregational churches of the time, Congress approved the "Indian Removal Act," authorizing forced removal of Native Americans to the western prairies.[394] The Nat Turner Revolt, a slave rebellion, took place in 1831, causing more deaths than any other event until the beginning of the Civil War. In other parts of the world, revolution broke out in Belgium, France, and Poland, the colonization of Australia and New Zealand was in its infancy, and Frederic Chopin was performing in the major music venues of Europe.

In ecclesiastical realms, the Second Great Awakening, a religious revival movement, swept across the nation led by Presbyterian minister, Charles Grandisson Finney. In addition to his emphasis on personal salvation, Finney promoted social equality, encouraging both education for women and the abolition of slavery. Higher education, albeit mainly for men, had long ranked as a high priority among the nation's religious leaders. In this era, Protestant denominations planted more than two dozen colleges in New England and throughout the expanding West, institutions such as Denison (Baptist), Wesleyan (Methodist), Gettysburg (Lutheran), Haverford (Quaker), and Grinnell (Congregational). The modern missionary movement was well under way throughout the world with Presbyterians in India and Palestine, Lutherans in Japan, Baptists in Thailand, and Congregationalists in Hawaii. The home missions movement gained momentum as denominations enthusiastically planted congregations in quickly expanding territories of the United States. In response to dereliction and poverty among young single Englishmen leaving rural England for urban areas, the Young Men's Christian Association was founded in London in 1844 by George Williams. In 1851, the first American YMCA was established at Old South Congregational Church in Boston by sea captain Thomas Sullivan.

The Boothbay region continued to experience steady growth in 1830, the region's population having doubled between 1800 and 1830. Local business developed and expanded, commerce overshadowing governance. Shipping and shipbuilding gradually eclipsed farming, while fishing continuing to be key to growth in commerce. As noted by Greene, "Damariscotta for beauty, and Bristol for pride; had it not been for codfish, Boothbay would have died."[395] This was a time in which most people practiced subsistence farming and, as Barbara Rumsey put it more generally, "a time when people did for themselves."[396] Much of New England, like upstate New York, was "scorched" by revivalism and Boothbay was no exception, the Congregational Church of Boothbay drawing several revivalist preachers to its pulpit.

1830 marked the beginning of a tumultuous, traumatic, and fractious era in the life of the Boothbay congregation. During this period, the church was challenged externally by the emergence of two other growing denominations, Methodist and Freewill Baptist, and internally by the troubling shadows that fell on the congregation following the brief tenure of the minister who arrived in the summer of 1830, the Reverend Charles Cook.

Rev. Charles Lewis Cook—1830-1832

Although Greene's history summarizes Cook's ministry in Boothbay with only one brief sentence, Charles Cook is a significant and provocative figure in the annals of the church.[397] His ministry and personal relationships led to his excommunication from the church, cast an unsettling shadow over the Boothbay community, and changed the course of local church history. In the Centennial Sermon of 1866, by which time Cook had been gone from the church thirty-four years and gone from this earth for twenty-five, Rev. Leander Coan wrote of Cook:

> This strange man has gone to his reward. It is said, whatever was his life, that he died a good man. Since he has gone to God's tribunal, it is useless to bring him again before man's.[398]

Coan was undoubtedly speaking to those who well remembered what had happened. In his own elegant and deeply pastoral way, Coan encouraged church members to leave judgment of Charles Cook in God's hands. Although the congregation was advised by the nineteenth century Maine Conference to "bury" what had transpired during Cook's ministry, some details of Cook's life and ministry have been unearthed, many from the court records of a troubling and consequential trial involving Cook that took place in Boston in 1835, three years after he left Boothbay.

Charles L. Cook was ordained in Boothbay on October 6, 1830, as a young man of twenty-eight. He served the church little more than two years but left behind deep feelings of betrayal, anger, and confusion, a legacy sadly typical of congregations that have discovered a pastor's "irregularities."[399] The *"American Quarterly"* summarized, "His ministry [in Boothbay] was disastrous."[400] Conference records indicate that Cook was dismissed from the church on October 31, 1832. In 1998, Rev. Joseph David Stinson wrote a brief history of the Congregational Church in Boothbay and Boothbay Harbor, in which he penned,

> Mr. Cook precipitated a crisis in the history of the church at the Center. He came in 1830 and left in disrepute in 1832. Before his troubles he oversaw a revival of piety, unequalled since Murray. He even got the Congregationalists to swear off alcohol! But in 1832 he committed some sexual sin, which resulted in his excommunication and the removal of his standing as a minister…
>
> But conflict over the Cook affair persisted for years. In 1848, forty-eight individuals withdrew from the Center Church and formed a second Congregational Church in Boothbay Harbor. They built a second meetinghouse and operated under the same covenant as the "Center Parish," as the Church on the Common came to be called. The large loss of members by the withdrawal of Baptists, Methodists and now most of the Congregationalists weakened the Center Parish. Add in this the conflict and fallout over Mr. Cook's situation and you have the reasons for the demise of the Center Parish…[401]

Stinson determined that Charles Cook's ministry was a significant factor in the congregational move to its present Boothbay Harbor location. Who was this man who changed the course of Boothbay's church history? To begin with, he was a New Englander with Boothbay roots, born on April 23, 1803 in Newburyport, Massachusetts. His father, Elias Cook, was part of a noteworthy and well-respected Newburyport family. His mother, Abigail Cook, née Davis, was from Boothbay. His maternal grandparents, Hannah Barter and Israel Davis, were both born in Boothbay (then called Townsend). His great-grandfather, Israel Davis, was a founder of the original Presbyterian congregation led by John Murray. It is likely, therefore, that Cook knew Boothbay well and was very familiar with the congregation, which had, in 1798, become a Congregational church. It is also likely that, growing up in Newburyport, he had heard stories of the great John Murray, who, having founded the church in Boothbay, left to serve the Presbyterian church in Newburyport, and who died ten years before Cook was born.

We know almost nothing of Charles Cook's childhood or education but it is recorded that, in 1827, he was ordained a Baptist minister in Hanson, Massachusetts.[402] The history of the Hanson church, written in 1962, notes that Cook was voted their pastor on December 30, 1826 and began service on February 21, 1827.[403] On July 7, 1827 the congregation voted to dismiss him, to put him under censure for speaking against the church and some of its individual members, and to form a committee to "labour" with him. Apparently, there was an argument over proper administration of the Lord's Supper. Additionally, it was believed that Rev. Cook had deceived the church regarding his credentials and that he had created further discord in the church by arguing about his salary.[404] The challenge that haunted him wherever he went, however, had nothing to do with sacraments, credentials, or salary; Charles Cook was homosexual.

Cook's vocation during the two years following his ministry in Hanson, 1828–1829, remains a mystery; but, according to his brother's account offered during the aforementioned 1835 trial in Boston, Cook moved to Derry, New Hampshire, then again to Plainfield, New Hampshire. One newspaper article refers to service in a Methodist church, but no data have been found to support this notion. We know with clarity that in 1830, Cook was called unanimously to become the pastor in Boothbay and that, according to one local newspaper, the *Wiscasset Citizen*, the church held great hope in him.

> The Congregational Church and Parish in Boothbay, have given the Rev. **CHARLES L. COOK** a call to settle with them in the Gospel Ministry, which invitation he has accepted, and preparations are making for his Installation. An unusual degree of unanimity has prevailed in the church and parish – the church were united, to a member, and the parish were unanimous, in their call.
>
> A reformation has already commenced under his preaching, with pleasing and encouraging prospects – a number have entertained a hope, and nearly sixty more are anxiously enquiring what they should do to be saved. – *Wiscasset Citizen*.

Rev. Charles L. Cook's Call to Local Ministry

Cook was a convincing preacher, "considered one of the most popular preachers in Maine."[405] He was a strong proponent of the temperance movement, the first temperance society having been founded in 1808 by Congregationalists. In the wake of the first Great Revival of 1800, the famous Congregationalist luminary, Lyman Beecher, railed against the use of alcohol by the clergy. Cook celebrated the anniversary of that first revival and its temperance message in Boothbay on July 5, 1830, committing members of the church to forsaking alcohol.[406] At that celebration, a collection was taken up for the American Colonization Society, also known as the Back to Africa initiative. The American Colonization Society raised awareness and funds for the purpose of freeing slaves and sending them back to their homelands.[407] In addition to temperance and abolition, Cook also demonstrated an interest in education, serving on the local school committee in 1832. He enjoyed both preaching and writing and was a noted contributor to *The Christian Mirror*, a widely read religious newspaper published in Portland at the time.

By church growth standards, Cook had a notably successful ministry in Boothbay, leading a spiritual revival that engendered an increase in both membership and baptisms. In the September 18, 1830 minutes of Boothbay church records, Cook wrote the following prayer: "O God, make this the set time for thy power." Such power was evident in minutes of the Maine Conference, which, in 1831, recorded thirty-three members received by profession of faith, two by letter of transfer, and twenty-eight baptisms, all in the Congregational Church of Boothbay. These minutes glowed with Cook's successes as a pastor, yet foreshadowed trouble ahead:

> Since that time [referring to the previous year], a revival of religion has been witnessed at Boothbay, which began auspiciously and was proceeding prosperously, till interrupted by a division which was excited by the interference of members of another communion. The consequences were deplorable; still the grace of God was not wholly frustrated, as it resulted in the addition of nearly 40 members to the congregational church.

One wonders if the interruption and division mentioned in these Maine Conference minutes were related to the storm that would blow full force the following year, the storm around Cook's sexual identity. The first hint of a problem with Rev. Cook came on August 28, 1832, when, during a special church meeting, his wife, Sophia, confessed, "I have shamefully abused my dear husband… so that I could not bear, nor would not have him in my sights. I left his bed and table." Sophia Cook's extended and poignant confession claims that a woman named Sarah Hilton had accused her husband, Rev. Cook, of lewd behavior, and that, initially, Sophia had believed Hilton. In her public confession, however, Sophia Cook no longer judges these accusations to be true and condemns Hilton as a liar, defending her husband as an "innocent sufferer." At another special meeting on September 18, there was a call to investigate "certain reports respecting their pastor." Only church members were permitted to attend this meeting, all others being asked to leave. In a beautifully composed letter to the church, Cook asked for a dissolution of his relationship with the church, expressed his regret in leaving, commended them to God, and closed with the hope, "May we all meet at length in the brighter and better world, where trials and weepings are no more."[408]

By 1833, the Maine Conference Minutes recorded what happened with shocking clarity:

> Soon after the last meeting of this conference unfavorable reports were in circulation respecting the conduct of Mr. Cook charging him with gross and abominable lewdness by the mutual practice of Onanism with young men of his own and neighboring towns, the details of which could not be spread before the public without danger of corrupting the minds and morals of the community. On the eighteenth of September last a public investigation of his conduct in relation to this charge was ordered by his church which took place in the meetinghouse at Boothbay on which occasion he had the benefit of legal advice and assistance and which resulted in his full convic-

tion. On the 30th of October he was tried by an Ecclesiastical Council mutually chosen by himself and the church and found guilty by abundant proof and subsequently by his own confession of conduct of which for disgusting vileness it is presumed the annals of New England do not furnish another example in a professedly Christian minister.[409]

The charges against Cook were as follows:

Charge 1st. That the Rev. Charles L. Cook has uttered expressions in relation to his wife, highly criminal in a minister of the gospel.

Charge 2nd. That said Rev. C.L. Cook has been guilty of lewd conduct, of a highly aggravated and unchristian character.[410]

Rev. Daniel Kendrick, pastor of the Edgecomb Congregational church, served as moderator of the Ecclesiastical Council that brought charges against Cook. He signed the document that convicted Cook and encouraged him "…to undo as far as in him lies, the injury he has done…and to serve God…in some other calling apart from the ministry."[411] This same document sympathizes with the church and encourages them to exercise: "…candor and forbearance towards him who now ceases to be their pastor; and especially sympathy and kindness towards his distressed family."[412] Finally, the document recommends that the church conceal the matter and "…cease from conversation about what has passed; to bury it, as soon as may be, in oblivion." [413]

The accusation of Onanism refers to the biblical figure, Onan, found in the 38th chapter of the Book of Genesis, who refused to be intimate with his brother's widow (as was his family responsibility). In the common parlance of the nineteenth century, the sin of Onanism was the sin of homosexuality.[414] All evidence points to Charles Cook being perhaps the first gay pastor of the Congregational Church of Boothbay. The very same year he was ordained in

Boothbay, he married Sophia Ann Horton, also of Newburyport; but this was, according to his own later testimony, to satisfy the wishes of his mother. This decision may also have been part of the desire to conform to social and church expectations. The marriage, however, was very unhappy from the start and, at times, publicly conflicted. 1835 Boston trial records document Cook's claim that he married at the insistence of his mother and believed the marriage to be a mistake. According to Cook's brother, Charles left Sophia in the fall of 1834. During the Boston trial, one of the witnesses for the prosecution, William Jordan, "stated privately that Dr. Cook had often expressed to him his aversion to the female sex."[415]

Having first been ordained a Baptist, Cook then became a Congregationalist in Boothbay. After he was forced from Boothbay, he became a Restorationist (Unitarian),[416] was called to a church in Watertown, Massachusetts,[417] and was dismissed following complaints similar to those leveled in Boothbay.[418] This time, however, while serving in Watertown, complaints were again brought by his wife, Sophia, and had to do with a young man identified as Benjamin Baxter. A defense witness in the aforementioned trial, George P. Bigelow, who knew Cook from his service to the church in Watertown, indicated that "The affair with the young man was the cause of the difficulty, and of his [Cook's] leaving Watertown." [419] Another defense witness, an officer who took a complaint from Sophia Cook against Charles regarding his relationship with Baxter, testified that Cook had resolved the complaint by removing Baxter from their home. Charles left Sophia and their child for good in the fall of 1834, whereupon she returned to Newburyport and lived with her father. Eventually, Sophia remarried.

Cook had met Benjamin Baxter when Baxter was a printer at the Independent Messenger in Mendon, Massachusetts.[420] Baxter was, at the time, twenty-four years-old and Cook was thirty-one. Cook's brother describes Baxter as "a smart, active boy, and had a quick discernment of medicines."[421] Baxter and Cook seemed to have formed an immediate bond. When the church in Watertown discovered this relationship, Cook left the ministry. Using family money, he set up shop on Broad Street in Boston, and "commenced operations as a physician and an apothecary."[422] Cook and Baxter lived beneath the apothecary. Benjamin Baxter, apparently in short order, resorted to thievery of expensive linens, perhaps as a way of making ends meet. Baxter was not alone in this criminal activity. There were two other young men involved in the thefts, and all would eventually be charged, tried, convicted, and imprisoned. Cook testified that he had no knowledge of the thefts. Following a very interesting trial, which focused more on Cook's personal life than on the official charge of "reception of stolen goods," Cook was convicted in 1835 and sentenced to seven years of hard labor at the State Prison. According to state records, he died of consumption on July 13, 1841.

Had Cook not departed Boothbay under the shadow of scandal, he would long be remembered for his enthusiastic revivals, lively sermons, ability to draw members to the church, and fervent commitment to ending slavery and addiction to alcohol.

Sabbath Schools and Revivals

The same year Cook's "distressing" dismissal was reported in Maine Conference minutes, the Lincoln Association report included an increased interest in Sabbath schools, now known as Sunday schools, which included adult education: "Many adults have formed themselves into classes and there prevails a feeling that this is a privilege."[423] In spite of an evident shortage of pastors, a general optimism was noted in the same report: "The eyes of the church it is believed are turned to this institution with greater hope and expectation…Of the eighteen churches connected with the conference only eight now have pastors."[424]

The optimism recorded in Lincoln Association minutes was undoubtedly correlated to the spiritual revivals taking place in Maine and throughout the country. Church historian, Robert Handy, wrote, "Revivalism in its many forms was the most powerful force in nineteenth century Protestant life."[425] The spirit of revivalism is seen in brief reports about the Boothbay church printed in Maine Conference minutes of this era, starting with Isaac Weston, who preceded Cook.[426] Notes of revival are attached to the ministries of: Charles Cook; Joseph Sessions, one of the many ministers who breezed in and out of Boothbay after Cook was dismissed; and David Cushman, who settled as the pastor in Boothbay in 1836. American revivalism, in Boothbay as elsewhere, almost always incorporated the call to end slavery and to improve opportunities for higher education for all.

Voluntarism

Thomas Jefferson wrote of "a wall of separation between church & state."[427] This constitutional divide, referred to as "disestablishment" in Massachusetts records (1833), changed the relationship between church and government and altered the role of churches in American society. Churches would no longer receive state funding, would no longer be expected by the government to care for the poor or educate the young, and would no longer be responsible for maintaining the law and administering punishments for infractions thereof. In the earliest records of the Boothbay congregation, it is clear that officers of the church were responsible for managing community complaints and for holding drunkards, adulterers, thieves, and other identified sinners accountable for their offenses. Disestablishment removed these responsibilities from the town parish and placed them in the hands of town boards and officials. The transition of responsibility and authority from church to state did not take place overnight. As articulated in one legal review,

> Disestablishment was not an abrupt legal development advanced at the national level as a consequence of the Revolution. Nor was it the work of the First Amendment, which bound only the lawmaking authority of the new federal government. Rather, disestablishment unfolded more gradually, state by state, and somewhat differently in each state, depending on the state's unique colonial background.[428]

In the State of Maine, the wall of separation between church and state was not yet fully constructed. It was still the job of the constable of the town of Boothbay, for instance, to call everyone to each congregational meeting of what was still identified as the town parish. "Protestants generally accepted the separation of church and state, but stoutly resisted any sense of the separation of religion and morals from public well-being."[429] The church in Boothbay grew slowly away from being the center of town governance and education to being separate yet supportive, as local government became more and more institutionalized. The shift away from government support for churches in America and away from mandatory support for the church from town citizens was seismic. The church would have to learn how to encourage voluntary associations with the church, voluntary financial support from members and friends, and voluntary concern for the poor—thus the term "voluntarism."

In the mid-1800s, public school was well established, but many local boys continued a long-standing pattern of attending school during the winter while heading to the cod banks with the men in the warmer months to work. The church was supportive of education, its ministers expecting to serve on small supervisory school boards and most classes for children taking place in the homes of church members. The days were coming, however, when the separation between church and public education would be carefully maintained.

Rev. Thomas Bellowes—1832-1833
Following the painful dismissal of Charles Cook from Boothbay, the church had no small amount of difficulty settling a pastor. In four years, at least four different ministers served the congregation in Boothbay, most of them as supply preachers. The first was the Reverend Thomas Bellowes in 1832, a third generation descendent of Col. Benjamin Bellows, founder of Walpole, NH.[430] Bellowes was an 1827 Dartmouth College graduate, who studied theology in Andover and at Yale. He preached in Warren and Boothbay

and was then ordained to the pulpit of the Second Congregational church in Greenfield, Massachusetts. Poor health followed him wherever he went, and, eventually, he returned to the family farm to rest and regain his strength, dying there at the age of 83. Never married, he left his entire estate to the American Board of Missions. No written materials have been found regarding his brief tenure in Boothbay, but his pastorate was undoubtedly challenging as the church struggled to recover from their experience with Charles Cook. Of Bellowes, it is written,

> He had a quaint humor, the effect of which was increased by a slowness of utterance resulting from an early impediment in speech. He inherited from his father an unusually retentive memory. He was a thorough scholar, well read in the classics, and of the early English authors in prose and verse. The writings of George Herbert gave him constant satisfaction and a large part of them was retained in his memory. He admired and read the authors whose works engaged his interest in his early manhood. Wordsworth and Coleridge were his special favorites…He was keenly interested in the public questions of the day and kept himself thoroughly informed by constant reading of the newspapers. His opinions upon political and religious subjects were carefully formed and tenaciously held.[431]

A good friend wrote of Bellowes, "I never failed to honor and love him for his upright integrity and his downright abhorrence of humbug in every form."[432]

Rev. Joseph Washburn Sessions—1833
Bellowes was followed in 1833 by revivalist Rev. Joseph Sessions, who provided buoyant supply preaching. Sessions was born in Vermont, studied for college at Phillips Academy, and graduated from Bowdoin College (1829) and Andover Theological Seminary (1832). He preached in Boothbay in 1833, the year following his graduation from Andover, the same year he married Mary Sewall

of Brunswick. Inspired to ministry during a lively tent revival, his spirited ministerial career was spent primarily in churches in Massachusetts and Connecticut. Andover Theological Seminary's obituary report offers the following acclamation:

> The many revivals, which blessed his labors, prove that his genial nature, his energetic disposition, and his warm heart were consecrated supremely to the Redeemer and the work received from his hands. When he had been in the ministry forty-two years, he had only missed preaching five Sabbaths.[433]

Rev. Nathaniel Chapman
1833–1834

Nathaniel Chapman, who provided supply preaching from May 1833 to July 1834,[434] was not a college graduate but was privately educated[435] before becoming part of the first class to graduate from Bangor Theological Seminary (1820).[436] He was ordained at the church in Bristol in 1824, where he preached nearly ten years. From Bristol, he supplied the pulpit in Boothbay Harbor before being called to the Camden church for fourteen years. After Camden, he occupied pulpits in Warren, Unity, Thorndike, Freedom, and Pittston, where he died in 1858. He was remembered as, "the genial pastor so full of sympathy with all in affliction, a type of many ministers in Maine who won a lasting place in the hearts of their people by their eminent pastoral gifts."[437] The Maine Conference obituary offers a descriptive report of his style of ministry:

Rev. Nathaniel Chapman

> Mr. Chapman was a man of sound judgment and discretion; eminently humble, devout, meek, kind and sympathetic, a peace-maker, a wise counselor, much loved in his domestic

and social relations; distinguished above most others as a son of consolation to the bereaved and afflicted; one who in simplicity and godly sincerity, had his conversation in the world. His preaching was such as might be expected of the man; not dealing in matters abstruse, and hard to be understood, nor effecting (sic) pomp of style, or impressiveness of delivery,—but simple, earnest, scriptural, practical.[438]

Rev. Henry Merrill—1835

The Reverend Henry Merrill began his brief ministry to the people of Boothbay in May 1835. He was educated at Hebron Academy and was in the second class graduated from Bangor Theological Seminary, 1822. Merrill was ordained in Shapleigh, Maine, and served congregations in Norway and Bremen before coming to Boothbay. Of his ministry in Norway, it is noted that "Near the commencement of Mr. Merrill's ministrations, there was a great awakening." Nineteen members were added to the Norway congregation, all but three of them, women. From Boothbay, Merrill served churches in Biddeford and Limington before moving to Johnston, Ohio. Of his faith and ministry, it is said, "An earnest desire to see men converted and Christ's kingdom advanced manifested itself to the end of his life. Rarely was he absent from the prayer meeting and rarely silent when there. He died with the words of the Doxology on his lips. Praise God from whom all blessings flow."[439]

Rev. David Quimby Cushman 1836-1843

Between 1829 and 1836, Andrew Jackson presided over an increasingly conflicted United States. The U.S. banking system was troubled, John C. Calhoun threatened nullification of tariff legislation pushed by Henry Clay, the West lured pioneers from poor states like Maine, and access to public lands was

Rev. David Q. Cushman

a looming issue. In 1832, Daniel Webster, in response to a verbal attack by a southern states righter, Robert Hayne, delivered one of the most important speeches in Senatorial history ending with "Liberty and Union, now and forever, one and inseparable." Before he left office, in contrast, Jackson had committed appalling atrocities upon the Cherokee Nation.

In 1836, as Andrew Jackson was preparing to complete his troubled term as President and around the time Americans were being defeated by Mexico at the Alamo, the church in Boothbay finally settled a pastor, Rev. David Quimby Cushman. Cushman was born and grew up in Wiscasset, then Pownalborough. His brother, Sidney, was a doctor in Wiscasset and his sister, Sarah Munger, a missionary in India. Cushman was central to a religious revival reported in 1840. Like so many pastors who came to Boothbay, he was a Bowdoin graduate (1830) and an Andover Seminary graduate (1834). Cushman was ordained as an evangelist following his acceptance of the call to Boothbay on February 8, 1836. He ministered seven years and, during that time, served as scribe of the Lincoln Association of Congregational Churches. From Boothbay, Cushman moved on to pastor churches in Richmond, Newcastle, and Warren, before retiring in Bath. Following the death of his wife, he moved to his daughter's home in Warren.

Cushman was very interested in history and wrote an ambitious work published in Bath in 1882 entitled *History of Ancient Sheepscot and Newcastle, Including Early Pemaquid, Damariscotta, and Other Contiguous Places, From the Earliest Discovery to the Present Time, Together with the Genealogy of more than Four Hundred Families*. Wherever he went, Cushman was a leader in the revivalist tradition. In 1852, Cushman was elected Supervisor of Schools in Newcastle. In 1860, he organized a temperance society for young people called "The Band of Hope." While serving the Warren congregation, he took a decided and vocal position in favor of the Union in the fight against slavery and was dismissed from the church over this stand.[440]

The Fishing Industry

Thomas Hodgdon, a successful Westport fisherman, moved his business to Hodgdon's Island in 1842. He had three or more Grand Bank schooners (called "bankers") and used to fish on the Grand Banks off the coast of Newfoundland, perhaps the richest fishing ground in the world. His son, Stephen G. Hodgdon, took over the business. Hodgdon joined a host of thriving fishing businesses in Boothbay, owned by such legends as Capt. William Barter, Isaac Barter, and Edward Barter, all of Barter's Island; Warren and George Reed of Campbell's Cove; Marshal and Stevens Smith of West Harbor; and Paul and Joseph Harris and Capt. Sewall Wylie of Boothbay Harbor. Cod was the original catch, but that would be expanded to include mackerel, menhaden, and sardines. In the nineteenth century, fishing expeditions to the Grand Banks, usually in the spring, could last two to three months. They required tons of ice farmed from local ponds; and, while at sea in angry Atlantic storms, fishermen coveted the ardent prayers of Boothbay worshippers. A significant portion of the catch was taken to Portland, where it was purchased and shipped to the West Indies and the American South to be fed to slaves.

While the call to end slavery echoed from pulpits throughout Maine, the connection between the fishing and shipping industries of coastal Maine and slave-holding plantations in the South complicated local feelings about the abolition of slavery. Revivalists such as Charles Cook and David Cushman openly opposed slavery, and there are indications that the Boothbay region may have been part of the underground railway for escaping slaves.[441] Boothbay, however, was not known as a center of abolitionism.

Rev. William Tobey—1844-1847

James K. Polk defeated Henry Clay in 1844 on the slogan "Fifty-four forty or fight,"[442] calling for America to make both Oregon and Texas part of the nation. Thousands of pioneers pushed into Missouri, Arkansas, and Illinois. In 1846, Brigham Young led twelve thousand Mormons toward the Great Salt Lake of Utah, while Yankee Clipper ships bearing New England trade goods and often Congregationalist missionaries beat around tempest-racked Cape Horn toward pre-gold-rush California. Meanwhile, during the 1840s, back in the relatively new State of Maine (1820), the congregation that remained in Boothbay Center limped along, perhaps never fully recovering from the feelings of confusion and duplicity left in the wake of Charles Cook's pastorate. The Reverend William Tobey, recognized as an excellent preacher and, as Francis Greene put it, "one of the ablest pastors ever connected with that church," brought hope into the church once more, skillfully ministering from March 1844 to April 1847.[443]

The minutes of the Presbyterian Church record Tobey as having served congregations in Hanover, New Jersey in 1832; Stillwater, New York in 1834; and Greenport, Long Island, in 1843. He was a graduate of Union College (Schenectady, NY), Amherst College, and Auburn Theological Seminary in New York City. One of his sermons, "Subservience of Eloquence to the Cause of Divine Truth," was published and survives. While still a member of the Presbytery of Long Island, Tobey became the Stated Supply Pastor of the Boothbay church. At that time, the church had 174 members.[444] Tobey, like several ministers in Boothbay before him, was an abolitionist and a vocal proponent of "colonization," the previously noted movement that sought to return slaves and freedmen to Africa. In 1839, the year of the ship *Amistad*'s capture in Connecticut, Tobey delivered an address to the Honesdale Colonization Society in Honesdale, Pennsylvania, saying:

> It gives me much pleasure to address you in behalf of that cause whose interest it is the object of your association to promote. Among the great philanthropic enterprises of our age and country, I have ever regarded it as holding a high place. I have never doubted either the integrity or the motives of its advocates, the importance of its object or the practicability of its plan. It professes to be a benevolent enterprise and certain-

ly it has all the external characteristics of one. What can be more benevolent than to restore the oppressed sons of Africa to the land from which they have been torn by cupidity and lawless violence? What more proper or more just than to seek to repair as far as practicable the wrong that has been done by sending back the children to the same land from which their fathers were taken furnished with the blessings of civilization, Christianity and freedom? What portion of the globe more adapted to their residence than those regions where their race has dwelt from immemorial time?

Tobey left Boothbay in 1848 to serve the Congregational church in Scarborough. It is said of Tobey that he was, "a preacher of uncommon excellence...His eloquence, when preaching the great truths of the Gospel, was of that persuasive nature that proved his own entire interest and belief in them, while it moved the minds and hearts of his hearers to solemn reflection and deep feeling. In the midst of a life of usefulness, at the age of 41, having been but one year the Pastor of this people [Scarborough], he died of a prevalent disease, Sept. 10, 1849."445 There were many prevalent diseases, including mumps and influenza, but cholera was the greatest epidemic of the time.

Conclusion

The years represented in this chapter were tumultuous and troubled in the life of the Boothbay congregation. The church was, nevertheless, a place of great spiritual excitement as revivalists brightened the pulpit of the Congregational church and called for social change. The church became a place of enthusiastic support for mission and education, as Congregationalists moved westward, and church education developed and increased. Based on its consistent choice of pro-abolition pastors and its ongoing support for the antislavery American Missionary Society, it is fair to suggest that sermons condemning the practice of slavery were preached regularly from the pulpit and that the Congregational church was a place in which justice and equality were sought. The church was also a place of great resilience, as the congregation responded to challenges, within and beyond its walls, with enduring faith.

CHAPTER 6

AGE OF PROSPERITY AND SORROW: 1848–1870
by Sarah M. Foulger

Introduction

To paraphrase Charles Dickens' classic novel about London and Paris during the French Revolution, these years were the best of times, they were the worst of times. Under any circumstance, they were revolutionary times, politically, socially, and scientifically. In 1848, revolution shattered the once stable, largely monarchical political establishments in much of the world, in places like Hungary, Sicily, France, China, and Sri Lanka. Elsewhere, in the more politically stable British Empire, a potato famine continued to devastate Ireland. Louis Napoleon, the nephew of Napoleon I, took power in 1852 as Napoleon III. Seven years later Charles Darwin published his *Origin of the Species*. And, as nations struggled to bridge the vast chasm between rich and poor, German philosopher Karl Marx, living in teeming London, published *Das Kapital*, better known as the Communist Manifesto. Telegraph lines crossed the Atlantic. The Suez Canal was constructed. Artists Camille Corot and Honoré Daumier refined realism in the 1840s; Monet and Renoir invented Impressionism in 1865. Verdi, Wagner, and Liszt stretched music in thrilling directions. Shakespeare and Jane Austen were still very popular, and the early Victorian Age brought a fresh wealth of literary voices into the English-speaking world, including Charlotte Bronte, Robert Browning, Charles Dickens, Mary Ann Evans (better known by her pen name, George Eliot), Louisa May Alcott, Herman Melville, and Emily Dickinson. In America, the 1849 Gold Rush to California began and the Mexican-American War ended. The latter expanded the nation's territory, making the Rio Grande the new Texas border, and New Mexico, Arizona, and upper California part of the United States. Wisconsin became the thirtieth state in 1848, and the Oregon territory was annexed. The historic Women's Rights Convention took place in Seneca Falls, New York, and the first medical school for women opened in Boston. The Whig party gained traction, and Frederick Douglass became the voice of freedom for African Americans. The railroad quickly became a primary means of transportation, swiftly spreading commerce, population and urban growth into the rapidly developing West. Westward expansion, especially into Kansas, alarmed abolitionists opposed to the escalation of slavery. The issue, always volatile, turned violent, first in Kansas, then in 1859 when John Brown, fresh from Kansas, raided the Harper's Ferry armory in West Virginia. The Civil War that followed shook the nation violently, cruelly swallowing at least six hundred and forty thousand of its sons and forever altering the face and foundation of the American economy.

Revivalism, a force in nineteenth century American religion, intensified as the nation moved fatefully toward civil war. Sometimes termed the Second Great Awakening, revivals swept America, even as Congregationalist Horace Bushnell boldly challenged essential tenets of orthodox theology and condemned revivalism as a specious means of spiritual growth. Nineteenth century theologian Theodore Munger wrote that Bushnell was "a theologian as Copernicus was an astronomer; he changed the point of view, and thus not only changed everything, but pointed the way toward unity in theological thought."[446] Protestant theology engaged every major issue of the time, from abolition to temperance to women's rights. Slavery was condemned from Northern pulpits, temperance was widely embraced in Protestant churches, and, in 1851, in the Congregational church in Butler, New York, Antoinette Brown became the first woman ordained to Christian ministry. The Millerite Movement reintroduced the notion that the end of the world was imminent, and, from this movement new churches arose, including Adventist churches. As the nation expanded westward, churches started important new colleges. International mission continued to swell throughout the Near East, the Far East, and South America. Congregationalist missionaries were supported in Thailand and Hawaii.

The motto of the State of Maine is Dirigo, which means, "I lead." With respect to the prohibition of alcohol, the abolition of slavery, and the suffrage of women, Maine was truly a leader during this era. Propelled by the tenacious efforts of Neal Dow, elected mayor of Portland in 1851, the State of Maine led the way in the movement to prohibit intoxicating spirits. Dow, sometimes referred to as the "Napoleon of Temperance," campaigned tirelessly for a ban on all alcohol in the state and was celebrated in Congregational churches for his good work. In another grand cause of the period, Maine provided critical routes along the Underground Railway, offering sanctuary for slaves seeking liberty in the North. And in 1854, a women's suffrage event took place in Bangor, where none other than Susan B. Anthony offered the keynote speech.

For Boothbay, for the State of Maine, for the nation, the world, and certainly for the Church, the mid-1800s were both exciting and conflicted: exciting in terms of growth and prosperity but conflicted by social change and civil war. Boothbay had become a successful center of shipping and shipbuilding, retained a productive fishing industry, and had developed a highly lucrative ice trade. By this time, Boothbay had also become a favorite health resort with a dramatic increase in tourism to follow.[447] Most of the beautiful older homes in the Harbor were constructed during this period of time, even as rusticators in less conspicuous locations continued to build more humble dwellings. Sabbath school, later called Sunday school, was growing dramatically in the region and throughout the nation. Alcoholism, slavery, and women's suffrage were popular topics in the news and, very likely, in sermons and conversation at social gatherings. New England writers Ralph Waldo Emerson, Nathaniel Hawthorne, Henry David Thoreau, and especially Harriet Beecher Stowe, profoundly influenced culture and socio-political priorities as, through their writings, they championed individualism and freedom for all.

The years 1848–1870 would be industrious, productive and successful, in spite of the fact that Boothbay ultimately decided against a railway line down the peninsula. Abundance sailed on rolling tides of sorrow as ninety-six men were lost at sea during this time period, many with the surnames of prominent church families, names like Adams, Auld, Hodgdon, McDougall, Reed, Sargent, Tibbetts, and Weymouth. Fifty men of the church would serve in the Civil War, many who never came home. Ultimately, fifty-six local young men died in service to the Union during the Civil War. Elizabeth Reed, in a 1948 historical address, wrote, "The generation of young men who fought in the Civil War and helped save the Union, grew up in this Parish." [448]

The Congregational church, located in the center of Boothbay, continued to be both haunted by the Charles Cook scandal and impacted by the emergence of new churches on the peninsula. During this era, the increase of commerce in the harbor area of Boothbay placed additional pressures on the church, since the center of population had moved two miles south to the harbor waterfront. This business and population shift was a significant factor in the formation of a second congregation, initially called the "South Parish," situated in its present location at the corner of Townsend and Eastern Avenues. South Parish would thrive and grow during this period of time even as the original church in Boothbay Center would essentially close its doors.

Congregational Church of Boothbay, c. 1910, and 1768 Session House

The Church in Boothbay Center (The Original Church)

Rev. Samuel Lamson Gould—1848–1851

In 1848, the Reverend Samuel Lamson Gould, nephew of former pastor Jonathan Gould, was called to serve the Congregational church in Boothbay. He was an 1832 graduate of the Medical School of Maine at Bowdoin College and practiced medicine in Searsport and Orrington before entering ministry. He served congregations in Dixmont and Bristol, where he was ordained in 1839 and stayed for nine years. After his three years of ministry in Boothbay, Gould went on to serve churches in New Portland, Phillips, Biddeford, and Albany. Of Gould it was written, "He was an earnest and faithful minister and his medical knowledge aided in making his pastoral visits especially helpful."[449]

Rev. Samuel L. Gould

In the first few weeks of Gould's tenure, forty-eight members of the congregation were dismissed to form a second Congregational church, known as South Parish, two miles closer to the harbor. The mass departure of so many members dealt a traumatic blow to the already beleaguered congregation, but surely came as no surprise, as plans for a congregation in the Harbor village had been developing for several years.

Rev. Jonathan Adams—1852–1861

Gould was followed in 1852 by the Reverend Jonathan Adams, a native of Boothbay. He was the youngest son of Samuel Adams, one of the earliest settlers and a founding member of the original Presbyterian church led by Rev. John Murray. Adams graduated from Middlebury College in 1812, married Hannah Antoinette Clough of Westport, studied at Andover Seminary, and started his ministry in Woolwich in 1817. He remained in Woolwich until 1832, when he took a call to the church in Deer Isle before coming to Boothbay. He served the center church for six years, during which time two of his six sons were lost at sea. Sadly, Jonathan and Hannah Adams had already lost a son at sea several years earlier. From Boothbay, Adams was called to New Sharon. It is said that his was a voice of influence in Congregationalism and of him it was written,

> Mr. Adams was a strong and able defender of the faith once delivered to the saints, during a ministry of forty-six years. He was an impressive preacher. Of courteous and dignified manner, he won the affections of the people. He loved them, and was beloved in turn…He could praise God, even in the agony of death.[450]

While Adams served the church in Boothbay, the national Congregational Church, at the American General Convention of Congregational Churches, made a consequential decision (1852) to drop the "Plan of Union," a long held agreement between Congregationalists and Presbyterians to plant churches along the nation's expanding frontier. Congregationalists came to believe they had drawn the short stick in this plan, giving Presbyterianism the more fertile acreage in America's evangelical garden. After 1852, support for "Home Mission," bolstering Congregational ministry in the expanding west, increased dramatically, as Congregational ministries grew all the way into the Washington and Oregon territories. The church in Boothbay Harbor supported such missions enthusiastically. Church records in 1860 indicate a clear mission-mindedness on the part of the Harbor congregation, which offered monthly concerts for mission purposes and also supported Bangor Theological Seminary in its preparation of ministers for service to the Church.

Rev. Horace Toothaker—1861-1864
Born in Oldtown in 1832, Horace Toothaker grew up in Holden, Maine, where he "early manifested an eager thirst for knowledge and marked intellectual ability."[451] He studied at a preparatory school in Meriden, NH, now called Kimball Union, and in the fall of 1855 entered Dartmouth College. Unable to pay his tuition, he left Dartmouth at the close of his junior year, taught for a year in Athol, Massachusetts, and then entered Bangor Theological Seminary, graduating in 1861. Toothaker was ordained as an evangelist at the struggling Congregational church in the center of Boothbay on September 5, 1861.[452] Three years later, he received a call from the Congregational church in New Sharon, where he remained nearly eight years before taking a call to the congregation in Deering (after 1899 part of Greater Portland). According to the Congregational Quarterly of 1877, "…he labored one year…and was then permanently laid aside from preaching by failing health." He travelled to Georgia hoping the milder climate might improve his health, but died there of tuberculosis, then called "pulmonary consumption." It is written that,

> Mr. Toothaker was a man of persevering industry, scholarly tastes and habits, and of marked integrity and force of character; as a preacher he had a clear vigorous style and a direct

earnest impressive manner; as a pastor he was genial, affable, fond of children, strong in his sympathies and attachments, and greatly beloved and as a citizen interested in all good things, and very highly esteemed. Versatile and ingenious in plans and methods resolute, energetic and richly endowed in mind and heart, his loss is deeply and widely felt."[453]

While in Boothbay, Toothaker worked side by side on the small local school board in 1863 and 1864 with Rev. William Leavitt, then pastor of the new "South Parish" congregation in the Harbor. Toothaker was the last minister to serve the center church exclusively. From 1865–1867, Rev. Leander Coan served both congregations; but eventually the church became fully consolidated in the Harbor, and the center church building would become the site of a public school.

South Parish (also known as Second Congregational Church)
A dynamic and definitive shift into the Harbor occurred in 1848 with the establishment of the South Parish or Second Congregational Church located on Townsend Avenue in what is now Boothbay Harbor. The Charles Cook scandal had driven some members to other Congregational churches, many to Edgecomb. The formation of a Freewill Baptist Society north of Boothbay Center and the spirited rise of Methodism drew even more members away from the original church. "But," as Elizabeth Reed wrote in her 1948 history of the church, "the most serious loss came in 1848 when 48 members of the First Congregational Church requested dismissal in a body in order to form a Second Congregational Church at Boothbay Harbor. The Mother Church at the Center, never recovered from that blow."

Planning for the new church had begun some years before, and worship often took place at the home of Ebeneezer Fullerton, then a deacon. On June 4, 1845, thirty-nine individuals contributed funds amounting to $1,512 for the new church building. The following year, pews for the new sanctuary were sold, raising

Congregational Church of Boothbay Harbor, Memorial Day, c. 1880

$2,382.62 in additional funds. There was, at that time, a distinction between "legal voters" (church members) and "pew holders" (those who had paid for pews), both groups being eligible to vote at congregational meetings.[454]

The new sanctuary was constructed in 1846 by John W. Weymouth, a founding member of the Harbor congregation. George Gannett was called to be the first pastor, beginning his service on January 14, 1847, but the church was not formally organized until August 1, 1848. The church had a single bell tower that, to this day, houses an extraordinary bell forged by respected bell maker, Henry Northey Hooper, an apprentice of Paul Revere. Hooper manufactured bells, chimes, chandeliers and, later, artillery for the Union Army. His highly prized bells continue to grace towers in Nova Scotia, on Martha's Vineyard, throughout Boston and Cambridge, and as close as Monhegan, the latter bell made famous by Jamie Wyeth's 1978 painting, "Monhegan Bell."

There are differing lists of those who moved their membership from the Congregational church in the center of Boothbay to the new church. Greene uses the figure of forty-eight but lists only forty-seven members:

> Andrew Anderson,* John Andrews,* Martha Andrews,* Susan S. Andrews,* Edwin Auld, Eliza G. Auld, Eunice F. Auld,* Frances M. Auld, Jacob Auld, James Auld, John Auld,* Mary Ann Auld,* James T. Beath, Lydia P. Beath,* Mary Beath, Benjamin Blair,* Margaret Fullerton Blair,* Mary Campbell, Mary Dockendorf[455], Martha J. Harris, Mary Holton, Willard Holton,* Charles Knight, Mary Ann Knight, John Love, Jr., Susan Love,* Jane McCobb,* Paul McCobb,* Margery S. McFarland,* David Newbegin,* Mary Newbegin, Nathaniel Pinkham, Jr., Mary J. Pinkham,* George Reed,* Martha Reed,* Samuel Miller Reed, Sarah M. Reed,* Caroline F. Sargent, Charles Sargent, Eliza Sargent, Sarah Sargent,* Stephen Sargent, Elizabeth Weymouth,* Elizabeth Fullerton Weymouth,* John W. Weymouth,* Mary J. Wilson,* Parker Wilson.*

In church records transcribed by Elizabeth Reed, a second Charles Sargent is added to the list. In an 1881 publication of the Articles of Faith, Covenant, Discipline, and Membership of the church, only twenty-seven individuals are named as subscribing to the creed and covenant of the church when it was first organized on August 1, 1848. An asterisk has been added to these names in the list above. In addition to these lists, Reed notes from church records that the following were also organizing members of the new church: William Holton, John Gove, Daniel Auld, Thomas Boyd, Luther Weld, Margery S. McFarland, and Rev. George Gannett, the first minister of the new congregation. In the sanctuary, the stained glass window to the left of the pulpit honors the names of four original founders: Margaret F. Blair, Elizabeth F. Weymouth, John

W. Weymouth, and Willard Holton. John W. Weymouth was the architect and builder of the church. He and his wife Elizabeth gave $175, a significant sum in 1846, to help pay for the construction of the sanctuary.

On March 9, 1848, Parker Wilson, Justice of the Peace for Lincoln County, and soon-to-be church member, handled the application required by the state to establish a new "Meetinghouse." James T. Beath, a farmer and descendant of John and Mary Beath, founders of the original Presbyterian church, became the first clerk and sexton of the new congregation, Three assessors were chosen: Luther Weld (Clerk of Boothbay, school board member, and selectman for many years), John W. Weymouth (architect and builder of the church and owner of a thriving shipyard and hotel); and John Auld (farmer from a family of Boothbay farmers). The aforementioned Parker Wilson (shop owner and first merchant to sell a line of ready-to-wear boots and shoes, Treasurer of Boothbay, and Justice of the Peace) became the treasurer.

The new congregation named itself "The South Parish." Isaac Reed, Constable of Boothbay, announced all parish meetings. The following year, Charles Sargent took on the role of sexton, and a committee of five was formed to procure preaching and raise "a subscription," that is, the funds to pay a preacher. The procurement committee consisted of James T. Beath, Parker Wilson, John Weymouth, Benjamin Blair (Town Clerk, postmaster, and husband of the beloved Margaret Fullerton Blair, named in stained glass in the sanctuary), and George Reed, (sea captain and descendant of founders of the original Presbyterian church). The names of these important local citizens and church members appear again and again in the early records of the South Parish church. In short order, the new congregation called the Reverend George Gannett to be their first pastor. Other leaders who emerged in the new congregation include Charles Fisher, John McClintock, Paul Harris, and Willard Holton, who is also named on the stained-glass window nearest the choir loft. Holton was the faithful Clerk of the Church for many years. He was a community leader who served as Representative to the

Maine Legislature in 1860 and as a customs official in 1865. He was also contracted by the United States Postal Service to deliver mail in Boothbay, Edgecomb, and Wiscasset. He and his wife, Mary, were among the founders of the South Parish congregation.

Rev. George Gannett—1847-1850

Rev. George Gannett served the fledgling congregation for more than three years from January 14, 1847 to May 1850. Originally from Belfast, Maine, Gannett was a Bowdoin graduate who started his career as the principal of Austin Academy in Strafford, New Hampshire. Sensing a call to ministry, he entered Bangor Theological Seminary and, upon graduation, accepted the call to Boothbay. According to a biographical sketch, "he labored with much comfort in his ministry three years until health failed and compelled his resignation."[456] According to church records, "the declining health of Gannett's wife was the reason he wished to resign."[457] Gannett requested dismissal from his call on April 22, 1850. From Boothbay, he moved to Boston, where he started a highly esteemed private school for young women. While Gannett retained close ties to Congregationalism, Boothbay was both the beginning and the end of his career in the church.

Gannett's ministry was followed by a series of short pastorates, none lasting more than three years. The church continued to thrive, nevertheless, as a community of faith, with church minutes recounting significant additions to its membership and active support for mission at home and abroad. With frequent changes in pastoral leadership, more than the usual number of congregational meetings were called, and, while the wall between church and state had long ago been drawn, the Constable of Boothbay continued to issue official public announcements prior to each one of these meetings.

Rev. Joseph Smith—1850-1852

In 1850, the Reverend Joseph Smith, an 1842 graduate of Bangor Theological Seminary, served for little more than two years. Born in Cornish, Maine in 1810, he was ordained in Old Town in 1842, serving churches in Denmark and Wilton before coming to Boothbay. Following his ministry in Boothbay, he was called to congregations in Lovell, Buxton, Minot, and Kenduskeag. During the Civil War, he served in Tennessee on the U. S. Christian Commission, a religious organization that furnished supplies, medical services, religious literature, and support to Union troops. He retired from ministry to Orland and then to Bangor, where he died in 1889.[458]

While Smith ministered to the South Parish, there were a number of tragic deaths and catastrophes. "For fatalities to our town," writes Greene of 1851, "that year has eclipsed all others, and its disasters were severely felt."[459] The fishing schooners Grampus and Forrester were lost at sea, probably in the same storm. Among the dead were Augustus and Elup Auld, the eldest son and grandson of James and Sarah Auld, and James Love, son of founding members John and Susan Love. Later that year, the C.G. Matthews sank in a gale off the coast of Prince Edward Island, and all thirteen on board were lost at sea, all of them residents of Boothbay, including Charles E. Weld, eldest son of Luther and Frances Weld, and James R. Weymouth, son of founding members John and Elizabeth Weymouth. Luther Weld and the Weymouths were pillars of the Harbor congregation and, surely, all of these losses were profoundly felt by both the congregation and its pastor.

Rv. John Kendall Deering—1852–1853

The Reverend John K. Deering arrived in Boothbay in 1852. Deering was born in Paris, Maine in 1828, graduated from Bangor Theological Seminary in 1849, and was ordained a Presbyterian minister in Murphysboro, Illinois in 1850. While in Illinois, he helped to found the First Presbyterian Church of Metropolis. He returned to Maine in 1851 to serve congregations in Farmington Falls, Mercer, Boothbay, and Gilead. He went on to serve congregations in Assabet and South Franklin, Massachusetts, before returning to Maine to preach from pulpits in Solon, Bingham, Holden, and Minot.[460] Deering then left the ministry, co-owned a grocery in Portland with his brother for several years and did some traveling in the South during three successive winters.[461] It is noted that he went into business with his brother because he was "unable to preach."[462] Following the Civil War, Deering moved to the South, where he taught theology at two newly founded Black colleges, Tougaloo University[463] in Mississippi, and Straight University in Louisiana. Both colleges were founded after the Civil War by the American Missionary Association for the expressed purpose of educating freed slaves and their families. Deering moved to Perrysburg, Ohio in 1875, founded the J.K. Deering Coal Company, and remained in Ohio until his death in 1894.[464]

Rev. Edmond Burt—1854-1855

John Deering was succeeded by the Reverend Edmond Burt, who was a Congregational missionary in Newfield, Maine when he received the call to Boothbay in May, 1854. He was an 1839 graduate of the Theological Seminary at Gilmanton, New Hampshire, part of what was Gilmanton Academy. He started ministry in Franconia before coming to Maine. While in Boothbay, Charles F. Sargent was the elected scribe of the church, responsible for maintaining congregational minutes and rolls of membership, baptisms, marriages and deaths. Sargent, an important founder of the South Parish, died on April 30, 1854, leaving a significant hole in the leadership of the church. There were other notable losses, including Luther and Francis Weld, who moved to New York, and Jacob Auld, who moved to Bath. Edmond Burt ministered to the South Parish congregants less than two years. According to Burt's obituary,

> Brother Burt went from Newfield to Boothbay. His services were very acceptable to the people of that place and they would have retained him longer in their midst, but as the sea air proved injurious to his health he was obliged to leave and seek a field of labor in the interior of the State. In June 1856 he was sent to Gilead by the Maine Missionary Society.[465]

Gilead, Maine, bordering New Hampshire near Gorham, where Edmond Burt had family, was his last call. He suffered bouts of prolonged illness throughout the remainder of his ministry. His obituary beautifully summarizes his work and his death:

> As his bodily strength was not equal to his labors, he went to Gorham NH in June to visit his family and to regain his weakened strength. But his work was then done. He survived departure from his little precious field by only three weeks. He died with the harness on. And it was well burnished. His divine Master called him suddenly. And he summoned him while in the midst of marked usefulness. But he was ready. His lamp was trimmed and burning. His end was peace. His conversation was heaven.

Rev. John Forbush — 1856-1857

Mr. John Forbush arrived in April, 1856 from the mission field in Farmington Falls. An ecclesiastical council of the Lincoln Association was convened to receive and install him. Representing the Boothbay church were the Rev. Jonathan Adams and church deacon, David Adams. Papers were presented to the council demonstrating that a call to ministry had been issued and accepted by Forbush. When the council asked to see his credentials, Forbush "explained that he had no credentials with him but that published documents proved him to have been a missionary of the American Home Missions Society."[466] That statement was sufficient for the council, which voted to dispense with the "usual formality of requiring credentials."[467] A committee of the parish comprised of John Auld, John W. Weymouth, and George Reed offered Forbush an annual salary of $400 to be paid in quarterly installments. In relation to his call, and as recorded by elected clerk of the church, James T. Beath, Forbush announced,

> May the God of all grace grant that it may be a connection which shall be for his glory and your salvation. Wishing you

grace, mercy and peace I subscribe myself yours in the bond of the gospel.

Those bonds were short-lived as Forbush stayed in Boothbay but one year, another victim of disagreeable sea air. A genealogical work about the Forbush family includes the following summary of his life:

> Rev. John Forbush was born in Upton (Mass) Sept. 4, 1800… ordained at Westboro, Massachusetts on October 6, 1830. Sometime during the same month, he left his native place for the State of Ohio to labor as a home missionary and as such laboring in different places, mostly in the southern part of Ohio for nineteen years returning again to his native place in the spring of 1850. In the fall of 1852, entering the home missionary field again in the State of Maine, he labored in Farmington Falls a little over three years when he was called to settle at Boothbay. He accepted and was installed but the sea air not agreeing with his health he resigned after about two years (sic) when he entered the home missionary field again and labored in Mercer, Solon, and East Madison until the summer of 1863, at that time receiving his first attack of the disease general paralysis which finally ended his life. He left the ministry and returned again to his native place where he died July 19, 1871.[468]

Monthly mission concerts continued in the church, generating funds to support the American Bible Society, Bangor Theological Seminary, the Seaman's Mission, Home Missions, the Congregational Church in San Francisco, and church development in the U.S. West.

Rev. Jonathan Edwards Adams—1858-1859
In April 1858, another one-year pastorate began, this time with the Reverend Jonathan E. Adams, eldest son of previous minister, Jonathan Adams, of the center church, and grandson of Samuel Adams,

who, in 1766, was a founding member of the original Presbyterian fellowship. He arrived in Boothbay two years after his brother Charles died at sea.[469] Twelve years earlier, another brother, William, had also perished at sea. One month after Adams began his ministry in Boothbay, William Holton, son of Willard and Mary Holton, founders of the South Parish, drowned off McFarland Point when his boat was overladen with mackerel, a heartrending event for the church and community. Fishing remained a profitable industry in Boothbay but at the wretched cost of young lives lost at sea.

Adams was a Bowdoin graduate (1853), a Bangor Theological Seminary graduate (1858), and was ordained in the church in New Sharon. He was very involved in the Maine Conference of Congregational Churches and served as secretary of the Maine Missionary Society. Having pastored in Boothbay for exactly one year, Adams left to serve the church on Deer Isle, mirroring the move his father had made from Deer Isle to Boothbay. In the years ahead, Adams would become a trustee of Bangor Theological Seminary and a member of the Board of Overseers at Bowdoin College.

When Adams arrived in Boothbay in 1858, Harriet Beecher Stowe's Uncle Tom's Cabin was widely read, and there was an increasing religious fervor to end slavery in the United States. The year of Adams' service in Boothbay was a year of impending crisis in the nation. Abolitionists were stocking up on "Beecher's Bibles," rifles to be used in the cause of ending slavery. Beecher, the esteemed brother of Harriet Beecher Stowe, was arguably the most popular preacher in the mid-nineteenth century. In an 1856 article in the New York Tribune, Beecher had written that there was "more moral power in one of those instruments (referring to rifles), so far as the slaveholders…were concerned, than in a hundred Bibles," thus the term, "Beecher's Bibles." Talk of war was in the air as a period of intense revivalism brought the message of freedom for slaves to a fevered pitch. While there was some sympathy for southern plantation owners among leaders in the shipping industry, there is every reason to believe most Congregationalists in Boothbay held strong abolitionist views.

Rev. John Johnson Bulfinch—1859-1862

Rev. John J. Bulfinch served the South Parish church from 1859 to 1862. Born in Waldoboro, Bulfinch was an 1850 Bowdoin graduate, who initially studied law with his father.[470] Deciding on a career in ministry, he became part of the Class of 1858 at Bangor Theological Seminary, where he was selected to be the "Commencement Orator."[471] According to church minutes, on February 3, 1860, the church in Boothbay and the Maine Conference of Congregational Churches voted unanimously to ordain Bulfinch as an evangelist. Ordination was set for February 21, but a severe snowstorm prevented the event. Lincoln Association minutes report that Bullfinch was ordained as an evangelist to the South Parish church on April 27, 1860. That same year, Maine native Hannibal Hamlin was named as Abraham Lincoln's vice president, increasing regional support for an end to the practice of slavery and marking the beginning of Republican dominance in the State of Maine. After Boothbay, Bulfinch accepted a call to the church in Newcastle, where he pastored for eight years. In 1865, he supported the Union troops on the U.S. Christian Commission and, following his pastorate in Newcastle, ministered to churches in Freeport and Waldoboro, where he died in 1914. While in Boothbay, Bulfinch pastored the church through the tumultuous early years of the Civil War, a challenging and worrisome time for the church and for the entire community.

The Civil War

Approximately 73,000 Mainers served the Union during the Civil War, either in the Army or the Navy, the highest population percentage of any state in the North. Tragic and disproportionate losses were felt in every town in the state, Boothbay being no exception. As attested on the monument in Boothbay Center, 256 men volunteered to fight in the Union Army and Navy, and 56 died in what is identified on the monument as "The War of 1861-65." More than one-fifth of those who served did not return. With regard to the Congregational church, Elizabeth Reed, in her 1948 history, stated that "more than 50 sons of this Parish served in" what she, like many others, termed "The Rebellion."

A great and patriotic passion for the Union was stirred early in 1861 by the secession of South Carolina, Mississippi, Florida, Alabama, Georgia, Louisiana, and Texas, and the surrender of Fort Sumter in Charleston Harbor. As Francis Greene summed up the prevailing feelings about the secessionists, "The crisis first produced this spontaneous outburst of indignation and patriotism combined, and then settled down to a legal, formal, systematic effort to stamp out treason in the land."[472] The Maine Memory Network summarizes the challenge well: "At home the war hung like a cloud over most Mainers. In 1861 President Lincoln asked for 75,000 men to serve in the Union Army, and in 1863 the federal government issued a draft law calling on all men between ages eighteen and forty-five to enroll in local militia units. Draftees were selected by state lottery, and to distribute this burden equitably each town in Maine was given a quota."

The town of Boothbay voted to pay volunteers who served in the Union Army or Navy. Special committees were formed to recruit soldiers and to provide support for them and for their families. The women of the South Parish church played a compassionate role. As Reed wrote, "The women of this Parish worked indefatigably for the U.S. Sanitary Commission and the hospitals, meeting frequently in this church to make bandages and collect vegetables, money and supplies for the soldiers."

Rev. William Leavitt—1862-1864
Bullfinch's successor at South Parish, soon to be called the Congregational Church of Boothbay, Rev. William Leavitt stood in the watchtower of the church through the most devastating years of the Civil War. Leavitt faced the sad privilege of honoring the fallen and committing their lives into eternal realms. William Leavitt was born in Buxton in 1829, was an 1862 graduate of Bangor Theological Seminary, and was ordained in Boothbay on January 27, 1864. He ministered to some of the

most heartbroken of his flock during the relentlessly miserable years of war.

The Civil War affected many families in the church and community. Multiple losses of primarily young men in their twenties were sustained in the Corey, Tibbetts, and Williams families, and none felt more deeply than the losses suffered by the Sargent and McCobb families. Four Sargent brothers, all shipbuilders in their father's yard in the Harbor, served on the battlefield: Edward, Edwin, Oscar, and Weld. Edwin was a private in the 38th Massachusetts Regiment and died on May 27, 1863, following the Battle of Chancellorsville. Weld, a sergeant in the 19th Maine, was killed in battle on June 6, 1864 at Cold Harbor and would be long and proudly remembered as a Civil War hero. The GAR Hall (Great Army of the Republic) that stood on Commercial Street until 1942 was renamed in his honor and memory. The McCobb family lost three members in the Civil War: Armitage, Charles H., and Charles S. The latter was a graduate of Bowdoin College, identified in Bowdoin Medical College graduate records as a teacher and hospital steward. Weld Sargent and Charles S. McCobb served in different locations in the bloodiest battle of the Civil War—Gettysburg. Weld Sargent went on to fight bravely nearly one more year, being mortally wounded in the Battle of Cold Harbor, just shy of his thirty-second birthday. Charles S. McCobb died on July 4, 1863, at the age of 26, the only Bowdoin graduate lost at Gettysburg.[473]

Weld Sargent

Elizabeth Freeman Reed, the great twentieth-century Boothbay church archivist, wrote beautifully of Corporal Weld Sargent, local hero, who enlisted early in the war, served in many major battles, and, though severely wounded, recovered to rejoin the effort, dying in "General Grant's Hammering Campaign" in 1864. He had three brothers, at least one sister, and was the son of Elizabeth and Stephen Sargent, owner of the largest shipyard in the Harbor and a founding member of the South Parish church. All of the sons, including Weld, were shipwrights in their father's yard, and Weld

Age of Prosperity and Sorrow: 1848–1870 165

was chief ship joiner on his father's vessels. Weld is remembered for his piety and "Sabbath keeping." He arrived at his family's pew at the Congregational church in Boothbay early on Sunday mornings and sat in silent meditation until worship began.

Weld Sargent enlisted soon after the outbreak of civil war, served in the Army of the Potomac, and was struck in the forehead by a bullet that went through his upper skull near Richmond on May 31, 1862. He returned home and recovered, enlisting again in August, serving with the 19th Maine. He returned to the battlefield in Virginia, fought in the battles of Fredericksburg and Gettysburg, and died at Cold Harbor. His brother, Edwin, died from heat exhaustion on the march to Gettysburg on May 27, 1863. Weld served alongside Rufus Ault, another son of the congregation who would later assume leadership roles in the church. There were several Ault pews, and eight members of the Ault family were founders of the South Parish church in the Harbor.

Charles McCobb

Charles McCobb

According to John R. Cross, Secretary of Development and College Relations, "The only Bowdoin alumnus killed in the battle (Gettysburg) was Lt. Charles McCobb of the 4th Maine and the Class of 1860, who fell during the fierce fighting in Devil's Den."[474] More than 150,000 soldiers fought in the three-day battle, resulting in approximately 50,000 casualties. Gettysburg remains the largest battle ever fought in North America. When the smoke and blood of the battle settled into the ground at last, 2nd Lieutenant Charles S. McCobb was among the countless fallen. He was honored in his hometown as no less a hero than Brigadier General Joshua Chamberlain.

Charles was a fourth generation McCobb from the original line of Scots-Irish settlers on the Boothbay peninsula. The first

McCobb, Samuel, is described as "the leader of the Scotch-Irish settlers" to the area.[475] He was a founding member of the original Presbyterian congregation. There are 121 McCobbs listed by name in Francis Greene's History of Boothbay, Southport, and Boothbay Harbor; yet not one resident with this surname survives on the Boothbay peninsula today.

Referring to Charles S. McCobb in a 2013 *Boothbay Register* article, Barbara Rumsey wrote, "It was rare for any dead Civil War soldier to be returned to his hometown, but Charley was—maybe."[476] Given the enormity of the task of locating one particular body among thousands, questions remain as to whether the body brought home was truly that of Charles McCobb. What is certain is that his brother Abial traveled to Gettysburg and, with devoted determination, located the body believed to be that of Charles. On the day of his funeral, August 6, 1863, at the thoroughly packed Congregational church and throughout the community, the Hooper bell tolled and businesses closed out of respect and with gratitude. McCobb's burial took place on Sept. 25, 1863 in Wylie Cemetery in Boothbay.

Abial McCobb

Abial, like his brother, Charles, was a fourth generation McCobb from the original line of Scots-Irish settlers on the Boothbay peninsula. Arthur McCobb, father of Charles and Abial, was a merchant in Boothbay. Their mother, Elizabeth, descended from the Fullerton family and was the niece of Dr. Charles Fisher, one of the first ministers of the Congregational church in Boothbay Center. When Abial was but eleven months old and his brother Charles, not quite three years old, their mother died at the age of twenty-three. Their father died later that year. Who adopted these young orphans is unknown, but it is likely that they were incorporated into one of their six uncles' homes.[477] It is certain they grew up in the nurture of the Congregational church. Abial's brother Charles, as already established, studied medicine at Bowdoin College, enlisted in the service of the Union, and died in the Battle of Gettysburg.

Soon after the untimely death and burial of Charles, the bereft Abial left for California. Having lost both parents and his only brother, he journeyed with his childhood friend, Ambrose Plummer, also of Boothbay. According to Richard Helin, a California historian who researched an interesting double headstone that carries Plummer's name on one side and McCobb's on the other, Plummer ran a ship's chandlery and McCobb worked for him as a sail maker.[478] In 1883, at the age of 44, Abial died in the town of Vallejo. Plummer had died the year before. Abial never married and did not leave any children. The only descendants he left behind are in his spiritual family at the Congregational church in Boothbay Harbor. Abial was the only survivor in his line of McCobbs.[479] He wished to be remembered in the Congregational church by the community of faith that his family had helped to found and which he continued to support financially throughout his life. In 1883, the church learned that Abial had bequeathed all of his property, including the property his brother Charles had left to him, to the South Parish.[480] In gratitude, a memorial plaque in his name was placed in the church and remains to this day.[481]

Effects of the Civil War

The Civil War stole lives by the thousands and left an indelible mark on both church and community. It also strained the local economy, troubling the shipping industry with blockades and attacks, and created both an increase in insurance premiums for shipping companies and an increase in shipping prices. This resulted in a devastating decline in shipping. For many years, Maine shipping had flourished and, prior to the Civil War, had achieved a peak of success. Maine had developed particularly strong cotton shipping business carrying southern slave-picked cotton. This trade was brought to a halt during the Civil War by Union blockades.

Some business prospered nevertheless. Shipping to and from Canada increased, for instance. As is written in the article, "Maine and the Civil War,"

In some ways the war brought prosperity for Maine shippers. While foreign trade declined in other northern states during the war, it tripled in Maine due to intensified commercial links with the Canadian provinces. Portland became the fourth busiest harbor in the country. Beneficial connections in Washington brought gunboat contracts to Portland and Bath. In general, however, Maine shipping and shipbuilding was declining, reflecting the national pattern in which U.S. imports were declining steadily.[482]

Other businesses that developed and flourished during the Civil War include canning, following the invention of hermetically sealed containers (useful in wartime), clothing, and produce. Dramatically expanding rail lines enlarged the market for Maine crops such as blueberries and potatoes and for Maine-manufactured products such as boots and cloth.

The war caused federal and local taxes to rise steadily between 1861 and 1865, and towns were strained by the burden of providing salaries to soldiers in order to meet quotas. To share the burden of the war more equitably, towns in Maine were expected to fill assigned quotas of soldiers based upon population. War casualties and westward expansion caused the population of Maine to decrease dramatically during the war years, the 1870 census indicating the first decline in population since records had been kept. Lee's surrender at Appomattox on April 9, 1865, came as a grief-laden relief. The State of Maine would never be the same. Boothbay would never be the same. It is fitting that the largest monument on the Boothbay peninsula is the one placed in the center of Boothbay, a visible reminder of the courage mustered by its citizens and the depth of sorrow that remained.

The Assassination of Abraham Lincoln

As the nation was beginning to tend to its deep wounds, John Wilkes Booth took aim at its heart, killing the battle-worn but resolute president of the United States. It is impossible to measure the shock waves that emanated from Washington on Good Friday, April 14, 1865, the day Lincoln was assassinated. However, the passionate sermon preached by Rev. William Leavitt in Boothbay on Thursday, June 1, a day of national fasting and mourning for Abraham Lincoln, is a poignant indicator of the depth of feeling in Boothbay. Leavitt preached,

> At last the long agony was over—agony such as no people in modern times have felt. We had watched through the long dark night of war, sometimes O how wearily. The promise of the morning, the morning had come. We looked upon the black retreating storm which had found us at the first so unprepared to meet it, which had swept over us with such terrific fury. We saw our ship of State, in which so many and such precious hopes were centered, which had been so tossed and Strained in rebellious mad tempest her decks often swept by the waves, whose freight so much of it had been cast over and sunk forever, once more riding buoyantly upon untroubled seas…Hardly had the echoes of our rejoicing ceased to vibrate in the air when like a thunderbolt from a cloudless sky fell that news upon the nations which for the moment stopped its beating ear and throbbing pulse. They have shot the president. Mr. Lincoln is killed. The president is assassinated…And the blow that produced it, what a cruel blow. Not that Abraham Lincoln's life was more precious to him than the lives of tens of thousands of others who have fallen on the battlefield or wasted away in hospitals or been murdered by inches in Southern prisons but because he held so large a place in every loyal heart so that when he fell, then "You and I and all of us fell down." Our hearts become linked with his were convulsed when we fairly knew it had ceased beating forever. The blow was aimed at us…Never since the world began has the death of any one man produced so profound and widespread a sensation.

Leavitt believed that the war was divine punishment for its complicity with human slavery, and he held utmost admiration for Abraham Lincoln. Near the end of his sermon, he spoke to Lincoln directly, saying,

> O great heart, thou art still now great, commander in chief, brave soldier, thy warfare is accomplished. Rebellion must glut its fierce appetite with blood and thou almost its last victim. One more sacrifice for the sons of the people and thou its highest oblation. Martyr of liberty, rest thee well.

This remarkable and very lengthy sermon exudes an impassioned literary style and gives an indication of the weight Leavitt carried during his ministry in the church. A biographical note in a family history is revealing:

> William Leavitt 3rd, became a Congregationalist in 1860, and graduated at Bangor Theological Seminary, class of 1862. From the Seminary he went to Boothbay, ME, where he preached for a little over two years, and then broke down from overwork, being laid aside for six months.»[483] When he recovered from his ministry in Boothbay, Leavitt took a call to the church in Presque Isle and then travelled west to Minneapolis, Minnesota, where he helped found a Congregational Church, and south to Monticello, Iowa before taking a westward move to Nebraska.[484]

Leavitt ended his ministry in 1892 in Norfolk, Nebraska but kept in touch with the people of Boothbay, to whom he was bound by deep and abiding ties. Following Leavitt's challenging ministry, the Rev. Leander S. Coan answered a call to serve both congregations, the all but dead church in Boothbay and the lively growing church in the Harbor.

Rev. Leander S. Coan[485]
1865–1867

Rev. Leander S. Coan

Leander Coan was a Civil War veteran, having fought with the 61st Massachusetts, where he was duly nicknamed, "The Fighting Parson." Coan was deeply patriotic and took pride in his service with the Union forces. Like many ministers of his day, he was also a strong proponent of the temperance movement. The *Granite Monthly*, a popular New Hampshire magazine that discontinued publication in 1918, offered a brief and revealing biography composed by his brother, Dr. E. S. Coan:

> Leander S. Coan was the eldest son of Deacon Samuel Coan a descendant of Peter Coan who came to America from Worms Germany in 1715. He was born in Exeter, Maine November 17 1837 and claimed on his mother's side direct descent from a Pilgrim ancestor who came over in the Mayflower. His parents were in humble circumstances but they realized the importance of a thorough education and fostered in him a desire to acquire it. At the age of twenty, he resolved to adopt the law as his profession and with that end in view he went to Bangor to enter the office of ex-Governor Kent as a student. Feeling himself deficient in preparation to enter upon his professional studies, he accepted a school in Brewer for a season.
>
> While there his plan for the campaign of life underwent a radical change he felt called upon to give up all and follow the Great Teacher. With the utmost zeal he entered upon his chosen calling and pursued his preparatory studies at the Theological Seminary at Bangor where he graduated in 1862. The following year he was ordained over at the church in Amherst, Maine. In August 1864, while spending his vacation at Cohasset, Massachusetts, he acknowledged the debt he owed

his country and enlisted [during] the darkest days of the rebellion as private in the Sixty- first Volunteers. During the months that followed, his brave patriotism won for him the title of fighting parson. During his term of service, he acted as chaplain of the battalion to which he was attached but not commissioned.

After the war was over, he preached the gospel of peace in Maine and Massachusetts until 1874. He accepted the charge of the Congregational church at Alton on the borders of Lake Winnipiseogee (sic) where he remained until his death [at the age of 42] in September 1879. During his residence in New Hampshire he was widely known and loved. His voice was welcomed at many a reunion and literary gathering while his facile pen guided by genius patriotism and love of humanity helped him to mould public opinion and gather about him a host of sympathetic friends. His beautiful poems will ever be treasured in many a New England home where their pathos was duly appreciated…It is poetry of a high order and would enrich and ennoble every home where it is read and treasured.[486]

From July 27, 1865 to July 28, 1867, Leander S. Coan served both the vanishing center and prospering Harbor parishes and was privileged to be the pastor during the Centennial celebration of the church in 1866. Church minutes reflect the fact that when, in August 1865, Coan celebrated the Lord's Supper with the congregation, it was the first time holy communion had been served in two years. On September 23, 1866, Coan preached a special centennial sermon, recounting the history of the church and offering poetic words of encouragement and healing to parishioners who were still in mourning following the Civil War and for whom the pain of the Charles Cook ministry persisted. On the day of the centennial celebration, Isaac Weston, one of the first ministers of the original church, was also invited to preach. It would be his last sermon.[487] In Leander Coan's centennial sermon, he penned questions that are timeless for this and any congregation: "When in one hundred years from now, they look back, what shall they have to record of us? Will we have been worthy of the past, equal to the future?"[488]

Rev. Andrew Jackson Smith—1868-1872

In August 1868, the Reverend Andrew Jackson Smith, minister in Rockport,[489] was called to serve the Congregational Church of Boothbay and stayed nearly four years. Like so many fine ministers in Maine, Smith went to Bowdoin College (1863) and Bangor Theological Seminary (1866), receiving all but the last year of his degreed education during the time of the Civil War. Perhaps because the name, Andrew Jackson, was so closely associated with the South, with a particular style of democracy, and with the Indian Removal Act of 1830, Smith discontinued regular use of his first or second names, preferring to be known simply as A.J. He left Boothbay to serve the church in Waldoboro, from there answering a call to the church in Waterford.[490] Four years later, he died at the age of forty. Nothing more than a "temporary illness" is mentioned in Maine Conference minutes.

Conclusion

During the 1860s, significant repairs to the South Parish church were made, and new leadership emerged in the church, including the following: Rufus Ault (Civil War veteran who fought in the 4th and 19th Maine Regiments at Gettysburg, Chancellorsville, and Cold Harbor), Dr. Alden Blossom (Civil War veteran and surgeon with the 6th Maine Regiment, who became a popular local physician and apothecary), Thomas Boyd (prominent Republican in Lincoln County who established the summer colony in Bayville), Charles Carlisle (carpenter and town leader), Ezekiel Hodgkins (blacksmith), Charles Kendrick (shop owner in Boothbay and in the 1880s, also on Squirrel Island, who would become Proprietor of the *Boothbay Register*), George Kenniston (lawyer and Civil War veteran who served as a lieutenant in the 5th Maine Regiment and worked to place a Civil War monument in the center of Boothbay),

Sewall Maddocks (bookkeeper, accountant and business manager, seller of marine insurance and real estate), Leonard McCobb (founding member of the South Parish church, shop owner, and postmaster), Newell Merry (Civil War veteran who fought with the 28th Maine Regiment and local brick maker, who would later be hired to take extensive land measurements in the division of the town), Dr. Otis Rice (dentist and surgeon who served with the 9th Maine and later in the Franco-Prussian War), Robert Sproul (sea captain, whose bright and vivacious wife, Mary is one of few women remarked upon in any historical account of Boothbay),[491] and Moses White, (teacher and ship carpenter, who would become president of the Boothbay Savings Bank). These church leadership names show up in positions of town authority, on school boards and town committees, as selectmen, representatives to the Maine Legislature, and moderators of annual town meetings. Then and into the present time, members of the Congregational church tend to be lively, engaged, and highly involved in the community.

During this chapter of the history of the Congregational church in Boothbay, pioneering spirits led the way through a demanding period of dramatic social change, searing grief, and steady growth. The brutal battle to end slavery in the United States was over. The fight for women's suffrage was under way. The drive to ban or manage alcoholism continued to generate both spirited enthusiasm in churches and violent resistance in communities. By 1870, the Congregational church, known for its deep caring and mission-mindedness, was firmly planted at the Harbor end of Townsend Avenue, the main connector between the Harbor and Boothbay villages. The church was filled with community-minded leaders, many of them veterans of the Civil War. Greater growth was to come for the Congregational church, now thoroughly consolidated in its present location, and for the village of Boothbay as it moved into its second hundred years of governance.

CHAPTER 7

THE RISE OF TOURISM AND INDUSTRY: 1870–1892
by Sarah M. Foulger

Introduction

In the post-Civil War era, Boothbay Harbor's fishing and boatbuilding economy, boosted now by a few budding summer colonies, left the quaint seaside village with its white clapboard Congregational church little changed from the 1850s. Elsewhere in America, however, a vibrant urban industrialism emerged and met a surge of European immigration. Change, in fact, swept the globe in the latter part of the nineteenth century. The world became more closely connected as the Suez Canal opened, work on the Panama Canal began, global communication blossomed, and railways connected America in every direction. A spirit of adventure was given a platform in literary works such as Robert Louis Stevenson's *Treasure Island* and Jules Verne's *Around the World in 80 Days*. George Eliot's *Middlemarch* broadened thoughts about women in society and introduced the Victorian heroine. Artistic sensibilities continued to be expanded by the French Impressionists. The Eiffel Tower, the Brooklyn Bridge, the Statue of Liberty, and the first metal-frame skyscraper, the Home Insurance Building in Chicago, became symbols of a new day. Medical advancements, from the manufacture of aspirin to the creation of vaccines, forever altered the human response to disease. Technological breakthroughs abounded as Alexander Graham Bell patented the telephone and Thomas Edison, the phonograph, with electricity soon to follow. Inventions, from barbed wire to blue jeans, from the cash register to the "qwerty" keyboard, kept patent offices busy. In the realm of music, Tchaikovsky and Wagner were wowing audiences, Beethoven had become a staple in church music, and Fanny Crosby, the "Queen of Gospel Song Writers" ("Blessed Assurance, Jesus Is Mine"), enlivened singing in church sanctuaries.

During this same period, priorities and theology changed the Church in significant ways. In response to industrialism, urban poverty, and alcoholism, Catherine and William Booth started the Salvation Army in the East End of London. Existentialism, the philosophical idea that each individual person is responsible for bringing meaning into this life, first espoused by the Danish theologian Soren Kierkegaard and subsequently developed by German philosopher Frederich Nietzsche gained a significant following. A bridge between Christian theology and Enlightenment thinking was developed by Bible scholar Friederich Schleiermacher, leading to fresh conversations in Protestant churches. Protestant scholars began to engage the findings of Charles Darwin in earnest. State by State, the wall of separation between Church and Government in the United States was thickening. Dispensationalism, the notion that God's revelation is time-bound and will lead to a «rapture» of saved souls on earth, was trending in independent Protestant circles.[492] Millerism, a movement that proclaimed the imminent demise of the world, continued to gain traction, launching the Jehovah's Witnesses. American Congregationalist Dwight Moody and British Baptist Charles Spurgeon were popular evangelical preachers and authors. In 1870, the Pope was declared to be infallible. In 1879, Mary Baker Eddy, in nearby Boston, stretched thoughts about faith and well-being, founding the Church of Christ, Scientist.

The Congregational Church became organized at the national level, holding the first of its triennial national meetings in 1871 in Oberlin, Ohio (National Council of Congregational Churches). At this meeting, the "Oberlin Declaration" and "Declaration on the Unity of the Church" were presented and adopted, both documents establishing "substantial unity in doctrine, polity, and work" among the churches. In 1873, the "Congregational House" was founded in Boston, the larger well-known edifice to be built in 1898. This became a center for National Congregationalism and home to Congregational organizations, including missionary associations, a bookstore, and the Congregational Library and Archives.

The missionary movement expanded dramatically, particularly in fields of education and medicine. In 1880, there were thirteen missionaries practicing medicine in fields established by the American Board of Foreign Missions. Within a few years, that number would grow to forty-six medical missionaries practicing in twenty-eight newly established medical facilities around the globe.[493] Turkey became the primary mission field of the Shepard family of Boothbay Harbor, led by patriarch and matriarch, Dr. Frederick and Mrs. Fanny Shepard, both Congregational medical missionaries who travelled by horseback, bringing medical treatment to Turks, Kurds, and Armenians, and who founded the American hospital in Gaziantep in 1884.[494] Their son, Lorrin Shepard, and his wife, Virginia (nee Moffat, also a well-known missionary family), followed in their parents' footsteps, serving as medical missionaries in Turkey. The Shepard/Moffat family purchased a homestead in Boothbay Harbor late in the 1800s. A number of Shepard missionaries and their descendants, including Dr. Robert Shepard, who was born in Turkey, and his brother, Dr. Barclay Shepard, who for a number of years directed the hospital in Gaziantep, became important and beloved members of the Congregational Church of Boothbay Harbor. In addition to former Ottoman Empire countries, such as Turkey and Bulgaria, Congregational missionaries focused their attentions in China, Japan, and India.[495]

The highest liturgical holy day for Christian congregations around the world was established from the very beginnings of the Church as Easter. During the 1880s, however, some Congregational churches on Cape Cod would begin to celebrate Christmas in worship as well as Easter. This practice would gradually work its way into New England and throughout the country, changing the face of worship and reprioritizing the liturgical calendar. During this same period, there were important theological changes as well. In 1883, the National Council of Congregational Churches adopted the "1883 Declaration of Faith," also called the "1883 Commission Creed." This creed marked a theological departure from Calvinism, eliminating any reference to predestination.

As a nation, the United States, South and North, struggled to heal from the Civil War. In 1872, Congress granted amnesty to most Confederates, and reconstruction was officially concluded in 1877. However, debilitating sorrow and pain remained in the hearts of those who had sacrificed so much. The West continued to expand in population and commerce, nearly unaffected by the Civil War, but the East, both North and South, continued to mourn overwhelming losses and to pick up the shattered pieces in war-torn states.

Growth on the Boothbay Peninsula

In the Boothbay region, the latter part of the nineteenth century brought a swell of tourism, industry, and construction. As Francis Greene put it, "No town in Maine of equal population and valuation enjoyed a greater degree of prosperity than Boothbay during the period from 1866 to 1878."[496] This is also the time frame in which the Congregational church building was completely renovated and rebuilt. Construction supplies and workers were much in demand on the Boothbay peninsula as the number of houses and businesses increased. Shipbuilding and fishing industries remained strong, although during this period, it became clear that the area could be dangerously overfished. By the 1890s, the ice trade was at its peak, with 650 men employed on ice ponds in Boothbay and Boothbay Harbor. Tourism grew dramatically, with resorts and hotels constructed in Boothbay Harbor, Bayville, Murray Hill, Ocean Point, Squirrel Island, and Isle of Springs. There was dramatic growth in the number of summer cottages. Approximately two dozen summer homes were constructed at Ocean Point in the 1870s alone. Squirrel Island was established as a summer colony in 1870, its chapel being added in 1881.

During the 1880s, the mackerel catch was so spectacular the existing fleet of schooners could hardly keep up with it. However, with large steamboats entering the fishing industry, fears abounded that the stock of menhaden, used to produce fish oil, would be depleted. The catch of menhaden, also known as pogy, or porgy, was excellent between 1866 and 1876, but quite suddenly local fears were realized when the swarms of porgy in Maine waters disappeared. By 1878, the menhaden were gone. For the Boothbay fishing industry, this change was catastrophic. Large fish oil processing plants along Linekin Neck were forced to close. This event sounded a wake-up call to the fishing industry and to the entire community about the importance of economic diversification and responsible stewardship of the ocean.

Local residents continued to house or "board" tourists in the summer, but the hospitality industry was off and running, attracting seasonal visitors to large hotels and resorts. Steamboats were an important source of transportation and tourism, travelling back and forth to Bath, Samoset, Ocean Point, and nearby islands.[497] Ubiquitous growth brought inevitable conflict, leading to the division of Boothbay into two towns in 1889. Also, in this time of economic development, it is to be remembered that, in 1879, the Town of Boothbay was still having trouble paying promised income to Civil War veterans. Full recovery from the cost of the Civil War would take many more years. Significant measures were taken to entice businesses to locate in Boothbay, including a policy of 10-year tax forgiveness.

Congregational church members made the most of this period of growth, upgrading the church building with a more steeply pitched roof, a forward shift of the bell tower, and the addition of a chancel area, vestibule, chapel, and wood-burning furnace in 1881. Church membership increased to 101 in 1892. In 1888, the women of what was now being called the Second Congregational Church formed a Pipe Organ Society. Through fundraising socials, they purchased the old pipe organ from Grace Episcopal in Bath and hired a boy to pump the organ for 25 cents per Sunday. Tourism not only brought visitors to the Congregational church, it carried celebrated guest preachers into its pulpit. Elmer Hewitt Capen, third president of Tufts College and a Unitarian minister, often preached, as did Professors Harmon and Woodruff, also of Tufts. All three summered in Bayville. Thus began a tradition of excellent guest preaching in the summer.

Alcohol continued to be a source of moral conflict on the peninsula and in the Congregational church. On April 15, 1885, B.T. Cox, founder and editor of the *Boothbay Register,* was publicly whipped on the street for his support of temperance. Portland and Lewiston papers reported that "Mr. Cox has incurred the displeasure of the anti-temperance people of that vicinity to such an extent that he was horse-whipped on Saturday noon in the street in the presence of twenty or more. It is stated that the assailant's fine will be paid by the friends he has gained." The temperance movement was closely aligned with Congregational churches and clergy but, within the local church and certainly on the Boothbay peninsula, alcohol consumption continued to be a contentious subject.

The Congregational church was, during this period, central to the Memorial Day Parade. The Weld Sargent Post of the GAR (General Army of the Republic) was located on Commercial Street, and on Memorial Day, Union veterans assembled and marched up to the church, where many veterans were members and elected leaders. Just as the names of those lost at sea are still read on the Sunday afternoon of the annual Fishermen's Festival, the names of the fallen were once annually read and remembered from the Congregational pulpit. Eventually, the practice of reading the names of those lost in war was discontinued, and the practice of speeches delivered at war memorials located in Southport, Boothbay Harbor, Boothbay, and East Boothbay was initiated.

Rev. Ezra Barker Pike— 1873-1877

In May 1872, Rev. Andrew J. Smith completed the ministry he had started nearly four years earlier at "Second Congregational Church" (previously known as South Parish), and in June 1873, Rev. Ezra Barker Pike arrived. Born in Hiram, Maine in 1833, he was a graduate of both Bowdoin College (Medical School of Maine, 1857) and Bangor Theological Seminary (1862). He was ordained in his hometown of Hiram in 1863 and served churches in Stow, Sweden, and Brownfield, Maine, and in Chatham, New Hampshire before coming to Boothbay, where he ministered for four years.

Rev. Ezra B. Pike

Rev. Pike was interested in music, composed several hymns, and compiled and edited two widely used collections: Happy Home Songs, which were to be sung by families at home and in camp and revival settings; and Better Than Gold, a hymnal often used in revivals. He was also the author of Bible Heroes, a book published in 1917. Pike left Boothbay Harbor in 1877 for New Hampshire, serving congregations in Northwood and Atkinson, then proceeded to Newbury, Massachusetts and Morris, Connecticut, before retiring in Brentwood, New Hampshire.[498]

Rev. Richard William Jenkins[499]—1878-1883

In the mid-1870s, the church built a parsonage at 56 Oak Street, which was lived in by every pastor and family until 1965, when Alexander Tener gave the church a building lot on Roads End in Boothbay Harbor along with $15,000 toward the construction of a parsonage. In May 1878, the Reverend Richard William Jenkins arrived, having served Congregational churches in Winthrop and Yarmouth. 1880 Conference minutes indicate that he served both the First and Second Congregational churches, in Boothbay and Boothbay Harbor respectively, although the church in the center was by then no more than a ghost.

Jenkins was born in Wales in 1853, worked in the Welsh coal mines as a boy, and moved to Pennsylvania to live with his father, arriving first in New York in 1869, then joining his father in the mines of Pennsylvania. Having sensed a call to ministry, he travelled to Maine to preach to the Welsh church which had been formed among iron workers at Ligonia (now a neighborhood in South Portland).[500] From there, Jenkins soon entered Bangor Theological Seminary, from which he graduated in 1874. He became a naturalized citizen in Portland, Maine, on April 3, 1877.

In 1878, when Jenkins began his ministry in Boothbay Harbor, deaconesses were, for the first time, elected to serve the congregation, the first two being Susan Wells Lewis and Antoinette Eliza Kenniston. Susan Lewis was married to Giles Lewis, a store owner who went into the coal business and owned much real estate in the Harbor. Antoinette Adams Kenniston was the granddaughter of Rev. Jonathan Adams, a former minister of the church and part of the Adams family, founders of both the church and the town. Her husband was Judge George Kenniston. The movement to place women in leadership roles was mounting in congregational churches across the nation, but at the local level pastoral encouragement was essential to its success. Jenkins was clearly supportive of the movement.

Christian education was also important to Rev. Jenkins. He kept in touch with his contacts in Wales and, in 1879, gave a talk to the Lincoln Association regarding "Sabbath Schools and the Training of Children in Wales." Development of the Sabbath School, which would come to be called Sunday school, was a priority in his ministry. While Jenkins was pastor, the Civil War monument was dedicated in the center of Boothbay, with General Joshua Chamberlain delivering the dedication speech on October 1, 1879. George Kenniston, himself a Civil War Veteran and a central figure in the life of the church, worked with great resolve to get this monument financed and placed.

1881 was a trying year for the nation, as President James A. Garfield, twentieth president of the United States and a Union general in the Civil War, was fatally shot by an assassin. He had appointed several African Americans to key positions, but his efforts to initiate integration in the capital were cut short when he was killed by a disgruntled and probably mentally ill supporter. Garfield was succeeded by Vice President Chester A. Arthur. That same year, there was a great flurry of activity in the Harbor church. Three congregational meetings were held in April 1881 for the purpose of improving the church, including lifting it and creating a vestry beneath the sanctuary, all meetings being publicized in the *Boothbay Register* and most taking place on Friday evenings. Warren Dolloff, Samuel Boyd, and Moses White reported that the floor of the church was sufficiently strong to raise it. It was voted at a ratio of ten to four to remodel the church. John Blair, Keyes Richards, Samuel Boyd, Charles Carlisle, Warren Dolloff, William McCobb, and George Kenniston were appointed to be the Remodel Planning Committee. At that same congregational meeting, the clerk recognized those still living who had organized the South Parish, renamed Second Congregational Church: Leonard McCobb, James A. McCobb, N. C. McFarland, Benjamin Blair, James T. Beath, and Andrew Anderson. William McCobb resigned from the Remodel Planning Committee and was replaced by John H. Carter.

The price of change is sometimes a measure of conflict. On April 14, Alden Blossom asked to be removed from the rolls and records of the parish, "as," he said, "I do not wish to be considered a member of Said Parish." He also requested the clerk, William Fisher, to erase his name from the parish record. The record was, of course, penned in ink. Fisher could not, therefore, erase Blossom's name. He elected, instead, to cross out every instance of Alden Blossom's name with two strokes of a bright red pen, perhaps symbolic of the pain Blossom's decision caused. It may be that Blossom, a beloved physician on the peninsula, took this action as a protest against the remodeling of the church, but the reason for his decision to leave the church remains unknown.

In order to pay for the renovations of the church, sixty-six pews were sold at auction, creating choice seating. This action was taken as a way of raising funds for renovations, with some of the original pew purchasers buying pews afresh to support their church.[501] Church clerk, William Fisher, carefully recorded which pews were purchased by whom and for what amount. The choicest locations, pews 22, 23, 24, 39, 40, and 41, raised $40 at auction; the least desirable pew, number 49, was auctioned for $2. The total amount raised was $1,484, a significant sum at the time.

On April 23, an invitation was extended from the Methodist Episcopal Church in the harbor, later renamed the United Methodist Church, to use their sanctuary while church repairs were being made. The next day the invitation was accepted. On October 4, the following letter was sent:

> To the trustees of the Methodist Episcopal Society, Boothbay, Maine
>
> At the close of the Jubilee service, held by the Second Congregational Society last Sunday evening the following motion was unanimously adopted:
>
> Whereas; the members of the Methodist Episcopal Society have so generously permitted us to occupy their place of worship during the last four months be it therefore;
>
> Resolved That we return them a sincere vote of thanks for this cordial favor; especially as it discloses a Spirit of Christian fraternity; that it is our desire as well as our prayer as a Society that the pleasant relations now existing between us, may be continued; and that we hold ourselves ready to reciprocate this marked courtesy; whenever we have the opportunity of so doing.
>
> Yours fraternally For the Society,
> William H. Fisher, Clerk

Rev. Jenkins had been invited to take an extended vacation during the renovations,[502] but, with the kind offer of the Methodists, following a much abbreviated vacation, worship took place in the Methodist church on Sunday afternoons. In this same time period, a new version of the church's Articles of Faith and Covenant was published. As a result of the often-heated prohibitionist debate, a sentence was added to the covenant agreement, calling church members to "abstain from slander, profaneness, and from all manner of evil speaking; and from all intoxicating drinks as a beverage."[503]

Completed in 1881, the remodeled white clapboard-sided church featured a new roofline and a forward-facing steeple. Straight-backed numbered pews with doors were replaced by the elegant curved pews now in place. The raised singing gallery at the back of the sanctuary was removed. Winged pews on either side of the pulpit and a mahogany table that held the Bible were replaced by upholstered oak chairs and a pulpit. A chapel was added south of the sanctuary, a space that came in time to be called the vestry. A furnace was installed, eliminating the sanctuary stove. The women of the church stitched a red carpet into place, red remaining the color of the floor covering ever since. Original receipts show that the paint was purchased from W.T. Marr, but the painters were all volunteers. A sign-up list for painters was posted in the church, and a great painting party ensued.

The following year, 1882, the congregation voted to raise additional funds to repair the parsonage. Captain John Emerson, an internationally respected commander descended from a long line of maritime ancestors, joined the church.[504] The church voted to use an "envelope method" of raising funds for the first time. Moses White, John Blair, and Albert Kenniston, brother of George, were elected as a committee to repair the parsonage. A year later, in 1883, William J. Winslow, owner of a town shoe and boot shop, assumed a leadership role as part of the "committee to procure preaching." Winslow was also elected auditor. The parish offered Rev. Jenkins $750 that year as a salary, plus the use of the parsonage. To put his salary into perspective, according to the American College and Public School Directory, 1883, the average male teacher in Maine earned $29.59 per month, approximately $350 per year.

Richard Jenkins left Boothbay in 1883 to serve the Gardiner church. His letter of resignation was accepted on December 17, 1883 and took effect the first Sunday in January 1884. It appears that Rev. Jenkins kept in touch with members of the Boothbay flock, sending a young Elizabeth Reed a card dated January 16, 1884. On one side, he wrote the Welsh, "Yr Jesu a wylodd," meaning, "Jesus wept," the shortest sentence in scripture (John 11:35), followed by his name, location (Gardiner), and the date. On the other side, he wrote, "Dear Bessie" and followed with three verses of Longfellow's ballad, "Maidenhood."

> Like the swell of some sweet tune,
> Morning rises into noon,
> May glides onward into June.
> Gather, then, each flower that grows,
> When the young heart overflows,
> To embalm that tent of snows.
> Bear through sorrow, wrong, and ruth,
> In thy heart the dew of youth,
> On thy lips the smile of truth.

Jenkins remained faithfully connected to friends in Boothbay and to his Welsh origins. In 1885, a church comprised entirely of members with Welsh roots was formed in Brownville, Maine, and at its founding worship service, all music being sung in Welsh, Jenkins served as interpreter. He continued at the Gardiner church until 1892, when he accepted a call to Rockland. He was acting moderator of the General Conference at its meeting in Machias in 1893 and married Abigail Chapman of Bangor in 1894. He died later that same year at the age of 41, as a result of peritonitis.

Rev. Lewis Darenydd Evans— 1884–1889

Rev. Lewis D. Evans

Before departing Boothbay Harbor, Jenkins passed the mantle of ministry to his lifelong friend, Lewis Evans, who also had grown up working the coal mines of Wales. Evans travelled to the United States to earn funds for a theological education and, like Jenkins, moved to Maine to study at Bangor Theological Seminary. Jenkins left Boothbay early in January 1884, and by the end of February, the congregation had offered Evans the pastorate and a salary of $900 per year plus use of the parsonage. Evans had been ministering to the Bristol congregation, and in his new post in Boothbay Harbor, he participated in Jenkins' installation as the pastor in Gardiner. William Fisher resigned as clerk of the church that year, and William J. Winslow was elected to replace him. That same year, 1884, Captain Benjamin E. Pinkham, Civil War veteran who had served in the 5th Maine, was elected to the committee to procure preaching.

Like many of the Boothbay Harbor Congregational church's future ministers, Evans seems to have been concerned about a lack of young men in the church and raised this as an issue at a Lincoln Association meeting in 1886. The title of his topic for this meeting was: "How Shall the Young Men Be Retained?" Like many Welsh people, Evans had a soul that was steeped in music. In 1885, he formed both women's and girls' choirs.

In 1886, Fred Huff, owner of a tin and stove store, was elected church treasurer. At the same meeting, it was voted to sell a piece of property "near the old school house" bequeathed to the church by Abial McCobb and to use a portion of the funds raised through this sale for the purpose of "procuring a tablet in memorial of Abial McCobb." Four unsold pews were successfully auctioned, raising additional funds for the church. In 1887, Norris Hussy, proprietor of a dry goods store, was elected auditor. That same year, with great encouragement from their pastor, the church elected a "Committee to Procure Singing." Antoinette Kenniston, who had been playing the organ for years and was one of the first elected deaconesses, resigned from her music responsibilities effective April 1888, and it was decided to pay for the services of a new organist. The "Ladies of the Pipe Organ" were invited to "assist in paying the organist." The first paid organist was Elizabeth Fullerton Blair, mother of future church historian, Elizabeth Reed.

For the first time in 1888, ushers were elected: namely, Charles Kendrick and Albert Kenniston. The congregation voted to insure the church for $3,000. On March 18, 1888, the trustees "closed up their duties in regard to the Legacy of Abial H. McCobb" with bequeathed lands being sold to church member Moses White. In March 1889, William E. Reed, Boothbay selectman and descendent of Andrew Reed, founder of the original Presbyterian church, was elected moderator of the congregation. Greene wrote of Reed, "He was a man who held the esteem and confidence of those who knew him to a remarkable degree."[505] That year, the congregation voted not to insure the church. All of these activities suggest that the church was financially healthy and continuing to attract citizens of energy and distinction to its membership and leadership.

In June 1889, Evans left Boothbay to serve the Camden church. While the minister in Camden, Evans delivered a talk entitled, "How to Raise the Standards of Music in the Church."[506] He ministered to the Camden church for twenty-five years, longer than any minister before or since. Of Evans it is written, "Being an eloquent speaker, he was sincerely devoted to his congregation and the town of Camden, making him a valuable and well-loved citizen."[507] The depth of his faith is revealed in the first few lines of a poem he wrote:

The Man of Galilee by L. D. Evans[508]
I have walked a rugged pathway
In the darkness thru my life;
All my gropings have been painful,
Every step has been a strife.

But I have felt the road grow easier,
And my gloom and sadness flee,

As I walked by faith in darkness
With the Man of Galilee.

On November 2, 1886,[509] there was a terrible fire in Boothbay Harbor, leveling what Greene called, "the severest blow to business the village had ever experienced." It nearly devastated the business district and caused insurance rates to skyrocket. This event stirred inevitable interest on the part of business owners in securing a town water supply. Town meetings, debates, and actions regarding water were heated. Those with businesses and homes in the commercial district of the Harbor claimed Adams Pond by "eminent domain" to be the source of their water. There was a protracted struggle between business owners, many of whom were relatively new to the town, and longstanding families of the area. Business owners stood passionately in favor of a water plan while others remained vehemently opposed. Church members participated from both sides of the question, but many if not most of the vocal "pro-water" proponents were members and leaders in the church. This rancorous battle for water eventually led to the division of Boothbay into two towns, Boothbay Harbor becoming its own municipality in 1889.[510]

Having witnessed several years of deep division in the town, Rev. Richard Evans left Boothbay Harbor the very year it became legally separated from Boothbay. Following more than a year in which the church had no settled pastor and relied on supply preachers, in July 1890, the Reverend John H. Matthews became the pastor of the church at a salary of $800. Matthews was ordained on May 5 but would stay less than two years, moving from Boothbay Harbor to the Congregational church in Madison. The church in the harbor had by then effectively navigated many of the shifting currents of American culture, embracing the pipe organ, electric lights, and more modern heating, welcoming both war veterans and women into leadership positions, and becoming a popular Sunday morning tourist destination with an established choir and Sunday School. Having been hit by great waves of theological change, social upheaval, and unremitting conflict within the church and the community, the church remained buoyant in the grace of God.

CHAPTER 8

CHARTING THE COURSE: 1892–1919
by Robert W. Dent

What a fascinating and diverse almost three decades fall between 1892 and 1919! Some have looked at this period and felt it reflected the rise of parochialism and a turning inward. Others have considered that maybe it was the end of isolationism and moving outward. At the very least, it would seem that the Congregational church in the Boothbay community was able to chart a successful course through some very turbulent times.

Maine author Sarah Orne Jewett, in 1919, through her representative character Captain Littlepage in *The Country of the Pointed Firs*, pointed to the spread of parochialism in "a community which narrows down and grows dreadful ignorant when it is shut up to its own affairs," and when most Mainers could not "see outside the battle for town clerk." Local Damariscove Island and Boothbay Harbor resident Alberta Poole Rowe, born in 1910, later recalled the reluctance of area residents during the early 1900s to switch their diets from the traditional salted codfish to the novel fresh cod, unlike "city people," who quickly adapted to this new "whitefish." A few Boothbay area residents during this period joined the Ku Klux Klan and held biases against Catholics, Jews, and blacks. On the other hand, such prejudices likely were more explosive outside Maine's Midcoast region. In fact, the only local deed restrictions against "people of Hebrew or Negro parentage" were in some of the more exclusive summer colonies established by developers from outside Maine during the early twentieth century.[511]

As a group in general, the Congregational church seemed to be far more forward looking. Not that the diet of the average parishioner then is known today. But the fact that the congregation invited Rev. Dr. Harry Emerson Fosdick to preach suggests that they were willing to listen to a progressive and liberal theologian. Although he supported the nation's participation in World War I, his position toward war and peace began to shift toward the end or after the war. By the 1920s, Fosdick was a formidable spokesperson for pacifism. The influence of the great Quaker teacher and writer Rufus Jones undoubtedly contributed to Fosdick's emerging passion for peace. In addition to visiting with Jones in Maine, Fosdick frequently invited Jones to speak from his pulpit at the Riverside Church in New York City.

Still, one might make a case for the reluctance of the community to look toward the future and a wider perspective in the area of education. In the *Boothbay Register* of June 25, 1915, an article was entitled: "No new school building. Voters in town did not feel like accepting extra burden in taxes." Co-author Carl R. (Chip) Griffin, reflecting on this article said:

> The voters rejected the proposed new high school. [It] must have been the old 1860s-vintage high school on School Street in Boothbay Harbor, where I attended grades one through eight in the 1960s. Similar ideas to build a new school on Kenneyfield Drive were defeated in the 1950s, but the new and present high school was finally built around 1957. It appears, then, as to education, Boothbay historically lagged in terms of providing the most up-to-date facilities. However, it is possible that this lack was at least partially offset by the small size of the classes and the quality of relationships that were formed between student and teacher.

Another issue of concern during the war years was that apparently a mixed message was being sent to visitors. Note excerpts from the following article from the *Boothbay Register*:

August 29, 1914: Correspondence Between Selectmen and the U. S. War Department In Relation to Abatement of a Harbor Nuisance: Selectmen aim "to abate the long-continued practice of dumping rubbish into our harbor and upon our water front, since the Army is in charge of our River and Harbor Improvements [hence our Army Corps of Engineers jurisdiction today]. We invite the vacationers to come in; we erect a barrier to keep them out. We publish broadcast [sic] our local charms and attractions but knowingly create conditions to materially impair them." The Army responded to the selectmen with an expression of cooperation but no money to appoint a person to watch these matters. The Army recommended that the selectmen appoint a harbor master.

It was roughly a half-century or more later that the Army's suggestion was implemented.

Turning to the bigger picture, 1892 through 1919 was a fascinating period nationally, internationally and locally. According to co-author John Bauman, "It was not only one of the most tumultuous, but one of the most significant periods in American history." It was during this period that in the wake of Darwinism there were some major shifts in the social sciences and in philosophy, with pragmatism taking center stage. William James, while open to religious experience, also introduced a relativistic epistemology when he defined 'true beliefs' as those that prove useful to the believer. John Dewey transformed education with a pragmatic emphasis on child-centered education with interdisciplinary studies and a more hands-on, learning-by-doing approach.

Socially, this era experienced some major crises. From the post Civil War years into the early 1900s, the so-called Gilded Age produced new opportunities, which, unhindered, turned into greed and a quest for power and money. The "robber barons" latched onto Social Darwinism and the Gospel of Wealth to justify their actions. Greed and sanctimonious feelings of entitlement justified by pseudo social science led to reactions of outrage toward monopolistic corporate industrialism and the living conditions of the immigrant poor and the working class. In 1892, the tension exploded in Homestead, Pennsylvania, with a work stoppage at Andrew Carnegie's steel plant. The result was one of the most violent episodes in the American labor struggles of the late 1800s. Although many could sympathize with the workers' complaints of unfair treatment, there was fear of more and similar labor violence around the country. At the same time, the rising income inequality within American society threatened the middle class as well as the working class, leading in the late nineteenth century to a wide range of increasingly professionalized middle-class organizations seeking reforms. Extensive foreign immigration, exploding industrialization, and accelerating urbanization led to more problems. Racism and xenophobia erupted in 1919 with the Chicago race riots—among the worst such riots in American history and the worst of the twenty-five riots that erupted in the "Red Summer"[512] of 1919 across America.

The late nineteenth century and early twentieth brought political change also. The Progressive movement emerged as a reform movement in the late nineteenth century and bloomed during the first few decades of the twentieth century. Names like Sinclair Lewis and Frank Lloyd Wright were associated with it and, in politics, Theodore Roosevelt and Woodrow Wilson. "While the Progressives differed in their assessment of the problems and how to resolve them, they generally shared in common the view that government at every level must be actively involved in these reforms."[513]

While many of these social-political issues may not have affected Boothbay directly, awareness of what was happening clearly impacted Boothbay through its many visitors and the homiletical endeavors of its ministers, who attempted to bring the Bible into dialogue with the contemporary world. Some key dates during this era were:

1890–1914 Immigration became a major factor.

1893 The Charles A. Briggs trial took place, drawing lines regarding a rigid Biblical interpretation of Scripture, leaving no room for other educational disciplines, prohibiting genuine scientific thought with the resultant fundamentalist-modernist divisions.

1893 The Foreign Missions Conference of North America was extremely important in developing interdenominational understanding and cooperation regarding the cause of missions. As the century turned, the churches grew in their interest in foreign missions. It was thought by church historian William Sweet that this interest came about because of the Spanish American War and the new imperialistic policy developed by the United States.[514]

1895 The World Student Christian Federation was started by a Methodist layman who helped prepare the way for the World Missionary Conference held in Edinburgh in 1910.

1897 Congregationalist Charles Sheldon wrote *In His Steps* exploring the theme: "What would Jesus do in addressing the sins of the city?"

1898 Spanish American War and increasing interest in missions.

1837–1899 Evangelist and publisher, Dwight Moody opined: "The principal business of religion is to change hearts not to reform society."

By 1900 An urban consumer culture and a gospel of prosperity were in place.

1901 The assassination of President McKinley occurred on September 6, inside the Temple of Music on the grounds of the Pan American Exposition in Buffalo, New York.

1906 The Student Volunteer Convention was held.

1908 The Federal Council of Churches was founded by thirty denominations.

1910 The World Missionary Conference was held in Edinburgh.

1914 Beginning of World War I.

1917 *A Theology For the Social Gospel* was published by Walter Rauschenbusch, and his thinking subsequently became quite popular.

1917 On April 6, the United States entered World War I following German torpedoing of U.S. ships.

1919 On June 28, the Treaty of Versailles was signed, ending the war.

1919 Karl Barth published his *Shorter Commentary on Romans*.

It is quite obvious that in these several decades change was accelerating. The industrial revolution of the late nineteenth century reshaped the nation. Transportation, communication, agriculture, domestic life, the labor market, and shipping were all affected.[515] As a result of industrialization there was also a population shift. By the 1880s the population began to move from the country to the city. Throughout the nation as a whole, one third of the population in 1890 was living in towns of 4,000 or more inhabitants, while there were 272 cities with a population of more than 12,000. In 1900, forty percent of the total population of the country were urban dwellers. By 1910, urbanization had increased to 45.7 percent, and in 1930, 56.2 percent of the total population were living in cities.[516] The rise of the city threatened the life of many country churches. Within the city, the trend was toward secularization of the Sabbath. The fast changes in the American city helped to bring about the institutionalization of the church.[517] The result was often a trend toward enthusiastic life in Christ giving way to an organization about Christ, which could generate committed growing Christians, but also risked becoming all about structure, rules and procedures.

Such change must have been a concern for residents of the Boothbay region. For in the *Boothbay Register* on February 21, 1906, there was an article about an interesting debate that had occurred at the Boothbay Harbor Methodist church on the subject "City life is more Desirable than Country Life." The weight of opinion was more on the negative than the positive side. However, it is rather interesting that as a result of the Theodore Roosevelt Commission, the Federal Council of Churches (1910–1912), along with some federal agencies, began to lift up "the importance of maintaining the country church as a conserving force in American civilization."[518] The primary focus of the Commission was divided into seven working groups; forestry, lands, fisheries, game and wildlife, water and waterpower, minerals, and public health.

Rev. David Stimson once noted about the Boothbay church that "it has over its long history prospered and/or suffered along with the fortunes and population of the region. Church membership was at 48 in 1848. By 1892 it had grown to 101. In 1916 it dropped to 78. By 1929 it was up again to 105 members." Was the cause of these changes industrialization, immigration, war, or theological controversies? The 1890 census showed that the Episcopal and Congregational churches had moved from dominant positions in American culture to seventh and eighth positions, respectively.[519]

Religious diversity was growing. During this era, the Episcopal church arrived in Boothbay when, on September 29, 1906, All

Saints By the Sea was consecrated. By 1914 the Catholic church was under construction. In Boothbay, however, from all accounts, it seems that the Congregational and the Methodist churches were the driving forces on the spiritual and cultural scene in the area.

Industrialization's Impact on the Region

Clearly, there was a long established fishing industry in Boothbay as well as boatbuilding. Soon though, boatbuilding would take on a new urgency, as will be indicated later under the subtheme: The First World War in the Region. (see page 204)

However else industrialization affected Boothbay, it had a secondary effect on the church. In the post-Civil War era, there was a consolidation of federal power (e.g., federal regulation of the railroads) and creation of large business organizations. Many of the leaders in these corporations were also staunch church members. A notable example was John D. Rockefeller. The successful businessman became the symbol of modern America, and his ideals and methods began to permeate every phase of American interest and life. In turn, the church began to emphasize efficiency, systems, organization, and responsibilities delegated to boards and committees.[520] The great subject for discussion was Christian efficiency.[521]

The concern for efficiency and order filtered down to the Congregational church in Boothbay during this period. At the annual meeting on April 30, 1904, a committee was appointed to look into the reorganization of the parish society under a constitution and bylaws, shaping them into a legal and revised form. Of special note, Judge George B. Kenniston moderated that meeting.

Judge Kenniston was obviously a very prominent, important and influential member not only of the church but also of the community at large. The importance of Judge Kenniston to the church and the community was stated in a 1918 *Boothbay Register* article following his death:

> Judge George Beaman Kenniston, born in 1836, was the son of William and Mary Kenniston. Educated at Bowdoin, he was

in the Fifth Maine Regiment at Bull Run, was imprisoned at Libby Prison, released on a deal and rejoined his regiment for the Battle of Fredericksburg. He was a local lawyer, owner of land in Boothbay, Southport, and Monhegan, a member of the Maine State Legislature, superintendent of schools, and inspector of customs. He had six children, one of whom died November 28, 1898, when the steamer *Portland* foundered in a fateful storm. He was a deacon of the Congregational church for many years. A former pastor, Rev. L.D. Evans of Camden, presided at the funeral service. Pall bearers were A.R. Nickerson, C.J. Marr, Edward Knight, F.B. Green, and S.T. Maddocks.[522]

If the concern for efficiency was one by-product of industrialization that filtered down into the church, another was increasing wealth. From 1880 to the end of the century the most significant single influence in organized religion in the United States was the tremendous increase in wealth. Poor men's churches were being transformed into churches of the upper middle class.[523] While the wealth entering Boothbay may have been quite different from that which entered the larger cities, still it is notable that there were many enhancements to the church property during these years. In 1890, a pipe organ was installed at the church. In 1901 a "steel [probably tin] ceiling" was added to the sanctuary. These were major and costly undertakings that might not have been considered during less affluent times. But other significant improvements were made for the church during these years. For example, on May 27, 1911:

> Notwithstanding the lightnings and thunderings, there was a good attendance at the semi-annual parish meeting on Monday evening. Three new members were received. It was voted to purchase a Franklin wood and coal furnace and place it in the choir loft. No more cold, shivering singers during the winter months. The grounds to the entrance to the church are to

be graded up and the driveway to the church stalls changed. George Lewis is the man to whom the oversight of this work was assigned. There will be a grading bee some day in the near future, and the ladies will serve dinner in the church vestry. Several of the ladies met on Thursday afternoon and cleaned the ladies' parlor, and everything was made ready for weekly meetings on Thursday afternoons from 2 to 4:30 o'clock, until their annual sale.[524]

At a parish meeting on November 11, 1904, action was taken with regard to lighting the church by appointing a committee to investigate costs with the local lighting company. On November 16, a proposal was presented to wire and furnish all the fixtures for the "audience room and vestry" for $100, to be accomplished in three weeks. The company would also install a meter and charge the same rate charged the Methodist church of $.15/ kilowatt hour. An alternate proposal was accepted to install gas lights at a cost of $90, the gas to be furnished for a year at a total cost of $35. With the latter proposal, six light chandeliers were installed in the main room, eight double wall lamps for the sides and ends. One drop-shade light was placed over the pulpit, one light in the vestibule and three double wall brackets for the vestry.

Another direct influence of growing wealth was the building of costly churches in many places and larger gifts to benevolent causes.[525] Services became more formal, yet cushions were placed in the pews, including in Boothbay. The era of Calvinistic austerity for the sake of spiritual discipline was giving way to the concept of becoming more inviting and welcoming to the visitor as well as to the member.

The comfort of the pastor and his family were not neglected during these years either, for the church showed great interest in providing a suitable parsonage. On April 14, 1906, Pastor Hyde and family moved into the new parsonage on Oak Street. The next evening, nearly 100 parishioners and friends gathered at the new parsonage to join Pastor Hyde and his family in a grand house warming and social evening. All were delighted with the modern beautiful parish home. Pastor Hyde gave an address of welcome and thanks to all who had worked so hard to complete the project. Pastor Gray of the Methodist church in Boothbay Harbor was also present and gave a few hearty and kindly words for the occasion, wishing life and much happiness to the pastor and the people. Dainty "ices and cakes" were served and a "very social time enjoyed."

It is worth noting in connection with this open house, that the relationship between the Congregational and the Methodist churches during this era, as in so much of their histories, was exceptionally congenial. Year after year the *Boothbay Register* makes note of frequent union services and special joint programs. Furthermore, there are many references to joint statements in the paper by the ministers of both churches, encouraging the increase in spiritual concerns in the community. When the Methodist church had a fire, the Congregational church was quick to respond with assistance.

Apparently, the Methodist and Congregational churches were tapping into a kind of ecumenical spirit that was developing nationally. The Federal Council of Churches had been formed in 1908 seeking greater cooperation among the churches. Perhaps the interest in unity was furthered by a statement Teddy Roosevelt made in 1900 at a meeting of representatives of New York churches seeking to form a state federation. Roosevelt said, "There are plenty of targets that we need to hit without firing into each other."[526] Eventually, in 1908, the Federal Council of Churches was formed to seek greater cooperation among the churches.

The Spiritual Life of the Church

Much of the focus up to this point has been on the church as an institution. What about its spiritual life?

One index of the spiritual life of a congregation is the health of its corporate worship. In 1904 it seems quite clear that Rev. Hyde was trying to improve worship. In May he initiated experiments with the service and asked the congregation for suggestions to make improvements. What exactly the experiments were we don't know.

The *Boothbay Register* reported many of Rev. Hyde's sermon titles. On Feb 10, 1906, Rev. Hyde began a series of Sunday morning addresses to the young people of the Sabbath School under the rubric "The Sensitive Age." The title that day was "The Glory of Young Men Is Their Age." On February 17 the topic was "The Great Builder," in which children were reminded that their service was to bring their friends to church. The sermon on February 25 was "The Friendship That Saves."

The vibrancy of the church at that time was reported by the *Boothbay Register* :

> The recent evidence of revived interest in our morning choir is noted with great satisfaction. What a blessing it is to have a religious service with appropriate music and song. The apparent renewal of interest in the Sunday morning service is also particularly encouraging and also eloquent of the truth that in every successful religious meeting everyone has his part and place.

In addition to worship, a further index of the spiritual life of a congregation is its concern for mission. Clearly, larger giving to benevolent causes was also a direct influence of growing wealth.[527] The era this chapter covers is an era that saw the emergence of a great number of mission efforts nationally and internationally. And the Boothbay Harbor Congregational church was no exception.

By 1914, three million American women were involved in worldwide mission work.[528] Women missionaries were evidently on the radar of the Boothbay Harbor Congregational church as well. On August 30, 1914, during the morning services of the church, the reported: "Miss Annie E. Pinneo, for many years a missionary in Turkey, will speak on present political conditions in Turkey, and the story of up-to-date American mission work, especially the life of a Missionary Heroine in the Interior, who has recently died. A cordial welcome will be extended to all who come."[529]

A third index of the health of a church is its youth activity. It's quite evident that there was a significant amount of such activity during the pastorates of Rev. Hyde and Rev. Post in particular. In 1917, much youth activity was reported in the *Boothbay Register*:

> BOYS' DAYS plans for both the usual 10:45 AM morning service and 7:00 PM evening service on Sunday, February 18 featured two Bowdoin College young men. "Our own Austin MacComick [sic], and his friend, Mr. Foster, will each give a short address. Austin McCormick, a Boothbay resident, delivered a sermon, "Christian Living Seven Days a Week," while Foster gave an account of the young men's conference in Kansas City. The young men's choir sang at both morning and evening services. Arthur Blake was the violinist, and Leslie Marr played coronet. We expect that the message these two young men from college will bring us, will be one that will touch on inmost life and help us to live better. Their hearts are just brimming in zeal and love and enthusiasm for Christian service, and we are sure that their coming to us will be very helpful to all who attended.[530]

The Austin McCormick referred to above was the son of the Reverend Donald McCormick. From the age of seven he had lived in the church parsonage until soon after his father's death when Austin was about fifteen. A Children's Day program was held on June 10, 1917 at the church. Early preparations were also under way for a celebration to be held in 1920 of "the Pilgrim Tercentary Movement." At a Sunday service in June 1917 "young people in costume interpreted through song and speech the Pilgrim Spirit."[531]

As suggested above, one of the youth about whom the church and town seemed to take great pride was Austin McCormick. He was a 1915 graduate of Bowdoin College and entered Columbia University, "having been awarded a large scholarship at Bowdoin for postgraduate work at any institution he might select."[532] There were signs that Austin was a creative individual who likely would enter some form of Christian ministry. However, all that was cut short by World War I.

The First World War in the Region[533]

As early as 1916, Washington created the U.S. Shipping Board to establish a merchant marine with enough tonnage and manpower to deal with the German threat to free shipping. When war was declared in 1917, the United States seized ninety-eight German ships, and a delegation visited Boothbay Harbor looking for deck officers and engineering officers to sail those ships. Sixty-one from Boothbay and twenty-two from Southport agreed to do so!

Boothbay Harbor shipyards became involved, including Townsend Marine, which worked for the U.S. Shipping Board. Officers from the Boothbay Coast Guard station patrolled for submarines that had been spotted, presumably reporting their findings to the Shipping Board. Captain Fred McKown, returning from Boston at the helm of an Eastern Steamship liner in early 1918, reported seeing German U-boats.

Many local boys enlisted for service in World War I. "Our Young Men Stepped to the Front Tuesday" the paper reported. In Boothbay Harbor, 141 men came forward, filled out papers and received their card and buttons—in Boothbay, 61, and in Southport, 22. The *Boothbay Register* made a point of saying "Few slackers. Our young men are ready if called."

As the war dragged on, the news was not always good. Twenty-one of those who enlisted lost their lives, and some of those were from the Congregational church. Among the war dead were: Charles E. Sherman, Willis Brewer, Kilburn Sherman, Harold Hagget, Walcott Marr, Harold Lewis, E.A. Gamage, A.G. Snowman, John Snowman, Arthur Rand, H.W. Bishop, S.T. Maddocks, Joseph McKown, Ray Pennoyer, Ernest Reed, Arthur Auld, Weston Farmer, Warren Payson, Raymond Decker, and Waldo Decker. The *Register* noted that those who lost their lives were not only people from the Boothbay region, but also seasonal residents of Squirrel Island and other summer colonies. One of the first to see battle was Willis Brewer, Co. K 301 Infantry. But other Boothbay boys were also in the thick of it. The first to die from the Boothbay area was Charles E. Sherman. He died on July 21, 1918.

Of course, war always brings with it intense debates over the ethics of war and peace. What position did the ministers of the Congregational church take during World War I? The evidence is rather scarce. Apparently there was a different minister every Sunday over many months. For example, in June 1917, Rev. Henry P. Woodin preached at 10:45 a.m. In the evening there was a union service at the Methodist church, where Miss Hall spoke on Armenian relief. Then on July 20, 1918 the minister was Rev. Frederick E. Heath. On August 17 Rev. Leopold Nies preached at the Congregational church on "A Parent's Gift to a Soldier." On another Sunday, Rev. L.D. Evans of Camden preached, and the following Sunday, the Reverend Harry Emerson Fosdick, just back from France, spoke about what he had seen. At the same service Mr. Hayden sang a solo, and in the evening there was another community song service including a solo by Miss Woodbridge. Those community sings had begun earlier in 1918. The program for a Sunday evening song service on July 20 began with the "Star Spangled Banner," followed by "Old Black Joe," a solo of "The Long, Long Trail," then "Flow Gently Sweet Afton," a reading of the "Soul of Joan of Arc" by Miss Mary Kenniston," a solo of the Marseillaise; a reading in French; then "Over There," "Keep the Home Fires Burning," "Love's old Sweet Song," followed by a solo of "Rule Britannia," and ending with "God Save the King."

With the large turnover of ministers during the war years, it's hard to create a profile of what the leadership of the church was thinking. The one sermon entitled "A Parent's Gift to a Soldier" would lend support to the notion that there was some degree of support for the war. That Rev. Fosdick preached might also indicate support, since he strongly supported our involvement in the beginning and during most of the war. However, by 1920 Fosdick began to shift his position, and from that time on became a stronger and stronger advocate of pacifism. As described in the following excerpt from an article entitled, "Harry Emerson Fosdick's Role in the War and Pacifist Movements:"

> After resigning from the First Baptist Church of Montclair [NJ] in 1915 to teach at Union Theological Seminary as a professor of practical theology, Fosdick entered headlong into the debate over America's entrance into World War I. In a country firmly committed to neutrality and isolationism, Fosdick advocated for the United States' involvement. Far ahead of his clerical colleagues, he stumped in pulpits across the country rallying support for America's intervention in the Great War. "Sad is our lot if we have forgotten how to die for a holy cause," Fosdick preached. He criticized President Wilson for dragging America's feet. Finally, Fosdick got his wish, and America entered the war in 1917. In order to stir up support for the war, he wrote a treatise, "The Challenge of the Present Crisis," which quickly sold over two hundred thousand copies. Fosdick donated the proceeds to the war effort.
>
> In "The Challenge of the Present Crisis," Fosdick acknowledged the complicated interaction between war and faith. He admitted that modern warfare had clearly made the current war the most appalling one in history. Yet, Fosdick noted that world leaders now understood war's destruction and had begun to question the harmony of Christianity and war. In his defense of American and Christian involvement, his liberal optimism asserted that in a war to end all wars, humanity now "will learn to handle the new relationships for fraternity and not for war."
>
> Alongside his optimistic idealism, however, Fosdick mixed in a healthy dose of realism. He belittled the idealism evidenced in extreme pacifism and remarked that Jesus did not face the same questions of war that modernity endured. Instead, Fosdick insisted that "the morale of our people de-

pends" upon their ability to harmonize Christ's ideals with the "necessities of action in a time of war."

Fosdick's engagement sprang from his belief in internationalism over isolationism. He asserted that each person shares mutual responsibility in war, and he offered specific guidelines about how countries might prevent future wars by developing an "international mind" in contrast to provincial nationalism. The challenge for both America and Christianity, however, was not prevention but rather to make the world "safe for democracy," winning both the war and the peace. Ultimately, Fosdick would not dare allow his church, his nation, or himself to miss out on the greatest issue of his generation.

Taking a semester's leave from teaching, Fosdick traveled to Europe under the auspices of the Y.M.C.A. in order to encourage Allied troops in the trenches and to be able to recount the war effort for citizens at home. Watching troops return from the front lines, he experienced firsthand the horrors of modern warfare. While continuing to extol the valor of American soldiers, Fosdick soon began to reevaluate publicly his Christian position on war. Explicit examples of the horrors of modern warfare repeatedly appeared in his articles and sermons. After the war's end in November 1918, Fosdick made reference to the war in each consecutive sermon for the next eight months. With each passing day, Fosdick became more disappointed in the war's inability to unite the world. By 1921, Fosdick could preach from the pulpit, "we cannot reconcile Christianity with war anymore." By 1923, he fully embraced a commitment to peace....

Whereas modernism's Social Gospel and American culture had once walked hand in hand accommodating one another, Fosdick now understood that the church might have to stand alone and speak prophetically against the prevailing culture. He focused on the impact of each individual Christian's ethic on the world while also serving as an apologist for the legitimacy of the Christian faith. The stakes were never higher for Fosdick, for he believed that if Christians did not end war, war would end Christianity.

In becoming a self-proclaimed pacifist, Fosdick did not wholeheartedly identify with the absolute position of the historic peace sects. He found the issue of pacifism much more complicated and distrusted people who felt that their positions escaped inconsistency. From citizens paying taxes to America's own economic practices, Fosdick believed no persons could avoid self-contradiction in attempting to dissociate themselves completely from war. He believed that renouncing war was never simply an individual decision but rather a public one made with the world in view. [534]

Although there was much support for the war efforts in Boothbay, it is notable that the *Boothbay Register* carried the reproduction of an article on July 9, 1915 entitled "Panama and Peace: Interesting Article Suggestive of Relative Relationship." The article highlighted the words "acquaintance softens prejudice." Material from the article was supplied by R.B. Hale., Vice President of the Panama-Pacific International Exposition of San Francisco; and it quoted the Honorable Elihu Root when he was about to leave office as Secretary of State: "It was impossible for any nation to be at war if the peoples of the conflicting countries understood each other." In the article there is an evident longing for the end of the hostilities in Europe and for peace to reign.

Pastoral Leadership

Who were the called pastors of the church during this era and how exactly did the ministers during these decades relate to many of the current day issues? *Boothbay Registers* for the first decade of this era are for the most part not available. And identifying the exact dates of service of the ministers in this time period is very difficult. However, the following appears to be accurate:

- Rev. Arthur G. Pettingill: June 5-August 2, 1892

- Rev. M.O. Patton: June 1893-February 1, 1895

- Rev. Donald McCormick: May 5,1895-November 27, 1902

- Rev. Frank B. Hyde: July 26,1902–1906

- Rev. George H. Hull: March-September 13, 1908

- Rev. Stanley Post: May 1, 1910-August 29, 1915

- Laity and Supply Pastors occupied the pulpit: September 1915–1919

- Rev. Walter P. Bradford: 1919–1922

Rev. Arthur G. Pettingill—June-August 1892
While not much is known about Rev. Arthur G. Pettingill and his very brief stay in Boothbay, he was invited back a decade later, on July 24, 1904, as a guest preacher. At that time he was living in Waterville.

Rev. M. O. Patton—1893–1895
Rev. Patton had only an eight-month stay in Boothbay as the pastor of the church. Little is known about him. Unfortunately, a huge gap of information exists in the church records from the years 1892 to 1903. Perhaps he was simply a regular supply pastor.

Rev. Donald McCormick—1895–1902
Sadly, most of the information available about the Reverend Donald McCormick is from articles written after his death and from naturalization records in the State of Maine Archives. He was born in 1842 and was from the Island of Islay on the west coast of Scot-

land. He was the oldest of fourteen children. Having attended normal school in Glasgow, he received his theological training from the Theological School of Nottingham, England. Married to Jane Greene in 1878, they had five sons and three daughters. Their children's names were Agnes, Ishe, Donald D., Winnifred, Darsy, William A., Austin, and Franklin.

Rev. McCormick arrived in Maine in 1894 and was naturalized in 1900. Prior to coming to Maine he served a church in Castleford, England for seventeen years. Then, due to climate-induced illness, the family moved to Canada. Rev. McCormick moved to Waterford, Maine from Canada because alcohol was not as accessible there as a temptation for his growing sons. Two years later, he moved to Boothbay because he wanted a better education for his children. It was in his eighth year of service as pastor of the church in Boothbay, on November 21, 1902, that Rev. McCormick died. It appears that his was the longest pastorate at the Congregational church of Boothbay in many years. The average length of stay from the church's beginning up to that point had been three and a quarter years. It was said that Rev. L.D. Evans of Camden preached an eloquent funeral sermon from the words of Job, "He knoweth the way I take, when He hath tried me I shall come forth as gold." Two of his children, Austin and William, appear to have played a prominent role in the Boothbay community in the years after their father's death. Of him Francis Green wrote, "His life was a continual benediction. He loved his church, the town and its people, and his death was the cause of universal mourning in the community."[535]

As to the ministers who followed Rev. McCormick, although few sermon titles were reported in the local paper, there are glimpses into the life of the church from some of the articles of the period.

Rev. Frank B. Hyde—1902-1906

The *Boothbay Register* in 1904 reported much more about the Methodist church than the Congregational church. Moreover, in that year and for several thereafter, the paper carried the entire sermon of the Reverend Dr. Frank Dewitt Talmadge on a weekly basis, as did newspapers across the country. Talmadge was the pastor of the Jefferson Park Presbyterian Church in Chicago.[536]

However, though the sermons of local ministers were not printed in the paper, it did report the Congregational church schedule frequently, showing that the church was quite active with worship at 10:45, Sabbath School at noon, Sunday School at 1:00 p.m., Christian Endeavor at 6:00 and an evening service at 7:00 p.m. Furthermore, in 1906, Rev. Hyde's sermon titles were often noted, for example:

> April 30: "The Ruling Characteristic, The Christian Faith and Service."
>
> May 14: "Christian Attitude Toward Death"
>
> June 3: "The Christian Program: Its Claim Upon US."
>
> June: "In What Way Is the Church of the Present Superior to the Church of the Past?"
>
> August 6: "The Meaning of God's Purpose In Redemption"
>
> October 9: "The Nobility of the Gospel and Our Response to It"
>
> October 23: "The Drawing Power of Christ"

Attendance may have fluctuated and the pastors in the village clearly collaborated in attempting to encourage better attendance. The June 3, 1906 *Boothbay Register* reported a union evening service that week to be held at the Methodist church. An article also appeared in the paper indicating that the pastor would like to suggest to any needing the information that the cold weather is not altogether over. "Hence he will expect his cold weather congregation still to sustain him." Noting the "enervation of the spring season," he goes on to suggest that the pastor's job is to preach and that the people's job is to make available "a congregation to preach to" and that "some of the best influences to be felt in any sermon emanate from the congregation." Likely quite intentional was the July 7 follow-up sermon: "Christianly Tested By Its Fruits."

Rev. George H. Hull—1908
In 1908, a new pastor arrived, the Reverend George H. Hull. Some of his sermon titles might seem a bit tedious to us today. On March 8, Rev. Hull spoke in the morning on the subject, "Is man part of the material system, subject to physical law or is he a separate creation?" In the evening his subject was, "The Man That Had a Good Beginning." Curiously the paper stated that the rear seats of the church are not to be used. Does that mean they were concerned that there might be low attendance and were encouraging people to sit up front?

Some additional sermon titles of Rev. Hull's in 1908, and far more captivating, were:

> March 22, morning service: "What Is Genuine and True Liberty?"
>
> March 22, evening service: "We Get Out of Life All that we Put Into It."
>
> April 12, morning service: "The Lifting UP of Christ."
>
> April 12, evening service: "Lessons Drawn from the Legend of King Arthur's Round Table."
>
> June 7, morning service: "What the Church is For."
>
> June 7, evening service: "A Tribute to Ulysses S. Grant and some Historical Facts about the Civil War and its Battles."
>
> June 15, morning service: "With Fire"

June 15, evening service: "My Companions, Who Shall They Be."

July 12, morning service: "The Difference Between the Artificial and Ideal in Life, or The True Act of Right Living."

July 12, evening service: "Hamlet and Lessons Drawn from the Great Tragedies and Dramas of Shakespeare."

Music was very important to Rev. Hull. At the July 12, 1908 service, he invited Lillian Gleason and Rosetta Hennessey of Boston to perform a viola and piano duet. Those two ladies were members of the Menwarment Hotel Orchestra in Boston. And then on Tuesday evening, August 12, Rev. Hull was a prime mover in bringing about a major summer concert. According to the *Boothbay Register*, "The Summer Concert of the Congregational Society held at the Pythian Opera House was a great success. Pastor George H. Hull had the matter in charge and with his well-known hustle and ability to get there, had assembled a program of visiting and resident talent that is seldom equaled." The performers included the Boston Ladies' Orchestra.

It also appears that Rev. Hull had a variety of musical interests, for the *Boothbay Register* also reported: "The new *Pentecostal Hymns* which were used last Sunday evening for the first time were received with much favor and the singing morning and evening was greatly enjoyed. The young men's singing in the evening did them credit."[537]

During Pastor Hull's time at the church, there was a close connection to Bowdoin College. The paper reported that he was hoping to get Professor Henry Chapman, D.D., of Bowdoin to give his inimitable lectures on Robert Burns—"he is one of the ablest lecturers of English Literature in New England and a most eloquent speaker," the paper stated.

Apparently on March 31, 1908, at 8:00 p.m., Professor C.C. Hutchins of Bowdoin College and his wife gave a "stereopticon lecture on a tour they had made of Austria and Germany. Professor

Hutchins was an instructor of chemistry and physics at Bowdoin and "one of the strongest men on the faculty." They had over 100 slides. To enable them to make their presentation on the equipment they wanted to use, the Honorable Luther Maddocks agreed to run electric wires into the church for the occasion. This may have been the first of a series of lectures sponsored by the Young Men's Club of the Congregational church. On May 18, Professor Woodruff and Professor Stone of Bowdoin presented a lecture on the subject "Ancient and Modern Athens." This lecture was used as a fundraiser. With his own academic and historical bent, Rev. Hull was preparing his own series of lectures on "Great Preachers and Statesmen of the last Century." Perhaps his lecture in June on U.S. Grant was one of those.

Rev. Hull did not isolate himself with his books all the time, however. In June 1908, the Congregational church held a Sunday School field day rally on the "south end ball grounds." Attendance was impressive. The paper reported that there were 125 present. The *Boothbay Register* went on to state, "Great credit is due our hustling and live pastor, George H. Hull, for his interesting work and interest for the young people."

Just when life at the church was picking up and in the prime of Rev. Hull's ministry in Boothbay he needed to resign and move away. The August 29, 1908 *Boothbay Register* stated:

> Rev. Hull deeply regrets leaving his parish and kind friends just at this time when his service is most needed with all the departments of the church; but his throat seems to be growing worse in this climate and it seems useless to fight against the elements. He has a warm place in his heart for all his parishioners especially those who have shown their sympathy and loyal support. He is preparing a farewell address to be delivered at the union service of the churches in his church on Sunday evening, September 13, subject "Some Impressions of Boothbay Harbor."[538]

From all reports Rev. Hull must have done an extraordinary job in the time that he served as pastor at the Congregational Church of Boothbay Harbor. When Rev. Hull left Boothbay he moved with his family to Seattle, Washington, where he hoped to find relief from his serious throat troubles. He apparently planned to pursue light agricultural work so that he could be out of doors much of the time along with limited ministerial duties in his new location.[539]

After Rev. Hull's departure, various people filled the pulpit: Rev. H.J. Newton of Bowdoin College, on October 18, and again in December along with Herbert Boyd on a different Sunday. Quite some time later, in March 1910, the Rev. F.M. Pickles "occupied the pulpit" as a candidate for the position of pastor. He apparently was highly spoken of, although he was not invited to become the church's settled pastor. A follow-up article in the *Boothbay Register* reported that he delivered two able sermons and:

> He is a ready speaker and intensely interesting as he gets warmed up to the heart of the subject he has at hand; sometimes sublimely eloquent in his portrayal of solid scriptural truths. He has 12 years of experience in ministry in the far Northwest.[540]

Rev. W. Stanley Post—1910–1915

On April 2, 1910, the Reverend Stanley Post of Ludlow led worship as a candidate. He was very well received by the large congregation that had gathered and was said to be "a ready, eloquent and polished speaker." A unanimous call was extended to him at the congregational meeting on Tuesday evening, April 5, 1910. Rev. Post accepted the call and began his duties as pastor of the church on the first Sunday of May 1910.

There were glowing reports of his work. On July 30, the *Boothbay Register* spoke about the previous Sunday as "another day of very interesting and well attended services at the Congregational Church." Of his sermon "Peculiar People," the assessment was that he handled it in a very able manner. And glowing reports of Rev. Post's August 15 sermon "Hereditary Piety" included these words from the local editor of the paper: "last Sunday at the Congregational Church there was an eloquent and interesting sermon." Another well-publicized sermon was delivered on September 13, 1910: "A Common Sense Letter to Common Sense Christians," based on James 1:1–27. On November 13, the service was shaped around observing World Temperance Sunday.

Other sermons of Rev. Post include:

August 16, 1914: "Odd-Job Christians."

June 6, 1915: "The Power of a Great Conviction" at the morning service.

June 6, 1915: "A Character Story of St. Paul" at the evening service.

On Christmas Day 1910, Rev. Post invited Rev. Fredrick Leavitt, president of the Franklin Academy in Nebraska, to preach. Rev. Leavitt's father had been the pastor of the church during the Civil War (1862–1864). Franklin Academy was a pioneer Congregational school west of the Missouri River on the frontier.[541]

It appears that the finances of the church were in good or perhaps increasingly better shape with the presence of Rev. Post. The report on the 1910 annual meeting states:

> The annual meeting of the Congregational parish was held Thursday. Hon A. R. Nickerson was chosen Moderator; B. S. Perkins Clerk; Wm. M. Smith, Treasurer; Irvin C. Kenniston, H. S. Perkins, Miss Mabel Smith, Committee. It was the unanimous vote of the meeting that Rev. Stanley Post be engaged another year, the salary to be raised by the same weekly envelope system. It was voted to increase his salary to twelve hundred dollars. The meeting adjourned for three weeks that

the committee might obtain subscriptions. The finances of the parish were reported in fine condition and the year will close, it is thought by Treasurer Smith, free of debt."

Rev. Post set high goals for his ministry, not least with regard to church attendance. On November 13, 1910 the *Boothbay Register* ran an article probably submitted by Rev. Post that "at last week's prayer service there were 18 women and 2 men in attendance. We were short by 16 men. Where were they? At social functions they are in evidence." Then, two months later, in January 1911 there was a follow-up: "The Congregational Church has a seating capacity of 340 adults. The pews are comfortable, rooms well ventilated, heated and lighted…Last Sunday evening we could have had three times as many people present. That means that there were 200 or more vacant seats. One half of the audience was men. We invite you to come again and to bring the other men with you."[542]

Rev. Post likely submitted these words to the paper on January 28, 1911: "We want the welfare of the church to become a topic of conversation in the home and upon the street." While Rev. Post's work must have been outstanding, unforeseen circumstances sometimes got in the way. The *Boothbay Register* reported on Saturday, November 9, 1912: "On account of needed repairs on the furnace the services at the Congregational Church Sabbath morning and evening will be held in the vestry."

Apparently Mrs. Post was quite capable in her own right:

> In the absence of the pastor Rev. W. Stanley Post, the pulpit at last Sunday's services at the Congregational church was occupied by Mrs. Post, who took for her morning theme, "The Still Small Voice" and delivered a most instructive sermon before a good-sized audience. In the evening, Mrs. Post led a song service, and although the congregation was not large, all appreciated fully the recital of interesting facts about many of the old songs, which have long been held in great favor.[543]

During those years, the Sunday School was quite active and was connected with organizations supporting its work. An article appeared about a Sunday School convention held at the church on November 10, 1914.

> *CONVENTION HERE. FINE PROGRAMS* at the Congregational church Tuesday afternoon and evening. The Southern District Convention of Lincoln County Sunday Schools will be held at the Congregational church on Thursday afternoon and evening next. There will be several out of town and local speakers [the local speakers were the pastors of Boothbay Harbor and Boothbay, Lyman M. McDougall, Esq., and Principal C. E. Merrill]. Hundreds of boys, aged 10 to 15 years, marched, accompanied by a cornet, from the Methodist church vestry to the Congregational church.[544]

Clearly, music was at the heart of worship at the Congregational church. On July 4, 1915, the *Boothbay Register* seemed impressed that there was an evening service with full orchestra and chorus. The chorus filled the choir loft to overflowing, and there was standing room only for those who arrived close to the hour. The service, with the accompaniment of the organ and large orchestra, made it "one long to be remembered." On August 16, 1914, the anthem accompanying the service was "Great We Beseech Thee" by W. Heaton, and a trio (Miss Wilkins and the Misses Chapman) performed excerpts from Mendelssohn's "Elijah."[545]

Over the decades covered by this chapter, there were so many different concerts held at the Congregational church that a separate chapter could be dedicated to the music and the musicians. Accessibility to Bowdoin College provided some of them, but musicians from far and wide lent their musical talents in concert with the local talents indigenous to Boothbay.

A special service took place on August, 29, 1915. "The Reverend Dr. Nathaniel W. Conkling, former pastor of the Rutgers Presbyterian church of New York City, was the guest minister of the

Congregational church on Sunday morning. Dr. Conkling was one of the oldest living alumni of Princeton University, a graduate of the Allegheny Theological Society, and a recipient of an honorary degree of divinity at the University of the City of New York. He had traveled extensively throughout Asia, Europe, and the Americas, and in the summer of 1914, he was in Switzerland at the outbreak of the Great War."

Eventually, it seems, all good things come to an end. And so a farewell service for Rev. Stanley Post was held at the end of August 1915. Rev. Post had accepted a call to the Biddeford Congregational church. According to the *Boothbay Register*, "The Congregation again heard two very able and interesting sermons; for Pastor Post is one of the best preachers we have ever had in this section."

The Laity and Pulpit Supply Ministers Carry the Church Forward—August 1915-1919

Life went on despite the loss of a very popular pastor. Not many details are available but on January 21, 1917, the Congregational church held a "Get Together Day." The morning sermon was "The Way To Be Happy." The evening address was "The Power of Friendliness." The weight of war began to be reflected in the sermons. The sermon on July 22, 1917 at the morning service was "The Conservation of Humanity." In the evening, the title was "Pan-Americanism."

Lay speakers were used at times in these years between ministers. The *Boothbay Register* indicated that on September 1, 1918, "one of our boys, Willis Moore, will speak at a Union service. He is doing valiant work among the great army of labor. Since the 1st of June he has addressed 35,000 men weekly in shipyards and shops. His job is to help the men to connect their jobs with the winning of this war as the only thing that counts today."

Since the heart of church life for Congregationalists had been for some time in the Harbor, it was not surprising that the first Congregational church, located in Boothbay center, was no longer used for services. On May 23, 1919, the church at Boothbay center was transferred to the town for $1 for use as a school house.

Vacationing clergypersons continued to be a help to the Harbor churches. On August 15, 1919, the *Boothbay Register* noted that "Boothbay Harbor is fortunate in having many distinguished clergymen who spend their vacations in this vicinity. These men are generous and kind in giving up a part of their time by preaching; let us show appreciation by filling the church to overflowing on August 17, 1919, when Dr. Nies of Worcester, Massachusetts will be preaching." On August 24, the Rev. Herbert Woodin of Brattleboro, Vermont was to preach. Soon thereafter Dr. William Scudder of New York preached at a morning service, and in the evening Professor William Stearns Davis of the University of Minnesota delivered an address.

Rev. Walter P. Bradford—1919-1922

From August of 1915 until 1917, there is no evidence of a settled pastor at the Boothbay Harbor Congregational church. The Maine Conference minutes of 1917 contain this notation: "Boothbay Harbor Church is happy with the Rev. Walter P. Bradford who recently left the church at Bristol for that in Boothbay Harbor." But then on April 14, 1919, the church authorized a search process for a minister. Is it possible Bradford left for a short time? By September 19, however, the *Boothbay Register* noted: "Rev. W.P. Bradford is expected home today from Rutland, Vermont and unless further notice is given, there will be services at the Congregational Church next Sunday as usual." Then it was reported that Rev. and Mrs. Bradford have announced the birth of a son, Walter P. Bradford, Jr., in Rutland Vermont. Perhaps they had returned to Rutland for some reason for the birth of a second child.[546]

October 28, 1919 marked the beginning of a series of evangelistic services, which were held alternately between the Congregational and the Methodist churches. These services were led by two Salvation Army workers along with the local pastors.

November 9, 1919, was Armistice Sunday. The sermon title was "The War's Aftermath?" The preacher was not specified. This would have marked the one-year anniversary of the Armistice signed on November 11, 1918.

The Work of the Women

Scattered throughout the local newspaper are numerous references to the work of the women of the church. Often they were doing fundraisers for various church projects or as part of the church's mission elsewhere. Interestingly, in the middle of the time period where little else is mentioned in the *Boothbay Register* about the church in general, there is an extensive article about the Dorcas Guild. It seems to have been a very active women's group for many years. The March 11, 1911 edition of the *Boothbay Register* reported:

> The entertainment given by the Dorcas Guild last Friday evening in Townsend Hall was a success financially and socially. The illustrated songs were exceptionally good, the "Ten Little Indians" picture calling forth loud applause as the ten tiny children dressed as Indians marched around the stage until there was only "one little Indian" left, the smallest of all, Reginald Orne, who gave the soldier salute and took his departure. The readings by Mrs. Post were excellent, as was Mr. Hammond's mirth-provoking story. Mr. Post as usual, made interesting remarks and the selections by the male quartet were excellent and loudly applauded. Wylie's orchestra furnished good music. The entertainment was followed by a food and candy sale.[547]

Then, barely a month later, on Friday April 7, at 8:00 p.m., the Ladies Mandolin Club presented a musicale at the Congregational church as a benefit for the church. Men's, women's and mixed quartets, along with readings, were the substance of the event. Following the program a social hour was held, where homemade candies were for sale. Admission was 25 cents.

The work of the Dorcas Guild continued through the years and is described in some more extended articles, but often in just a brief reference like this one in 1917: "The Dorcas Guild will meet with Mrs. Mary Kenniston Monday evening and the Junior Guild will meet with Mrs. William Simpson."[548] Sewing circles, social gatherings, and numerous fundraisers for various projects around the church and beyond peppered across these years with references to women's meetings and to the work of the church for which the women were responsible.

Conclusion

During the period from 1893 to 1919 there were clearly some outstanding pastors, a very active laity, significant progress in the upkeep and improvement of the church facilities as well as the church parsonage, improvement to organizational structure, a vital music program, a very active women's group, and indications of active youth programming. Both nurture and mission seemed to be cultivated. During this period, the life of the church caught the attention of the local paper on numerous occasions. Perhaps no endorsement could have been stronger than the one that appeared in the January 21, 1917, *Boothbay Register,* where the editor said of the congregation "the church's aim is to make its life a practical expression of the religious ideal interpreted in the terms of everyday life, to relate itself to the community and wider interests and to make its influence felt during the seven days of the week."[549] It seems clear that amidst all the radical changes of industrialization, theological tremors, the horrors of war, disruption in community life, changing social patterns and the stresses of significant changes in family life, the church was able to chart a successful course and be a beacon of light in the community. The numbers may have been down at times, but a faithful witness continued, and the stage was set for the coming years.

CHAPTER 9

TOUGH TIMES AND GOOD TIMES: 1919–1941
by Robert W. Dent

Introduction

The third and fourth decades of the twentieth century were pivotal ones. The 1920s were a time of economic progress for many. Transportation, new conveniences, electricity, refrigeration, communication, the radio, entertainment—all of these created a new climate. Along with progress came some social tensions. And the economic bubble of the 1920s burst in the 1930s with the Great Depression. Indeed these were tough and transitional times. The Boothbay region and the Boothbay Harbor Congregational church were affected, but certainly not in the same way as were the large cities or those communities without some of Boothbay's special assets such as shipbuilding and strong tourism. So while Boothbay shared many of the stresses and strains of changing times, as well as looming and sometimes real financial challenges, life in Boothbay also enjoyed some very good times. People from near and far found solace from the sea and beautiful shoreline, and there were increased opportunities for social interaction at the Strand movie theater, at the Pavilion (a gathering place for youth), and at the Opera House, all of which provided numerous opportunities for young and old to come together for various events. The Congregational church reflected many of the social, economic, and to some degree the theological changes that impacted America in the era 1919 to 1941.

All of this also meant that the region was no longer isolated from the rest of the world. Gaustad and Schmidt in their religious history of America declared that "in the last two decades of the nineteenth century and the first four of the twentieth, the United States entered upon the world stage in a way that had not been true in the first century of her history as a nation...and rediscovered the Monroe Doctrine. The United States had come of age as a global power." [550] Some churches responded to globalization as a calling or an opportunity for expanding missionary activity. In 1919, Robert E. Speer was one of the strong voices contending that missionaries should go forward in greater numbers and with greater boldness to help heal the wounds of war and to counteract the political imperialism of the time.[551] By 1922, about $750,000 in special offerings were sent from United States churches to China. As part of the mission focus, Protestants operated 219 kindergartens, 700 elementary schools, and over 300 high schools in this country and around the world. And in 1923, the American Bible Society sent 20,000 Bibles to China. [552]

By the mid–1920s, missionary thinking began to shift slightly. In part, with the work of E. Stanley Jones in India, questions were raised about culturally imperialist assumptions behind the missionary movement. As a result, mission thinking shifted toward mutuality in missions that emphasized enlisting the cooperation of indigenous populations in the development of mission projects. By 1932 a more dramatic shift in thinking was introduced by William E. Hocking of Harvard. In his report entitled *Rethinking Missions: A Layman's Inquiry After One Hundred Years*, he suggested that while the missionary enterprise began with the attempt to save souls, missionaries had been drawn into efforts to strengthen minds and bodies and to improve the social life with which these souls were engaged. The report recommended "a greater emphasis on education and welfare, transfer of power to local groups, less reliance on evangelizing, with respectful appreciation for local religions. And it was also recommended that missionary efforts in the United States be reorganized for better coordination, working toward a single organization for Protestant missions."[553] As a result, main line denominations shifted more toward an educational and social emphasis, while evangelical denominations picked up the traditional evangelizing.

These were also major pivotal years for theology. Comparing the first two decades of the twentieth century with the second two, there was a seismic shift within theology. And, as with missions, some of that shift was felt in Boothbay Harbor, stimulated by the presence periodically of the nationally known Reverend Harry Emerson Fosdick. Reflections of those changes are also evident in the life of the Congregational church and in the sermons of the ministers of those times.

Changes in the Theological Landscape

At the end of the nineteenth century and into the era of the First World War, theology was strongly influenced by a liberal movement that was fed by a spirit of optimism initiated by Friederich Schleiermacher, pursued by Walter Rauschenbusch, and also associated with Washington Gladden. The Social Gospel movement was a Protestant enterprise prominent in the late nineteenth and early twentieth century in the United States and Canada. It applied Christian ethics to social problems, especially to issues of social justice such as economic inequality, poverty, alcoholism, crime, racial tensions, slums, unclean environment, child labor, inadequate labor unions, poor schools, and the danger of war. Theologically, Social Gospel adherents sought to operationalize the Lord's Prayer (Matthew 6:10): "Thy kingdom come, Thy will be done on earth as it is in heaven."[554]

Many women identified with the movement. People like Jane Addams and her companion Ellen Gates Starr may have been motivated by the movement to found the Hull House settlement in 1889 as a center for social services for poor immigrants in Chicago.[555] The Social Gospel movement made a positive impact on both the Church and the world by responding to human suffering and by trying to make a difference for those who were hurting.

Nevertheless, the movement's tenet that the Second Coming could not happen until humankind rid itself of social evils by human effort, along with disillusionment accompanying World War I, led to the Social Gospel's being viewed with skepticism in the succeeding neo-orthodoxy era.

In 1918, when Karl Barth, usually identified as the founder of the Neo-Orthodox movement, published the first edition of his "Shorter Commentary on Paul's Letter to the Romans," the tide began to turn. In his commentary and in subsequent revisions, Barth broke with liberalism and asserted that the God who is revealed in the cross of Jesus challenges and overthrows any attempt to ally God with human cultures, achievements, or possessions. He re-emphasized Paul's claim that "we are saved by grace alone." Barth's commentary was the first volley in a theological battle that would change the landscape of much of religious thought for the rest of the twentieth century. Barth's influence was first made apparent in his challenge of the then popular theological liberalism and what was sometimes perceived as Schleiermacher's "feel good-do good" theology. The Social Gospel however, reappeared in the Civil Rights movement and in the Theology of Liberation, although perhaps readjusted by Barth's corrective lenses.

The year 1919 was a time of turmoil in many ways. That was the year of the Chicago race riots. The Russian Revolution led to concerns over the effects of radical political agitation in American society. The alleged spread of communism and anarchism in the American labor movement generated a general sense of paranoia. The Volstead Act was debated in Congress, and the eighteenth amendment to the Constitution was passed on 10 October 1919, making prohibition the law of the land. Although typically associated with the South and with prejudice against African Americans, the Ku Klux Klan surfaced in Maine about this time. "With a negligible African-American population but a burgeoning number of French-Canadian and Irish immigrants, the Klan revival of the 1920s [in Maine] was chiefly a Protestant movement directed against the Catholic minority."[556] In *The Great Gatsby*, F. Scott

Fitzgerald exposed the excesses of the 1920s, a prosperous age in which many Americans came to enjoy the blessings of consumerism and excess, only to see it all crash around them with the Great Depression that arrived in 1929.[557] The "Spanish influenza" devastated many communities in 1918 and 1919.

Of course, what was taking place in the world also had an impact on Boothbay. Influenza struck in Boothbay Harbor and environs as elsewhere. As noted by co-author Chip Griffin, "In the winter of 1918–1919, about 20 million people, including 500,000 Americans, died due to that deadly disease. [During that time period] the *Boothbay Register* reported 'eleven dead in two weeks, the most in memory for such a short period of time.'"[558] Alberta Poole Rowe told Chip Griffin about losing her sister Josephine to that epidemic. Alberta was nine and her sister eleven. She said, "Old Doctor Gregory came with medicine, and someone took her [Josephine] to the hospital. That's the last time I saw her. She was taken to the hospital, and she was running the corridors. There were too many sick, and they just couldn't take care of her…In the Woodward House, we'd look out at the wooden cart drawn by a horse with four or five dead bodies piled in the back, being brought back home. No one could help you because they didn't dare to. We were like rats, shut in, and nobody could help us sick people."[559]

Pastoral Leadership Through the Ups and Downs

Between 1919 and 1939, there were seven ministers who served the Congregational Church of Boothbay Harbor. Who were they and how did they process the changes we have noted?

Rev. Walter P. Bradford—1919–1922

As reported in chapter 8 of this book, the Reverend Walter P. Bradford had served the Congregational church in Bristol prior to coming to Boothbay in 1919. He appears to have served successfully as minister in the Congregational church for about three years, although the ending date of his ministry in Boothbay is difficult to pin down with any precision. Reference is made to his discussing proposed new bylaws at the April 28, 1922 parish meeting.[560] Nevertheless, a year later the notes of the parish meeting state that the parish was voting on raising money for a pulpit supply, indicating that Mr. Bradford had moved out of Boothbay.[561] Another small mystery relates to the Bradfords' announcement while living in Boothbay of the birth of their son Walter P. Jr. in Rutland, Vermont. What their Rutland connection was is not clear.

The titles of a number of Rev. Bradford's sermons are rather intriguing: "Two Great Fundamentals of Life," delivered on March 19, 1920; "The Common People," on Oct. 14, 1921; and "The New Christian Internationalism," on Nov 11, 1921. Perhaps the latter sermon was inspired by Robert E. Speer or other people from the missionary movement.

Evening services during Rev. Bradford's time were quite varied. Some were filled with music as on March 21, 1920. It was a praise service, with music provided by an orchestra. The subject of the evening sermon was, "A Review of J. M. Keynes' book: *The Economic Consequences of Peace*.[562] The book was written and published by John Maynard Keynes, who attended the post World War I Versailles Conference, where, as a delegate of the British treasury, he argued for a generous peace. The book was a best seller throughout the world and was critical in establishing a general opinion that the Versailles Treaty was a "Carthaginian," that is, a brutal peace."[563]

Another evening service, on December 5, 1920, had a strong musical emphasis. The *Boothbay Register* suggested that "this would be an unusual service: The Rock of Ages, a beautiful illustrated lecture, combining three special features, Story, Song and Sermon…The scenes represent the storm, lightning and rainbow in dissolving effect, shipwreck and safe on the Rock of Ages. The views furnish opportunity for old familiar hymns, which are sung with effect as the story-sermon moves on. One or more of the hymns will be sung as solos, with orchestral accompaniment." The article concluded: "You cannot afford to miss this service," and added, "Good Sundays make good Mondays."[564]

On May 29, 1921, an evening service featured "Boothbay's own Austin McCormick," as the *Boothbay Register* proudly stated. During this service McCormick shared his experiences as associate director of the Naval Penitentiary in Portsmouth, NH. The subject of his address was "From the Scrap-heap to the Repair Shop."

While Rev. Bradford was pastor, the following editorials appeared in the paper, likely reflecting the feelings of the local clergy at that time:

> Great statesmen, churchmen and even those who do not take a very active part in religious work have said that there can be no real Christianity until man is brought to realize that he is but a steward of God; that everything he possesses, wealth and even life itself comes from God as a sacred trust, and that some day he must account for all that has been entrusted to him.[565]
>
> Let one fact in regard to religious education be burned into the minds of parents and church leaders: that a church or a home that cannot save its own children cannot save the world. Let us place greater emphasis on religious instruction.
>
> Fathers and Mothers! That boy of yours is trying to walk in his father's footsteps. You want him honest, truthful and fair. Where can he learn these virtues better than in the home and in Sunday school? "Why should I go to Church or Sunday School while Dad stays at home?" Many a youth has asked himself this. Take him to church. Give him the best moral foundation. He will go to church most willingly if you go also.[566]

Whoever wrote those articles, they resonate with the good intentions of President Wilson, son of a Presbyterian minister, for whom moral issues were paramount and who sometimes spoke about wanting "to save the world."

On November 6, 1921, Rev. Bradford invited the Reverend Dr. Peter MacQueen to conduct an evening program. Of this service the *Boothbay Register* reported, "The big audience which filled the Congregational Church again thoroughly enjoyed Dr. Peter MacQueen's great lecture on Japan and reporting his travels through Japan. His apt expressions pleased and he kept the audience in good nature throughout, which is half the battle of interesting. The pictures illustrated the exceptionally interesting lecture. The rest of the service of the evening was of song. Dr. MacQueen had been a well-known lecturer on the Chautauqua circuit and had spent seven years as the pastor in West Somerville, Mass." More will be said about him subsequently, as in early 1923 he became the called pastor of the Congregational Church of Boothbay Harbor.

Throughout the Bradford years and beyond, the women of the church were very active, with frequent reports in the paper. For example, the Dorcas Guild met at the home of Miss Anna B. Kendrick on a Wednesday afternoon and at Mrs. B. E. Kelley's home on another occasion. The Priscillas met on a Monday evening at the home of Mrs. Helen Lewis. Likely as a result of the work of one of the women's groups, a harvest supper at the Congregational church vestry was announced by the *Register* on Thursday, Nov. 17, 1921. The paper said to expect: "All the usual good things that go with a real harvest supper." The trend of women taking a leading role in the life of the Church would continue and eventually expand, culminating with the ordination of women. Women had received the right to vote only in 1920, and the church was sometimes one of the few places where women were given the opportunity to lead in public.[567]

Building improvements were part of the Bradford years. At the annual parish meeting in April 1920, it was voted to apply any funds received from the sale of the old organ toward new light fixtures. In October 1922, a meeting was called to discuss installing a new wood furnace. The agent responsible said that the furnace had been overhauled and repaired, and it was voted to try to get along without installing a new one that winter. About that time, the Dorcas Guild donated new chairs for the vestry. Modest attempts to improve the building show that money was tight. Following World War I, the economy nationally slipped into a serious recession. Boothbay and Boothbay Harbor had wartime shipbuilding contracts in WWI, as they would in WWII. However, in 1922 finances were a concern.

A very active congregation undertook a very ambitious program, which was presented on Monday evening, Feb. 21, 1923. It was a fundraiser to help purchase a new pipe organ. A cast of eighty people produced the "Pageant of Pilgrims." It was presented by the church at the Opera House. The *Boothbay Register* reported "This Pageant has been given recently in large cities—Brooklyn, N.Y., Providence, R.I., and other cities."[568]

A notable polity effort on the part of Rev. Bradford is reflected at the April 28, 1922, annual parish meeting. The pastor was asked to open the meeting with prayer (first time noted in these records). A new set of bylaws was presented. The bylaws appear to have been entitled or based on: "the Modern Church Organization and Parish System."[569] The bylaws were tabled, and a committee of three was appointed to study them and report back at a subsequent meeting. Nothing further is mentioned about this action in minutes for the remainder of the year. But presumably Rev. Bradford was instrumental in getting the leaders and congregation to think more about the need for orderliness in the conduct of the business of the church by way of clarifying and abiding by the bylaws.

These years must have kept the pastor quite busy. It was reported that many people in town had been on the sick list in 1922, the last year of his tenure in Boothbay. And then the face of war came home once again with the headlines of the paper on May 27: "Ready for Memorial Day—Program Complete for the Events of the Day"; "First of Soldier Dead—Body of Irving Sherman Arrives in Edgecomb and Military Funeral Held."[570]

Rev. Dr. Peter MacQueen—1923-1924

The ministry of the Congregational church was assumed by a long-term summer preacher and resident of East Boothbay, the Reverend Dr. Peter MacQueen, who accepted a call to the church in 1923 and was pastor until his sudden death less than a year later in Jan-

Rev. Dr. Peter MacQueen

uary 1924. The May 1, 1923, parish minutes[571] speak of raising money for a pulpit supply and of repairing the parsonage, but do not mention Dr. MacQueen specifically. Perhaps the arrangements to call him were made after this meeting.

Dr. MacQueen came to the church with quite a record. He had given 2,000 lectures in New England alone. The goal for his ministry in Boothbay was to build up the Sunday school and start a Boy Scout Troop and a Camp Fire Group. He once said, "there are as many elements of culture and idealism on 'Main Street' as there are in Broadway. In fact all that is best on Broadway came from Main Street. The small town should have as able men as the metropolis to lead the rising generation of youth in the country, because these men [youth] in the country will eventually own and control the big cities." Obviously, feminism had not yet impacted the use of exclusive masculine language; however, Sinclair Lewis' 1920 novel *Main Street* may have struck some chords with MacQueen.

Perhaps the good record Dr. MacQueen had and the impression he made upon the congregation prompted the action taken at the May annual parish meeting: it was voted to raise the support of preaching to $1,600 and to make necessary repairs to the parsonage. In 1919, the pastor's salary was $1,000. While the economy of Boothbay may not have improved greatly in 1923, MacQueen's preaching and pastoral leadership may have motivated the congregation to dig deeper and give more.

A glimpse into the life of the church in December 1923 shows that the church members gave a splendid performance of Dickens's "Christmas Carol." Dr. MacQueen read a touching Christmas story, translated from the French, called "François." This must have been a very special Christmas for the congregation.

The joy the congregation experienced with the prestigious leadership of Dr. MacQueen was abruptly interrupted. On January 11, 1924, Dr. MacQueen died very suddenly. He was attending a banquet at the Hotel Weymouth[572] when he died. The *Boothbay Register* said of him:

> He was a world-famed traveler, lecturer, war correspondent and author. His death shortly following his happy participation in a banquet at the Hotel Weymouth on Thursday evening has shocked the whole community." His heart attack started just before he was going to make a speech at this banquet. He had 2 very severe heart attacks in the past 18 months, one at Dr. Fernald's Hall at East Boothbay and the other while bathing at Murray Hill, and he had experienced less severe heart attacks during this period as well. [This was the rationale for his accepting the pastorate at the Congo Church in September 1923, as he should no longer travel widely in his speaking engagements.] The work and plans of Dr. and Mrs. MacQueen for the church were fast maturing and perhaps never before had the activities of this church been so cheerfully and earnestly entered into by all. For the moment the people of the church are stunned. The whole community in this section is stricken by the loss of this man.
>
> Dr. MacQueen is well known to our readers and to the whole world and more than a brief sketch of his career is unnecessary. He was born in Scotland on January 11, 1863 and would have been 61 years of age had he lived but a few hours longer. He came to America in 1881 and was graduated from Princeton University in 1887 and from Union Theological Seminary in 1890. His first church was at Bronxville, New York. He was later called to the West Somerville, Massachusetts Congregational Church. In 1898 he was with Roosevelt in Santiago in the Spanish War, for Leslie's Weekly. In 1900 he was in the Philippines, and later produced his first book, *Tramping in the Philippines*.

In 1901, Dr. MacQueen accepted a call to the Harvard Church in Charlestown, Mass, where he remained until 1908, when he went to Central Africa for explorations. He later produced his second successful book, *In Wildest Africa*, which later was used by British army officers as a guidebook of the wilds of Africa in the Boer War. He joined the Boer Army in South Africa in their war against England, as a war correspondent. He later performed important service for our government in making reports to President Roosevelt on the Panama and Venezuela sections. In 1911 he was a war correspondent in the battles between Madera and Diaz in Mexico. Further travels took him through Russia, where he was accorded signal honors through his friendship with the Czar and Tolstoy. He was in Turkey when the World War broke out and was a prisoner, released through friendship of an officer after his death had been decreed. He reached France in time to join Marshall Foch at the First Battle of the Marne. In 1919 he reported the Peace Conference for *Leslie's Weekly*.[573]

Dr. MacQueen had given close to 3,000 travel lectures and his work in the Chautauqua circuit was in great demand. He had lectured in every state but two in the Union and in many other English-speaking countries." His funeral service was held at the Congregational Church in Boothbay Harbor on January 13, 1924, at 2 PM, led by the Wiscasset Congregational Church minister and the Boothbay Harbor Methodist minister, with interment at Ocean View Cemetery in Boothbay.

The Congo Church was filled to capacity. Only a small number of his friends were able to attend. His wife had received a flood of telegrams and letters. Dr. MacQueen had prepared a funeral for that Sunday: "Faithful unto the End." Pallbearers were Richard Matthews Hallet, famed local author and writer [who co-author Chip Griffin remembers lived on Atlantic Avenue just across from Road's End]; Benjamin E. Kelley [who co-author Chip Griffin believes was the publisher of the *Boothbay*

Register]; Dr. George S. Nevins, who had tried to save Dr. MacQueen [Dr. Gregory was too late in arriving]; and K. Weston Farnham.[574]

Whether it was the legacy of Dr. MacQueen or not, the Congregational church almost always headed the list of churches in the *Boothbay Register* in 1924, though not always in 1926. The other places of worship at the time were the Methodist Episcopal Church, Boothbay Baptist Church, East Boothbay Methodist Church, and Southport Methodist Episcopal Church. The church calendar for a given week in the *Boothbay Register* might well include the Junior Guild, Dorcas Guild, Abenaki Boys Club, and Pomona Club, all meeting at the Congregational church.

And whether it was the legacy of the Scots-Irish influence in the region or of Dr. MacQueen, on January 11, 1924 the *Boothbay Register* ran this article, entitled "Scotch and English: Four separate wrecks had cast up four men on a lonely island of the South seas. There were two Scotchmen and two Englishmen. After several years a passing steamer hove to and took the four men aboard. Sandy and Donald found their way to the skipper's cabin and in telling their experiences Sandy said 'It would grieve you, mon, to see the Englishmen. Never a word did they speak all the time they were there; they were not introduced.' 'And hoo did ye lads muck oot?' inquired the skipper. 'Aye, mon, the dee I found Donald on the beach we organized a Caledonian society, a golf club and a Presbyterian church.'"—*Cappen's Weekly*."[575]

Rev. George H. Woodward—1924

The Reverend George Woodward began his pastorate March 9, 1924, after delivering a series of successful sermons as a candidate over the previous weeks. He and his wife had five children ranging in age from nine to nineteen. He made a "very fine impression on his hearers...and was making friends rapidly in town," according to the *Boothbay Register*, which also said, "It is hoped and confidently believed that a preacher of his power and sincerity will have no difficulty carrying forward the work of the church effectively and in keeping up that strong interest in its activities which the short pastorate of the late Reverend Peter MacQueen had wonderfully kindled."

Rev. Woodward was born in Winthrop, Maine and had always lived and worked in this state. He graduated from Winthrop High School and Fryeburg Academy, then attended Colby College for two years, and graduated from Bangor Seminary in 1897. In that year he was ordained a Congregational minister. His pastorates had been in Princeton, South Freeport, Phillips, South Bridgton, and in Denmark—all in Maine. Around March 27, he moved the family to the parsonage in Boothbay.

Unfortunately, few of his sermons were reported in the paper. However, on March 30, 1924, The *Boothbay Register* listed one of them: "Back to the Blanket." A review of current events in early 1924 provides little help in uncovering the content or concern of this sermon.

The ecumenical tradition so evident in Boothbay was continued under Rev. Woodward. On May 30, 1924, he and the congregation hosted a Union Memorial Day service at the Congregational church. Rev. Woodward delivered the address. He took as his theme "America's Part in the World's History" and declared that "a divine providence had decreed that America should not be discovered until religious wars were nearing the end and not strongly settled until the persecutions of the Pilgrims had led them to seek a new land where they might have a freedom of thinking and worshiping not granted to Europe. From the Pilgrims and the Puritans had been born our hope of liberty…" He then reviewed the wars in which the United States had been engaged and said that "in some of these the might was against our country, but the right was with us." He characterized the Mexican War as the only shameful warlike effort ever participated in by the United States—a war seeking more land for slave states.

However, on August 10, 1924, once again the Boothbay Harbor Congregational church experienced a tragedy. After another short-term pastorate, the church lost its pastor to sudden death. Rev. George H. Woodward died that Sunday morning: He was the second pastor the Congregational church had lost within eight months. According to the *Boothbay Register*, Rev. Woodward, who had been pastor since March 9 "at the age of 54 passed away quickly at the parsonage, on Sunday about six o'clock following a heart attack which came on during Saturday when he was in his strawberry patch. He had been born March 18, 1870. His funeral service was at his prior pastorate, in Denmark, ME."

Rev. Woodward was said to be "a student of modern political life and kept well versed in social problems." His sermons were most interesting and helpful…His short pastorate in Boothbay had won him high esteem, both as a citizen and as a pastor. He was described as a tireless worker, unsparing on himself, attempting things for which he should have asked for assistance.[576]

Rev. Woodward or the deacons of the church invited Rev. Dr. Harry Emerson Fosdick to preach in the summer of 1924. In 1923 Fosdick had delivered the Lyman Beecher Lecture at Yale entitled "The Modern Use of the Bible." The following year, those lectures were published in book form. "The book focused on modern biblical scholarship, linguistic, historical, and archaeological, persuasively arguing to many Protestants the contemporary relevance of the Bible. Fosdick believed in his earlier years that the Church was a moral community that cultivated the only force that could ever morally transform society…The mission of the Church was to nourish the development of personality and redeem the world through the care and idealism of morally regenerated communities."[577] Fosdick's interest in the development of personality is reflected in his book, *On Being a Real Person*, where Fosdick attempts to integrate psychiatry and religion in ways that could help the individual achieve his or her greatest potential.

The Evangelical Dictionary of Theology says of Fosdick that he "was one of the most influential clergymen of the first half of the twentieth century. He was among the major popularizers of modern theological liberalism…He greatly influenced preaching through his problem-centered theological style."[578] Not surprisingly, the *Boothbay Register* ran this article on August 8, 1924:

> DR. FOSDICK PREACHES NOTABLE SERMON: NEW YORK DIVINE AND SUMMER VISITOR HAS OVERFLOWING CONGREGATION: "The 10:45 service...was to include a sermon by Rev. Dr. Harry Emerson Fosdick of New York, a summer resident of Mouse Island...The chancel and vestry were filled, many sitting on the steps of the altar, in the choir loft, and in the chairs placed in the aisles, while hundreds stood in the side aisles and at the rear of the pews and filled the vestibule. Some unable to get near enough to hear the sermon, remained outside on the lawn to await members of the family who got inside.
>
> [Rev. Fosdick] carried a message to the congregation that will not soon pass from memory...[Christ's] approach to a personal problem was like that of a stranger in a boat approaching an island. He rowed around it all and found the best place to land. Christ rowed around every problem and found the spot to touch at and landed there.
>
> He urged his hearers to find the spots where they should change their ways of living that they might make life more abundant for those about them; forget grudges and wrongs in bringing richer life to others. Dr. Fosdick said doctrines were experiences translated: that if Jesus should come upon earth today and find the churches with their narrow boundary lines and rules he would look out as of old for primary individual needs and seek to make life more abundant. There are 40 different denominations and there is no reason for any of them. Jesus would say, 'Nothing of all this matters.'"[579]

In October 1924, the *Boothbay Register* published an extended article about Dr. Fosdick's famous resignation on May 21, 1922, from the pulpit of the First Presbyterian Church in New York City: "Dr. Fosdick has been the center of a storm for some time," said the *Boothbay Register*. "He is a free thinker and entirely unafraid to express his views. In the furor over the Fundamentalists he has been attacked from various sides. An ordained Baptist preacher with modernist views, he has been for several years filling the pulpit of the very important Presbyterian Church. Now the New York City Presbytery requests that in accordance with a ruling of the General Assembly five months ago, Dr. Fosdick should renounce his Baptist membership and become a Presbyterian...Many who heard Dr. Fosdick's sermon at the Congregational Church here last summer will feel that in a way the remarks Dr. Fosdick then made were prophetic of this later event."[580]

In New York, on that May Sunday he had delivered his famous sermon, "Shall the Fundamentalists Win?" in which he presented the Bible as a record of the unfolding of God's will, not as the literal "Word of God." He saw the history of Christianity as one of development, progress, and gradual change. To fundamentalists, this was rank apostasy.

Rev. Dr. Harry Emerson Fosdick

Guest preachers in Boothbay must have found it a daunting task to follow Harry Emerson Fosdick's presence there. Some of the ministers who supplied the pulpit at that time were no slouches themselves, however. Among them were: Dr. Charles H. Beale of Milwaukee, whom the *Boothbay Register* called "the most noted preacher of the Mississippi Valley" and a frequent summer guest preacher at the Boothbay Harbor Congregational church. In the 1920s he was pastor emeritus of the Grand Avenue Congregational church in Milwaukee. The *Boothbay Register* even described him as one of the country's most distinguished preachers and referred to him as being widely known, having filled many preaching and speaking engagements outside his own church. Other guests included Rev. Horace H. Hayes, of Providence Rhode Island.[581]

In the midst of growth in theological inquiry and frequent very forward-looking guest preachers at the Boothbay Congregational Church, on the national scene there was a reactionary, constrictive, orthodox response to new scholarship in science and theology. It found a voice in the Scopes trial, a famous American legal case, the first day of which was July 10, 1925. Perhaps coincidentally, that case followed soon after Fosdick delivered his Beecher Lectures at Yale on the Bible. John Scopes was a substitute high school teacher, who was accused of violating Tennessee's Butler Act, which made it unlawful to teach human evolution in any state-funded school. Scopes was found guilty and fined $100 (equivalent to $1,345 in 2014), but the verdict was overturned on a technicality. The trial drew intense national publicity, as national reporters flocked to Dayton to cover the big-name lawyers who had agreed to represent each side. William Jennings Bryan argued for the prosecution, while Clarence Darrow, the famed defense attorney, spoke for Scopes. This trial was the beginning of major theological battles between what were beginning to be called fundamentalists and modernists. The latter did not see evolution as necessarily inconsistent with religion. But the fundamentalists insisted that the word of God as revealed in the Bible took priority over all human knowledge. The issue could be crystallized in questions like: Is the Bible intended to be a scientific textbook? Is God big enough to include the possibility that evolution could be part of God's creative process?"

Meanwhile, despite the sudden deaths of two of their own ministers, life went on in Boothbay in the mid–1920s. Some families were concerned about the negative effect of the movie house on young people. Bootlegging had become an issue. Chip Griffin's book *I'm Different* about the life of Ethelyn Giles, highlights the latter problem with delightful tales of Ethelyn helping the government track down stills. It's clear that Boothbay posed some interesting challenges for a new minister.

Another major change occurred at the church prior to the Scopes trial. On September 19, 1924 there was a special meeting of the parish. The resignation of Henry Perkins as parish clerk was accepted, and a note of thanks extended to him for his 21 years of faithful service from 1904 to 1924—a notable achievement. He had been a remarkable member and leader of the church over those decades. Along with his family, Perkins was about to move out of the area. Millicent Maddocks was then elected as clerk. At that same meeting the question was raised about obtaining the services of a pastor. A vote was taken to purchase the coal in the cellar of the parsonage belonging to Mrs. MacQueen, and the treasurer was instructed to pay her what it was worth.

In the spring of 1925, the Dorcas Guild was given permission to redecorate the interior of the church. A committee was appointed to get samples of carpet and report to the guild. Another committee was appointed to get estimates on the painting of the ceiling and walls of the church and vestry. In April, a vote was passed to accept the report of the painting committee on estimates for the walls and ceiling and to authorize the work. It was also voted to buy a fabric carpet and to have a candidate preacher come as soon as could be arranged.

During this interim period the church benefited from the will of Archer W. Hodgdon, who bequeathed the sum of $100 annually to the Congregational church for twenty years. His estate also gave $5,000 to the Boothbay Harbor Memorial Library.[582]

Rev. William G. Kirschbaum, Jr.—1925–1928

On Easter Sunday, April 12, 1925, Rev. William Kirschbaum, then a candidate for the position of pastor, preached two sermons—one in the morning and one in the evening. Apparently, he was very well received. Prior to his coming to Boothbay, Rev. Kirschbaum had been the chaplain at the National Soldiers' Home in Togus. He came highly recommended. Following morning worship, a concert was presented by the Sunday school. Mrs. Millicent Maddocks held an informal tea at her home at four in the afternoon so that many might meet Mr. Kirschbaum informally. About thirty attended. There seemed to be a consensus that the church should endeavor to secure his services as pastor. On April 20, the parish voted to hire Rev. Kirschbaum at a salary of $1,800. At the same meeting it was voted without explanation to mortgage the parsonage for $1,000.[583] That would seem to be a drastic decision, suggesting that finances were still tight or that the needs were bigger than the budget.

Rev. Kirschbaum began his Boothbay Harbor pastorate on July 1, 1925, which is when his wife and three children moved to town. Quite popular, especially with young people, he attracted new members. The local newspaper reported, "These two young pastors [Rev. Kirschbaum and Rev. L.D. Porter of the Methodist church] are doing much excellent work in their churches and in the community—both earnest workers and excellent preachers."

The church trustees of this time made some major improvements during the spring and summer of 1925. At a meeting on April 20, it was voted to allow the carpet committee to show samples of carpet to the members of the parish after the supper to be held on April 24. A decision was made to repair and paint the ceiling of the church. On July 16 the installation of the carpeting was authorized and authorization also was given for the pew cushions to be recovered at the best price available. A November report shows that the cost of carpeting was $937.80. The cost of painting walls and ceiling was $438.89 and the cost of recovering the cushions was $120.90. Likely these important improvements were possible in part due to the mortgage on the parsonage.

The financial picture of the church received a boost in June 1925 through the aforementioned will of Archer W. Hodgdon. He had been one of the most successful businessmen in the town, had worked for his father and eventually took over the family store— R.G. Hodgdon. It was common knowledge that if one could not find something anywhere else in town one likely could find it there.[584]

During this era, there was a very colorful and fascinating layperson who attended the church. His name was James B. Perkins.

The *Boothbay Register* noted "James B. Perkins of this town is being mentioned as a candidate before the Democratic primaries for congressman from the Second District. Mr. Perkins has also often been mentioned in the political talk of this state as a candidate for governor." In addition, "James Blenn Perkins headed the Congregational church committee formed to finalize arrangements for Congregational and Methodist joint services to be held during Holy Week. During the 1930s and 1940s Perkins was a bulwark of the church. He was also a six-term Lincoln County attorney, president of the Bath Savings Bank, and a partner with his son James Perkins Jr. in the Harbor-based law firm Perkins and Perkins. Both Perkins were leaders in the Congregational church."[585]

A June 1926 *Boothbay Register* revealed that James B. Perkins was a candidate for the state senate. Chip Griffin had a conversation with Vice Admiral James B. Perkins III, in which the Vice Admiral recalled a story of his grandfather's participating in the life of the Boothbay Congregational Church. James Blenn Perkins, Sr., would always sit in the last pew in the rear of the church on the right side. At the beginning of the service he would take out his pocket watch and lay it on the pew next to him. When the hour was up, he would snap shut his pocket watch, get up, leave the church, and walk to his home on West Street. Apparently for Jim Perkins, one hour was ample time for a church service![586]

Union services of Holy Week were held Sunday through Thursday, March 29 to April 2, 1926—the first two at the Methodist church and the next three at the Congregational church. At the first service Rev. Kirschbaum preached. There were 350 people in attendance. On successive nights the pastors of the Baptist church and of the East Boothbay and Boothbay Methodist churches preached. Apparently, these services were of exceptional interest, and so many people attended that the local pastors were greatly encouraged and large numbers indicated their intention of being confirmed at one or the other of the churches.

On Easter Sunday, twenty new members were received into membership of the Congregational church—the largest class ever received into the church at one time in the memory of anyone present at the service. Of the 254 people attending the service, twenty-three were received into membership. The group consisted of people who had attended for thirty or forty years as well as some young people who had become interested in the church only during Rev. Kirschbaum's ministry. In addition there were fourteen baptisms. Perhaps encouraged by this upsurge in participation in church life, the church in 1926 undertook major repairs, including a new carpet, new lighting, and repairs to the ceiling.

Rev. Kirschbaum's sermons were described as deeply interesting and instructive. Services were well attended. Furthermore, the other activities of the church were also enthusiastically described as being at a high point. The physical church plant was also flourishing with hundreds of dollars having been raised in the prior year and expended for a new carpet throughout the church along with new decorations. Additional repairs included a new lighting system and, as a result of a special gift, the addition of a new furnace. It was in the midst of this that Rev. Kirschbaum organized a Markon Club for boys and a Christian Endeavor Society. The Markon Club likely was one of the many predecessors to what later became The Boys Club of America. The Young People's Society of Christian Endeavor was a nondenominational evangelical society founded in Portland, Maine in 1881 by Francis Edward Clark. Its professed object was "to promote an earnest Christian life among its members, to increase their mutual acquaintanceship, and to make them more useful in the service of God."[587]

Not surprisingly, the congregation voted on April 29, 1926, to extend call to Rev. W.G. Kirschbaum to serve the church as pastor for another year. The parish also asked him to "get up" a concert to obtain money to complete the amount needed for the "electocler" in the church. Perhaps the reference is to "electrolier," which was the name for a fixture, usually suspended from the ceiling, for holding electric lamps. The word is analogous to chandelier, from which it was formed.

Eager to initiate a daily vacation Bible school program, Rev.

Kirschbaum wrote an article for the *Boothbay Register* in May, making an appeal to the town to join him in starting one. He referred to the movement as "spreading rapidly in the country throughout the last 25 years." He suggested that Boothbay Harbor would want to be as progressive and up-to-date as any other town in the State of Maine. That expression "up-to-date" was significant in the 1920s, a decade that despite the rise of fundamentalism, appeared to worship modernism. Permission was secured from the "School Committee" to use the public schools as the locator for the summer Bible school program. The plan was to enroll two hundred students and to conduct the program from July 12 to July 30 between 9 and 11:30 each weekday morning. Young people aged four to twelve were eligible to enroll. He concluded by saying "It will be one of the best investments the town has ever made."

Yet, despite his success with the youth and an upsurge in membership early in 1926, there seemed to be some problems. Later that year, the evening services seemed to lose strong support, and B.S. Fifield, the Sunday School superintendent and the manager of the Union Mutual Life Insurance Company, resigned as superintendent! What were the issues? The evidence is not clear. It was said about this time that Rev. Kirschbaum was also pushing for an increase in salary.

Perhaps the slump in the evening service is what prompted the editorial that appeared in the paper on November 19, 1926. It reported that the local pastors spoke on Sunday evening about the problem of decreased attendance at the evening church services. While precise knowledge of the cause it not available, we might speculate about some of the new lures that kept people away from church—the movies, radio shows, dances at the Pavilion and gatherings at the Opera House. Whatever it was, Rev. Kirschbaum "did not mince words" as the paper said. Since the summer, only two evening services were held due to lack of attendance. He assured his congregation that unless attendance improved materially and at once, he would feel called upon to resign his pastorate. The editor of the paper went on to comment, "No wonder the pastors are calling for help. There are 2,000 people in town and possibly a hundred at church services…We all need to resolve to attend church services regularly or as often as possible…Be at church somewhere next Sunday!"

Likely as a follow-up to these concerns, we find a notice in the paper with this heading: "GO TO CHURCH SUNDAY, Nov 27, Dec 4, and 11." This special emphasis on church attendance was to be observed by the churches represented in the Lincoln County Ministerial Association on Sunday December 4 with a Bible Sunday. The notice was followed by the statement: "Let This Be Your Invitation" and was signed by the Pastors' Committee: Wm. T. Bennett, W.G. Kirschbaum, F.W. Hovey, M.W. Russell.

On, January 13 1927, Frank S. Killin was elected Superintendent of the Church School. At the annual parish meeting on April 27, 1927, the call of Rev. Kirschbaum was extended for another year. And there was a vote to buy shades for the parsonage.[588] Does that mean the parsonage was truly a fish bowl prior to that action?

In the spring and summer of 1928, pastoral changes were in the air. Two other ministers had moved away and in July 1928 Rev. Kirschbaum accepted a call to a church in Houlton with a salary of $2,500. As a result he submitted his resignation to the Boothbay Congregational Church and the congregation accepted his resignation on June 25. Prior to his resignation it was said that the church found it increasingly difficult to meet his salary demands. However, the *Boothbay Register* noted that "Rev. Kirschbaum has been pastor of the Boothbay Harbor Congregational Church for four Years. Kirschbaum has been very helpful in Lodge work here and for two years was Commander of the Charles E. Sherman Post [of the]American Legion" (which explains why he attended the Great American Legion Convention in October 1926 as one of Maine's delegates in Philadelphia.) [589]

On Sunday, August 27, 1926, during the pastorate of Rev. Kirschbaum, the newly completed Our Lady Queen of Peace Roman Catholic Church was dedicated. The officiant was Bishop John Gregory Murray. Land for this church had been secured in

1916 and Roman Catholic families had been gathering for Mass in various locations around the community for some years prior to this special occasion. "Though there had been only a few Roman Catholic families in the area, a large congregation attended this service." [590] A truly ecumenical spirit must have been present from the start.

Rev. Louis Lincoln Harris—1929-1930
The Reverend Louis L. Harris was called as the pastor of the church on May 7, 1929. The call was approved at the annual parish meeting on that date.[591]

During his pastorate, one notable accomplishment was the incorporation of the church. On May 30, 1929, the Boothbay Congregational Church applied for and received incorporation. The committee members drafting the incorporation papers were: Millicent Maddocks; Thaddeus Orne, T.H. Stevens; K. Weston Farnham; Marcia Kenniston; Fannie Perkins,[592] and Rev. L.L. Harris. The name of the new corporation was the Congregational Church of Boothbay Harbor. Its officers were clerk, treasurer, and a business committee of seven persons. The treasurer's duty was to keep accurate records; the business committee, to be elected annually, was to hold a meeting on the first secular day of each month at 7:30. They usually met at the home of one of the members. The first business committee consisted of Natalie Nickerson, Mrs. William E. Bartlett, Mrs. Mabel Rand, T.H. Stevens, and K. Weston Farnham. Curiously, one of the first issues raised was the question of placing a signboard in front of the church advertising Boothbay Shores Properties. A motion to incorporate had been requested previously by Rev. Kirschbaum, but had been laid on the table only to be removed and acted upon at this meeting several years later. The purpose of incorporation was "to bring the church organization up to "modern standards" used by most "progressive" churches."

Life at the church seemed to be going well considering the crisis nationally and internationally caused by the Great Depression.[593] Change must have been in the air. Attendance likely had improved, and giving must have been satisfactory. At the annual meeting on January 6, 1930, the reports were "commendatory of a very successful year." Following discussion, a vote was taken to make a church survey of the town in cooperation with the Methodist church. It was to be undertaken "to interest the people in the town who do not now attend the church often to become interested in one of the churches and help with the work." In addition it was stated that "a good reason for the survey is that no survey has been undertaken for many years, if ever, and the pastors need to identify which families actually come under their charge or not at all." The paper then indicated that some of the pastors have been out of touch with some of the older members and newer families.[594]

Rev. Elton K. Bassett—1930—1936

In October 1930 the church hired Elton K. Bassett at a salary of $2,000. He continued to serve the church until April 1936. An unusually large congregation gathered for both the morning and evening services at the church on November 9, 1930, as the Rev. Basset began his "church duties as the new pastor." It was reported "He is a very pleasing speaker from the pulpit and very anxious to meet the people of the parish and town. He has always elsewhere received most hearty cooperation in all branches of church work so that his efforts have always been crowned with success."[595] His sermon that day was "How Much Is Education Worth?" based on Proverbs 8:11. On November 23, his sermon title was "My God I Thank Thee." Later that day at the Community Union Thanksgiving Service, Rev. Bassett spoke on "Remembering God's Blessings." The *Boothbay Register* reported that he did so "in a most interesting manner."[596] The evening service on December 21 was a "White Gift Service." The community was invited to come and bring gifts wrapped in white and place them beneath an immense Christmas tree, which would occupy the normal place for the pulpit. Each gift was to be marked indicating whether it was suitable for a boy or a girl. The gifts would later be given out through the community Christmas tree project sponsored by the town. The offering received at the service was also to be used in community work. Rev. Bassett's sermon was "Gifts of God & Frankincense & Myrrh." Symbolic of the ecumenical spirit that was so typical in Boothbay, around this weekend the Congregational and the Methodist churches together went out into the community to sing Christmas carols in various people's homes.

Some insight into the life of the church can be attained from the Congregational meeting held on May 3, 1931. The business included changing the church services to daylight savings time[597] with Sunday School at 9:45, worship at 10:45, a roundtable discussion for high school boys at 12:15 and evening services at 8 PM so that people "can get home from their afternoon rides and have their supper before it is time to be in church."[598] Apparently, Vacation Bible School in 1931 was a huge success. It was reported that the enrollment had been the largest in the history of the movement in "this locality." Enrollment had reached one hundred eighty-nine.

Some of Rev. Bassett's sermon titles were particularly notable: "References Required, Ask Me—I Live Here," preached on January 4, 1931. For the next several weeks he did a series of sermons with the overall theme: "Jesus, The Royal Redeemer." During Holy Week of 1931, the Congregational and Methodist churches held union services each evening, Sunday through Friday. Rev. Basset's sermons on two of those nights were entitled "Riding Toward the Cross" and "Carrier of the Cross." On another night Rev. Basset was the soloist. On Friday of Holy Week, Rev. Basset held a special children's Good Friday service, which included a children's choir and a story hour for the children.

But how were world events impacting the life and worship of the congregation? By the fall of 1929, the Great Depression had begun in the United States. It may not have impacted Boothbay immediately or entirely in the same way as it did in the big cities across the country. But the Great Depression was one of the most serious financial crises in the history of the country, and of the world for that matter. As John Bauman notes in his book, *Gateway to Vacationland,*

On October 27, 1929, securities plunged by forty-three percent. By November, the stock market was down 228 points ending the Roaring Twenties. Nearby Portland endured none of the large-scale misery, but hardly avoided the Great Depression…By 1933, Maine paper-mill production had dropped 50 percent. That same year, three of Portland's principal banks closed and along with that went declining real estate values.[599]

As Bauman observes further, "Maine tourism, sluggish in the early 1930s, had inched upward by 1936…During the Great Depression, teachers, ministers and others from Philadelphia, Boston and elsewhere, their wages slashed, found the beautiful coast of Maine with its inexpensive lodging, cheap seafood dinners, and cool, healthful air an affordable as well as relaxing vacation."[600] While Boothbay was not affected in the same way as Portland, times were tougher, although some of that was offset by tourism.

It wasn't just economies that had turned upside down in the 1930s, however. It went beyond that. More dark and ominous clouds were on the horizon. "The radio was becoming a staple in many American homes. For the first time, citizens did not have to wait until the evening paper to get the latest news—radios brought breaking news right into people's living rooms. The airwaves carried talk about jobs and the economy during the Great Depression, but Americans also heard news about incredible advances in science and technology, celebrities of aviation exploration, and political changes afoot in Europe."[601] Adolf Hitler's rise to power, which began in the 1920s with his joining the Nazi party, was increasing steadily.

These developments didn't go unnoticed at the Congregational church in Boothbay Harbor. On March 30, 1931, at the evening service, Rev. Bassett's sermon was "Breaking God's Laws." The sermon reviewed the news of the week as reported in the daily papers. Accounts of wrong doing presumably were identified. However, the paper noted that no items related to prohibition would be included. And the paper stated, "There will be an evaluation of the various magazines found on the newsstands today."[602] Whether world events or the spiritual temper of America, Rev. Bassett may have been inspired by Karl Barth's instructions to his students that they should enter the pulpit with the Bible in one hand and the newspaper in the other to bring the Word of God to bear on the events of the day.

On Mother's Day that year the sermon was "Mothers: The Stewards Of A Nation's Future." On June 14, his sermon was "Only Four Children In The World." During the sermon that day the *Boothbay Register* indicated he would be speaking about a proposal being presented to the country by the Child Welfare Committee appointed by President Hoover.[603] Sermons in 1932 included "Limelight, Spotlight, Searchlight" on June 26 and "A Gracious Host" on July 3.

A group with a novel name called the "Ninety Nine" was formed in the early thirties. Rev. Bassett apparently attempted to bring together ninety-nine or more men in the evening service. They were to sing one of the hymns together. On March 15, 1931, the desired number of men was not reached; however there was a large attendance at the church that evening and more than half of the congregation present consisted of men.[604]

Church suppers were very much a part of the picture in the 1930s. On July 7, 1932, a very successful supper was held with ninety-six people attending. On the menu were spiced ham, potato salad, cucumbers, tomatoes, sandwiches, strawberries and cream, cake and coffee. Also a very successful flower sale was held outside the church in the afternoon.

A notable first happened in August 1931, unique to the region. The event was successful enough that it was repeated the following year with even greater attendance. In the first year, forty-three ministers gathered. The following year it was reported that fifty church workers gathered on an August afternoon. These were some of the comments made by the local paper:

> Thursday afternoon the Congregational Church here was the

scene of the most unusual gathering of religious leaders ever held in this part of the state. It was a Ministerial-get-to-Gether (sic) and it was the getting together of ministers and their wives from all over the United States...[It was designed] to let the ministers of the various denominations in Lincoln County have a chance to meet some of the nationally known men who summer in the Boothbay Region...ministers from the pulpits of twenty states are spending their vacations in the immediate locality.

(Among) the forty-three ministers attending were: the Rev. Dr. Harry Emerson Fosdick as well as four other ministers from New York City or its Burroughs; the Rev. John Henry Wilson from Littleton, MA; the Rev. John M Weber from the St. James Episcopal Church in West Philadelphia; the Rev. George E. Gilchrist from the Congregational Church of Tilton, NJ; the Rev. Dr. Arthur H. Beale from the Grand Ave. Congregational Church of Milwaukee, WI; the Rev. Charles H. Beale from the First Congregational Church of St. Petersburg, FL; the Rev. Lester W. Stryker from the Episcopal Church of Youngstown, OH; and the Rev. Dr. Charles W. Gilkey, Dean of the Chapel at the University of Chicago; as well as Rev. Bassett.[605]

One of the indications of the high regard for Rev. Bassett can be seen in a *Boothbay Register* article on July 1, 1932. Rev. Bassett "was selected by the State Congregational Committee on Religious Education to teach at the YMCA Camp at Cobboseecontee from August 22 to August 29. He will teach the Seniors Social Work for young people. This award is a great and much sought for honor, and it is an example of the fine name Mr. Bassett has made for himself throughout the state."[606]

The celebration of Memorial Day in 1933 included various parades and gatherings and a special program at the Strand Theater with bands and choirs. Rev. Bassett was the speaker. The title of his address was "Our National Soul," described in the paper as interesting and inspiring. One wonders if he mentioned anything about Hitler's burning of the Reichstag only two months before, or if he had begun to see the dangers ahead with Adolf Hitler's becoming Chancellor of Germany four months previously, when he proposed eliminating traditional party politics, creating a unified one-party state, and eradicating all opposition to the Nazi party. News of the power shift had begun to worry American leadership and political analysts who believed Hitler's extremism could lead to a dark future.[607] And were Karl Barth, Dietrich Bonheoffer, and Paul Tillich's thinking about the evil of the Nazi cause influencing Rev. Bassett's thinking?

Barth's rejection of nineteenth-century liberalism for an objective Christ-centered faith made it possible for him to see clearly the evil of Hitler's propaganda and politics. Barth wouldn't let Schleiermacher redefine Christianity, and he wasn't going to let Hitler do it either. 15,000 pastors had already thrown their hat in with Hitler. Barth was not one of them and authored the Barmen Declaration of 1934, which proclaimed:

> 8.09, In view of the errors of the 'German Christians' of the present Reich Church government which are devastating the Church and also therefore breaking up the unity of the German Evangelical Church, we confess the following evangelical truths:...8.11, Jesus Christ, as he is attested for us in Holy Scripture, is the one Word of God which we have to hear and which we have to trust and obey in life and in death...8.12, We reject the false doctrine, as though the church could and would have to acknowledge as a source of its proclamation, apart from and besides this one Word of God, still other events and powers, figures and truths, as God's revelation.[608]

Barth reclaimed the traditional Reformed church's position of the otherness and holiness of God, the centrality of the Word and the pivotal significance of Jesus Christ.[609] Barth is often regarded as the greatest Protestant theologian of the twentieth century, and his work had a profound impact on twentieth century theology and on notable persons such as Dietrich Bonheoffer, who, like Barth, became a leader in the Confessing Church.[610] Perhaps Barth is best known for his response to the question, "What has been the greatest theological insight you have ever gained?" His answer after a brief pause, "Jesus loves me, this I know, for the Bible tells me so."

Among theologians, Karl Barth was not alone. Others joined in changing the course of theological thought over the next couple of decades. Among them were Emil Brunner, Martin Buber, Reinhold Niebuhr and Paul Tillich.

The Christian faith, Brunner maintained, arises from the encounter between individuals and God as God is revealed in the Bible. The sense of personal encounter through the scriptures with Christ perhaps came into even sharper focus with Brunner's writings than with Barth's. Enhancing Brunner's thinking in some ways was the Jewish theologian Martin Buber, whose famous book *I And Thou* brought into focus the distinction between I-it relationships and I-Thou relationships. It is only through personal encounter with others that we can create community. But the yearning for connection happens most completely in an I-Thou relationship with God. The Divine encounter is a transforming experience that enables persons to stop treating others as "its" and to engage in a true caring experience of the other. According to Buber, one can meet God at any time and everywhere in one's everyday existence.[611] Barth's emphasis on the otherness of God and Brunner and Buber's emphasis on the immanence of God would become more synched in twenty-first century theology in some ways to be explored further in the last chapter of this book.

Joining Barth and Brunner in their reclaiming the power of the Word and re-emphasizing the sinfulness of humankind and the need for redemption was Reinhold Niebuhr. Starting as a minister with working-class and labor-class sympathies in the 1920s and oriented to theological pacifism in the 1930s, he shifted to a neo-orthodox realist theology, inspired by Barth, and developed a "theo-philosophical" perspective known as "Christian realism."

Niebuhr attacked utopianism as ineffectual for dealing with reality. The direction he took is reflected in these words published in 1944: "Man's capacity for justice makes democracy possible; but man's inclination to injustice makes democracy necessary."[612]

Still another theologian opposing Hitler was Paul Tillich. He was Professor of Theology at the University of Frankfort from 1929 to 1933. While at the University of Frankfurt, Tillich gave public lectures and speeches throughout Germany that brought him into conflict with the Nazi movement. When Adolf Hitler became German Chancellor in 1933, Tillich was dismissed from his position. Reinhold Niebuhr, learning of Tillich's dismissal, having visited Tillich in Germany and impressed by Tillich's writings, contacted him and urged him to join the faculty at New York City's Union Theological Seminary. Tillich accepted the invitation and captured the imagination of students with assertions such as: "'Faith as ultimate concern is an act of the total personality. It is the most centered act of the human mind…it participates in the dynamics of personal life." [613]

The Reverend Dr. Harry Emerson Fosdick routinely vacationed in Boothbay and supplied pulpits. He also brought with him the experience of having met with, listened to and developed a personal knowledge of many of these new theologians. Rev. Fosdick had been invited to be a full professor in homiletics and practical theology at Union Theological Seminary starting in 1915, and he continued on the faculty of Union in one capacity or another until he retired in 1946.

1934, appears to have been a busy year. During Lent, Rev. Bassett offered a series of sermons on "The Meaning of Lent." In one of those sermons he said that God had nothing to do with the hate, prejudice, and cruelty which devised and perpetrated Christ's death on the cross."[614] Is it possible that any of these thoughts were also connected with the horror of Hitler's rise to power in Europe? And what prompted his sermon entitled "The World's Greatest Ailment" on March 18, or, what about his sermon, "Men of Vision" on April 6? Was he encouraged by some of the speeches and policies of President Franklin D. Roosevelt? And was his own sense of personal security in his position as pastor at the church being challenged when he preached the sermon, "What Is A Successful Church" on April 15?

Strikingly, Rev. Bassett's sermon on June 30, 1934, was: "Peace." About this time it was reported that throughout the land, the churches and colleges had been uniting their forces in peace movements. These efforts had gained power steadily, and ministers in the United States had answered a questionnaire confirming that many would not again sanction or participate in any war.

On May 4, for the first time during Rev. Bassett's pastorate at the Congregational church, the young people conducted the morning service. Attendance was unusually large, reflecting the interest the church constituency had in its young people. Each part of the service was conducted by a different youth, building up to the sermon, which was preached by the president of the Christian Endeavor Society, Richard Story. He used the theme "Christian Youth Building a New World." The *Boothbay Register* reported that Story presented his material in a very able manner, having mastered his subject, and "presented convincing arguments, using Italy's and Germany's Youth Movements compared with the Christian Youth Movement in America."[615]

Given what was happening in Europe at the time, it would be fascinating to know exactly what was said. Were these youth up on current events? Was information about what was truly happening in Europe available to the general public in the United States? Was the arrival of the radio into the area having any impact? Were they and Rev. Bassett on the same page regarding the peace movement?

Later in 1934 on November 4, National Education Week was observed at the Congregational and the United Methodist churches in cooperation with the public schools. Both churches held morning services with students from the elementary school singing two hymns. At the evening service the high school participated with the Methodist church at the Congregational church. The liturgy preceding the sermon was led by the residents of the high school classes. The Superintendent of Schools, Harold B. Clifford, also a church organist, played the organ for the service. The high school principal and a faculty member served as ushers. Special music was provided by the high school chorus. [616] Thankfully, some of those connections continued even into the twenty-first century between the public school and the churches in the area.

On November 11, an Armistice service was held in the evening at the church. In effect it was a peace rally. Rev. Bassett secured, with the help of the American Legion, flags of allied countries along with 12 large U.S. flags, which were used to decorate the sanctuary. In the morning, there was a service in memory of those who "gave their lives that there might be no more war."[617]

Apparently, Rev. Bassett was a capable singer. For on November 17, 1934, he sang the National Anthem at a special community ceremony of the Daughters of the American Revolution in the old Congregational cemetery. The purpose of this event was to mark the graves of three Revolutionary War soldiers: Samuel Adams, Ichabod Pinkham, and Robert Wylie. Interestingly, on more than one occasion the paper noted that the evening service would be a "Long Song Service and Short Sermon."

Rev. Elton Kennedy Bassett was the minister during the worst years of the Great Depression. He lost the support of the business committee, resigned and moved to North Woburn, MA. Possibly that was the context of this sermon "Facts On Financing Religion" delivered on December 9, 1934, and "Taking Account of Stock" preached at the end of 1934. That people in Boothbay were affected by the Depression was noted by Jack Bauman when he said, "My parents were here in Boothbay in 1931, and the reason these school teachers came is that you could go down to the docks and the fisherman would give you all the fish you wanted for twenty-five cents."[618]

The year 1934 concluded with a "Reflections Service." The *Boothbay Register* said that on Sunday, December 30, the morning service was devoted to a review of the outstanding happenings in the Christian work of 1934. Emphasis was laid on the great gain in church membership made during the year nationally, when people were turning to the church for solace and comfort after the Great Depression. A total of 655,482 members was the gain at the close of 1933, making a total of 60,812,874 in Protestant membership at the beginning of 1934.

The *Boothbay Register* continued to be attuned to the unique programs or worship services at the Congregational church during these years. It referred to another "Novel Program at the Congregational Church"—this time on March 2, 1936. There was a young people's choir, a quartet and several instrumentalists, who joined with Rev. Bassett in presenting a service of poetry and music— Biblical and sacred poetry, responsive readings and prayers.[619]

Rev. Bassett's pastorate concluded around April 13, 1936, since that was the date of the last check written to him for his services on that Sunday. There is a letter dated January 7, 1936 in the church files from Millicent Maddocks (clerk) addressed to Rev. Bassett, informing him of an action taken at a parish meeting the previous day indicating that his term would expire in three months from that date according to the bylaws and that he be notified of this action at once. The vote had been taken by ballot. Over the next several weeks there were at least eight candidates who were paid to conduct worship on successive Sundays. No mention is made in church records as to the circumstances surrounding Rev. Bassett's departure.

Rev. Kenneth Vernon Gray—1937-1944

Kenneth Vernon Gray served the Church at War from January 8, 1937, to July 23, 1944. Gray graduated from Bangor Theological Seminary, May 28, 1935, and from Bowdoin College, cum laude in 1938. He attended Bowdoin while pastor at the Boothbay Harbor Congregational church and filled the pulpit even prior to his ordination.

1937 was a year for changes. On December 6, Harold Clifford sent a letter resigning as the church organist. In the letter he said: "This will terminate a several year period which has been both pleasant in a social and spiritual way and profitable to me musically." He noted his skills gradually lessening. But then he went on to say,... "my relations with your pastors and congregation have been most cordial."

Mr. Gray seems to have made a good impression, for at an Annual Meeting held on July 31, 1938, the congregation was asked to act on matters having to do with his ordination and to invite the Lincoln County Association of Congregational Churches to hold their annual meeting at the Harbor church in October 1938.[620] The church historical files contain a letter from the Lincoln County Association inviting the churches to participate in the special meeting on October 3 at 7:30 PM at the Wiscasset Congregational Church for the purpose of examining Mr. Gray as a candidate for ordination to Christian ministry. Apparently the examination went well for the *Boothbay Register* subsequently reported on Kenneth Gray's ordination, indicating that among the participants were the Rev. Rodney Rounty of Portland, Superintendent of the Congregational-Christian Conference of Maine and the Rev. Harry Trust, President of Bangor Theological Seminary, as well as the Rev. F. L. Littlefield, pastor of the Methodist Episcopal Church of Boothbay Harbor.[621]

Two of Mr. Gray's sermons listed in early 1937 include "The Greater Man," and "Double Choice." And two in 1938 were "Is Christian Goodness Reasonable?" (Was that a touch of Reinhold Niebuhr?) And later in the year: "God the Good Provider." The sermon for January 1939 sermon was: "Strength for the Day." Beginning in February 1939, Rev. Gray announced an upcoming series of sermons under the theme: "Inward Perfection," following the order of the Beatitudes and reaching its climax in the sermon for Easter Sunday, April 9: "The Enduring Life." Rev. Gray's children's sermon that day was entitled, "What The Grub Found Out." The sermon on November 19 was "Two Kinds of Faith" and on November 26 it was entitled, "Be Ye Thankful."

1939 concluded with a joint Union Watch Night Service held at the Boothbay Harbor Methodist church on New Year's Eve. Both pastors preached "sermonettes." Rev. Gray's theme was "Forgetting The Past," and Rev. F.L. Littlefield's was "Reaching Forward." Under "Congregational Notes" in the paper the prior week, this thought appeared: "The Church is the best place to watch the Old Year out and the New Year in."

In 1940 some of Rev. Gray's sermons were: "The Freedom of the Christian Mind," "Thanks Plus," and "Born A Savior" with the children's choir singing the offertory anthem entitled "Glory Be To God." The sermon titles available for 1940 don't reveal much of what was going on in the church and the world around it. However, the *Boothbay Register* reported some details about the Thanksgiving service which are of interest. The special offering to be received at that service was to assist war victims. The giver could designate on an envelope which of the following causes they preferred to help through their offering: starving children in Europe; homeless European refugees in the U.S.; impoverished European churches; or relief of Chinese war victims. The latter concern probably arose from the news that "there were thousands of biological and chemical warfare attacks by the Japanese army in many parts of China during the Sino-Japanese War of 1931–1945." [622]

Rev. Gray displayed creative innovation. For example in stewardship, on December 16, 1938, he introduced a new way of pledging. A parish letter was sent out to the homes rather than initially doing a house-to-house visit. Members were asked to bring the pledge card on Christmas Sunday. The cards were to be placed on the altar as an act of worship, much as the wise men brought their gifts to the manger at Bethlehem. The sermon for the occasion was entitled "The Quest."

In December 1937 there is reference (in a letter from Mabel Rand in the church archives) that money received from Dr. George K. Blair's widow was to be used to purchase and install communion cup racks in memory of Dr. Blair's mother, Mrs. Mary Blair.

During the summers while Rev. Gray was pastor there were many supply pastors. A notable event occurred on August 20, 1939, when the supply minister was Dr. Charles Beale of Milwaukee. He filled the pulpit on many occasions in the summers over the years. But what was so special about this particular Sunday was that he was conducting worship on his eighty-fifth birthday. The title of his sermon was: "The Enchantment of the Disenchantment, and the Enchantment of Life." The title sounds a little complex, but it does peak one's curiosity as to what he might have said.

Also in 1939 a wonderful addition to the life of the church was the development of a newly organized children's choir. They sang for the first time on January 15, 1939, under the direction of Katherine Lewis. Their anthem on that day was: "God Will Take Care Of You."[623] In adult education that year, Rev. Gray initiated the first of four Lenten Pastor's classes, which met at the parsonage. The topic for this series was "Christian Belief about God." The subjects to be considered subsequently were: Jesus, the Bible, the Church, prayer, Christian growth, church membership, the sacraments and the rights and duties of church membership.[624] Likely this was a new members' class or a class for persons who wanted to understand more about their church membership.

Apparently Rev. Gray's efforts didn't go unnoticed. At a congregational meeting on January 9, 1939, Rev. Gray was invited to serve the church for an indefinite period of time with an increased salary.

During the Gray years the organizations and committees of the church were very busy. On October 10, 1937, the business committee voted to make the church vestry available to the high school band one afternoon a week during the school year for their "practice sessions." At a congregational meeting held on October 27, 1938, a proposal was discussed regarding shingling the south end of the church roof.

The women of the church as always were holding up their end of the work of the church during this era. On November 18, 1938, they planned a McGuffey party and entertainment. A costume tableaux and dramatizations based on selections from the then famous McGuffey reader were built into the event. They also presented a one-act play. The chairperson of the event was Mrs. Walter Reed. Admission was twenty-five cents. The proceeds from the event were to go to the roof fund. [625] In February 1939 the Dorcas Guild held a colonial tea.[626] That fall the Dorcas Guild and the Congregational Guild sponsored harvest suppers. And, in December, the Dorcas Guild sold wreaths at the Christmas fair. The Congregational Guild held a rummage sale in early November at the Benoit Company store on Townsend Avenue. Mrs. Madeline Mudge was in charge of the sale. Any gifts of used clothing, books, shoes, furniture, knick-knacks, etc., were gladly accepted to be offered at the sale. Members of the parish wishing to donate items were encouraged to leave them at the parsonage or at Miss Kendrick's store, or they could be "called for" if Mrs. Mudge or any member of the guild were notified.

The Christmas season in 1940 was lively. A Christmas pageant, "Watchers on the Hills," was presented on Sunday afternoon, December 22, by the Sunday school and the children's choir.

> "Watchers on the Hills" concerns four girls, who are discussing their Christmas purchases. One of the girls, having recently read a book entitled "Watchers on the Hills," hears in a realistic way the question repeatedly asked by the Shepherd Boy in the book: "Have you found Christmas?" Asked to explain what the question means, she begins to do so. The Shepherd Boy appears as in a vision, and proceeds to tell his own story. He tells of the ancient watchers on the hills, the shepherds and the Wise Men, and then he shows some modern "watchers" on the hilltops of life, i.e., those who find the real meaning of Christmas through the Christmas stories, through worship, forgiveness, goodwill, and helpfulness. The girls realize that, although they have found many Christmas things, they have not found Christmas itself. Resolved to find it, they begin, as did the ancient watchers on the hills, by hearing the angel's message and the song of the heavenly host. The several musical selections in the pageant were prepared under the direction of Mrs. Katherine B. Lewis, who served as organist for many decades. [627]

On Christmas Eve in 1940, the library lawn became a bit of holy ground with children singing carols. It was about this time that the church received a gift of $1,000 to be used in remodeling the room under the vestry for the use of the Sunday school. The balance of the gift was to be used for further improvement in the church property. The generous giver wanted his name withheld, but the officers of the church and members of the parish were quite intentional about expressing their gratitude to their anonymous benefactor.

The conclusion of Rev. Gray's ministry falls within the time period of the next chapter. But the twenty years just reviewed obviously included some tough times and difficult years, with one war just ended and another one brewing, economic disasters, and major social changes. Theology was going through major transitions in Europe and trickling onto the American scene, as translations from the German were not instantly available. But the Boothbay church traversed these difficult waters with the assistance of some able leadership, some of whom especially were able to connect the Bible and the emerging theology to some degree with the changing times. Hindsight is always so much easier than foresight. There are things we might wonder why they didn't do differently. But given their circumstances, we might well have been equally struggling to find our way through the chaos of those days. And through it all we see that in Boothbay there were many really good times despite the tough times in the region, the country and the world.

CHAPTER 10

THE CHURCH AT WAR AND PEACE: 1942–1965
by John F. Bauman

Introduction

"The forces endeavoring to enslave the entire world now are moving toward this hemisphere. Never before has there been a greater challenge to life, liberty, and civilization." With these grim words, President Franklin D. Roosevelt announced on December 11, 1941, four days after the Japanese had attacked the American naval base at Pearl Harbor, that the United States was officially at war with Germany, Italy, and Japan, a triumvirate declaimed as the "Axis." With Roosevelt's words, World War II began, men were drafted, factories were retooled to produce tanks rather than refrigerators or trucks, and the nation mobilized, in New York, Chicago, Philadelphia, Boston, and across the nation, as well as in Boothbay Harbor, Maine, home to the Congregational church, perched on the Atlantic coast, and vulnerable to the whims of German submarines prowling the coastline.

This chapter examines the twenty-three year period, 1942–1965, an era beginning with the opening of World War II and one important for the history of modern Protestantism, Congregationalism, for the Boothbay Harbor Congregational church, and for the town of Boothbay Harbor. It explores how the Boothbay region and the Congregational church, having weathered the Great Depression, now became a cog in the "Arsenal of Democracy" that ultimately defeated the Axis. Victory in World War II not only brought renewed prosperity to the region, and ultimately to the church, but also, heralded significant change. From a busy wartime shipbuilding center in 1945 (with a struggling, but extant ground fishing industry), picturesque Boothbay Harbor evolved into a busy, but primarily tourist town. Meanwhile, as this chapter makes clear, the postwar Congregational church, after enduring a decade of instability—marked by a spate of brief pastorates (three shortened by deaths)—ultimately installed a long-term minister, stabilized itself financially, and undertook much needed major improvements to the church building.

Sluggish during the 1930s, Boothbay Harbor's economy surged during the 1940s. The town became a small but important wartime production center. Lest enemy ships prowling the North Atlantic be advantaged, the Coast Guard darkened all navigational aids, including the Ram, Burnt Island and Cuckolds lighthouses at the entrances to Boothbay Harbor. East Boothbay shipbuilders Goudy & Stevens and Hodgdon Brothers teamed together and, with Boothbay Harbor's Sample Shipyard, won federal contracts to build wooden-hulled minesweepers. Shipbuilding boomed and labor from other areas flowed into the two towns. Weather-beaten old hotels like Boothbay House accommodated some of the new single workers, as did some of the Harbor's large older homes, which were subdivided into apartments. But, family units proved scarce, making Boothbay Harbor, like Bath and South Portland, eligible for war housing under the 1941 federal Lanham Emergency Housing Act. Called the Dunbar Homes, a 23-unit "temporary" war housing development arose not far from the Congregational church on the Ocean Point Road just above its intersection with Route 27, where it remained a government-owned war housing development into the late 1950s. In addition to the construction of minesweepers during World War II and well into the postwar era, the local economy was sustained after 1945 by a resurgence of the town's fishing industry (mainly lobster harvesting) and by the revival of its prewar tourism. Simultaneously, the enduring mystique of the town's historic fishing and boatbuilding industry and the Harbor's eighteenth- and nineteenth-century architecture—including its white-spired Congregational church—preserved the prewar aura of New England coastal authenticity that so enchanted the cosmopolitan tourists and cottagers from Philadelphia, Boston, Hartford, and New York who populated the region during the summer months. Likewise, audiences who watched the 1956 movie version of the Rodgers and Hammerstein musical *Carousel*, filmed in part in Boothbay Harbor, found the place irresistibly charming. Nevertheless, as this chapter explains, the war engendered enormous change, change that inevitably enveloped small towns like Boothbay Harbor and small churches nationwide.

The era 1945 to 1965 witnessed not only the rise of the Cold War, which kept the Boothbay region's shipyards humming, but also the Marshall Plan to financially aid the rebuilding of war-torn Europe and the government-sponsored hunt for communists known as the Red Scare. The "GI Bill of Rights" gave veterans "no down payment" mortgages, which, together with working-class affordable Federal Housing Administration (FHA) mortgages, intensified suburbanization, engendering the dawn of a mass-consumption culture. Television, first viewed at the 1939 New York World's Fair, but becoming ubiquitous after 1949, further promulgated the mass culture. Television shows such as "Leave it to Beaver" brought into the homes of Congregational church members such as J. Blenn Perkins, Sr., Wilder Blake, Norman Hodgdon, Jr., Weston Farnham, and Archie Campbell, images of the consumer-driven suburban culture profoundly transforming America. Television, likewise, exposed small town America to the lives of the "gray flannel-suited Organization Men" ensconced in those ever rising, gleaming glass office towers of growing metropolises such as Philadelphia, New York and Boston. Inevitably, by 1965 the Harbor became increasingly a small, charming, but now thriving tourist town and very much part of America's growing mass consumption society.[628]

The Boothbay Harbor Church at War

Rev. Kenneth Vernon Gray—1937-1944

The Reverend Kenneth Vernon Gray was nearing the end of his fifth year in the pulpit of the Boothbay Harbor Congregational church when America declared war on the Axis. While war-driven shipbuilding now stabilized the towns' economy, the draft and local enlistments, shift work in the yards (including a number of "Rosie the riveters"), gas rationing, and contributions to a succession of war bond drives, all detracted from the weekly total in the church's collection plate. More and more it was the women of the church whose efforts sustained the welfare of the wartime church.

Indeed, in the wake of the Great Depression church finances remained strained, and the war exacerbated the situation. Rev. Gray confessed at the January 1943 annual meeting that church membership had dropped from 126 to 121 and that because of gas rationing church attendance for the year 1942 had likewise suffered. Gray hoped to recruit new members from among the many new shipyard workers and their families who daily moved into the town. Moreover, the young minister with his young family had received no pay increase. In fact in the spring of 1942 Gray had informed the business committee that with wartime prices rising, despite inflation controls, he and his family could no longer live comfortably on his $1,400 salary. The committee reluctantly boosted his salary to $1,500, adding just $66 to the church's annual budget.[629]

There were a few bright spots. When church member Archer W. Hodgdon died in 1925, his estate bequeathed to the church $100 annually for twenty years; however, "not for operating expenses." Several benefactors, Rev. Dr. Harry Emerson Fosdick for one, regularly mailed checks to the church, Fosdick's for $25. And, Frank Spencer, a summer resident from New York City, periodically mailed the church $250 for "improvements," but "not operating expenses." Nevertheless, in 1943 the church had barely $650 in its checking account and faced immediate needs. For one, it lacked a decent vestry.[630]

Frequently during the 1930s church organizations had bemoaned the inadequacy of the small vestry, the place where the guilds, business committee, Sunday school, and other bodies scheduled meetings and events. In truth, rather than meet in such a cramped space, church guild and business committee meetings ordinarily took place in members' homes. As early as 1941 Gray proposed to enlarge the vestry, and he actually secured cost estimates from several masons and from Pierce and Hartung Hardware. But, Pearl Harbor quashed the plans. Instead, in 1943 with the one hundredth anniversary (of the founding in 1848 of the Second Congregational Church in Boothbay Harbor) in sight, Gray initiated a five-year plan to raise funds for a new vestry. Still, the existing vestry needed painting, and the "buckling floor" of the church vestibule begged to be repaired. To make matters even worse the years 1941–1945 brought record cold weather, bringing blizzard-like snow storms almost weekly and sub-zero temperatures. To heat the church meant running the oil burner all day Saturday and having a raging fire burning in the vestry fireplace.[631]

Worsening conditions culminated on January 11, 1943, when Gray submitted his resignation effective April 1944. A Navy Reserve chaplain, Gray told the congregation that he imminently expected to be called to active duty. The historical record, however, becomes somewhat opaque here, because a month later, in February, the church not only voted to recall Gray, but to award him a new, higher salary of $1,600. Gray apparently never served as a Navy chaplain in World War II.

At the same time as he resumed his pastorate, in light of frigid temperatures, rationed fuel- oil supplies, and a severe firewood shortage (no one was cutting firewood), Gray took the lead in collaborating with the Boothbay Harbor Methodist church to hold alternating joint services. The host church would provide the music, and the loose plate offering would be divided. Separate services would recommence Easter Sunday.[632]

The arrangement was unusual enough to be the subject of a story carried on WGAN, a Portland radio station. A long-serving deacon, James Blenn Perkins, Sr., headed the Congregational church committee formed to finalize the arrangements for the unusual Congregational-Methodist joint service. During the 1930s and 1940s Perkins was a bulwark of the church. Surprisingly, in an overwhelmingly Old Guard Republican state and Boothbay Harbor community, places where he carved a very successful business and political career, Deacon Blenn Perkins remained staunchly loyal to the Democratic party. Born in 1881, a 1906 Bowdoin graduate holding a law degree from the University of Maine, a six-term Lincoln County attorney general, representative in the Maine legislature, 1919–1920, 1942, 1946–1948, president of the Bath Savings Bank, and partner with his son, James Blenn Perkins Jr., in the Harbor-based law firm Perkins and Perkins, he loomed in stature not only in the Congregational church, but also in the town and state.[633]

Perkins' magisterial presence notwithstanding, it was the women of the church who during the difficult wartime years kept the institution steered steadily forward. At the January 5, 1942 church annual meeting, with J. Blenn Perkins, S. and Benjamin Rand being prominent exceptions, all those elected to church offices were women: Addie Dolloff, Stella McKown, Mabel Rand, Grace Labbie, Claire Miller, Grace Lewis, Mrs. James Blenn Perkins, and Mrs. Grange. The same women constituted the Dorcas and Congregational guilds, whose labors proved vital in sustaining the work of the church during the grim war years. Founded October 11, 1933, the Congregational Guild met monthly, usually at a member's home. The dozen or so women attending the meetings (if they missed they had to pay a token fine) ate lunch, often macaroni salad and scalloped potatoes. "Who could want more?" They dropped their coins in the "penny basket," held their business meeting, which mainly dealt with the guild's next fundraising event, then turned either to charitable sewing, bandage rolling for the war effort, or to games, most frequently bridge, but, once or twice, the game of "Cootie."[634]

"Cootie" aside, these women were hardly frivolous, but instead deadly serious people. Their "penny basket" raised $5 or more for the church; their many covered-dish suppers brought in $10 to $15, as did their minesweeper trials luncheons held the day that the ship trials took place at Sample's Shipyard. For one minesweeper's trials in early 1943 the women produced for the church $15.06 by making 180 sandwiches, bowls of salad, and ten dozen doughnuts. Another trials event grossed $19.05. Their 1943 food and "May Box" sale on the Boothbay Harbor Memorial Library lawn raised $38.37, while a combined white elephant sale and church supper earned slightly less, $36.72. They also held rummage sales ($48.15), sold Christmas candy, and made and sold Christmas wreaths.

Some of the women's wartime charitable ventures aided the town's war chest drives; others helped the Red Cross ($25); the Sunday School; and in 1944 women's money boosted Gray's "Building Fund" for a new vestry ($50). Significantly, much went into the church operating fund.[635]

The Reverend Kenneth V. Gray would not witness the building of the new vestry. Nor would he be in the pulpit in early May 1945 to cheer with his congregation "Victory in Europe." Gray preached his final sermon at the Boothbay Harbor church on Easter Sunday, April 7, 1944, shortly after which he and his family moved "Down east" to the Congregational church in Calais.

Rev. Aubrey Hastings—1944-1945

Three months later, July 15, 1944, accompanied by his wife and their newborn child, the Reverend Aubrey Hastings arrived in Boothbay Harbor to take the helm of the Congregational church. Having yet to complete his coursework at Andover Theological Seminary, Hastings for some reason insisted upon being installed by means of what had once been a familiar service that involved having the Lincoln Association convene a church council to oversee the installation. The church requested Blenn Perkins' opinion on the implications of such a ceremony for the sanctity of church autonomy. Perkins found nothing objectionable, and Hastings was installed. However, Hastings stayed in the pulpit less than a year before returning to Andover in June 1945, a few days after VE Day.[636]

Still in wartime mode, the rhythm of church life under Hastings resembled the rhythm under Gray. During the cold winter months from November through April, the union worship services with the Methodist church continued. The Dorcas and Congregational guilds continued to raise money at ship trials, library lawn sales, and at pot-luck suppers. [637]

One event did break the veritable calm. The annual meeting held January 8, 1945, came one day after what was called "The Town's Worst Fire." Occurring on Sunday morning, the inferno must have interrupted or even cancelled the church service. The waterfront blaze destroyed six buildings and twenty-seven boats, and forced many families to evacuate the most densely settled part of the town.[638]

Despite the inferno, the annual meeting, held while the waterfront ruins still smoldered, oozed optimism. The Sunday School flourished, the church treasury showed a "good balance," and as the gender of the newly elected church officers revealed, Benjamin Rand and J. Blenn Perkins, Sr., aside, it was still the church women—so vital during the Great Depression—whose labors and dedication kept the church afloat.[639]

Hastings left the Boothbay Harbor church that June, and the pulpit sat empty that historic August 1945 when U.S. B–29 bombers dropped atomic bombs on the Japanese cities of Hiroshima and Nagasaki. Six days later Japan surrendered, and two months later in October 1945 the Reverend Ernest Whithall, the church's first postwar pastor, accepted the call to the Boothbay Harbor Congregational church. [640]

The Boothbay Region and the Congregational Church in the Postwar World

Fearful that postwar demobilization might thrust the nation back into an economic depression, Boothbay Harbor, like the nation, faced the future with some trepidation. Yet, the years 1945–1965 proved to be not only prosperous, but also transformative. Thanks to the Marshall Plan to rebuild war-ravaged Europe, countries like

England, France, Belgium, Italy and Western Germany, and even Japan, became highly lucrative markets for American goods and services. The 1944 Servicemen's Readjustment Act (the so-called GI Bill) enabled many GIs, especially those with a high-school degree and some prewar college, to earn college diplomas at no-cost as well as to purchase homes with "no money down." For millions of industrial workers, the wartime demand for labor had greatly bolstered the union movement and, thus, decent middle-class earnings. Affordable mortgages (both GI-Bill and Federal Housing Administration (FHA)), especially for white Americans, impelled the trend toward suburbanization and also homeownership, which rose to 62 percent of Americans by 1960.

America's middle class burgeoned, and foreign policy events helped undergird this prosperity. Winston Churchill's 1947 address at Fulton, Missouri, observed that thanks to the threatening actions of the Soviet Union, an "Iron Curtain" now separated Communist Eastern Europe from the free West. A new "arms race" had begun and for Boothbay Harbor and nearby Bath, except for a brief postwar interlude, military shipbuilding continued to flourish.

Prosperity fueled cultural change. Despite the aura of traditional domesticity fostered by the television craze for shows such as "Leave it to Beaver," women steadily moved into the workforce and helped form the backbone of the growing consumer culture. Emblematic of that culture was the automobile. Thanks to the 1944 Federal Aid Highway Act and to Eisenhower's Highway Act of 1956, by 1960 a nascent network of multilane turnpikes and freeways spanned the country, connecting—and in many cases—encircling cities and making the suburban mall, not the historic but embattled downtown department store, America's new meeting place.[641]

But, this new market-propelled culture, from which Boothbay Harbor was hardly insulated, challenged older social and religious norms and values as well as ingrained racial and sexual attitudes. Books about sex by Bowdoin-graduate Alfred Kinsey, and on child rearing (namely Dr. Benjamin Spock's 1946 *Baby and Child Care*), movies such as "Rebel Without a Cause," and novels such as J.D. Salinger's *Catcher in the Rye* (1953), as well as court cases such as the 1954 Brown v. School Board, which banned racially segregated education, all foreshadowed serious social change and the revolutionary Civil Rights Movement and Youth Rebellion of the Sixties. [642]

Behind much of the postwar social and cultural change stood larger macrocosmic forces such as modernism and deindustrialization, which physically restructured American cities, redefined the organization of work, and foretold the computer age and globalization. These forces also impacted the American religious experience, not only for urban and suburban churches, but also for those in smaller coastal villages like Boothbay Harbor.

Religious trends among "mainline" churches (Lutherans, Presbyterians, Congregationalists, and Evangelical and Reformed, among them), led by theologians such as the Evangelical and Reformed Church's Reinhold Niebuhr, continued, as they had during the 1920s and 1930s, to espouse modernist thinking and to raise doubts about the hopeful theology of the early nineteenth century, which preached the perfectibility of man. Niebuhr, a Christian "realist," stressed the imperative of human justice and saw the church as an instrument for its attainment. While, after World War II, modernists like Niebuhr and Riverside Church's Harry Emerson Fosdick still clashed with Fundamentalists such as the youthful Reverend Billy Graham, both religious schools of thought saw church membership in their individual churches grow. Indeed, observers spoke of a "religious revival." Niebuhr called it "phenomenal," but saw the proliferation as an example of "religion emotion" not of "religion per se." He imagined postwar religious fervor as "a heightening [of] faith in religion, any religion," part of an American "search for community," a yearning "to belong," one that had spurred the exodus of urbanites to suburbia and produced the commonly heard phrase "the family that prays together stays together."[643]

Churches in the postwar era summoned parishioners "back to God" and proclaimed faith to be "a [Cold War] weapon against atheistic communism." Billy Graham loudly exhorted a religion that was both personal and social. Conversion, he preached, enabled men and women to work to overcome social ills. Other postwar TV clergy like Bishop Fulton Sheen (1895-1979) and Norman Vincent Peale (1898-1993) saw religion as therapeutic, a foundation for success in the modern world of big cities and big organizations. Whatever it was, religion in the postwar period, 1945-1965, filled churches. During these years 65 percent of the nation's population professed church membership, the highest ever recorded before or since. In 1957 the U.S. Census reported that 96 percent of Americans identified with some religion. [644]

The Boothbay Harbor Church in Postwar America
Although an hour and a half from Portland and over three hours from the metropolis of Boston, postwar Boothbay Harbor readily absorbed urban culture. During the 1950s, television sets mushroomed, streaming modern culture into the living rooms of Boothbay Harbor's Congregational church parishioners. Harbor Congregationalists owned cars, traveled to Portland, Boston, and New York; and welcomed tourists from those cities into their guest houses, hotels, restaurants, and gift shops. Moreover, every summer a prince of modernist theology, Harry Emerson Fosdick, D.D., in the nineteen fifties, now "Pastor Emeritus of New York's Riverside Church," preached to enormous crowds at the Congregational Church of Boothbay Harbor. Thus, the same forces of change at work in America's cities and suburbs inevitably enveloped the rural, coastal Boothbay Region, albeit somewhat more slowly.

Although at the turn of the nineteenth century the Boothbay region had prospered because of a mix of relatively small shipyards, an established ground fishing as well as lobster-fishing industry, and a fledgling, but steadily growing tourism, its economy had sputtered through the 1920s and 1930s. During those years the Harbor's population actually declined twelve percent, from 4,219 in 1900 to 3,729 in 1920, before rising four percent to 3,896 in 1940. However, after the war it rose almost ten percent by 1950, reflecting the wartime boom in shipbuilding and resurgent postwar tourism. It rose another seven percent by 1960, sustained increasingly by tourism.[645]

During World War II, Sample's Shipyard at Signal Point in Boothbay Harbor employed over 700 workers. By the late 1940s Sample's workforce had dwindled to about thirty men, about the same as Hodgdon's. In East Boothbay, Hodgdon and Goudy and Stevens employed over 300 during World War II, all building wooden-hulled minesweepers and other small craft. In 1950 after communist North Korean armed forces invaded South Korea in what was described as a "Police Action," President Harry Truman enlisted America in a United Nation's action to push the North back over the 38th parallel. [646]

Amidst the "Welcome Home Johnny" celebrations for returning World War II veterans and the ratcheting down of war-based shipbuilding, commercial fishing had resumed, and the towns painted and fixed up in full anticipation of a welcome revival of tourism. For the Congregational church and its new pastor, Ernest Whitnall, that meant preparing for the church's much anticipated one hundredth anniversary celebration.

Rev. Ernest Whitnall—1945–1948

Born in Southwold, England, Whitnall graduated from London University's Hackney Seminary. As an enlisted man, Whitnall, in August 1914, had joined the "London Irish Rifles." Fighting on the Western Front at the very heart of the notorious mud-caked and blood-soaked trench warfare, Whitnall attained the rank of corporal, but before being discharged at the war's end suffered serious battle wounds from both gunfire and exposure to mustard gas. Together with his Canadian bride, the Reverend Whitnall immigrated to America in 1919 and had served pastorates in Florida, Massachusetts, and at the St. Lawrence Congregational church, located on Munjoy Hill in Portland, before accepting the call to Boothbay Harbor in 1945.[647]

Involved in the Christian Endeavor Movement in London, which had been founded at Portland's West End Williston Church,

Whitnall brought with him to the Harbor church strong conservative convictions about religion, morality, and ethical behavior. After only a month in the Harbor pulpit and having conversed with parishioners such as J. Blenn Perkins, Sr. and Norman Hodgdon, Whitnall recognized the church's elevated stature in the community. However, like many vexed Americans during those years immediately following World War II, he feared that the war had undermined moral values, especially among the young. During the war, nearby Portland, having become crowded with a host of war workers and enlisted personnel, bemoaned the "girl problem," the presence, that is, of single military personnel, unattached male war workers, and young, equally unattached women. Portland feared an epidemic of immorality. Social critics also fretted that husbands and wives working round the clock on shipyard shifts left their children at home unsupervised. These same critics denounced the wartime increase in the number of teenage gangs, the rise in juvenile delinquency, and youth garbed in outlandish "zoot suit" attire, and blamed much of it on comic books.[648]

Whitnall discerned evidence of these same social evils lurking in the streets and byways of picturesque Boothbay Harbor. He accused the church's young people of being uninterested in religion. "A mere seven youths attended his Sunday evening's young people's meeting," complained Whitnall. "How can we interest these young people who never come?" he asked. "Too many are pleasure bent at night to be building a solid Christian character, a character they will never build in the movie houses or on the streets of the town. Young people of Boothbay Harbor," bemoaned Whitnall, "say church is where women go and it's not for men."[649]

Like many religious Americans, Whitnall regarded the popular wartime movie genre, *film noir* (stark crime-themed films like the "Maltese Falcon" and "The Big Sleep," both starring Humphrey Bogart) as symptomatic of cultural decline. "Morality and religion have suffered a staggering blow in these past few years," exhorted Whitnall, "and it will be what you and I of the great church of Christ do now that will make this world possible for us to live and grow in on the morrow."[650] Whitnall's sermon topics reflected his fears about the shallow depth of America's religious convictions. In March 1947 he preached about "My Responsibility as a Christian," "a timely subject for these days," he added. A few months later, in an eschatological musing, he spoke about "Thy Kingdom Come," following that, a half-year later in January 1948, with a sermon entitled "The Way of the New Life," which implored his listeners to believe in the need to be born again.[651]

Whitnall's poor health, a legacy of his service in World War I, not only rendered him absent from the pulpit on many Sundays, but also drew him to contemplate the next life. Nevertheless, he fully expected to be standing in the pulpit on August 1, 1948, when the church planned to celebrate its centennial. It was Whitnall who wrote Mouse Island summer resident and New York pastor emeritus Fosdick, inviting him to preach the centennial sermon. And, it was Whitnall who urged the importance of completing the considerable number of critical repairs to the church in time for the festivities. Not incidentally, the superintendent of the Sunday School, Dorothy Abbott, in her annual report for 1945, inveighed—not for the first time—about the inadequacy of the church school facilities. "We are like well-packed sardines in here each Sunday," she lamented, "and the noise is often terrific…[A]t present we have no piano."[652]

With the war just over, Whitnall in 1946 had seemed optimistic about actually accomplishing those repairs and improvements. As during the war, the church women, with J. Blenn Perkins, Sr., and Benjamin Rand as cheerleaders, proved no less diligent in their fundraising, holding food sales, making and selling Christmas wreaths, organizing rummage sales, raising $97 here, $46 there, and as much as $215 from the 1947 summer sale on the town library lawn. Sustained by this assiduous fundraising, Whitnall contended that church finances were now fairly stable. Some of the guild-raised money went to the minister's fund and to missions; some went into the vestry account that Vernon Gray inaugurated, and some went specifically for the 1948 centennial celebration.

However, neither J. Blenn Perkins, Sr., nor Ernest Whitnall would be present for this centennial event. In mid-January 1948, at age 66, James Blenn Perkins, Sr. died. Four months later, in May, his heart failing, Whitnall died in Bridgton, Maine.[653]

Rev. Dr. William James Campbell—1948-1949

As the supply pastor secured to fill the new vacancy in the Congregational church pulpit, Dr. William James Campbell hailed from prestigious Vanderbilt University, where he had taught "Practical Theology." Before Vanderbilt, Campbell, a native of Prince Edward Island, had served churches in Detroit, Port Huron, and Kalamazoo, Michigan. In September 1948 the church named Campbell its settled pastor.[654] Except for the centennial, Campbell's brief pastorate proved uneventful. Held Thursday, August 12, 1948, the day one hundred years earlier that marked the founding "on the hill" of the Second Congregational Church of Boothbay Harbor, the "Centennial Celebration" featured Rev. Dr. Harry Emerson Fosdick's sermon, as well as a reading on church history by local historian Miss Elizabeth Reed. It also featured greetings from both the Reverend Orville O. Losier of the Congregational Christian Conference of Maine and the Reverend Forest Littlefield of the Methodist Church of Boothbay Harbor. An evening music program, hosted by the Congregational Guild, followed, capped by a talk, "Looking Forward," by newly arrived clergyman, Dr. Campbell.[655]

As usual, in January 1949 the church held its annual meeting and elected a familiar slate of officers, Mrs. Benjamin Rand, Mrs. John Dorr, Mrs. Paul Abbott (Church School superintendent), and Mrs. Addie Dolloff (auditor).

There was, however, a new deacon, James Blenn Perkins Jr., the son of the late Blenn Perkins, Sr. Born in 1912, the younger Perkins graduated from Boothbay Harbor High School and spent a year at Hebron Academy before attending and graduating first from Bowdoin College and then from Harvard Law School. Following Harvard, he became the other half of Boothbay Harbor's Perkins and Perkins law firm, and in 1938 succeeded his father as the Lincoln County attorney and as deacon in 1949 of the Congregational church. During World War II, Perkins Jr. served as part of the U.S. Naval Force Command in Europe and in the Office of the Naval Attaché in London. Unlike his father, Perkins Jr. voted and ran for office as a Republican. [656]

The Boothbay Harbor Congregational Church and the Creation of the United Church of Christ

Strangely, with the exception of a brief mention in the Congregational Guild minutes for February 5, 1948, almost nothing appears in local church records about the number one issue raging that year among the clergy and academic cadre of the Congregational, Christian, and the Evangelical and Reformed (E&R) churches: namely, a "Merger."[657] From April 17, 1948 through the spring of 1949, Campbell almost weekly received mailings, for and against the proposed merger. However, no evidence exists either that he took a stand on the issue, or that he communicated anything in particular about this controversial merger to his Boothbay Harbor congregation. This is significant, because nearby Hallowell, Maine, like Cleveland, Ohio, Chicago, Illinois, and Pasadena, California, was a center of the "Antimerger" movement.[658]

Congregationalists had earlier united. In 1931 the Congregational Church had merged with the Christian Church to form the Congregational Christian Church. Liberal, ecumenical-minded clergy, like Reinhold Niebuhr of the E&R Church and Raymond Calkins of the prominent First [Congregational] Church of Cambridge, Massachusetts, argued forcefully for a unified Protestantism to boldly confront the evil and injustice abroad in the world. At a meeting in Grinnell, Iowa, in 1946, church leaders from both the Congregational Christian and the Evangelical and Reformed (E&R) churches had approved a merger, based upon an "agreed upon interpretation" of the "Basis of Union." The "Basis" created a General Synod of the United Church that in Calkin's words "would not violate or endanger or obscure the essential witness of Congregationalism and its historic contribution to Protestantism, namely, the freedom and independence of the local church." A subsequent meeting of both church bodies in Oberlin, Ohio, established that, to be consummated, the merger would require that seventy-five percent of the Congregational Christian and E&R churches vote their approval of the merger by January 1, 1949.[659]

Dr. Marion J. Bradshaw of Bangor Theological Seminary, Rev. James W. Fitfield of the First Congregational Church of Los Angeles, and Rev. Malcolm K. Burton of New London, Connecticut repudiated almost every word of the so-called merger "Basis." They espied in the document "irreconcilable" differences between the forms of the two church bodies, especially the fact that the Evangelical and Reformed Church's synodical organization challenged historic Congregational church polity, whereby individual churches (not regional synods) owned their own property and voted approval of all church policy. Bradshaw detected in the "Basis" "Presbyterial leanings" and a "Calvinistic approach to impose a super-church, which shall give orders to both individuals and the state."

By November 1948 the merger opponents, a body that Calkins deemed "small," had created a pamphlet entitled the *ANTI-MERGER*. Simultaneously, the pro-union forces, at a meeting in Cleveland, established the Committee of Fifteen to aggressively secure the seventy-five percent vote from the two denominations. Bradshaw branded the pro-merger forces "Totalitarian." Reams of broadsides from both sides piled up on ministerial desks, but by February 1949 the pile slowed after the vote showed the pro-merger forces had garnered only sixty-five and a half percent, not the seventy-five percent needed for merger approval. However, a positive event cheered the pro-merger forces: the anti-merger forces lost a court challenge to the Oberlin process. The pro-merger v. anti-merger battle had deadlocked by the beginning of 1957, when slowly but surely the tally of churches voting, congregation by congregation, inexorably produced victory. In the meantime, only silence prevailed at the Boothbay Harbor church.[660]

A Profile of the 1950 Boothbay Harbor Church

William James Campbell never received the April pro-or-anti-merger literature. He died in March 1949, having served the church for little over one year. It was toward the end of Campbell's pastorate that the church undertook one of its periodic surveys of church membership, assaying which members were active and which were inactive. From the handwritten, annotated membership lists, examined and tabulated by the author side by side with the 1940 U.S. manuscript or "enumerated" census, emerges a portrait of the Boothbay Harbor Congregational Christian church circa 1950.

Of the 115 members counted, forty-four or thirty-three percent can be identified in the 1940 manuscript census, including information (often complete) on age, gender, family status, occupation, annual income, and the value of an owned home. The persistence of this population cohort is remarkable considering the intervention of World War II and the opportunity for geographic mobility afforded by wartime military service and work in both munitions plants and shipbuilding firms in nearby cities. Postwar veteran mortgage and education assistance benefits also accelerated mobility.

Examining the forty-four members of the 1950 church cohort reveals that after World War II the Congregational church remained significantly female. Twenty-seven of the forty-four members identified were women, and only eight had husbands as co-members. This compares to the 1952 list of membership, which counted eighty-five women and forty-two men.

In concert with other mainline Protestant Christian churches (Presbyterian, Methodist, Baptist, Lutheran) the Harbor church between 1940 and 1950 retained its aura of status. Over three-fourths of the membership cohort possessed either a high-school degree or a post-high-school diploma. In fact, almost 42 percent had either attended or graduated from college. Of the thirty-one church members who identified an occupation in 1940 (not including those describing themselves as "retired" or as "housewives") the vast majority (over seventy percent) listed non-manual occupations. Sixty-one percent engaged in business, government work (customs office), or the professions (lawyers, teachers, doctors). Eight reported skilled trades (welders, automobile mechanics, ship builders). Only two church members identified in the 1940 census could be called unskilled. While communicants built boats and captained ships, only one (a lobster merchant) engaged in fishing for a livelihood in a town where in addition to tourism and shipbuilding, fishing (lobstering) represented a declining, but still important segment of the economy. About half of the twenty-nine heads of household (including retired persons) reported their income to the 1940 census taker. The $1,500 mean income of those reporting further confirms the solidly upper-middle-income, home-owning status of the congregation.[661]

Rev. George Gledhill—1949-1953, Another "Wartime" Minister
For the fourth time in less than five years, the Boothbay Harbor church searched for a new settled pastor. Two had died in office. Following an unsuccessful invitation to a minister in Duxbury, Massachusetts, recommended by the Congregational Board of Pastor Supply, the church received a letter from Wilbur Bull of Waterford, Maine, recommending to the Boothbay Harbor church Rev. George Gledhill of Winslow, a long-time summer resident of Fisherman's Island. Bull praised Gledhill, but, to be sure, somewhat fainteartedly. "He may not be an able preacher," confessed Bull, "but he is one of the most truly Christian men we have ever known. He is a faithful worker, and a good organizer...[He] meets people well, and I think most naturally can meet your summer residents."[662]

In August 1949 Gledhill assumed the pastorate of the Harbor church. He would shepherd the Boothbay Harbor Congregational flock for four and a half years, years during which the Cold War suddenly warmed. In 1949 Mao Zedong's People's Republic of China tested an atomic bomb, and soon, in June 1950, after North Korea attacked the South by crossing the 38th parallel, American-led, United Nations armed forces landed in Korea. In the fall of

1950 those forces, under General Douglas MacArthur, penetrated deep into the north, where they faced the armies of Red China. By the end of 1951 the war had settled into a bloody stalemate, which lasted until an armistice was reached in July 1953. That August Gledhill announced his resignation. Thus, as Gray did, Gledhill served as a wartime pastor.[663]

Called a "police action," for most Americans it was war, and in Boothbay Harbor and East Boothbay the shipyards hummed during those Korean "War" years. Orders for military vessels created another boom for Sample's, Goudy and Stevens, and the Hodgdon yards. In 1950 Washington awarded Sample's a contract for three 145-feet-long minesweepers, and then in 1951 it gave the team of Hodgdon Brothers and Goudy & Stevens a contract for eight more. For the new work Sample's boosted its workforce to 300; Hodgdon and Goudy & Stevens employed 250. Hodgdon added a new thirty-five-feet addition to its main shipbuilding shed. A year later, while finishing its work on four minesweepers, Sample's won a one million dollar government contract for twelve sixty-three feet Navy crash boats.[664]

Shipbuilding complemented the Harbor's other historic industry, fishing, which in the early 1950s plodded faithfully, but not vigorously along. The Boothbay Harbor Freezer continued to process whiting; but ground fishing, as it had for decades, remained precarious. The Boothbay Harbor Fishermen's Cooperative sent a delegation to Rockland to discuss "industry problems." In fact, lobster fishing remained the real staple. In 1951 a new seafood firm opened specializing in shipping canned and frozen lobster.

However, while Harbor and East Boothbay shipyards hummed, in 1951 dramatic and presumably welcome economic news splashed across the headlines of the *Boothbay Register*: a "new" industry might arrive. The town had created a blue ribbon committee (Asa Tupper, Dr. Philip Gregory, and Roy Kelley, publisher of the *Boothbay Register*) to negotiate with a Georgia industrial firm interested in bringing a shoe factory to Boothbay Harbor. After first documenting that the town possessed a suitable workforce, the town committee was charged to find and purchase a facility and lease it to the shoe company free for the first year. The prospect of a shoe factory excited the town. A workforce materialized, but the deal collapsed when the committee failed to raise the $35,000 necessary to buy the factory building it had located on Atlantic Avenue.[665]

The doomed shoe factory deal paralleled the failure of region voters in 1951 to heed school superintendent Harold Clifford's urgent plea to approve funding to replace the inadequate and crumbling School Street high school building. Shipbuilding and fishing aside, the real direction of the Boothbay region economy in those years veered ever more sharply toward tourism, a direction especially apparent after the Maine Turnpike construction reached Augusta, and the state had rebuilt and modernized Route 1 all the way to Brunswick.

The Boothbay region had attracted summer people in the nineteenth century when Southport Island, Capitol Island, Squirrel Island, Bayville-Murray Hill, and Ocean Point all hosted colonies accessed by regular steamship service. Tourism burgeoned in the twentieth century with the advent of the automobile, but slackened during the Great Depression and World War II. It quickened after the war when the Harbor, with the help of the Chamber of Commerce and the state, sponsored a much ballyhooed tuna fishing tournament. When the state bowed out in 1952, Boothbay Harbor resident Rupert Neily, Sr. tried to replace the tournament with a two-week-long international regatta and water sports festival. Tuna tournaments, water festivals or not, tourism flourished in the fifties. New gift and candy shops, restaurants and hotels opened, as well as art studios, and excursion boats like the *Richard T* and Captain Eliot Winslow's new *Argo*.[666]

Despite Cold War atomic bomb drills and daily press updates on the progress of U.N. troops led by McArthur moving north of the 38th parallel into North Korea, the early fifties in Boothbay Harbor were marked by its white-spired Congregational church, and an apparently prosperous people living up to the stereotypic

"Happy Days." With war work again, but this time without the gas, butter, or other rationing of World War II, church attendance, especially in the summertime, rose. Gledhill's weekly sermons followed current upbeat themes of religion and were uplifting and therapeutic; for example, "Religious Certainty," "Christian Liberty," and "Church-Going Families are Happy Families." For "Race Relations Sunday," February 8, 1953, Gledhill preached on "Christian Brotherhood;" and on Memorial Day, May 24, 1953: "Our Vision of Peace." Significantly, the early 1950s witnessed the return to vacationland and to the Congregational church pulpit of a summer line-up of distinguished preachers, including Dr. Harry Emerson Fosdick, Dr. James Willis Lenhart (then of State Street Congregational Church in Portland), the Reverend Dr. Wallace W. Robbins (a Unitarian, and president of Meadville Theological Seminary at the University of Chicago), Dr. Arthur Baldwin of Philadelphia's Chestnut Street Baptist Church, and Dr. Charles Whitney Gilkey, dean of the University of Chicago chapel. [667]

Improved attendance and a resurgent local economy resurrected the old World War II discussions about enlarging the church vestry. In the spring of 1953 the church's business committee solicited architectural drawings for a much larger vestry including basement space to accommodate Sunday School rooms. On July 17, 1953, the distinguished Portland architectural firm of John Howard Stevens and John Calvin Stevens II submitted plans. However, the church deemed the plans too grandiose and expensive. Before a simpler plan appeared, the Reverend Gledhill announced his resignation. On August 28, 1953 he preached his final sermon and left to assume the pastorate of the Congregational church in Thomaston. [668]

Rev. Edward Manning—1954-1955

A new settled minister did not arrive at the Harbor church until almost seven months later, in the spring of 1954. Meanwhile, a series of guest preachers supplied the pulpit. One of those guests was the Reverend Edward Manning, the minister of Prides Corner Union

Church in Westbrook, a suburb of Portland. Ultimately, he became the Boothbay Harbor Congregational church's newest settled pastor on March 14, 1954.[669]

While a new suburban, mass consumption culture tightened its grip on America, and tourism strengthened in the Harbor, several events in 1954 foreshadowed a more tumultuous decade to come. Both occurred just months after Manning's arrival. On May 8, in distant Indochina, the French colonial fortress of Dien Bien Phu fell. For two months the communist Viet Minh forces under General Giap surrounded, tunneled, and undermined the bastion defended by the elite French Foreign Legion. Despite parachuted supplies and reinforcements, the battered French force suffered a terrible defeat. The French left, and Indochina split into a communist North Vietnam and a noncommunist South Vietnam, the latter increasingly under the protection of the United States. Year by year the American presence in South Vietnam and the guerrilla war against Vietcong infiltration from the North escalated until at the cost of 58,220 American lives and years of social protest, the United States, like France, departed. [670]

A week after the fall of Dien Bien Phu, the U.S. Supreme Court, in the case of Brown v. the Board of Education of Topeka, Kansas (1954) declared racially segregated education in America unconstitutional, accelerating a Civil Rights Movement begun during World War II and leading to seamstress Rosa Parks' protest against Southern bus segregation in 1955 and to the Reverend Martin Luther King's decisive leadership of the bus boycott in Parks City, Montgomery, Alabama.[671]

The Cold War, and the Korean war had kept the Boothbay region's shipyards busy through the first half of the fifties. In 1954 Sample's and Goudy & Stevens won a $9 million contract to build four 171-feet minesweepers. However, in January 1954 a costly fire temporarily shut down shipbuilding at Hodgdon Brothers.[672] More big economic news for the town arrived in 1955, especially regarding the town's second largest business, tourism. That year Hollywood selected Boothbay Harbor as the site for an important scene in its movie production of the Rogers and Hammerstein musical "Carousel." Specifically, Hollywood chose an East Side site, formerly Brewer's Lobster Shack, for the song number "Spring is Busting Out All Over." Initially, the song scene featured crooner Frank Sinatra as Billy, the barker at the carousel. Holed up briefly on Landing Road on Southport Island and detesting the local Maine weather, Sinatra abruptly flew back to New York. Gordon McCrea replaced him, and the show went on, to the glory of Boothbay Harbor. Meanwhile, a new motel, the Midtown, appeared in the bustling town, and the House of Logan opened a new sportswear shop.[673]

Rev. Manning arrived in March 1954, a year before the "Carousel" film crew. Unlike Sinatra, he stayed. Despite the shipbuilding boom and the aura of "new" tourism, the church that year faced unanticipated heavy expenses. A damaged steeple required repair, and the church exterior desperately needed to be repainted. The business committee put the cost for both at $2,500, a number it included in the church's total estimated budget for the year 1954 of $8,973. But, the estimated income in pledges, loose offering and dividends for that year came to only $4,723, leaving a gap of $4,250. On July 10, 1954, only three months after Manning's arrival, the business committee, chaired by Norman Hodgdon and still composed mainly of church women, mailed out an urgent appeal imploring the congregation to "carefully and prayerfully" increase their pledges.[674]

Six months later, with thanks to the successful July appeal, and to the towns' improved economy, and, furthermore, to several generous bequests, the church's financial situation substantially improved. At its annual meeting on January 3, 1955, thirteen years after Pastor Kenneth V. Gray had first urged its building, the Boothbay Harbor Congregational church voted unanimously to raise the sum of $20,000 to build an addition to the vestry that included a new vestry and Sunday School. The church selected Gleason Gamage to build it and appointed a "Building Committee for the New Vestry" chaired by Raymond Pennoyer, with the Reverend Manning, George Vaughn, Dora Greenlaw, Norman Hodgdon, Blenn Perkins Jr., and Miss Bea Groves as members.

The two-level addition provided 24-feet by 43-feet vestry, an "auditorium," a 14-feet by 30-feet "assembly room," three Sunday-school classrooms, and two lavatories. Thanks to a bequest in the will of Susan B. Russell, the church as of January 10, 1955 had already raised $11,222. Gamage estimated the total cost of the project to be $16,927. Subsequent to the estimate, the committee voted not only to enlarge the proposed vestry two feet toward the east, but also to include a second toilet on the lower floor and popular linoleum flooring in the new upper floor kitchen and in the pastor's study. The building committee also decided upon a cement-filled cinder-block foundation wall and a complete septic tank system rather than a rock-lined cesspool. Despite raising a total of $19,256 by April 1955, the total cost of the project had climbed to $27,353, forcing the church to take a $5,000 mortgage on the church parsonage.[675]

Albeit brief, Manning's tenure proved eventful, marked by the vestry project and a shipbuilding and tourism-fueled prosperity. His sermons reflected timely themes that were more secular than biblical, for example, "Jesus and the Hometown," "The Churches' Answer to Communism," and "Spiritual Preparedness versus Military Preparedness." Nevertheless, Rev. Manning left the church in December 1955 less than two years after arriving.[676]

Rev. Ivan Welty—1956-1965

Soon after Manning's departure the church on February 14, 1956 called Ivan Welty to be its next pastor. Welty preached his first sermon as settled pastor on May 12, 1956. The new pastor arrived in a Boothbay Harbor now rapidly transforming from a shipbuilding and fishing village, where old-fashioned charm itself attracted tourism, into a thriving Maine vacation town that actively lured tourism as its primary business. In 1960 lobster hauling comprised 90 percent of the town's fishing industry. As for shipbuilding, however, with a 1956 armistice in Korea and with advisors only in Vietnam, Cold War tensions eased, and thus, less demand existed for minesweepers. At Sample's, labor issues, formerly unknown in Boothbay Harbor, flared in 1956. In fact, workers at Sample's walked out on strike. Soon after the strike had been settled, the Navy temporarily suspended funding for Sample's two unfinished minesweepers, idling 250 workers. When funding resumed, and the firm had launched the last two of its four-ship order, Sample's ended its Naval business. It switched to building tugboats in 1958.[677]

Meanwhile, having recovered from its devastating fire, Hodgdon won a government contract to build seven 30-feet steel Navy workboats. However, that order aside, in November 1958, Hodgdon announced a new "3-Point Shipyard Program" to "steer the 131 year-old shipyard back to pleasure and small boats." For years during the 1950s Hodgdon's had emblazoned the image of its signature product across its weekly, half-page advertisement in the *Boothbay Register*. The image had been a Naval minesweeper, darting intrepidly through a heavy sea. That quickly changed. Hodgdon's new 1958 advertisement featured its "Newly Designed," "Unique" 21-foot sloop, "The Fastest [sail] Boat of Its Size."[678]

Like the town, Hodgdon now saw its future in America's consumer society, in middle-class vacationers or summer residents, people with paid vacations and with rising disposable incomes, in short, in tourism. In 1956, the same year the new high school opened on the Wiscasset Road adjoining the community athletic field, Boothbay Harbor earmarked monies for expanding tourist parking. In 1958 the rebuilt, modernized Route 1 at last reached the intersection with Route 27 South to Boothbay Harbor, and *Boothbay Register* columnist Sidney Baldwin reminded his readership that "Tourists Benefit Everyone, Not Simply Hotel and Motel Operators." [679]

The Harbor Passenger Boat Association announced in early 1958 that pleasure boats would operate through September. Yearly, the colorful palette of town gift shops, candy emporiums, restaurants, and other tourist businesses expanded. In 1956 the Lake View Motel had opened, soon joined by the Linekin Lodge and the Dodge Inn. Unfortunately, in February 1958 a flash fire caused $300,000 in damages to the Wharftel owned by the Fishermen's Wharf Inn. The *Boothbay Register* called the Wharftel "one of the most popular spots in the region and one of the 'Harbor's' biggest industries." It urged the town to help it to quickly rebuild. [680]

Buttressed by a sizable $5,000, bequest from the Jessie Dow estate, by growing summer church attendance, and by its enlarged vestry and Sunday School space, the Congregational church, like the town, enjoyed halcyon times during the Welty years. Welty gave sermons with snappy and often intriguing titles whose content sometimes proved difficult to decipher. Consider the following: "Spiritual Dust," "Try it On," "The Weakness of Giants," "Haunted Houses," "The Lure of Pagan Incense," and "Hidden Gods." A host of illustrious summer preachers continued to mount the pulpit, including Dr. Wallace Robbins, Dr. Charles Gilkey of State Street Congregational Church in Portland, the Reverend James Lenhart, and Dr. Loren A. Shepard, who served for thirty-eight years as a medical missionary in Turkey.[681]

However, nowhere in 1957, neither in Welty's sermon topics, nor in the content of guild or business committee minutes or correspondence can one discover that on Tuesday, June 25, in Cleveland, Ohio, the Evangelical and Reformed Church and the Congregational Christian Church, "a fellowship of Biblical people under a mutual covenant for responsible freedom in Christ," joined together as the United Church of Christ. "The union was possible," stated the message forwarded to all the united churches, "because the two companies of Christians hold the same belief that Christ and Christ alone is the head of the Church."[682]

Under Welty's pastorate, the church officers with few exceptions, including newcomers Eugene Tavenner and Richard Conant, remained familiar persons. In 1959, Mrs. Robert Walbridge served as treasurer, J. Blenn Perkins Jr., Wilder Blake, and Hallman Russell were deacons, and Mrs. Eldred Lewis, Mrs. John Dorr, and Norman Hodgdon sat on the business committee. That April, however, Wilder Blake, deacon, as well as assistant treasurer and cashier of the First National Bank of Boothbay Harbor, died. [683]

But, while Welty's pastorate, the membership, and the soaring white steeple of the 112-year-old Congregational church edifice, proclaimed enduring small-town stability, change inexorably beckoned. In a close 1960 presidential election, John F. Kennedy, a Catholic, defeated Richard Nixon. Youthful, handsome, articulate, the war hero of P.T. 109, Kennedy especially excited young America. Seemingly, the Bay of Pigs fiasco in Cuba (1961), and the Cuban Missile scare (1962) hardly ruffled the spirits of the prosperous nation. Summer travelers in ever larger numbers drove their Fords, Chevys, and increasingly, Volkswagens to places such as Boothbay Harbor.

During the summer before the November 1960 election, the Harbor witnessed several auspicious changes. Founded as a sanitarium by Dr. Philip Gregory in 1906, thanks to Hill-Burton Act (1946) funds, and with $15,000 from a James Dow bequest, on May 12, 1960, a new Saint Andrews Hospital opened with thirty beds and both a nursing and obstetrical wing. Almost simultaneously the town celebrated the opening of the rebuilt and new "ultra-modern Fishermen's Wharf Inn" a two story, colonial-style, twenty-four-unit motel with a gift shop and very plush dining room.[684]

While not ultra-modern, the Congregational church in November proclaimed itself newly and "attractively redecorated." At the cost of $11,000, the church choir loft and pulpit platform were extended, a new red carpet laid down, and a new, forced-air heating system installed. The church gave much of the credit for the redecoration to "our pastor, Rev. Ivan Welty, who has brought us together to work as a family." [685]

Year by year new motels, new restaurants, gift shops and enlarged marinas and yacht repair and storage facilities opened. The town brashly advertised itself in 1961 as the "Boating Capital of New England." To protect visiting yachtsmen as well as excursion boat passengers from the stench of raw sewage, in 1962 the town, using a federal grant, built a needed sewage treatment plant. To protect its own youth, Boothbay Harbor vaccinated all school children with the Salk polio vaccine. However, the town voted against adding fluoride to its water. At the same time Southport summer resident Rachael Carson's 1962 *Silent Spring* suggested that to protect the environment, the region must reconsider its use of DDT spray to ward off summer mosquito pests. [686]

In the year 1962 those stiff winds of cultural change blowing through the nation seemingly arrived in the Harbor. First, on January 25, the United States Supreme Court in a six to one decision ruled in the case of Engel v. Vitale that New York's prescribed school prayer violated the Constitution's First Amendment. In a bold editorial, "Right is Right," defending the court's decision, the *Boothbay Register* stated that while its critics might condemn the court as "far left," "in this case as in the earlier Brown vs. School Board case outlawing school segregation," the *Register* believed that "the court ruled liberally with the idea of equality racially, politically, and religiously always of prime consideration." [687]

Asked his opinion on the court's prayer ruling, the Reverend Ivan Welty demurred. He hoped the ruling "only applied to official [government] prayers…[and would] not interfere with the free right of local schools to worship according to local customs [or] do away with the prayers opening Congress…I am not nearly as worried about the Supreme Court," charged Welty, "as I am about the ordinary, indifferent American citizen who completely forgets that our American civil society depends on church principles."[688]

Then in August 1962, in a hastily arranged visit, America's first Catholic president, and a Democrat came to historically Republican and Yankee Protestant Boothbay Harbor, Maine. Kennedy and his sister Patricia Kennedy Lawford spent the night on his boxer friend Gene Tunney's John's Island, and on Sunday morning, August 12, arrived by boat to attend church at Our Lady Queen of Peace Roman Catholic Church. A cheering crowd estimated at some 2,500 people awoke early to greet the president. The *Boothbay Register*, reporting on the event, observed that "political affiliations dissolved. For that matter so did other impressions harbored by people who had never experienced any direct contact with the man or the office. [The town] enjoyed the visit because it gave us a day unlike any other. It cast a spell that lingered." [689]

Fifteen months later, in Dallas, Texas, an assassin's bullet ended the life of John F. Kennedy. Then on November 28, the *Boothbay Register* boldly headlined "Region Joins World in Mourning Death of President John F. Kennedy." It poignantly titled its editorial that day "He Was Our Friend."[690]

We do not know whether on that early Sunday morning of August 12, Ivan Welty or, for that matter, any members of the Congregational church joined the throng of early risers who welcomed the president. During Kennedy's 1,000 days in office, however, the church, like the town, enjoyed continued prosperity. Weekly attendance in the early 1960s averaged between 122 and 126, up from 100. And in 1961 the Boothbay Harbor church, after four years, finally voted to become part of the United Church of Christ.[691] Its official name since then is the Congregational Church of Boothbay Harbor, UCC, although it is commonly known around the region as the Congo church.

The business committee had invested the $5,000 from the Jessie Porter Down bequest in the Tri-County Trust of New York. As a result by 1963 the church, in addition to the Dow Trust and other gifts, owned sixty-five shares of the Stanley Corporation, and thirty-four shares of Gulf Oil stock. The business committee, increasingly but not exclusively composed of men, in the early 60s voted to increase Welty's salary from $3,500 to $4,000. At the same time it voted "that Welty be retained as minister as long as he wished." His sermon topics: such as "Turning the World Upside Down" and "Giants in a Promised Land," remained as before, whimsical and highly palatable to a congregation seeking comfort and community in an increasingly tumultuous world. Indeed, Welty possessed a highly creative mind and authored a number of children's books as well as articles for religious journals. His nine-year pastorate was in 1965 the longest since the church had been built in Boothbay Harbor in 1884. [692]

The Weltys lived in the church parsonage at 56 Oak Street, an elderly building, which, much to the chagrin of the business committee, needed constant maintenance. Therefore, the church rejoiced in February 1965 when church member Alexander Tener, a retired judge from Sewickley, Pennsylvania, as a gift, deeded to the church, the Brewer property on Roads End. Tener was married to Ethel Logan, the founder in 1930 of the apparel store House of Logan and the gift shop, Village Store. Ethel had died in 1961. In the gift, Tener specified that the property be used for a new parsonage.

About the same time as the Tener gift, Welty announced his plan to leave the church pulpit in June 1965. The business committee accepted Welty's resignation "with regret." He left the church not to accept a new pastorate, but to serve as pastor/administrator of Gould Farm in Monterey, Massachusetts. The farm worked with "troubled souls" who found it difficult to cope with the pressures of life. [693]

Conclusion

The wartime and postwar years, 1942–1965, brought great changes to both the Harbor and its Congregational church. The Boothbay region in 1940 featured a picturesque sprinkling of summer colonies and summer guest houses, several large and old-fashioned summer hotels, a bevy of small shipyards, and a small but active fishing fleet, including many lobster boats. During World War II, three of the region's boat yards landed Naval contracts to build wooden-hulled minesweepers, contracts that during the Korean War, 1950–1953 were reinstated. By the late 1950s, with an armistice in place in Korea, the age of East Boothbay and Boothbay Harbor-built minesweepers ended, and the yards turned to the building, maintenance, or storage of pleasure craft and tugboats.

Indeed, by 1965, having gained fame as the charming setting for the movie musical "Carousel," now calling itself the "Boating Capital of New England," and the home of five marinas, fine hotels, motels, restaurants, clothing and gift shops, Boothbay Harbor imagined itself as primarily a tourist capital, which still sheltered a fleet of mainly lobster boats, insuring itself some patina of the past.

An important part of that patina was the iconic white steeple of the 1848-built Congregational church. Like the region as a whole, the church had weathered the harsh years of the Great Depression, and the cold winters, rationing, and long work shifts of World War II. Indeed, the war and postwar years proved difficult for the historic church. Between 1942 and 1965 no fewer than six ministers, two of whom died in office, served the church. But, these were also years during which the church overcame adversity, built a new vestry and Sunday School, redecorated the sanctuary, acquired land for a new parsonage, and emerged fiscally stronger than perhaps it had ever been.

CHAPTER 11

THE CHURCH IN AN AGE OF TURMOIL: 1965–1986
by John F. Bauman

Introduction: The Tumult and the Shouting

As Saint Paul's letters testified, Christian Churches have forever weathered change, and during this tumultuous era, 1965–1986, in America, change came relentlessly. The church's new minister in 1965, Richard Balmforth, arrived amidst President Lyndon Baines Johnson's "War on Poverty" (a part of Johnson's "Great Society"), while, simultaneously, America enmeshed itself deeper and deeper in what historians have called the "quagmire" of Vietnam. To salvage victory in Southeast Asia, Johnson, that same year, ordered a massive aerial bombing of fiery napalm aimed at literally removing the tropical jungle canopy of Southeast Asia.

Vietnam hardly occurred in a vacuum. While young American soldiers (disproportionately black) patrolled the Mekong Delta and swept through South Vietnam villages on "search and destroy missions," other youth—many of them members of a growing "counterculture" ("hippies" some were called) and many of them found on America's college campuses—staged demonstrations that were not always peaceful. Some marched on Washington, some burned draft cards, and others raided or even bombed government buildings, or held "summers of love" in places like San

Francisco's Haight-Ashbury district. At the same time that mostly white, college-age youth protested the war in Vietnam and rebelled against contemporary mainstream norms (short hair, and sexual constraints), African-American youth, the denizens of opportunity-bereft urban ghettos in cities such as in Newark, Philadelphia, New York, Washington, D.C., and Chicago, spent "long, hot, summers" rioting against poor housing, police harassment, and deepening poverty.

America during these years seemed thrust from crisis to crisis. Besieged by throngs of protestors, young and old, Johnson in 1968 refused a second term. Seeking respite, the nation turned for its next president to Republican Richard M. Nixon, who, contemptuous of longhaired antiwar protestors, promised to quell the social unrest. Tormented, perhaps paranoiac, fearful that "enemies" conspired to deny him a second term, Nixon took extralegal means to defeat his opponents. Facing impeachment for helping cover up a botched attempt to pilfer documents from Democratic Party headquarters at Washington's Watergate condominiums, Nixon resigned. Under Nixon's successor, his Vice President Gerald Ford, America abandoned Vietnam without victory; and under both Ford and his successor, Jimmy Carter, the nation endured an unprecedented severe energy shortage, a nuclear meltdown at Pennsylvania's Three-Mile-Island nuclear reactor, and a hostage crisis in Iran. By the time the Reverend David Stinson in 1982 became settled pastor at the Congregational Church of Boothbay Harbor, the nation literally begged for quietus. It came. By 1982 President Ronald Reagan had ushered in a long era of conservative politics, ending two decades of tumult, and closing the books on any policies even vaguely resembling Johnson's "Great Society."

Boothbay Harbor's white-steepled, Gothic-revival Congregational church, a part of the theologically liberal United Church of Christ, did not escape the social and political turmoil rending America in the 1960s and 1970s. Nor did American religion as a whole. Indeed, the 1960s resonated as a pivotal year in both political and religious history. In that decade American liberal Protestantism steadily pursued a more socially tolerant, more progressive, as contrasted with evangelical agenda—one described as "ecumenical" by David Hollinger, professor of American intellectual history at the University of California, Berkeley. Indeed, the United Church of Christ (UCC) leadership stood at the center of that movement. In January 1961 Martin E. Marty, professor of modern Christian history at the University of Chicago, had heralded John Fitzgerald Kennedy's inauguration as the "End of Protestant America" and the death knell of the "Protestant Establishment." Liberal, pluralistic, ecumenicists, harshly critical of the racism they perceived in the institutional American church, marched in the van of Rev. Martin Luther King, Junior's civil rights movement. However, the UCC leadership, along with many "mainline" Presbyterian, Episcopalian, and Methodist church leaders, had advanced far beyond the church laity seated Sundays now in increasingly less crowded sanctuaries. This widening gap between the ecumenicist church leadership and the laity, in Hollinger's view, reshaped not only American Christendom, but American politics as well. While liberalizing mainline churches like the UCC struggled to keep pews full, conservative, evangelical churches, from small fundamentalist rural sects to megachurches in California and elsewhere would—in postwar America—steadily boom. Meanwhile, the Boothbay Harbor Congregational church, since 1957 a part of the UCC, seemed in 1965 light years away from the theological debates raging in the Harvard, Princeton, Yale, and University of Chicago seminaries and in the work of religious thinkers such as Harvey Cox, whose "Secular City" epitomized ecumenicist discourse. [694]

Rev. Richard B. Balmforth—1965–1970

The Reverend Balmforth arrived at the picturesque New England Boothbay Harbor Congregational church bearing perhaps the most unusual background of any previous church pastor. He had spent most of his ministerial career in the Salvation Army. In 1930 Balmforth had entered London's William Booth Memorial College; however, he never graduated. Balmforth instead joined the Salvation Army, where for 25 years he served as a commissioned officer, attaining the rank of major. He spent fifteen of those years as a chaplain with British troops stationed in England, Cairo, Egypt, Calcutta, India, and from 1952 to 1956, in both Berlin and Bielefeld, Germany. During almost all of those tours, his wife Doris accompanied him, likewise as a major in the Salvation Army. Honorably discharged, Major Balmforth in the late fifties pastored a Congregational church in the seaside town of Paignton, Devon, England, where in 1963 he chose to participate in a three-month pulpit exchange with the First United Church of Christ in Ottawa, Canada. Obviously captivated by the experience, in 1964 he returned to North America, where he spent a year at Bangor Theological Seminary before accepting the call in 1965 to pastor the Boothbay Harbor Congregational church. Without formal academic credentials, Balmforth was forced to convince the Maine Conference that his experience as a Salvation Army chaplain alone warranted ordination. He succeeded and was ordained by the conference in February 1967. [695]

A major in God's army, who wore the uniform proudly, Rev. Balmforth never shed his martial demeanor. He served the Boothbay Harbor church as much a commissioned officer as an ordained minister. Church members recalled him as "no nonsense," a "disciplinarian," "stand-offish," and "not particularly involved" in the life of the church family. Nor for that matter was his wife, Major Doris, deeply involved. Church members remembered Doris as aloof, and the Reverend Balmforth as, in parishioner Leah Sample's words "positive," meaning "he was going to be the boss." [696]

A figure of authority, prepared to be respected rather than loved, Balmforth carried out his ministerial duties efficiently, visiting the sick, chairing meetings, officiating at marriages and funerals, and giving sermons about which little is known. At his ordination, Balmforth had unveiled his theology. He called himself a "conservative evangelical," a person "tolerant of the views of Fundamentalists as well as of Liberals, while maintaining his own stand between those extremes." He saw the scriptures as "the Divine Word of God, written and revealed for man," and he beheld "evil as a powerful force and Jesus as the Savior of the World." Finally, using words bound to impress his Maine Conference inquisitors, he viewed "unity among Christians, and social justice, and civil rights for all" as worthy ideals. [697]

His "From the Pastor's Desk" series in the *Boothbay Register* provided more illumination. As a person who had lived in several foreign countries and known the horrors of war, Balmforth suspected blind patriotism, and consistent with the UCC hierarchy, applauded ecumenicism. Writing a piece in the *Boothbay Register* on "Patriotism," Balmforth observed that "while patriotism can be…a refining thing, it can itself be poisoned and perverted." "John Wesley," he wrote, "claimed the world as his parish. Every land is my fatherland," argued Wesley, because every land is my Father's land. He [Wesley] saw Christ in the parable of the Good Samaritan, pleading for an all-embracing love for men [and women] everywhere."

But, Balmforth also possessed a millennial streak. In July 1969, on the occasion of Neil Armstrong's walk on the moon, Rev. Balmforth wrote in the *Boothbay Register* about what he called the "Cosmic Day." He noted that the "vehicle of science has brought us the Cosmic Day." However, convinced that evil lurked in the world, he dreaded that the Cosmic Day could be followed by a "blacker and more fearful day." Clearly in an eschatological mood, Balmforth wrote that "there have always been prophets who have foretold another kind of cosmic day, the day of the Lord."[698]

To a real degree, that latter more grim expression about "another kind of cosmic day" summed up Balmforth's core philosophy. Things could be better, but also worse. However, he saw the Boothbay Harbor church in 1969 as holding its own. He promised to give the Boothbay Harbor church community a "balanced ministry," that is to say, "to give as far as I am able, a good pulpit ministry and a good pastoral ministry, to make a good administration both at my desk and away from it." [699] Often to the dismay of the church's business committee, Rev. Balmforth could be overly rigid about assuring that good order. For example, he demanded that the church must be kept holy, uncontaminated by secular use. When the Lincoln County Choralaires in March 1966 asked to use the church for their April concert, Balmforth "urged strongly that we must take a stand as to whether the Congregational Church was to be a House of God, or a concert hall." For him, "there should be no doubt that the only appropriate use of the Church itself should be as a place of worship."[700]

Indeed, Rev. Balmforth's military-style ministry appeared to be mainly about stability and good order, a rigid order in the face of the national turmoil filling the screens of his parishioners' television sets. Yet, if there was any local church excitement during Balmforth's ministry, it involved a fairly mundane parsonage issue. He had refused to live in the church's Oak Street parsonage that he considered too small and too undignified. Auspiciously, on January 19, 1965, a month before Balmforth arrived, the recently widowed Alexander C. Tener offered the church his oceanfront lot (115 Atlantic Avenue) at Roads End on the East Side of Boothbay Harbor. However, on the lot stood a small cottage to which Etta P. Brewer had been deeded a "lifetime right of residence." Etta, who lived most of the year in Fall River, Massachusetts, died November 17, 1967, clearing title to the parcel. Meanwhile, the church proceeded to build a new parsonage. In fact, the Roads End gift of deed to the church came with another gift, a check for $15,000 to be matched by the church in order to build the new parsonage on the Roads End property.[701]

With Balmforth a settled pastor and adamant about not living in the Oak Street parsonage, the church in September 1965 voted to accept the Tener offer, match his $15,000, and build an attractive, albeit ordinary, one and three-quarter story Cape Cod-style manse. Unfortunately, while charming, for budget's sake, it was built cheaply out of scrap lumber.[702]

Clapboard-sided, the new parsonage boasted a full rear dormer, white-oak flooring, and a brick central fireplace. Demolition of the Brewer cottage began in 1966 and the Balmforths moved into the new parsonage in early 1967. In 1990 the assessor valued the house at $322,000. This new parsonage enjoyed spectacular harbor views and by arrangement even a slip for a skiff at the neighboring Carousel Marina. The church equipped the parsonage with a refrigerator, range, dishwasher and approximately $2,000 in furniture.[703]

Richard and Doris Balmforth found bliss in their waterfront parsonage. An amateur filmmaker, Rev. Balmforth was inspired by the parsonage's panoramic harbor views to make movies of the harbor with its blissful mélange of yachts and lobster boats. Alas, this bliss would not be uninterrupted. Their neighbor to the north was Pierce Marine, which in the late 1960s not only sought to expand its mooring field, but also planned to enlarge its dockage space northward, thus encroaching on the deeded parsonage waterfront. Balmforth vociferously protested, contending that Pierce's actions "disturb[ed] the natural amenities of the parsonage in violation of Judge Tener's desire that the property should be freed [from] and unmolested by commercial interests." The church fought Pierce's plans, but hardly to a victory. The battle added to Balmforth's disaffection, which had been building.[704]

Rev. Balmforth's determination to "administer" the church as if its members were Christian soldiers won very few adherents. Members, as already noted, viewed him as "cold" and "distant," and his wife, who played the piano in church, as too quiet and "uninvolved."[705] As early as May 1968 Balmforth reported to the business committee "that a number of individual derogatory criticisms had been brought to his attention and [that] he would like to have a vote of confidence from the church membership." Although one committee member readily confessed that "he was aware of the individual criticisms," the business committee concluded that no reason existed for convening a church membership meeting. Instead, the committee prepared a letter to be sent to the Maine Conference indicating its confidence in Rev. Balmforth. Nevertheless, undoubtedly a number of members of the Boothbay Harbor congregation balked at Balmforth's rigidness, at his stiff demeanor, and, for some, his obliviousness to the current national unrest, the Black Revolution, the student revolution, and the antiwar movement. Some in protest even left the church.[706]

Despite these signs of restiveness, church membership during the Balmforth ministry remained fairly stable. While there were 284 members in December 1967, membership had dropped to only 250 in 1970 and only 82 of those 250 members pledged. The treasurer's report of January 1971 stated that "the church is not insolvent, but the local reputation for being a rich church is no longer more than a legend." It is important to note that the Congregational Church's reputation derived from its large Harbor membership. However, historically, the church, especially in summer, drew from Boothbay, Southport, and as far away as Edgecomb. That trend continued. [707]

Richard Balmforth resigned effective October 31, 1970, a resignation that the church accepted "with regret." "While there has been only one perfect ministry," wrote the business committee in a letter of recommendation requested by Balmforth, "his [Balmforth's] vigor, forthrightness and strong convictions will long leave their mark on the church."

The Reverend Balmforth delivered his farewell sermon on October 25, 1970, and at the coffee hour that morning the church presented him with a purse of money. Soon afterward, the Balmforths returned to England and to the town of Paignton, where he been pastor before moving to Canada, then Bangor, and finally Boothbay Harbor, Maine. A number of years later, during Karl Phillippi's ministry, while on a holiday in America, Rev. Balmforth returned to Boothbay Harbor where he had "fond memories," and as a guest, stayed in the Dodge house on the footbridge.[708]

Two months before Balmforth's final sermon, on September 1, 1970, the church's search committee chaired by Dr. Joseph Graham, had called the Reverend David M. Laney, chaplain at the Maine State Prison, to be interim minister. Next, it launched a full-scale search for a new, "young" minister. While seemingly sympathetic to the ecumenical emphasis of the United Church of

Christ leadership, Balmforth had demonstrated general insensitivity to the social and cultural changes buffeting society. He especially alienated the town's male youth, whose hair appeared just as conspicuously long in the photographs of the Boothbay Region High School graduating classes, 1965–1970, as it was in graduating class photographs nationwide. [709]

Rev. Bruce A. Riegel—1971-1972

In response to the perceived need to appeal to young people, the search committee deliberately narrowed its scope to younger candidates. Yet, aided by the Maine Conference, it spread its net wide, examining seventeen prospective candidates, three of whom it interviewed. The Reverend Bruce A. Riegel, to whom the committee at last extended an offer, was not its first choice. Only 30 years old, Riegel had earned his bachelor's degree in 1964 from Moravian College in Bethlehem, Pennsylvania, and his Divinity Degree from the Moravian Seminary on the same campus. From 1964 to 1965 he had served as a student pastor at Saint John's United Church of Christ in Allentown, Pennsylvania, and from 1968 to 1970 as assistant pastor of Dubbs Memorial United Church of Christ in Allentown, where he was ordained. His ministerial experience had been primarily with youth, an important and positive consideration for the search committee. However, on the negative side, the committee expressed serious reservations about Riegel's preaching. They rated his trial sermon at the Boothbay Harbor church "not outstanding." Still, Moravian College had awarded Riegel "honors for his public speaking." He was young, his wife Barbara, a journal editor, expressed exuberance, and Riegel, after all, had somehow survived the church's rigorous search process. The committee regarded the latter achievement to be sufficiently "fortuitous." "Essentially," his approach to religion appeared "enthusiastic and optimistic," they wrote.[710]

From the start, Riegel's one-year tenure at the Boothbay Harbor Congregational church, April 1971-May 1972, proved disappointing if not calamitous. He quibbled with the business committee over his moving expenses and car allowance, and, albeit inexperienced, still negotiated a salary of $6,500, $1,500 over the $5,000 paid Balmforth. The search committee did advise Riegel that the salary figure might be "financially embarrassing," and any future increase "impossible."[711] Nor did things improve. The search committee's somewhat guarded assessment of Riegel's sermon proved prescient. While some thought his sermons occasionally "charismatic," most complained that they seemed "unprepared." The business committee minutes of October 18, 1971, gave David Parkhurst, the Church's auditor and member, approval to assemble a "Liaison Committee" tentatively entitled "Church Council," chaired by William McCormick, and consisting of church members, "to receive suggestions, comments, criticisms from the membership of the church, make recommendations to the pastor and/or business committee for the mutual good of the church, administration, and community and to consult with and advise the pastor on such matters as he wishes." Moreover, it commanded Riegel to submit his sermons for inspection in advance of his Sunday delivery. [712]

The experiment failed. Discussions with the deacons followed and in late December the Liaison Committee "on an unofficial basis" organized regular discussions with Riegel. Despite his presentation of an outline entitled "A Proposal of Ministry Based on a Personal Assessment of the Congregation's Needs and Desires," (which was "well received), at a "Special Meeting," February 18, 1972, "it was moved and seconded that the business committee recommends that Rev. Bruce Riegel be asked for his resignation." The motion passed.[713]

Young, someone who loved boating in the "Boating Capital of New England," Riegel successfully befriended and appealed to the church's youth.[714] However, he failed to adapt to the rhythms of a church ministry. After a few months of ministry, Riegel summed up his experience quite tersely in his "Pastor's Annual Report for 1971." "Whether or not my ministry here has had any highlights worthy of the impressive 'I have done this or I did that' of a formal report," he wrote, "I am not sure." A few months later in March 1972 the 31-year-old Riegel reached his own verdict and announced that he was ending his career in ministry.

In parishioner Donna Closson's words, Riegel "was the most unlikely person for a minister...[she had] ever experienced." That May 1972, he and his wife moved to Brunswick, Maine, where he would open a successful counseling practice focused on youth. Riegel specialized in Jungian therapy and was instrumental in starting a Jung center on the campus of Bowdoin College. Carl Jung (1875–1961), Swiss psychiatrist/psychoanalyst, famous for his dream analysis believed that the human psyche was "by nature" religious. [715]

Riegel's tenure also proved financially disappointing for the church. No new members joined the church during his tenure, and the church spent $1,100 more than it received in pledges and loose change. A December 1971 business committee missive to "Dear Friends and Fellow Church Members" stated that the year 1971 finds us with a budget which will not have been met, together with rising costs...[O]ur bank balance at the year's end will show a sharp reduction. Some of our members have passed on while others have moved from the area contributing to a bleak outlook for 1972." While the church still possessed a stock portfolio worth over $125,000, plus savings of almost $25,000, the church had only $1,376 in its checking account.[716]

Rev. Charles S. Hartman

Rev. Charles S. Hartman—1972-1978
From May to October 1972, several guest preachers acted as interim ministers, including Dr. Walter Eastwood, and, for two months, September to October 1972, the Reverend Gerald Weary of the Newcastle United Church of Christ. Meanwhile, a new search committee headed by 82-year-old Sumner C. Fairbanks and including William A. MacCormick, whose father had been the minister of the church in 1895, Thomas Tavenner, William

Van Allen, Laura Blake, and Leah Sample, resumed the quest for a new minister, now more concerned about restoring stability to the church than about the future pastor's age.[717] MacCormick stated as much in a letter he wrote to the Reverend Arthur Rice early in August: "We have had two troublesome ministers," he wrote, "and really need what I call now a 'healing minister.'" MacCormick characterized the congregation as composed largely of seasonal retired people "who are active in their home churches, have money… [and] a deep interest in our program." He felt "the whole enterprise can give a man a great deal of satisfaction." The committee had launched its search in April, but by August worried about "the lack of progress."[718]

The Maine Conference worked closely with the search committee and widely circulated the notice of the Boothbay Harbor opening. The letter proved crucial when it finally reached the mailbox of the Reverend Charles S. Hartman, minister of the 1,000-member, 176 year-old First Reformed Church (United Church of Christ) of Greensburg, Pennsylvania, a small city (17,000) just north of Pittsburgh in Westmoreland County. Once a bituminous mining center, "Rustbelt" Greensburg in 1959 welcomed a branch of the University of Pittsburgh, and in 1965 the large, Westmoreland County Mall arrived. Hartman had pastored First Reformed Church there since 1963.

Seeing the Boothbay Harbor opening, Hartman promptly contacted the Maine Conference minister, William Thompson, who in his letter to the search committee waxed enthusiastic at the "Caliber" of Hartman, who, Thompson had learned, "might be persuaded to step down a bit…and take a smaller situation. He is not interested in a semi-retired job, but would like a church with a less demanding pastoral role." [719] By early September MacCormick and the committee all shared Thompson's enthusiasm. They not only hastily arranged Hartman's mid-September visit to the Harbor, but even chatted about how quickly the Hartmans might sell their house in Greensburg. Curiously, someone in the Boothbay congregation raised the question of Hartman's possible "fundamentalism!" The Greensburg clergyman found the concern highly amusing. "My friends," he wrote MacCormick, "might classify me in a number of ways for my social and community interests, but not in their wildest dreams would they call me a fundamentalist. You know how I admired Dr. Fosdick, and how unhappy the fundamentalists always were with him. So I am sure we will soon minister to the worries of those few who were concerned." [720]

Clearly, for the search committee and Hartman, it was love at first sight, especially after Hartman visited Boothbay Harbor September 13 and 14, and preached his trial sermon. MacCormick was ecstatic, and so was the congregation. In a letter to Hartman and his wife Louise dated September 18 and addressed to "Dear Friends," MacCormick thanked the Hartmans "for bringing us so much joy in your recent visit." MacCormick told the Hartmans "that the listeners on Sunday all sounded encouraged. I think one woman covered it all when she said with deep sincerity, "Now, I feel that I have been in Church. Mrs. [Harlow] Russell expressed my personal feeling when she said that she was sure that we were being led by God in bringing us [Hartman, MacCormick, and the congregation] together in this place we love so much..., indicat[ing] an eagerness to get about the business of 'healing' of which I spoke to you so often."[721]

The attraction was reciprocal. Hartman told the committee that as a boy of ten he had visited Boothbay Harbor with his grandfather and spent a day on Monhegan Island. Enchanted by his visit to the region, he decided that this was the place for him to retire. When he received from the Maine Conference the list of vacant pulpits and saw Boothbay Harbor "he looked no further."

Just days after Hartman's visit and trial sermon, the church convened a congregational meeting to consider "calling" Hartman to the church pulpit. Ninety-six-year-old Harlow M. Russell, a long-standing member of the congregation and a legend in Boothbay Harbor with one of the largest libraries of recorded sermons from "outstanding Protestant leaders" including Harry Emerson Fosdick (Harlow weekly recorded the sermons of Boothbay Harbor Congregational church ministers), submitted to the church meeting his written thoughts on Hartman. "I believe," he wrote, "that the church cannot within our means find a better man anywhere, and I believe that the church has never had a better pastor. I believe that he can build up the church and repair the dark spots which have upset us during the last two pastorates." [722]

At that congregational meeting, October 1, 1972, members voted to make Hartman the next pastor at a salary of $8,500, plus the Roads End parsonage, $1,000 for fuel and telephone, and $600 for automobile allowance. The Hartmans promptly sold their Greensburg home, and in mid-October arrived in Boothbay Harbor. With the possible exception of John Murray, Hartman brought to the church the most impressive ministerial credentials to date. Indeed, much of the recent discussion at the search committee meeting had focused on why Hartman wished to come to the Boothbay church. His answer: It was the lure of an idyllic place, of an iconic Congregational church. In his own words: "[He] regarded a change to Boothbay Harbor as a completely exciting and challenging move to an inspiring location." [723]

Born in 1913, in Lancaster, Pennsylvania, Hartman graduated in 1934 from the town's Franklin and Marshall College. Rather than attending the United Church of Christ's Lancaster Theological Seminary, located adjoining the F&M campus, he attended Yale Divinity School, graduating in 1937. Ten years later Hartman earned a master's degree in history from Johns Hopkins. Ordained in 1939, he married Louise Showman the next year. Prior to his arrival in Boothbay Harbor he had pastored several large UCC churches in Baltimore, Maryland, Fort Wayne, Indiana, Rochester, New York, and from 1963–1972 the First Reformed Church of Greensburg. A warm and loving wife, and also extremely outgoing, Louise had actively volunteered in all the communities in which her husband served. Boothbay Harbor would be no exception. In addition, she loved flying, whether in hot air balloons, in propeller driven or jet- powered aircraft.

Describing himself as "liberal in theology, in training, and in heritage," his background revealed that he was socially liberal as well. He fully reflected the ecumenicist agenda of the UCC Synod. Hartman, in fact, served three times as an elected delegate to the UCC General Synod, most recently in June 1971. In Greensburg he had organized the Greensburg Council of Churches' Committee to Provide Better Housing for Low-Income Families. He also sat on the Board of the Westmoreland County Public Health Nurses, and as a member of the Council of Churches he had taken the lead in organizing numerous ecumenical events. In Fort Wayne Hartman had been active in a radio ministry. The Hartmans had four children: Edwin, a professor of philosophy at the University of Pennsylvania, Ira and Stewart, both high-school teachers, and Charlene, a student at Kalamazoo College. [724]

With the Hartmans' arrival, the year 1972 may have inaugurated healing at the Boothbay Harbor church, but not in America. Nationally, the Hartman years, 1972–1978, remained distressing, while at the same time witnessing a decline in campus revolts (after the fatal National Guard shootings of students on Ohio's Kent State University campus), and a waning of summer-long rioting in black inner cities,

The aforementioned suspicious break in at the Democratic Party headquarters at Washington's D.C.'s Watergate condominiums led to the 1973 televised "Watergate Hearings," and to President Richard M. Nixon's resignation in August 1974, making Vice-President Gerald Ford President. Ford faced a Vietnam War-inflated economy, exacerbated by the actions of the 1960-founded, Middle East-centered Organization of Petroleum Exporting Countries (OPEC). In October 1973 OPEC imposed an oil embargo, triggering in America an "energy crisis" which caused a severe oil shortage, greatly raised petroleum prices, and led to nine percent inflation and double-digit unemployment. Ford fought the crisis by launching the "Whip Inflation Now" campaign featuring the ubiquitous WIN button. Georgian James Earl Carter defeated Ford in the bicentennial presidential election of 1976. Carter inherited the same high-inflation, high joblessness, and sour economy that defeated Ford. He indelicately dubbed it "malaise." [725]

Hartman had abandoned the dying steel and coal industrial climate of the Pittsburgh region for the unscarred, pollution-free bliss of "vacationland." But, the tourist-dependent Boothbay Harbor region could not forever escape the repercussions of national social and economic change, especially an increasingly fragile economy. For example, in 1972, Carl Griffin, a long-haired, brilliant Boothbay Region High School senior who is a fellow author of this history, launched a movement to seat a student representative on the Boothbay Region school board. Griffin's demand (rejected by the school board) announced that students even in the tranquil Boothbay region were no longer politically docile. The politically conservative editor of the *Boothbay Register*, Mary Brewer, interpreted "Watergate," the "energy crisis," and even youthful long hair, as more evidence that the concentration of power in Washington is corrupting (even in Boothbay Harbor) and that the nation must renew its faith in states' rights and in the sanctity of individual rights.[726]

There was additional evidence close to home. Nixon's efforts in 1973 to cut federal spending threatened to close the National Marine Fisheries Laboratory at McKown Point in Boothbay Harbor. In March 1973 Maine Senator Edmund Muskie visited the laboratory and urged Augusta to save the valuable marine research facility by sharing its cost with the federal government. Ultimately, the State of Maine assumed the entire cost, making the McKown Point laboratories part of the Maine Department of Marine Resources.

In this Hartman era, Boothbay Harbor's dependence on tourism only grew. Luxury yacht building remained more and more a vital economic sector, while the region's century-old ground fishing fleet dwindled in importance. The Chamber of Commerce continued to emphasize not only the area's hotels and seafood restaurants, but that Boothbay Harbor was the "Boating Capital of New England." And, ensconced at the Road's End manse, settled pastors—like Charles Hartman—had a front row seat on that busy summertime yachting scene.[727]

But Hartman came to Boothbay Harbor more than for his love of boating. (They did, however, own a Lapstrake runabout moored by deeded arrangement at the Carousel Wharf.) As in Greensburg, he and Louise had a liberal ministerial agenda, not only to serve faithfully the parish, but also the people of the community if not the world. In his "Pastor's Report" for 1972 Hartman expressed joy and gratitude "for the opportunity to share with you the life and ministry of this church" and to take up the challenge of growing its membership. He also wrote that "One of my deepest concerns throughout my life…is to widen the horizons of our ministry through the work of the United Church of Christ as we reach out to those in need." He beseeched the membership to considerably increase its benevolence to Church World Missions. Reflecting Hartman's past work in Greensburg, he would share that benevolence as much with the needy of the Boothbay region as with those starving in Africa. He signed his 1972 report, "Yours in His Service." [728]

Spearheaded as much by his wife, as by Hartman himself, the Hartmans almost immediately started a "Meals on Wheels" project. It officially began June 18, 1973. Dorothy McEvoy, Leah Sample, and Judy Pinkham joined Louise Hartman in transforming the vestry kitchen into a beehive of meals production. Between 10:30 A.M. and noon, volunteer drivers transported meals to the elderly, disabled, and convalescents for whom the rapidly rising cost of living was proving disastrous. [729]

The Hartmans' community outreach even involved seeking federal help. Since 1973 Hartman had wanted the church to hire a youth worker, possibly in cooperation with other churches [730] and the YMCA. That very year Congress had enacted the Comprehensive Employment Training Act (CETA). Through county administrators, the act aimed to give job training to the rising population of unemployed. Washington gave the State of Maine over $2.5 million. CETA funneled federal grants to non-profit organizations to fill newly created positions with persons enrolled with the unemployment office and jobless for thirty days. Hartman believed funds might be available for a church "parish worker." In October 1974 he submitted a proposal to CETA for a such a worker, contending that in his parish of over 300 members, 165 elderly, sick, or shut-ins needed visiting to provide health and maintenance care. The Sunday school, he argued, also needed help as did, in summer, the church day camp. Obviously unmindful of any church and state conflict, Hartman in his application for a CETA worker stressed that the worker might also provide leadership for young people and "help the minister with clerical and secretarial work." Needless to say, the Lincoln County CETA administrator rejected his application. Undaunted, Hartman on March 11, 1975 reported to the business committee that Leslie Climo, an active church member, "had secured a CETA position with the "Y" doing some of the same things the church had in mind for her." Leslie had informed Hartman of her interest (on top of her CETA job) in working twice a month with the church youth at $30 a month for three months.[731]

Hartman was much more successful in his support for a twenty-one-unit, low-income housing project to be built on a 2.9 acre site located on Andrea Lane off Reed Road in Boothbay Harbor. Developed by Joseph Cloutier of Warren, Maine, and financed by the Farmers' Home Administration and with eight units subsidized by the Department of Housing and Urban Development's (HUD's) Section 8 program, Hartman enthusiastically backed the project and at meetings spoke publicly on its behalf. He worked closely with Cloutier to have the town grant the necessary zoning variances and permits. Within the church Hartman in 1974 pressed equally hard to have the congregation reach outward. When the United Church of Christ launched a "17/76" ($17 million in 1976) "Achievement Fund" campaign aimed at strengthening the denomination's historically black Southern colleges founded by the Congregational Church after the Civil War, Hartman rallied the church fully behind what he saw as a vital cause. Likewise, he prodded the church's youth to look outward. In 1973 he personally escorted a group of church youth on a trip to tour the United Nations in New York and visit Dr. Fosdick's Riverside Church. In preparation for the nation's bicentennial, in 1975 the church had created a committee that seemed only modestly active. In addition to framing a statement about the importance of "Freedom of Worship," the committee planned a covered-dish supper for Sunday, November 14, 1976; and on Sunday morning, July 4, 1776, church members dressed up in colonial garb for the planting of a "liberty tree" (a sunset maple) on the front lawn of the Congregational church. [732]

Despite Watergate, the energy crisis, and what Jimmy Carter called "malaise," Hartman's six years at the Boothbay Harbor Congregational church might easily be described as "golden." In his first year, 1972-1973, sixteen new families joined the church. Between 1972 and 1977 the church welcomed 122 new members. People lauded Hartman's success at extending the outreach of the church, not only his "Meals on Wheels" initiative to the community's elderly and disabled, but also his effort to increase the church's benevolence giving. In 1977, led by Hartman, the church formally honored its foremost missionary family, the Shepards, who had long served as medical missionaries in Turkey.[733]

Likewise, under Hartman the church expanded its real estate holdings, and thus expanded its space for automobile parking. Balmforth in November 1969 had approached Mrs. Cutts, a church member who lived in the small house on a sizable parcel situated on Eastern Avenue just behind the church. At the time she had no plans to sell her land, but promised the church first refusal. Three years later in 1976, upon Mr. Cutts' death, the business committee intensified its interest in the Cutts' property "provided it is put on the market." The committee envisioned in the purchase, first, space for needed parking, second, space in the Cutts' house for educational rooms and offices, third, an opportunity to lease out space in the house for revenue, and lastly, protection against an undesirable buyer.[734] One year later in August 1977, for $43,500, it acquired the adjoining Cutts property, which in addition to providing the additional space for parking, included the aforementioned 152-year old Cutts house, described by Hartman as "very small. One of the three bedrooms [is] quite tiny, and the other two [are] also small." It also needed constant and expensive repairs.[735]

The investment, meant to provide parking and rental income for the church, immediately stirred one of the few controversies in Hartman's tenure at the church. Some members espied an opportunity to further enrich the church by selling the now valuable Roads End property and converting the small Cutts house into the parsonage. Opposed to the idea, Hartman wrote "Brother Balmforth" about Judge Tener's intentions in deeding the East Side land to the church. He was sure Tener desired to keep the idyllic Roads End parcel residential and free of commerce, albeit still zoned commercial. "Was there a letter documenting this?" asked Hartman. Balmforth assured Hartman that no such document existed and agreed with him that the Cutts house was too old and too small to attract a prospective minister. A former member of the business committee, Harold Wood, sided with Balmforth and Hartman, contending that while Tener "attached no legal strings," he hoped that by constructing a parsonage on the former Brewer property, it would forever guarantee the residential character of Roads End. To Hartman's relief, the Roads End property was not sold in October 1978. [736]

Charles and Louise Hartman never promised the Harbor church a long ministry. On October 8, 1978, at age 65, Rev. Hartman, to the deep sorrow of the church and the town, announced his retirement. In November he moved to Fort Wayne, Indiana. However, the Hartmans regularly returned for summer visits and, ever popular, stayed rent-free at the cottage of Judy Pinkham's aunt. When Charles Hartman died in 1999, church members aboard George McEvoy's *Nellie G* scattered the pastor's ashes in the lee of Cuckold's lighthouse.[737]

Rev. Charles Montieth—October 1978-February 1979
The church's pulpit committee commenced its search for Hartman's replacement immediately in October 1978. For the interim minis-

ter they chose Charles Montieth from the Rockland, Maine, Congregational church, who contracted to preach Sundays and spend just two days a week on pastoral duties. Montieth and his wife Edna served the church from October 1978 to February 1979. At the close of his brief sojourn in Boothbay Harbor, Montieth and the Methodist minister shared a January 1979 ecumenical worship service at the "Our Lady Queen of Peace" Catholic church, a religious event encouraged by the strongly ecumenical Charles Hartman.[738]

Rev. Karl Phillippi—1979-1981

Against Hartman's advice that the church ignore past disappointments and select for his successor a younger pastor, the search committee chose a man in the waning years of his ministry. With his wife Vera, the Reverend Karl Phillippi, the committee's choice, on February 22, 1979, moved into the delightful oceanfront Road's End parsonage. Phillippi came from Georgetown, Massachusetts, an attractive "North Shore" community, where for twelve years he had served as the Conference Minister for the Northeastern Massachusetts Region. Before coming to Massachusetts, he had served churches in Connecticut, New York, and Ohio. Like Hartman, Phillippi came highly recommended. Since Riegel's brief ministry, inflation had steadily raised the church's ministerial costs, and the committee awarded Phillippi a salary of $12,500 together with the free use of the parsonage and $1,000 for automobile expenses. [739]

In January 1981, one year after Phillippi assumed the pastorate of the Boothbay Harbor church, Ronald Reagan, a conservative Republican, proclaiming "Morning in America," became President of the United States. The nation in 1980, under Carter, had faced not only a hostage crisis in Iran, but also a 7.4 percent unemployment, and a thirteen percent rise in the cost of living. Reagan in response called for cutting taxes, slashing federal spending, and dismantling the social welfare edifice erected since 1933 during the presidencies of Franklin Roosevelt, Harry Truman, John F. Kennedy, and Lyndon Baines Johnson.[740]

While Hartman had left the church financially secure, with a much larger congregation of 265, over half of whom pledged, inflation, especially the rising cost of fuel, raised the cost of church operations. The thirty-five year-old asphalt-shingled church roof leaked, a rotting sill was discovered in the rear of the church, the chimney needed to be repaired and the steeple painted. The church created a building repair fund committee, which in October 1980 raised $10,000.[741]

And in 1980 the fate of the Cutts house again arose as an issue. Having rejected the house as an alternate parsonage, the church separated it from the parking lot parcel and rented the house to a tenant, who in 1980 announced plans to vacate. But, it still needed extensive repairs, and the business committee proposed to sell the 155-year-old Cutts house with the understanding that the prospective owners move it. Although the congregation voted overwhelmingly for the business committee's proposition and advertised the house for sale, no offer came. In 1984 the church decided to repair the house, convert the first floor into two offices, and to rent the upstairs. [742]

The Phillippis spent barely two years in Boothbay Harbor. Like Hartman an ecumenical, Phillippi preached about Christian unity and held world prayer services at Our Lady Queen of Peace. He welcomed the opportunity to have the church host the federal Women's, Infants, and Children program (WIC) and continued Hartman's highly successful "Meals on Wheels." Modern in his theology and psychology, he based his January 1981 sermon on Karl Menninger's classic 1973 book *Whatever Became of Sin*.[743]

Also like Hartman, Phillippi filled the pulpit in summer with a bevy of distinguished preachers. They included Dr. Roger Hazelton, for twenty years Abbott professor of

Rev. Dr. Walter H. Eastwood

pastoral theology at Andover-Newton Theology School; Dr. Wallace Robbins, former president of Meadville Theological Seminary; James Lenhart, minister emeritus of Plymouth Congregational Church (UCC), Des Moines, Iowa; the Rev. Dr. Walter Eastwood, and on July 13, 1980, the vacationing Rev. Charles Hartman.[744]

The Cutts house and church repair issues aside, Phillippi's ministry at the church proved uneventful. He could be colorful, even theatric at times. Parishioners recall that he dressed up as Noah for a town parade in which the children of the church dressed up as animals. The Phillippis started a brown bag lunch program and at one of the luncheons attendees made advent wreaths. Members regarded Karl and Vera Phillippi as "a good team." They called Phillippi himself "a wonderful person," "very Christian, giving, and forgiving," a very nice man who wanted one more regular pastorate before retiring from the ministry. Thus, few were surprised when on October 12,1981, Phillippi informed the church of his intention to retire in January 1982. The new search committee included Margaret Pinkham, Paul Cushman, Caroline Parkhurst, and Marjorie Graham.[745]

Rev. Joseph David Stinson

Rev. J. David Stinson-1982-1992

The church, now heeding the advice of Karl Phillippi, again made youth the key criterion in its search. Thirty-two-year-old Rev. J. David Stinson moved into his new home at Roads End in mid-July 1982, after preaching a very successful sermon on May 9. Shortly afterward, the Boothbay Harbor church issued him a call.

The first minister of the Boothbay Harbor Congregational church to have been born in the South, in Bonham, Texas, Stinson had graduated magna cum laude from Texas

Christian University in 1972 and three years later from Yale Divinity School. From 1975 to 1982 he had been the minister of South Congregational Church in Lawrence, Massachusetts. In Lawrence, Stinson enlisted in the Naval Reserve and in 1979 was commissioned a chaplain in the United States Navy. He would retire from the Naval chaplaincy in 2010 as a rear admiral. [746]

Therefore, in 1982 the Harbor Congregational church had settled not only a devoted and devout, Biblically oriented minister, but also a committed and ambitious Naval chaplain. The presence in the Boothbay region of a host of retired and semi-retired summertime substitute ministers—for example, Walter Eastwood, Wallace Robbins, James Lenhart, Robert Luccock, and Charles Hartman—enabled Rev. Stinson's dual career. His wife Cynthia (Cindy) also fostered Stinson's two-career track. Married in 1980, they were veritably newlyweds in 1982. While at the Boothbay Harbor church she bore three children, all with Biblical names, Hannah in 1982, Phoebe in 1985, and Jesse in 1986.[747]

Like Rev. Hartman, Rev. Stinson brought a strong church faith, a solid theological foundation, and, notwithstanding his southern birth, a New England Congregational passion for doing good. As one of his first acts upon settling at the Boothbay Harbor Congregational church Stinson created the *Harbinger*, a monthly newsletter, which featured his theological ruminations, usually in the form of a Biblically based sermonette. Stinson believed—like the British Puritans who founded New England—that faith was learned. It was achieved and girded through the Word preached on Sundays from the pulpit by well-educated clergy, through the Sunday school to eager youth, and also through Bible study for adults. Stinson immediately launched an adult Bible study program. [748]

Doubt, Stinson believed, came to humans naturally. Unquestionably, the Bible contained what Stinson called "hard" [implausible] sayings and deeds; and, he contended, individuals have the free will to question them. As pastor, it was his job to "defend and teach the doctrines of the ancient Christian faith." Stinson spent little time teaching his flock about the pillars of theology and the key doctrines of Christianity. One of his first adult classes focused on Saint Augustine and his Confessions. Yet, claiming that religion was deeply personal as well as public, Stinson professed to be open to all theological sides, quoting freely from C.S. Lewis as well as from Reinhold Niebuhr and others.[749]

A lover of history, Rev. Stinson easily gravitated toward the great sixteenth and seventeenth-century Protestant reformers, including Martin Luther, John Knox, John Calvin, and other disciples of the Reformation, and moved swiftly into the eighteenth century with America's "Great Awakening," Jonathan Edwards, and, of course, the Reverend John Murray. Stinson both wrote and preached about the Presbyterian Murray's historic eighteenth-century ministry in the Boothbay region. As a historian and Biblical scholar, Stinson's sermons could often be profound, perhaps too erudite for some of the laity. A retired headmaster of a Maine boarding school, Andrew Holmes, who befriended Stinson and greatly respected his intellect and his ministry, characterized his sermons as perhaps "too much like Yale Divinity School lectures."[750]

However, as a United Church of Christ pastor, Stinson, like Hartman and Phillippi, espoused ecumenicism and urged support for such missionary endeavors as Church World Service, especially during the severe African famine of 1984. He also recognized the importance of home missions. During Phillippi's ministry Hartman's Meals on Wheels program still operated out of the Congregational Church, but with less intense church involvement. In May 1985 the meal preparation was transferred to the Saint Andrews Hospital kitchen. In its place, the church hosted what Stinson proudly called the "ecumenical" Boothbay Region Food Pantry,[751] which had been established jointly in 1968 by Our Lady Queen of Peace and the Congregational Church of Boothbay Harbor.

During Stinson's early ministry at the Congregational church, 1982–1986, the church prospered. The youthful Stinson grew the Sunday school by fifty percent, and in October 1985 the young high-school music teacher, Eugenia (Genie) O'Connell, became the director of the Sunday school's music program. In March 1984

Blenn Perkins Jr., for 36 years the church's senior deacon, stepped down to be succeeded by Robert Walbridge.[752]

With a young, energetic minister as its shepherd, and a growing congregation, the church began finally to address many overdue physical projects. The church steeple—tattered and peeling—was finally repaired and painted. Work began to replace the church's ancient and hazardous electrical system, and, with a gift of $5,000 from the Richard and Margaret Thorpe family, the church in 1985 hired Tom Hampson from Sawyer's Island to make new, teak, sanctuary doors. [753]

And, at last, after years of frustration, the business committee addressed the conundrum of the Cutts house. In December 1983 the Cutts' tenant informed the committee that she was moving out. Earlier, under Phillippi, the church had vowed to sell the small house and have it moved. Unable to find a buyer, opinion shifted toward retaining the house, converting its first floor into two rooms, one for the minister's office and another for committee meetings, and remodeling the second floor into a rentable apartment. The business committee estimated the cost of the Cutts' rehabilitation at $10,000 and welcomed donations, even announcing naming rights. "Smaller gifts are also welcome." Since no one proffered the $10,000 required to name the building, it became the "Murray House," and in February 1984, mirabile dictu, the Coast Guard announced that it would rent the apartment for $475 a month. By the fall of 1984 the business committee joined the Christian education committee in scheduling future monthly meetings in the Murray House.[754]

Conclusion

Nationally, this era began with both a "War on Poverty," and an intensification of the war in Vietnam. America's crisis-ridden cities, racially festering, rife with slums, spawned not only rioting, but also Lyndon Baines Johnson's antipoverty legislative agenda. None of this seemingly resonated in the seaside village of Boothbay Harbor. Occasionally, the photograph of a locally known young man now serving in Vietnam appeared in the *Boothbay Register*. As for America's ravaged urban battlegrounds, not a word appeared. Yet, violent student protests and summer-long African-American rioting in America's stultifying urban ghettos left the nation deeply rent socially and politically. Like the *Boothbay Register*, the imperious, British-born, ex-Salvation Army officer Richard Balmforth remained deaf to the social and political upheaval of the 1960s and insensitive as well to the fears, uncertainties, and questionings gestating among his communicants, whose televisions captured the national trauma on the evening news.

The church languished, and the next, and youthful, pastor, Bruce Riegel, only exacerbated the situation. It was not until 1972 that the vastly experienced and masterful Charles Hartman steered the church forward, boosting its membership, and despite an energy crisis and soaring inflation, stabilized the church financially, while bestowing upon it an enhanced outreach mission at home and abroad. While the minister following Hartman, Karl Phillippi, who served only briefly, preserved stability, his successor, David Stinson, revived the vitality of the Hartman years. As the next chapter explains, it would be Stinson's command of the pulpit, and his visionary energy that would inspire one of the largest church building undertakings since the Second Congregational Church had been established in Boothbay Harbor in 1848.

CHAPTER 12

FAITH FOR THE FUTURE: 1986–2003
by John F. Bauman

Rev. David Stinson—1986-1992 (continued)

It was 1986, the fifth year of the Reverend David Stinson's Boothbay Harbor ministry, and the dawn rising over Ronald Reagan's "Morning in America" still glowed, indeed, brightly. Just one year later, on June 12, 1987, the President would stand at West Berlin's Brandenburg Gate, and, staring at the graffiti-blanketed concrete edifice—undefiled since its birth in 1961—dared the Soviet Premier to "tear down this wall." While sounding defiant, Reagan had not necessarily meant his challenge to sound offensive. He had, after all, cultivated a good rapport with Mikhail Gorbachev, whose campaign for glasnost and perestroika warmed their relationship. In reality, Reagan was goading him to take action on his promises. The very next year, November 9, 1989, with Angela Merkel, a youthful future chancellor of a united Germany among the giddy watchers, the wall's dismantling began. Two years later the Stanford University political scientist Francis Fukuyama's *The End of History and the Last Man,* which celebrated the "universalization of Western liberal democracy [and capitalism] as the final form of government," served as an epitaph for both communism and what Reagan reviled as the "Evil Empire."

Reagan in the 1980s proceeded on his part to dismantle much of what was left of Franklin Roosevelt's New Deal and Lyndon Johnson's Great Society. Reagan slashed taxes and announced a new era of robust laissez-faire conservatism. But, America's slum-ridden cities now vegetated, while newer suburbs and more affluent small towns boomed, especially those in the shadow of increasingly prosperous "Sunbelt" metropolises, such as Charlotte, Dallas, and Los Angeles.

Almost as the Berlin wall crumbled into smoking ruins, another Republican president, George Herbert Walker Bush, who summered at Walker's Point in Kennebunkport Maine, a mere two hours from the white-spired Boothbay Harbor Congregational church, followed Reagan into office. Thus, for twelve years conservative Republican presidents steered the American ship of state through the collapse of the Soviet Union and, with Bush at the helm, through Operation Desert Storm in Iraq.

Captured live on CNN, "Desert Storm" informed Americans in 1990 that—absent the familiar Cold War—a new global threat loomed in the Middle East. Indeed, halting the aggression of Iraqi President Saddam Hussein against neighboring Kuwait ignited a cauldron of future political instability, religious violence, and, ultimately, terror. In fact, Operation Desert Storm had significant implications for the Boothbay Harbor Congregational church. On the first Sunday after Christmas 1990, with war against Saddam imminent, Rev. David Stinson, an ambitious and rising officer in the Naval Reserve chaplaincy, sure he would be called to serve in a combat-zone field hospital in Saudi Arabia, wrestled before a rapt congregation with "the moral and spiritual perspective that is proper for a minister of the gospel" about to go to war. He regarded Saddam as evil, a person comparable to Herod, the slaughterer of innocent children. Saddam aimed to control half the world's oil; he was an evil person who must be harshly "disciplined." Against the official position of the United Church of Christ, which favored "stepping back from the brink and letting diplomacy have more time," Stinson stood poised to serve. He fretted, for sure, about whether or not "he was on the Lord's side…Certainly military force," admitted Stinson, "is a grim option without our intentions getting all mixed up with religion…But, I know which side I'm on and I believe I know what is right. May God grant us the courage and resolve of our convictions." American military forces—countering Iraqi aggression—did attack Saddam, but Stinson was never called to test his resolve. [755]

Bush's short-lived Gulf War against Saddam Hussein had few economic benefits for a nation already enshrouded in economic gloom. Earlier in 1989—as a result of the "Savings and Loan" debacle—America was plunged into another economic recession, and, by raising gasoline prices, the Gulf War exacerbated the crisis. Inflation surged, while job growth remained sluggish. Unemployment rose from 5.4 percent in June 1990 to 7.8 percent in June 1992, reflecting a loss of 1.6 million jobs and ultimately causing George H. W. Bush to lose the presidency to William Clinton in the November 1992 election.[756]

Meanwhile, in 1986, several years before Bush jousted with Saddam Hussein, and when the morning sun still caressed America's shores, Boothbay Harbor's tourist-driven economy purred along smoothly. With an abundance of valuable oceanfront land, salubrious salt-water air, and New England charm, the Boothbay region enjoyed both a growing population and an economic surge in the 1980s. Since World War II the region had long experienced steady, albeit modest, population growth. Between 1940 and 2000 the combined population of the two towns of Boothbay and Boothbay Harbor rose fifty-two percent, with the bulk of that growth occurring in Boothbay. Neither the region's historic shipbuilding and fishing industries, nor its natural growth explains this. Rather, as in most Maine coastal communities, tourism and an influx of upper middle class retirees swelled the region's population. Given these prospects, and without any recession or war in sight, David Stinson and the church business committee assessed the church's future optimistically with undimmed faith for the church's future. [757]

There was reason for caution. Between 1990 and 2010 the region's population of twenty to thirty-nine year-olds dropped by over 200, while its fifty to sixty-nine year-old cohort rose by 600. The median age increased from 38.1 to 51.7. Indeed, in the millennial year 2000, family households of one and two persons comprised over sixty percent of Boothbay's population. The region had become what sociologists described as a "naturally occurring retirement community" (NORC). Not surprisingly, in the 1990s, Saint Andrews Village, an offspring of Saint Andrews Hospital, opened as the area's first continuing care retirement community.[758]

The region's growing, albeit aging, "summertime" population annually exploded between April and October. Boothbay Harbor with its Congregational church sparkled as the region's centerpiece for most of the nineteenth and twentieth centuries. The town scintillated as a picturesque, if not iconic, New England town with houses aligned along two major streets (Townsend and Oak) and with the essence of a town commons headed by a library rather than a church and surrounded by banks and grocery, clothing, and other stores, including, of course, gift shops. That tourist-driven prosperity spurred change in the 1990s. Growth shifted automobile-dependent commerce to the periphery, in Boothbay Harbor's case to the relatively rural stretch of Route 27 between the Harbor and the Town of Boothbay's common, an area of meadowland ripe for commercial development. The new high school, junior high and elementary school located there, as did the YMCA, a major supermarket, an electronics store, bank, pizza parlor, pharmacy, laundromat, and even (briefly) a Burger King, the region's first (and up-to-now only) chain restaurant.

Growth altered not only the periphery, but also the Town of Boothbay Harbor itself. Down Townsend Avenue and along Commercial Street on the west side of the busy waterfront and along Atlantic Avenue on the east side, in addition to tourist homes, a gasoline station, a hardware and a book store, an array of new boutiques, candy shops, gift shops, restaurants, motels, and real estate offices opened. The Harbor's chamber of commerce no longer portrayed the region as a summer colony. "Coastal Maine," proclaimed the chamber, is a "four season vacationland. Many [seasonal] businesses [remain] open [from] Columbus Day [through] Christmas. Maine is beautiful in the winter."[759]

The Boothbay region's weekly newspaper, the *Boothbay Register*, reflected the boom in the town. The paper in the 1980s was under the ownership of Howard S. Cowan, a veteran newspaperman with experience in Tulsa, Oklahoma; Kansas City; New York; and Toronto. Under Cowan the once eight-to-ten-page paper burgeoned in size and advertising. The paper grew fatter as spring approached and the Fishermen's Festival arrived followed by Windjammer Days, both meant to lure tourists as well as local residents. Advertising blossomed, not only for automobiles (Levitt's and Wiscasset Ford), but also for yachts (Hodgdon's, Goudy & Stevens, Pierce Yacht Sales), and, of course for the growing number of inns and motels: for example, Rocktide, Fisherman's Wharf, and the Tugboat Inn. Other advertising featured the Maine Trading Post, Bonnie's Cut Above, the Custom House, Maine Country Store, Crunchy Snail, House of Logan, and Orne's Candy Store, 135 years old in 2015.[760]

As the population statistics suggest, the region's growth was hardly confined to commerce. The region, especially the Town of Boothbay, increasingly attracted retirees, people like the Reverend Charles Hartman, the popular ex-pastor of the Congregational Church of Boothbay Harbor, who then wished to semi-retire there. Barters and Sawyers islands attracted retirees, but so did a new subdivision lining the Back Narrows Road. Forty units of oceanview condominium housing opened in the spring of 1987 on Mill Cove. But, growth bore consequences. Zoning to control growth loomed as an issue. The old open-burning trash dump near what had once been the popular Beath Spring (now closed) became, first a sanitary landfill, and then (after the local Bigelow Laboratory for Ocean Sciences testified about the health hazards of waste disposal dumps), a "trash disposal facility." [761]

One of the *Boothbay Register*'s 1987 photographic images of Boothbay Harbor showed a parade of motorcycles, mainly Harleys, roaring past the hilltop Congregational church, the gleaming chrome and black metal monsters nearly sideswiping the corner of the church as they whizzed by the roadside sanctuary's front entrance. In fact, the church had been damaged several times by motorists, some sober, some drunk. It was among the church's long-discussed concerns, but thus far one without resolution. That would at last change. Indeed, as earlier noted, for the Reverend David Stinson and the church business committee the year 1987 seemed an auspicious one for both the town and the church. [762]

The Advent of Faith for the Future

Under David Stinson the church had grown. Two hundred and seventy-two members strong in 1984, the congregation boasted 298 members two years later with a booming Sunday school of 119 in 1988. Stinson's youth program likewise expanded so much that, with approval from the business committee, in 1985 the church hired a part-time assistant youth minister, Dennis Burke, a student at Bangor Theological Seminary. The few pesky church problems seemingly eased in the mid-1980s. Renovations to the Murray House in 1985—painting, wall papering, and a new heating system—finally turned a liability into an asset when the Coast Guard committed to renting the second floor. Church income, $75,525 by the close of 1985, had exceeded that budgeted and left $4,042 cash on hand. The endowment reached $70,405. [763]

With a growing membership and a flourishing Sunday school, the moment seemed auspicious for the church to expedite long delayed projects, especially enlarging the vestry, expanding space for the Sunday school, and adding room for parking. In fact, Rev. Stinson saw some urgency about moving forward with church improvements, perhaps even replacing the church organ, an old Wurlitzer that had once served as the practice organ at Radio City Music Hall in New York. In 1985 Stinson had formed a church council, chaired by Andrew (Andy) Holmes, whose primary mission was long-range planning. In July 1985 the council held a two-day retreat at the beautiful Eastwind Inn located in nearby Tenants Harbor, with the Reverend David Glendinning of Concord, New Hampshire, as facilitator. An Episcopalian priest whom Holmes had recruited to be chaplain at the Oak Grove School where

Holmes was headmaster, Glendinning had widely known skills and experience as a facilitator. The retreat focused on the "responsibility of our church to its membership and equally to the community as a whole," as "outlined in the Church Covenant;" however, much of the conversation that mid-summer spotlighted the church's increasingly inadequate physical plant. As Stinson probably hoped, the retreat also produced energy and excitement, especially in Stinson's case. After the Tenants Harbor retreat, Holmes remembered Stinson telling him "Andy, we've got to move—Go for Broke!" Ultimately, the retreat culminated in an eighteen-month study that produced "The long-range plan for the future operating and physical needs of the church." Shortly, Stinson and the church council abbreviated that phrase to "Faith for the Future." [764]

Holmes, in his 1986 annual report of the church council, delivered on January 1, 1987, observed that an early outcome of the council's planning endeavor had been the hiring of the student minister, David Burke. Essentially, the 1986 "plan for the future," as Holmes explained it, addressed the church's "pressing needs," for additional parking, for parsonage repairs, and for more organ loft space to solve the problem of "communication between the choir director and the choir, where the former cannot hear the latter and the latter cannot see the former!" It addressed, as well, in Holmes' words, "the weakness of the present organ and suggests possible receipt and installation of the Moller Organ which Mrs. [Katherine] Cook [the choir director] has most generously offered to donate to the church." Although Cook's offer of her Moller organ generated a swirl of conversation, alas, according to Holmes, few members took it seriously. Cook's theater-size Moller had been trimmed down to accommodate her house, "it was a timid little thing" and lacked the power and verve desirable for a spacious church sanctuary.[765]

Holmes in his January 1987 presentation noted that the council's "plan" addressed more than the church's need for a new organ. Other urgent projects existed: new Sunday school classrooms, an expanded vestry, a rear entrance to the parking lot, facilities to help the disabled, space for a community room, and a redesigned and remodeled kitchen. However, Holmes, fiscally minded, emphasized that the plan "does not necessarily contemplate immediate or major expenses or expansion of the church programs or facilities." In conclusion, he "cautioned…that in the orderly development of Church facilities every effort must also be made to see that the budget can maintain and operate such additions and that none of the efforts conflict with other ongoing programs."[766] Those words of caution aside, as early as August 1986, council member Robert Kidd had quickly drafted a floor plan for an enlarged vestry and a choir loft large enough to hold Katherine Cook's proffered Moller organ.[767] With those caveats duly noted, but with a glowing "faith in the future," David Stinson, at the church's January 1987 annual meeting, formally announced the council's "Long Range Plan." Forthwith, Stinson officially christened the plan "Faith for the Future," and although it inaugurated seven years of fervent, often frenetic additional planning, building, and fundraising, the venture ultimately plunged the church into over a decade of turmoil. [768]

As early as August 1986, Robert Kidd had not only drafted a plan for church improvements, but mused as well about funding such a plan in the face of the Boothbay YMCA's proposal to massively enlarge its physical plant. Kidd estimated that immediate church improvements would cost around $110,000 and set a reasonable fundraising target of $22,000 a year for five years. "We are at a crossroad in the history of our church," proclaimed the church council; "We can worry, cry poverty, and stay where we are now, or we can plan, grow, and expand. If we don't plan for growth and work for it…we can be assured that growth will not occur."

In March 1987 the council officially created a Faith for the Future (FFF) committee chaired by Andy Holmes, which included Peter Mundy, Jack Hanselman, Charles Stewart, and David Walker. The FFF program remained fixed: Sunday school rooms, an expanded parking lot behind the church, an enlarged vestry, kitchen improvements, parsonage improvements, and a new organ. At that crucial juncture in the process, the council quoted the value of the church's endowment at $73,704.

Fundraising commenced almost immediately, and by January 1988 $31,000 had been committed, some of which was promptly allocated to pay for a new parsonage furnace and to paint the church steeple. Simultaneously, the choir formed a committee to decide whether or not a new organ might be preferable to the gifted Moller organ. Undiscouraged, momentum for the plan built. Two months later on March 8, 1988, a joint meeting of the church council and the business committee took place, focusing exclusively on how the church should move forward with the Faith for the Future program. The two committees commenced by itemizing the proposed improvements—now headed by the "new organ program." Next they established a "planning process," beginning with the selection of an architect who—in concert with the church council—can formulate a detailed plan for the proposed physical improvement to the church and its cost. With the architect's advice, the church should determine what it "has to have," concluded the two committees, and then decide what the church "can afford" and how these needs can be "sequenced."

As a direct consequence of the March 8 meeting, the congregation in April 1988 approved hiring the Scagliotti Associates architectural firm of Portsmouth, New Hampshire, and formulated a schedule of the capital improvements to be undertaken, beginning with enlarging the parking lot in the summer of 1988, and ordering a new organ in the fall of 1989, at which time the vestry enlargement would begin, the latter to be completed in the winter of 1990. Bob Scagliotti, a "high-powered" architect, owned a large summer house on Townsend Gut.

On June 14, 1988 the church appointed a planning and design (P&D) committee, headed by Harold Taylor and including Jack Hanselman, Charles Stewart, Priscilla Gillespie, Sally Walker, and Robert Kidd, which was commissioned to work directly with the Scagliotti firm. That team became the new face of the FFF campaign, and, in fact, replaced the FFF committee, which was dissolved due to "organizational confusion." In addition to working with Scagliotti, the P&D committee collected data from various church groups about the church's needs and desires, evaluated the information, and then made recommendations to the congregation, "leading to construction." Ominously, at the very moment in March 1988 when the church council and business committee had finally solidified plans and particulars for the Faith for the Future program, the business committee discovered a disturbing $3,000 shortfall in the church operating budget. To address the deficit it called for a series of church suppers. One roast beef dinner that year was advertised as "Beef Up the Budget." The discovery proved ominous and, alas, untreatable with church suppers.

Curiously, the church music committee operated independently of FFF, although its actions profoundly impacted the program. The choir deliberated *in camera* on the organ issue. For reasons already explained, it rejected Katherine Cook's offer of her Moller organ and, forthwith, raised $110,000 from five generous church members toward a "new custom made" $150,000 Austin organ, whose purchase was approved at a congregational meeting held in November 1988.

During the next year, new planning and the modification of existing plans proceeded apace, all of which drastically revised the original design and cost estimates of the FFF program. For example, in November 1989, Scagliotti, whose local representative on the church project was Earl Kincaid, presented plans for adding a new kitchen and bedroom to the Road's End parsonage, as Stinson's young family had outgrown the relatively small house.

Indeed, by the time a new fundraising committee, headed by the Reverend Dr. Otis Maxfield, and including Bob Memory, Jenny Logan, Don Walker, Michael Harrison, and George Fotos, had been formed in November 1989, the program's cost had seriously escalated. Before retiring to Boothbay Harbor, Otis Maxfield, whose wife Ginny was an active church member, had been a prominent UCC minister. Among his many talents, Dr. Maxfield possessed not only a flair for the dramatic, but also a gift for public relations (the subject of his doctoral dissertation) that he easily parlayed into a successful post-retirement business career, a career that took him veritably around the world. One of his biggest clients was Singer Sewing Machine. Maxfield's public relations skills were vital to his church fundraising role, one that daily grew more and more important.

As early as the spring of 1988, Harold Taylor, chair of P&D, reported to the congregation that the installation of an Austin organ required moving the church back thirty-five feet from its historic roadside perch to allow the necessary space to accommodate the enlarged choir loft, organ wind chest, and pipes. The move would also create a useful enlarged space beneath the sanctuary. Taylor estimated that the proposed move would cost $21,000. With the Austin organ already approved, the cost of moving the church became a new budget item. Originally, the church had quoted $250,000 as the cost of Faith for the Future. No longer. By November 1989 the new costs far exceeded that figure.

As chair of fundraising, Otis Maxfield on December 5, 1989 wrote to a prominent church benefactor, George McEvoy, informing him that the church has "reached the point where we shall soon need to make decisions and commitments to complete detailed construction plans and enter into construction contracts if we are to meet our objective of a spring 1990 start with completion in the fall of 1990." Maxfield had earlier spoken with McEvoy about FFF, and he now sought greater assurance that McEvoy's foundation was firmly committed to the FFF program. "We are extremely reluctant to commit to a building contract," wrote Maxfield, "until our ability to finance the project is certain or at least of high confidence. As previously discussed with you, we have to date secured $285,000 in firm or verbally committed pledges from our members; we estimate an additional $85,000 will be raised in our planned general campaign, for a total of $370,000 in congregation contributions…We are prepared to assume a mortgage of approximately $90,000. We are therefore confident we can raise on our own more than $500,000, or seventy percent of our project cost." Accordingly, Maxfield listed the latest FFF projects and updated cost figures for McEvoy to consider: [769]

Sanctuary $275,000
Vestry $140,000
Church School Class Rooms $40,000
Site Work/Landscaping $65,000
Parsonage $50,000
Organ $155,000
TOTAL $725,000

By June 15, 1990 Maxfield could report to George McEvoy that his committee had secured gifts and pledges amounting to $480,000, that it had circulated among building firms "requests for proposals," and had received bids from twelve "qualified" contractors. Awards would be made on July 1. That July the McEvoy Foundation pledged $120,000, and on August 3, 1990, the business committee, citing the bank's "greater flexibility," selected First Federal of Bath, Maine, for a $200,000 "line of credit" secured by a mortgage on the church's Road's End parsonage.[770]

Soon afterward, on September 6, 1990, Harold Taylor announced that for Phase II of the Faith for the Future program (moving the church and expanding the vestry and parking lot) the church had signed a contract for $299,000 with McCormick and Associates General Contractors of West Rockland, Maine and with Northern Building Movers of New Hampshire to separate the meetinghouse from the vestry and move it back 35 feet eastward and onto a new foundation and a new basement-level hall. There will be a new addition constructed behind the building to house a new Austin organ and parking lot for 50 cars. The vestry wing will remain on its present foundation…and [will be] made into new [Sunday school] classrooms, and a new entrance from the parking lot behind the church will be built.[771]

McCormick hired a local firm, Northern Light, to do the electrical work. The parking lot expansion necessitated removing the Murray House barn, which found a new home at the Boothbay Harbor Railway Museum.[772]

Since the moving project rendered the church sanctuary unusable for at least four months, the Boothbay Region YMCA offered its facilities for Sunday worship and for Sunday school. In a true ecumenical spirit, both the Catholic and Methodist churches volunteered the use of their space for non-Sunday programs. In September 1990 the business committee voted to give the "Y" the sum of $75 per week for expenses.[773]

However, beneath the euphoria of signing contracts for Faith for the Future projects, the receipt of sizable donations, and the expectation of shortly securing a $200,000 line of credit lurked unresolved and cantankerous fiscal problems that promised to fester. Beginning as early as 1989, the church operating budget, which kept the minister paid, the lights on, the building heated, and paper and pens on the church office desks, stood constantly and annoyingly in the "red." At the April 16, 1990 business committee meeting, Melodee Burnham, who acted in the unpaid capacity of assistant treasurer, reported on "procedures for handling the weekly offering." Burnham explained to the trustees "that it is not feasible for confidentiality and other reasons to have two people count and deposit [the collected money] every Sunday."[774]

The persistent financial dilemma confounded the business committee. Unquestionably, heating costs had risen, emergency repairs to the parsonage roof had proven somewhat expensive, and the Murray House tenant (who was expecting a baby) paid her rent only irregularly. Still pledge income versus expenses seemed fairly well balanced and, furthermore, church income met expectations. In August 1990 the business committee, looking for a culprit, speculated that tourism might be down. A month later, however, Rev. Stinson denied that church summer attendance had been down, but he added, "Loose plate [offering] is down." [775]

Troubles with the church operating budget notwithstanding, construction in December 1990 finally and fully got under way on the FFF projects. But, here too, problems arose. In excavating the basement preparatory to moving the church back from its historic roadside site, the contractor encountered more granite ledge than initially expected. The encounter, which involved blasting, raised costs. Later in December, upon the advice of the architectural firm and to save head room in the new basement, the P & D committee changed the plans to switch from hot air to, alas, more costly hot water heat, which eliminated ceiling ductwork. [776] Thus, while McCormick had successfully repositioned the church eastward thirty-five feet to its new permanent location, with costs rising, and with both the Murray House and the parsonage already mortgaged, the business committee now debated floating a bond issue—one limited to church members.

At the January 1991 annual meeting, held at the YMCA, the business committee presented its idea for the bond issue. To save on the exorbitant 10.5 percent interest on the church's $250,000 line of credit, the committee proposed issuing eight percent bonds to be purchased by members of the congregation. The ten-year, eight-percent bond program—overseen by a building bond subcommittee headed by Alice Thompson and Hildy Johnson—produced savings by reducing the costly principal on the church's line of credit. Approved by the congregation at its 1991 annual meeting, the program raised $125,000 and reduced the line of credit principal to $154,000.

However, it was not enough. From April through the summer of 1991 Stinson asked church members to "Dig Deeper" and even further underwrite the Faith for the Future program. To help even more reduce the burdensome debt of the FFF Phase II projects "special Sunday collections" were held. Many families, such as the Mundys and Florinis, indeed dug much deeper, and by January 27, 1992 Rev. Stinson reported that the congregation had in all raised close to $600,000. Yet, despite "digging deeper," the church failed to complete the projects designated in the "Faith for the Future" campaign. It would leave Phase III of Faith for the Future totally undone. [777]

Nevertheless, Stinson rejoiced with his congregation that the church could celebrate Easter 1991 in the moved sanctuary, with its enlarged vestry and a new fellowship hall; however, it had not relocated the kitchen to fellowship hall, and the vestry wing remained unrenovated. Neither was work on the rear entrance, additional Sunday school rooms, nor paved parking lot accomplished. Moreover, the financial problems, which originated in 1989, stubbornly persisted in 1991. From August through December 1991 the church got no rent from the Murray House. Operation Desert Storm (which did not see Rev. Chaplin David Stinson called to duty), plus rising fuel prices and a national economic recession in 1991, all depressed the value of the church's endowment. Recession or not, the church in 1991 faced the first payment of $8,362 in interest to its bondholders and another $10,000 payment on bond principal. The church's total indebtedness by the end of 1991 amounted to $161,500. More worrisome, as New Year 1992 arrived, the church operations budget remained agonizingly in the red, leaving a $5,121 deficit on the church books by year's end. [778]

None of these problems had disappeared on July 12, 1992 when the Reverend David Stinson received a call to serve the United Church of Christ of Glen Ridge, New Jersey. He submitted his resignation to the business committee effective September 1992.[779] Since he had served the Boothbay Harbor church for half of 1992 he dutifully submitted his January 1993 annual report to the church. He thanked all those who had helped him, including George Fotos, Franklin Poe, Katherine Cook, who in July 1991 had been replaced as organist and choir director by young Eugenie O'Connell, Otis Maxfield, Bob Memory, Harold Taylor, and Bob Kidd. "Any Regrets?" he wrote rhetorically. "Well, if I have by accident offended anyone in trying to accomplish what I thought was best, please forgive me. I have aimed to leave our church in better shape than I found it...In so many ways you are stronger than you know...Cyndi, Hannah, Phoebe, and Jess join me in thanking you for your many kindnesses."

Rev. Jack Perkins—November 1992-January 1993
Rev. Charles Svendson—February 1993-November 1993

The Reverend Jack Perkins became the church's interim pastor for the months of November and December 1992 and January 1993. In February 1993 the congregation welcomed the Reverend Charles Svendson as its interim, with Robert Luccock and Walter Eastwood, perennial summer preachers also filling in. These ministers served the church until November 1993 when the Reverend Peter Panagore arrived in Boothbay Harbor as the new settled pastor of the town's Congregational church, UCC.[780]

Rev. Peter Baldwin Panagore 1993–2003

Peter Panagore's decade-long ministry in the Congregational Church of Boothbay Harbor bestrode the millennium, and to the extent that the occasion conjured up apocalyptic imagery of a coming age rife with turbulence to be followed by one of harmony, Rev. Panagore's ministry was truly "millennial." Panagore's pastorate also corresponded nationally to the presidency of William Jefferson Clinton (1993–2001), "the man from Hope (Arkansas)." Clinton's youthful presidency promised hope and did produce economic prosperity, but unfortunately, also accusations and charges of unconventional behavior.

Rev. Peter B. Panagore

At the local level, charges of unconventionality of a different kind troubled Rev. Panagore's tenure, charges often leveled at the United Church of Christ, the larger denomination to which the Harbor church had belonged for the past forty years. Panagore was eclectic and experimental, but so was the UCC. In fact, Rev. Panagore, as much as any past minister of the Boothbay region's Congregational church, reminded the congregation of its UCC affiliation. For those members of the Harbor church who had never attended a United Church of Christ General Synod meeting, who were unaware of the denomination's strong commitment to ecumenicism, to foreign missions, and to welcoming diversity, who were oblivious to the church's strong presence in the Pacific Isles— in Samoa and Hawaii—and in the urban West and Mid-West, in Los Angeles, California, in Chicago, and in Indianapolis, Peter Panagore's much vaunted Catholic background, his frequent thespian approach to sermonizing, and his mysticism were sometimes unsettling.

This does not imply radicalism. A 2001 report issued by the Hartford Institute of Religious Research found only 5.6 percent of UCC parishes to be "Very Liberal," 3.4 percent to be "Very Conservative," 22.4 percent to be "Somewhat Liberal," and 23.6 percent to be "Somewhat Conservative." These were typical, unremarkable findings for a demographically older, "mainline" denomination facing a declining membership. What really distinguished the denomination was its ecumenicism and its much vaunted mission to be inclusive, to reach out to all who seek an encounter with God's living presence, to know that "God is Still Speaking." [781]

Robert Shepard, the son of a UCC missionary in Turkey, and in 1997 the head deacon of the Harbor church, in a letter to "All Members" succinctly and artfully explained the church's UCC connection. Unlike Presbyterian forms, explained Shepard, the United Church of Christ abjured hierarchical form. The resolutions of UCC synods and conferences, declared Shepard, spoke "to" not "for" local churches. Each church in the UCC existed basically for four purposes, purposes that in reality had remained unchanged for at least several hundred years: "to try to learn God's will for us through scripture, teaching, and preaching; to praise and petition God through prayers and hymns and anthems and offerings; to help the needy, as Jesus instructed us; to draw others into the joy of Christian discipleship." Beyond that, UCC churches were free to experiment, to improvise and to be creative. To the joy of some and the chagrin of others, the Reverend Panagore exemplified all three. [782]

After Rev. Stinson's resignation in July 1992, the Boothbay Harbor Congregational church had chosen Daniel Jameson, assisted by Dr. Otto Sommers of the Maine Conference, to head its search committee. The "Local Church Profile" revealed forty percent of the church's membership to be over age fifty; twenty-three percent of adult church members engaged in business enterprise or in the professions, while almost a quarter were retired. The "Profile" highlighted that in 1990 the church had been moved thirty-five feet back onto a new foundation and that the church's thirty year-old waterfront parsonage had recently been "extensively" renovated. In summing up Boothbay's economy, it noted that while fishing and boatbuilding provided important jobs, its base was tourism. Finally, the profile confessed that the Faith for the Future program remained incomplete and that "when all of the pledges have been received in 1994, a mortgage of approximately $80,000 will be sufficient for all the work accomplished to date." Nothing in the profile indicated a chronic deficit in the church's operating budget.[783]

The profile attracted attention. By the late spring of 1993 résumés from over forty candidates had arrived on Jameson's desk. Panagore added his to the pile at a time when the Town of Boothbay was completing work on a new, modern town office located opposite the Boothbay common, adjoining the lot once the site of Levitt's Chevrolet; and when Bath Iron Works was finishing another Aegis-Class Destroyer. Jameson and the search committee found Panagore's résumé sufficiently impressive that they invited him for an interview, during which Jameson drove the young minister out along route 96 to beautiful Ocean Point. Like Rev. Hartman, Panagore fell in love with Ocean Point and with the region. He compared his feeling upon beholding the breathtaking views from Grimes Cove at Ocean Point to a religious experience.[784]

On Sunday, July 8, 1993, Rev. Panagore preached his trial sermon at the Harbor church, after which the congregation voted to make him its next settled pastor. He and his wife Michelle Miclette, with their eighteen-month-old son Andrew and their four year-old daughter, Alexandra, moved into the Roads End parsonage in November, at which time he officially assumed the pastorate of the over 200-year-old church.

Peter Baldwin Panagore graduated in 1982 from the University of Massachusetts at Amherst with an English degree, and four years later from Yale Divinity School, after which he served two Connecticut UCC churches, first as a student interim and then as an interim associate pastor. His first full-time pastorate came in 1986 on Deer Isle, Maine, where he served two Congregational (UCC) churches, Sunset and First Church, each a five-minute walk apart. Rev. Panagore adored the beauty and charm of Deer Isle with its art scene surrounding the Haystack School of Crafts, an architecturally distinguished art community founded by the celebrated modernist architect, Edward Larrabee Barnes. Rev. Panagore formally studied glassblowing there. He worked intimately with the small Deer Isle community, which was beset by sharp social contrasts between the relatively affluent artists and retirees and the less affluent, often socially and educationally disadvantaged, local community. It was his ministry to the latter that entangled him as a mediator in an island murder case, whereby his own life was eventually threatened, motivating him to seek a pulpit elsewhere. [785]

From the outset, like a medieval mystic, Peter Panagore ventured forth on a personal quest for spiritual growth and fulfillment, a platonic journey toward God, a mission to, in his own words, "conjure God's presence through the Holy Spirit in me and around me." He told the search committee that he began each day with a half hour of "centering prayer" to "unplug" his "spiritual well," to "help the artist waters flow and fill my little internal reserve full of the Living Water from which I drink." He was never disingenuous with the committee. "In preaching," he told them, "I am Biblically based, direct, challenging, confronting, serious, [and, he added] comic. I try to keep the attention of the congregation at all times." And, he did, although to the consternation of some. He admittedly preached sermons (often in a series) on difficult subjects such as the plausibility of Biblical miracles, or on death and dying. However, none of these sensitive subjects shocked the largely over-fifty congregation half as much as when on one Sunday morning they beheld the Reverend Panagore strolling with ministerial dignity toward the pulpit, a gleaming gold bauble dangling from his newly pierced ear.[786]

A mountain climber, Frisbee instructor, glassblower, thespian, the bejeweled Panagore was also a talented and compulsive doodler (his father was an architect and he had taken art lessons in junior high school). His elaborate and artistic doodles, sketched amidst council, business committee, and diaconate meetings, in his own words, "enabled him to keep focused." After the often staid, academic, and philosophical Stinson, Rev. Panagore brought a creative theatricality to the church and the pulpit. His hand puppet "Mr. Moose" became a regular feature in the children's as well as in his adult sermons. Church members might even encounter their minister in town walking on stilts.

Panagore was indubitably unconventional, which from the start of his Boothbay region ministry alienated a certain discrete segment of the congregation whom he came to describe as the "cabal." After his first year at the church he insisted in 1994 that the church council conduct a written congregational evaluation of his performance. The evaluation undertaken by the pastoral relations committee revealed "enthusiastic approval" of his ministry from a large number of the respondents. "That fact, coupled with his success in drawing new members," concluded the pastoral relations committee, "bodes well for a healthy growth in the near future and beyond."[787] Members like Andy Holmes found many of Panagore's sermons, especially the adventures of Mr. Moose, "fun and enlightening." Rev. Panagore told Holmes that "some of [his] best sermons are built from stories and real life situations. To my way of thinking a short sermon, well stated and simple, but to the point is more effective ['and far better received and far longer remembered'] than an expansive theological discussion."[788] Youthful, Panagore was only thirty-five when he became pastor of the Harbor church. Like Rev. Stinson he appealed to youth, whom he regularly took on ski trips, kayaking, and on ice skating ventures.

Born a Catholic, and a subscriber to the *New Christian Century* and *The Ecumenical Weekly*, with other town clergy (and like the Reverends Hartman and Stinson before him) he participated in a weekly clergy breakfast and in many ecumenical services. Above all, Peter Panagore was the first computer-savvy, internet-wise, minister. From the start he had the church purchase for him a computer. Through a service called Ecunet, and in late 1994 Cyberchurch, he could circulate his sermons in cyberspace as he could via UCChristnet a year later. He would be the first Congregational Church of Boothbay Harbor minister to list his email address in the weekly announcement of church services in the *Boothbay Register*.[789]

Financial Purgatory

Peter Panagore denied having any knowledge of the church's financial problems when in November 1993 he took the pulpit his first Sunday as pastor. At Yale he had been taught to "distance himself from money issues," but early in his new ministry he suspected that the church faced serious financial difficulties. He recently recalled pointing them out to the business committee and—with one or two exceptions—was promptly told not to interfere. He did have allies who shared his anxieties.[790]

In November 1993 the business committee consisted of Hildy Johnson, Phillip Gittings, Melodee Burnham, Ned Freeman, Earle Kincaid, Donald Walker, Bud Harris, Andrew Holmes, and Susan Bogart. The severity of the financial situation faced them immediately. In January 1994 $109,500 of debt for Faith For the Future stood outstanding, with $8,760 in interest on the member-held bonds due in March. The church's remaining investment funds of $107,056 had been newly deposited in the Maine Conference Consolidated Trust Funds. Just $14,477 remained in the Phase III Faith for the Future construction account. Moreover, upon the insistent recommendation of the church's auditor, Walter S. Reed (who perennially delivered "a qualified opinion" on the reliability of the church accounts), the business committee had pledged for its 1994 "goal" to restructure its internal controls over the church's bookkeeping system. With a carpenter ant problem looming in the parsonage and the Murray House again about to be unrented, treasurer Melodee Burnham reported $3,727 in bills, but a piddling $158 balance in the checking account. [791]

In August 1994, with pledges ten percent below expectations, the value of the endowment down, and a $108,500 bond issue falling due in March 1995, the business committee, in concert with the long-range planning committee, created a tripartite "Plan to Resolve the Financial Situation." First it would launch another drive for "special gifts;" second, it proposed instituting a new "One-Write" accounting system; and third, it sought to secure a mortgage loan of $100,000 from First Federal. Although the "special drive" produced several generous gifts, including much desired bond forgiveness, it fell short of the goal. While the church paid off its line of credit, $14,000 remained of the church's bond principal, with interest due March 1995. Meanwhile, as of October 1994, pledge income stood at fifty percent making the church again $10,000 short on its operating budget.[792]

At the January 18, 1995 annual meeting, Jack Hanselman branded the church's newest proposed budget an "exercise in hope." Two weeks later a "special" business committee meeting voted to take $14,000 from endowment funds to retire the final Faith for the Future bonds (with the added interest, $15,120) on March 1, 1995. This was the same meeting at which the same committee voted that for the sum of $10,000 it would transfer the deed to the old Boothbay Center church lot to the Boothbay Civic Association rather than to the original suitor, the Boothbay Region Land Trust. The lot, opposite the Civil War Memorial, was the site of Rev. John Murray's Presbyterian Church, later the Boothbay's Center School. Shortly thereafter, the Civic Association carried out its plan to make the historic site a war memorial. [793]

That October, with the bonds at last paid off, but with the church confronting a $6,000 shortfall between pledges and expenses, and in order to better restructure its finances, the church revised its bylaws to terminate both the business committee and the church council and to create in their place a board of trustees. The bylaws change took effect September 1, 1996.[794]

However, at its January 1996 annual meeting, despite the church's heroic efforts, its "special" fundraising, borrowing from the endowment, its bylaws changes, etc., the "financial situation" remained just as dire. The "lame duck" business committee could proclaim "all bills paid in 1995," but they were in fact "paid" only by using the old line of credit. A few days later at the January 16, 1996 business committee meeting, Bob Memory again observed that the pledge monies were in arrears. "We can normally expect some 1995 pledges to be paid in 1996, but not to this extent!" exclaimed Memory. When the diaconate convened in April and heard that because of the church's poor cash flow neither the minister nor the choir director had been paid, they decried the situation as "inexcusable." At the very next business committee meeting in May 1996, Bob Memory responded to the deacons' charge by informing those assembled that the executive committee would meet the next day to discuss selling the parsonage. "It is the thought that funds from its sale could get us out of the financial bind that we are in." [795]

Built in 1965, and, alas, too cheaply, the parsonage, quaint, beautifully located on a harbor frontage, and recently refurbished with a new kitchen and added bedroom, had forever proven somewhat problematic. The roof leaked, pipes burst, ants invaded, doors fit poorly, and to make matters worse (or perhaps better!) from his first day in Boothbay Harbor, Peter Panagore had begged for a housing allowance so that he could buy his own home at Ocean Point, where he had had his mystical experience. Memory viewed the sale as alleviating several burdens, burdens made even lighter if the church added to its real estate for sale portfolio the equally problematic Murray House.[796]

With the Boothbay Harbor firm Tindal and Callahan as its real estate agent, the church set the price of $369,000 for the parsonage. At the same time it granted Peter Panagore a $15,000 annual housing allowance, and a $10,000 loan (at 6.75 percent) for a down payment on the purchase of a home. It priced the Murray House at $5,000, but that figure did not include the land. The purchaser was expected to move the house off the church land. Very shortly the Solarzano family successfully bid $4,000 for the Murray House; however, their inability to secure the money to purchase the lot and move the building delayed the settlement.

In fact, despite the business committee's decision to escape debt by selling the church's real estate assets, by January 1997, without a bid for the parsonage and with the Murray House transaction stalled, the church's financial tribulations persisted. Minus the cash from those transactions, during the year 1996 (a year "of frustration" for the new board of trustees) the church was forced again to borrow money ($60,000) from the endowment to replace the sanctuary roof ($22,000), to pay $20,000 on the line of credit, and to use $10,000 for operating expenses. It was not until the spring of 1997 that the parsonage finally sold, to Peter and Mary Lloyd, and for $280,000 not $369,000. With the proceeds of $162,000 (the realtor fee and the unpaid mortgage amount deducted) the church promptly repaid the $60,000 that it had borrowed from its endowment, paid off $5,000 on the church mortgage loan, and established a $10,000 reserve fund. [797]

Faith over Perfidy

Compounding the onus of debt, since 1986 the church had faced another equally severe and ominous financial problem: an annual shortfall in projected monies from pledges and a chronic decline in expected "loose plate" income. The church's auditor had regularly warned the church to tighten its financial controls and the church had ultimately responded, as stated above by revamping its bylaws, scuttling the old business committee and creating a new board of trustees. Never had it questioned either its treasurer or its assistant treasurer, who since 1986 had been Melodee Burnham. She served as assistant treasurer under Louise Holmes from 1986 to 1993, after which Burnham herself became treasurer. Long praised for her dedication, for her long unremunerated hours, and for her faithful service, Burnham was regularly and heartily applauded at the church's January annual meetings.

At the January 21, 1997 meeting of the board of trustees, that applause ended. Irena Prall had just been made treasurer and, in Burnham's absence, Bob Memory presented the past treasurer's report. "There are some questions concerning what appears in the annual report of the treasurer," confessed Memory. "To us [the Trustees] the 'balance sheet' does not add up, and the Line of Credit figure on the Income side should equate with the savings on mortgages when the parsonage and Murray House sales are complete." Much had not added up for a long time.[798]

However, if the Reverend Panagore, or anyone else at the Boothbay Harbor Congregational church suspected Burnham of theft, they failed that January to deter the board of trustees from re-appointing Burnham to the key fiscal posts of assistant treasurer and financial secretary. Every Sunday in 1997 she still took home the weekly collection, including checks and loose cash, counted it there, and deposited it in the First Federal Saving and Loan Bank either on a Monday or a Tuesday. Which is why a year later in March 1998, Irena Prall could inform the trustees that, despite upgrading the church's bookkeeping procedures, the church remained "VERY much behind in pledges." In order to pay the minister's salary, bemoaned Prall, "we must take it from the contingency fund." At the same time Panagore notified the trustees that the church computer would probably "succumb" to the "millennium problem" (Y2K) and that he had discovered a computer expert who would build the church a crash-proof computer for half price.[799]

Meanwhile, despite the popular disbelief that Melodee Burnham might be tampering with church funds, Panagore's suspicions hardened, and he prevailed upon Irena Prall to probe the church's past financial records for evidence. Irena's investigation soon uncovered a church "special account" oddly missing $8,000. That was enough. At the June 16, 1998 trustees' meeting, Bob Memory stated that "It was the [trustees'] consensus that the assistant treasurer be encouraged to give up the position…[and he] asked for names or volunteers who would do the recording of the weekly offering, deposit same in the bank, and give the report to Mrs. Prall who is willing to do the necessary bookkeeping and reports." No one had yet been directly accused, but for the first time in a dozen years the church's monies, its checks, stock certificates, cash and loose plate receipts had been safely secured. In her minutes of the September 15 trustees meeting, Susan Bogart wrote that "The treasurer is very happy because ALL THE BILLS HAVE BEEN PAID!"[800]

Despite the evidence, disbelief and silence still reigned in 1998. Panagore's and Prall's internal investigation actually continued into 1999. According to Rev. Panagore, in early 1999 he contacted a person at the Boothbay Water Department, where Burnham worked, inquiring about whether or not the department, like the church, might have experienced any similar suspicious financial losses. They had! One and one now added up to two, triggering both a Lincoln County Sheriff's and a local police investigation. Beginning in March Boothbay Harbor's Lt. Benner, in concert with the Lincoln County sheriff and county prosecutor subpoenaed the church's and the Water Department's financial records. In the wake of that action, the church held a special Sunday meeting where, before a stunned, even devastated, congregation, Rev. Panagore revealed details of the longstanding embezzlement. [801]

The prosecutor scheduled a grand jury hearing on the so-called "Burnham Case" for November 1999, but Burnham pleaded guilty and a December sentencing hearing was held instead. In the interim, Burnham was freed on her "personal recognizance." Although Burnham had been treasurer of the Congregational church, 1989–1998, and she had admitted stealing cash from the offering plates and cashing checks, because of the statute of limitations, the Boothbay Harbor Police limited its investigation of the subpoenaed church records to between 1993 and 1998. Lt. Benner admitted that he found $80,000 "to be suspicious," but the department charged Burnham with the theft of just $40,000. "We'll probably never know how much was taken from the church," concluded Benner. The church at the time estimated that Burnham likely stole between $70,000 and $80,000.

The theft may well have exceeded $100,000. Her plea agreement obligated her to repay the Boothbay Water District $75,000, but only $15,000 in restitution to the church.[802]

At the December sentencing hearing, Susan Bogart read the "Victim Statement" on behalf of the church. While Bogart prepared her statement, the church through its lawyer, Franklin Poe, seriously contemplated filing civil suits against both First Federal Savings and the Burnhams. Simultaneously, Melodee Burnham approached head deacon Ralph Prall and requested to be allowed to address the congregation at a special November 14 congregational meeting. Irena Prall, however, felt Burnham's action to be "manipulative" and advised the deacons to deny her request. Rather than demonstrating "to me any sincere remorse," Prall saw in her plea bargain and in her behavior in general, only "arrogance," a ploy, engineered to ease sentencing…An invitation should be extended in Christian love to Melodee, if she so desires," but, interjected Prall, only "after the sentencing. This may expedite the healing of all concerned."[803]

With the Burnhams filing for bankruptcy, and the First Federal Savings Bank denying any liability for Burnham's theft, the church, with Poe's advice, declined to file civil suits against either the Burnhams or the bank. However, Susan Bogart, joined by several church members, did appear at the December sentencing hearing, where Bogart read a strongly worded, somewhat impassioned statement. In it she reviewed the church's agonizingly long, financial nightmare, and articulated how Burnham's perfidy tested the boundaries of the church's faith and its powers of forgiveness. "The Christian church," exhorted Bogart "rests on TRUST, spelled in capital letters. The breach in trust we had in our treasurer has affected the congregation and the minister in a most negative way. It caused a rift in the church that has been difficult to heal." Bogart spoke of the distress caused when at each meeting of the trustees, members had to decide "which few of our local small businessmen creditors could get paid…Even our minister and the church secretary went without pay." The power company threatened to cut off any electricity; "we were a derelict floating on a sea of debts. It is a relief to say that with a new treasurer…a renewed spirit within the church, we are on a new path." Christians, she concluded, "teach forgiveness,…[W]e are gratified that the time of dissension is past, and we can minister to the community as we've been commissioned to by our Christian beliefs."[804]

Burnham's plea bargain brokered for her a lighter sentence in return for an admission of guilt and payments in restitution to the church and the Boothbay Water Department. In return, the Lincoln County judge sentenced her to four years in prison with all but 90 days suspended. [805]

Among those members of the congregation most grievously wronged by Burnham's breach of trust was the Reverend Peter Panagore himself. Unlike Rev. Stinson, he bore the full brunt of the financial imbroglio. Many members targeted him for the church's chronic monetary problems. Yet, he had faced—in his own words—"threats and intimidation" when he periodically pointed out the problems. On several occasions he had submitted his resignation, but was convinced by other church members not to surrender. Panagore contended that "in the face of strong opposition" he was not only instrumental in uncovering the embezzlement, but, once the crime was revealed, as a minister of the gospel he pastored and counseled both Burnhams and helped heal the festering wounds.[806]

Melodee Burnham's incarceration lasted barely three months, hardly retribution enough for some in the church. Moreover, the rift that Susan Bogart spoke of at the sentencing hearing resulted in a legacy of bitterness and some loss of church membership. On the other hand, as the last second passed at midnight on December 31, 1999, the 2YK-caused crashing of every computer did not happen, vastly relieving many in the church, the Boothbay Harbor community, the region, and the office of the *Boothbay Register*. The church, together with the larger community, moved smoothly into a new millennium, and church finances continued to improve. New members, such as the Bauman family, joined the church in 2000, and while gangrenous memories of the church's horrific financial past lingered, they were gradually, very gradually, obfuscated by time.

Some things didn't change immediately. Mr. Moose happily survived the millennium and so did the Reverend Panagore's promise to employ comedy and antics like stilt-walking and karate to enliven his sermons. But, by his tenth year, and with the financial crisis over, his spiritual quest resumed. After church one Sunday, a member informed him of the retirement of David Glusker, minister of the First Radio Parish Church of America, which featured a longstanding, Portland-based, originally radio broadcast, but now televised program entitled "Daily Devotions." Rev. Panagore seized the opportunity. In this teleministry, Panagore's appetite for communications technology, his theatrical skills, and his talent for storytelling, would prove invaluable in helping to make "Daily Devotions" a media success.

Conclusion

In 1986, the Reverend David Stinson, Andrew Holmes, Harold Taylor, Otis Maxfield, Robert Kidd, Priscilla Gillespie, Sally Walker, Peter Mundy and many others concurred that with a growing church congregation and a flourishing Sunday school, the time had come for a major expansion of church facilities. Two years later in 1988, the church launched "Faith for the Future," which, among other things, aimed to enlarge the vestry, add Sunday school rooms, and install a more powerful new organ. In late 1993, after David Stinson had left and a new minister, Rev. Peter Panagore, arrived, much of what Stinson had earlier envisioned was reality. The church, now moved back thirty-five feet from its original site, flaunted a much-enlarged vestry, expanded Sunday school space, a basement fellowship hall, a large kitchen, and a magnificent, concert-quality Austin organ.

At the same time, beset by mounting financial problems, the UCC Congregational Church of Boothbay Harbor faced enormous threats to its future. In many respects the era, 1993–1999, ranks among the darkest in the church's long history. Rev. Panagore, with his young family, inherited much of the onus of the church's fiscal crisis, a grave situation greatly exacerbated by the lengthy, unsuspected and undetected embezzlement of thousands of dollars of church monies by a long-trusted church member. Ultimately, as this chapter revealed, the perfidy was discovered, and with supreme trust in God, buoyed by its pastor and a loyal congregation, as well as with "Faith in the Future," the church survived and welcomed the new millennium.

CHAPTER 13

CELEBRATING THE PAST, CLAIMING THE PRESENT, AND PREPARING FOR THE FUTURE: 2003–2016
by Robert W. Dent

A new era was about to dawn. Perhaps part of the uniqueness of this new epoch in the life of the Boothbay Congregational Church was that it claimed the faithful witness of its past history, recognized the challenges and the opportunities of the present, and began to envision a new future rooted in its great ecclesiastical traditions. At the same time the church found fresh expressions for engaging developing issues and concerns that surrounded the church in 2003. Continuity and change were the order of the day. Rev. John Murray's focus in the 1760s on the church as comprising "living stones" (based on I Peter 2:5) was reclaimed as a guiding light during this period. Changing times, internal conflicts, and new social needs and norms needed a fresh look, new theological lenses, and a new vision for the future. The person who sensed a divine calling to make this happen with the help of staff and willing volunteers was the Reverend Dr. Sarah Foulger. She indeed had her challenges, as well as fulfillments, as will be seen.

This chapter begins midstream in what has been called the postmodern era, a term that carries varying meanings in different disciplines, including fine arts, literature, and theology. In 1991 theologian Dr. John B. Cobb, Jr. wrote a paper entitled "Theology in the Twenty-First Century" that effectively describes and clarifies the more than thirty year-old seismic shift in theological thinking that is known as postmodernism.[807] To understand that shift, a comparative view of the two eras, as developed by Dr. Cobb, is useful. (see Appendix A, page 473)

Cobb ends his paper with the statement: "There is a chance for Christianity to appear again as part of the vanguard of human thought and life, moving into a better world. For it to cling to its chains in modernity and refuse to lead into the twenty-first century would be a deep betrayal of its calling."[808] That would appear to be an appropriate context for doing ministry in the early part of the twenty-first century. The balance comes in recognizing the values of the past while seeing the needs of the present and the new things God is doing in the Church and in the world. The capacity to forge into the future while maintaining that balance was a special gift found in the pastor who was called to serve the Congregational Church of Boothbay Harbor as interim minister in 2003.

Of course, life in 2003 was very much affected by the post-9/11 era. In addition, climate changes increasingly impacted everyone, including populations around the world. The second Iraq War was launched by America against Saddam Hussein for good or ill with continuing consequences, and the space shuttle Columbia disintegrated over Texas upon reentry killing all the astronauts aboard. The next year NASA landed a vehicle on Mars. Back on earth, marital commitment seemed to hit a new low with the annulment of a pop singer's marriage only 55 hours after her wedding. In 2005, London experienced terrorist bombings, Katrina devastated Louisiana, and an earthquake killed 80,000 people in Kashmir. In ensuing years, natural disasters continued to be common; for example, 225,000 people in fourteen countries were killed in 2014 by one of the largest tsunami disasters ever recorded.

The year 2006 marked a communications revolution with eighty percent of the world's land surface covered by cellular networks for mobile phone use. As technology improved, the world would before long find that it had shrunk once again with the spread of cellular texting and photo sharing. New forms of social networking provided ways for people to grow closer together, to communicate more quickly, and to organize for better and sometimes for worse. It sometimes caused powerful divides by mobilizing propaganda and violent initiatives. By 2011, Facebook had 700 million members and Google Plus was launched. The political implications of new mobile technology and social networking were seen that year in both the "Arab Spring" and in the "Occupy Wall Street" movement. Technological advances that made life more convenient at the same time ran headlong into technological terrorism, with cyber attacks putting at risk the identity of millions of people, as well as credit cards and bank accounts. By 2014, the threat of the internationalist terrorist organization ISIS and the destructive uses of technology were becoming ever more apparent.

Recessions were nothing new, but the financial world looked particularly bleak for the West in 2007–2008. The "Great Recession" may have been the worst worldwide recession since the Great Depression of 1929–1931. The housing market was heavily hit and struggled for many years to recover. Furthermore, in 2008, global economic power began to shift from West to East. However, 2009 marked a significant first in American history with the election of the first black U.S. president, Barack Obama. In addition, global warming reached the agenda of world leaders in Copenhagen in that year.

The theological landscape of this period is different from that of earlier eras. At the opening of the 1900s, theology was often associated with names like Schleiermacher, Rauschenbusch, and Washington Gladden, who represented a form of liberal theology associated with the Social Gospel Movement. In 1950, neo-orthodox[809] theologians such as Barth, Brunner, Tillich, and the Niebuhrs were on the tips of the tongues of those discussing theology. Even an evangelical like Rev. Billy Graham was able to engage in a broad ecumenical dialogue. But by 2015, the landscape had shifted significantly. The ecumenism so evident in the

1950s and 1960s took a back seat while hotly debated issues became divisive rallying points within religious groups. Some theologians were associated with conservatives, others with liberals, and others still with the evangelical movement. Who could speak for the mission of Christ and engage these diverse groups while engendering a spirit of love, understanding and cooperation? Such theologians were hard to find. Scotland's John Newell[810] became such a voice as he attracted those receptive to the Celtic tradition[811] and approached life from a postmodern perspective. Marcus Borg's[812] Progressive Theology[813] had a strong appeal for many, encouraging readers within and beyond the church to take another look at Jesus, God, and the Bible. Perhaps a sign of hope for a new ecumenism was the election of the Argentinean Cardinal Jorge Mario Bergoglio as Pope Francis in 2013. With his election came signs of a new openness and perhaps the possibility of renewed interdenominational cooperation.

Rev. Dr. Sarah M. Foulger

Rev. Dr. Sarah M. Foulger— 2003-Present

In May 2003, the Reverend Peter Panagore resigned after ten years of serving the church in creative and very personable ways. Despite his efforts, as discussed in chapter 12, the church during the 1990s had undergone a serious crisis and had not yet fully recovered. The congregation, through an interim search committee chaired by Jackie Mundy, began looking for an interim pastor. Through a variety of serendipitous turns of events, later in 2003 a call was issued to the Reverend Dr. Sarah Foulger to fill the interim position. She was more than well qualified, holding a bachelor's degree in fine arts and languages from

Hofstra University, a master of divinity degree with an emphasis on systematic theology from Princeton Theological Seminary, and a doctorate in theology, worship, and administration from Boston University. Rev. Foulger also had published two books and composed numerous pieces of music. Ordained on June 24, 1979 into the Presbyterian Church, USA, her first parish was in Wilmington, Delaware, where she served from 1979 to 1984.

In 1975, Rev. Foulger met Russell Hoffman at the Community Presbyterian Church of Massapequa, New York. They were married on August 30, 1980 at the Wilmington church where Rev. Foulger was serving. Sarah and Russ moved to Maine in 1984 when Russ was offered a position as a naval architect at the Bath Iron Works. In 1985 she became the founding pastor of the Mid-Coast Presbyterian Church in Topsham, where she served until 1997. Prior to her arrival in Boothbay in 2003, she had served as interim in several churches, including in Annandale, Virginia, and in both Camden and Bristol, Maine.

When Russ Hoffman and Sarah Foulger came to Boothbay, their son Noah was a junior at Colby College in Waterville, Maine, majoring in biology, and Christopher was a first-year student at Colby majoring in history and German. Subsequently, Christopher settled in Brunswick and began teaching history and English at Greely High School in Cumberland. He and Courtney Reichert, a math teacher at Mt. Ararat High School in Topsham, were married in 2011. While Courtney grew up in Bowdoinham, she had deep family roots in Boothbay reaching back to Samuel McCobb, a leader in the early Scots-Irish settlement and a founder of the church. Noah went on to graduate from Dartmouth Medical School and become a physician at Children's Hospital of Philadelphia, specializing in pediatric gastroenterology. Noah was married to Sarah Goodrich, who had family roots in East Boothbay, in 2009. Sarah became a pediatrician with a specialty in sports medicine.

Like Rev. John Murray nearly 240 years before, Rev. Foulger arrived in Boothbay as a Presbyterian pastor in good standing, in her case with the Presbytery of Northern New England. She accepted the interim position with approval from the Presbytery. In addition, Rev. Foulger had gained dual standing with the United Church of Christ (UCC). As a trained and certified interim pastor, she was familiar with the rules and regulations governing interim ministry in the *Presbyterian Book of Order* and in the *Manual on Ministry* of the UCC. Rev. Foulger saw herself as coming to Boothbay in a temporary and specific capacity. The typical interim term varies from one to three years, depending on the speed with which the congregation clarifies its mission and future directions, and then searches for, finds, and invites a new pastor to serve as the called pastor in the church.

Rev. Foulger began her interim ministry at the Congregational Church of Boothbay Harbor on July 1, 2003. She quickly won the respect of the congregation and the community. From the start she understood that her role was to help the congregation and its leadership to discern identity, direction, needs, and mission. She sharpened the ministry focus of the church by identifying three central dimensions of the church's work: worship, education, and mission. In her interim minister's annual report for 2003, some aspects of her vision for the Boothbay church were clearly outlined, based on her experience with the church during the previous six months. In addition to the routine aspects of such a report, were these thoughts concerning what Rev. Foulger saw as necessary changes that she might help to facilitate:

- Oversee a cosmetic overhaul of the Sunday school area.
- Assist in the development of a church website.
- Encourage growth in church membership.
- Lead several Bible studies and promote adult educational opportunities.
- Participate in youth events.
- Work with the church trustees on important decisions regarding endowments.
- Encourage renewed adherence to the bylaws.

- Organize a communitywide effort to coordinate responses to residents in need, an effort that would include most local churches as well as town managers and other resource persons.
- Continue to develop trust in the handling of finances and to prioritize the work of stewardship through the stewardship committee (stewardship giving had grown by 15 percent in 2003).
- Encourage the church to look to the future and to bridge generational and cultural gaps with a revised hymnal.

Those who frequented the church during the years after Rev. Foulger arrived recalled how the seeds of her thinking blossomed one by one into new life under her guidance, not only as the interim pastor, but later as the settled pastor.

Staying on in Boothbay Harbor as the settled pastor of the Congregational church initially seemed impossible due to common mandate that an interim not be allowed to settle in a church permanently. The search committee, as they sought a settled pastor, found that the more the committee and congregation clarified its identity, its mission and its future directions, the stronger the feeling grew that their interim minister was exactly the person they had been looking for and whom they needed for their full-time "called" pastor. Convinced, however, that both Presbyterian and UCC rules prohibited her from becoming the settled pastor in a church where she was serving as interim, Rev. Foulger prepared to move on to wherever God was calling her next. Surprisingly, the Conference Leader of the Maine Conference of the United Church of Christ, David Gaewski, phoned Sarah and told her, "I have a sense that God is calling you to be the pastor in Boothbay Harbor." Gaewski knew that the congregation was energized to move forward, and he had come to believe that the leadership needed to help channel that energy was to be found precisely in Rev. Dr. Sarah Foulger. Rev. Foulger was so astounded she could not respond but, following a lengthy conversation with Gaewski, agreed to pray about it. A week later Rev. Gaewski met with Sarah but she still could not answer as she continued to struggle with the ethics of her contract with the church. She did admit, however, that she had "fallen in love with the (Boothbay) church." At that point, David revealed to Sarah his mantra: "Make rules that serve the church, not vice versa." Having met with the other interim ministers in Maine and received their unanticipated blessing, Sarah Foulger agreed that it might indeed be God's call for her to serve the Congregational church of the Boothbay region, despite strictures set by the *Presbyterian Book of Order* and the UCC *Manual on Ministry*.

Unknown to Rev. Foulger, David Gaewski's advice to Sarah encouraging her to accept the position as settled pastor had likely been influenced by a meeting Gaewski had had prior to his meeting with Rev. Foulger. At their request, Peter and Jackie Mundy, respectively, chair of the search committee for a permanent pastor and senior deacon of the Boothbay church, met with Gaewski in May of 2004. Conscious of the rules mandating the specialized and limited work of interim pastors, the Mundys explained to Gaewski, the extent of Rev. Foulger's accomplishments in the short time of her interim ministry in Boothbay. According to Jackie Mundy's account of the meeting, Peter and she presented Gaewski with a summary of the facts of Foulger's work and of the new and exciting things that had been initiated. They then looked at David and sincerely asked, "What should we do now? And where should we go from here?" Leaning back in his chair, with his eyes closed and after a very long silence, Gaewski said that he felt God had a reason for Sarah's coming to the Boothbay church. Gaewski, who, recalling the meeting, indicated that he did not feel pressured in any way by the Mundys, agreed with their spiritual sense of the situation and remembers asking, "What do you think God is calling us to do?"

On June 15, 2004, Pete Mundy and Peggy Pinkham, representing the search committee, met with the "Lincoln Association of Congregational Churches" Committee on Ministry, hoping to gain its support to offer the position of settled pastor to Rev. Foulger. Among other observations, the following words were included in the letter of endorsement subsequently sent to the search committee: "We were all impressed with the integrity of your search, and the plan to recommend Foulger for a call. We are glad that the impetus for the possibility of considering Rev. Foulger did not come from you or her, but from our Conference minister. We sense the work of the Spirit in this process. May God be with you and bless you as you begin this new adventure in faith." Then, on July 11, 2004, after her "candidating" sermon, at a special meeting of the congregation, it was voted unanimously to accept the recommendation of the search committee to call the Rev. Dr. Sarah M. Foulger as the forty-third settled pastor of the Congregational Church of Boothbay Harbor and the first woman to assume this position. On October 10, 2004, Foulger was installed as the settled pastor and continued to serve faithfully in that capacity with "energy, intelligence, imagination and love."[814]

The members of the search committee for settled pastor included Barbara Bauman (secretary), Kim Burnham, Bar Clarke (vice chair), Maurice Landemare, Jennifer Marden, Peter Mundy (chair), Peggy Pinkham, Leah Sample, Barclay Shepard, Carolyn Shubert, and Barbara Zarpentine. The committee had reviewed forty-eight candidate profiles, each of which was discussed at one of the twenty-six meetings the search committee held. In the committee's words, "We did not find a candidate among those profiles that met the congregation's criteria and had the qualifications needed to lead us into the future. The committee was unanimous in its opinion that the person God was calling to the Congregational Church of Boothbay Harbor was Rev. Foulger, who was already preaching from our pulpit!"[815]

There was something about this call that was perhaps unusually providential. Unlike some perceptions of providence, it was not a detached divine being autocratically forcing people and events into a predetermined mold, whether it be comfortable or uncomfortable. People of faith believe that providential occurrences happen from two directions—from God's direction, as God works to fulfill God's purpose, and from the human direction as persons find their greatest joys and hopes being fulfilled. Nothing captures the power of this particular call as well as Rev. Foulger's own words delivered in her sermon on the occasion of her tenth anniversary as the called pastor of the Congregational Church of Boothbay Harbor:

> Back in 1987, the year we were enjoying watching Brian Boitano and Katerina Witt, the year we were eating Ben and Jerry's Cherry Garcia ice cream for the first time, the year Russ and I had a 2-year-old and a 4-year-old, the year I helped found the Presbyterian Church in Topsham, I fell in love with John Murray, the first minister of the congregation here in Boothbay. I read everything I could lay my hands on about Murray, who was, in the late eighteenth century, the leader of Presbyterianism in the State of Maine.
>
> And on the day trips we took with the kids down here to the beautiful Boothbay peninsula, as we drove by this very church which was, at that point, still pressed right up against Townsend Avenue, my heart skipped a beat, and I allowed myself a moment of fantasy, wondering what it might be like to serve the congregation John Murray helped to found. Now I've been here eleven years, ten as your settled pastor. And it has been just as thrilling and interesting as I imagined it might be all those years ago.[816]

Visionaries help possibilities become realities. Within the church, visionaries who utilize simple, clear Biblical images often become the conduit for the Spirit of God to do amazing things. A powerful Biblical image Rev. Foulger employed which once again became a driving force for the church was that of "Living Stones." It comes from I Peter 2:5 "like living stones, let yourselves be built into a spiritual house, to be a holy priesthood, to offer spiritual sacrifices acceptable to God through Jesus Christ." The living stones image was lifted up by the founders of the congregation, who incorporated it into the original church covenant. This powerful image, so appropriate for the rocky coast of Maine, reminded the congregation of their interconnections with each other, with the past and with the future. Whatever the church might build, they would do so on stones that others had put in place before them, and they would build not only for themselves but for many they would never have the opportunity to meet in their earthly lifetimes.[817]

The Boothbay Region in the Early Twenty-first Century
As a new century unfolded, Boothbay continued to attract visitors from all over the world. Its beautiful coastline and shops, its tourist attractions and its unique eateries, as well as its hints of a quieter and simpler life were all part of its magical and magnetic powers. Restaurants came and went. The Boothbay peninsula blossomed into approximately 50,000 people in the summer and retreated to a hardy and faithful, tightly knit 5,000 residents in the winter months. Shipbuilding shifted, with Hodgdon Yachts in East Boothbay launching most of its super-sized luxury yachts after the year 2000. The crowded and outdated facilities of the Bigelow Laboratory for Ocean Sciences located on McKown Point gave way to a spectacular world-class research facility located on the Damariscotta River in East Boothbay. Boothbay's small nine-hole country golf course was transformed into an 18-hole championship golf club by Paul Coulombe, resulting in the relocation of the historic Kenniston Inn. The Boothbay Harbor Memorial Library was enlarged and improved. The Boothbay Region YMCA (where Rev. Foulger served two three-year terms as a trustee) undertook a major building fund campaign resulting in a new and enlarged swimming pool and the addition of a warm therapeutic pool.

Since 1766, the history of the Presbyterian and later the Congregational church, first in Boothbay and subsequently in Boothbay Harbor, has been inseparable from the history of the town, with frequent changes yet continuity in both. In the opening years of the twenty-first century, the groundfishing industry, once so prominent in Boothbay, continued to diminish dramatically. Lobstering, however, remained a significant part of the Boothbay DNA despite the challenges of climate change and more complex government regulations. Although businesses came and went, some disappearing, tourism continued to be a substantive segment of the region's economy and kept the community surviving, if not thriving, as it had since the 1880s.

As a result of tourism, the Boothbay Harbor Congregational church developed different congregations, a membership of year-round residents and a summer congregation of tourists, regular vacationers, and seasonal residents. Many of the year-round parishioners attended less frequently in the summer in order to help fill the many extra jobs and long hours demanded by Boothbay's part in Maine "Vacationland" or to attend seasonal chapels located in East Boothbay and Southport. The reality of cyclical populations, exploding employment opportunities in the summer, and the accompanying roller coaster drop in jobs in the winter created distinct social challenges. During the winter months, many families had a hard time making ends meet. As the colder months progressed, there were needs for assistance with food, clothing, basic household supplies and bills, as well as an occasional need for shelter. These were some of the opportunities and challenges facing the new settled minister. At the very core of Rev. Foulger's ministry was the corporate experience of worship, which formed the base for addressing many of the needs and problems in the church and the community.

Worship at its Best

The experience of worship can make or break a church. Boring or irrelevant sermons, lifeless liturgy or marginal music can torpedo church attendance and cause membership to decline. The opposite has been true in the Congregational Church of Boothbay Harbor over the last decade. Attendance at worship, as well as increasing membership, has been the reverse of all national trends. From

2003 through 2013, membership soared 49 percent, pledges skyrocketed 55 percent, and pledging units rose 34 percent. Jackie and Peter Mundy described it with passion:

> To see the church's continued growth, not only in the number of attendees of all ages, but in the scope of activities and outreach, is very heartwarming. Even though church attendance—especially among younger people—has declined dramatically everywhere, ours is still going strong. Thanks to our creative and hardworking minister, a tireless staff and volunteers, an outstanding children's program and superintendent, and a special music director and choir, our church is adapting to changing times and needs.[818]

Foulger's sermons were Biblically based, imaginative, and creative in their crafting. They were intellectually sound yet down to earth, filled with personal images and vivid stories, truly connected with the lives of the people and with the struggles and issues of local and world events. Evidence of the impact of the worship services is abundant in the booklet entitled: "Faith Stories" gathered by the Capital Campaign committee in 2014. Church member and co-author Chip Griffin wrote, "Sarah delivers sermons and takes actions that move me to plumb the depths and to reach out to others. Sarah is probably the most transformative, charismatic, and effective leader our church has ever seen since our founder, John Murray, almost 250 years ago."[819] Rev. Foulger's openness and willingness to wrestle with tough questions without forcing simple answers is clear in the response of campaign co-chair and adult education leader, Ted Repa, regarding his membership in the church.

He stated :

> I was reluctant to join a church here as I was disillusioned with the direction of many organized churches and religions around the world (especially in light of 9/11), as well as with some of the things I was supposed to believe to be a good

member. Betty [his wife] convinced me that if I didn't join, I would leave others to chart the direction of religion, and when Sarah said she welcomed members who were still asking religious questions, I said, "Sign me up. I continue to seek answers, especially in our adult religious education classes, but firmly believe in the power of our church to do good in our community, and I am proud to do my part.[820]

Perhaps the most telling witness to the power of worship at the Congo Church, as it has been affectionately called in the region, is the statement of Rev. Foulger's husband, Russ Hoffman. A clergy spouse presumably knows the clergyperson better than anyone else. Few could receive a better commendation than Russ's: "Sarah, the love of my life and our pastor, has been a vital part of my faith journey as well. From her I have learned the importance of personalizing faith, making it work for each of us as an inspiration and motivator."[821]

"Worship" and "fun" are not often located in the same sentence and some churches are anything but fun. However, in the summer of 2007, when Rev. Foulger was at St. Andrew's Village, she met the daughter of a new resident. When she introduced herself as the pastor of the Congregational church, the daughter said, "Oh, I hear that's the fun church." A significant factor in the "fun," or to use a more theologically rich word, the "joy" of worship, was the close working relationship between Foulger and Minister of Music, Eugenie O'Connell. They formed an immediate bond of friendship and teamwork that inspired buoyant and purposeful worship. O'Connell was very thoughtful in her music selections and preparations and was always ready with an appropriate musical response to any situation.

Foulger's willingness to make herself vulnerable and tell stories about moments in her life where she found herself embarrassed or mistaken or overwhelmed added to the fun of worship, not because the congregation wanted to laugh at her but because they saw her humanity and identified with her struggle to make sense out of her life. Such homiletic windows helped congregants to walk with the pastor in her journey and find the courage to examine their own journeys in the love of Christ. Moreover, like many of her parishioners, Rev. Foulger endured grief and uncertainty, in her case, when her son Noah was hospitalized for an extensive period with a rare cancer. She shared the trial she and Russ were experiencing with her church community, thus demonstrating to the congregation her humanity and efforts to deal with real issues, sharing what was appropriate, accepting the help that was needed, and humbly allowing the power of God to transform evil into good. As Paul worded it, "We know that all things work together for good for those who love God, who are called according to God's purpose."[822] Love for and trust in God opens our eyes to the truth that God is not willing to let bad things have the last word in our lives. Often in life in the midst of tragedy such words can sound trite. But some people are able to take these words and show how they ring true over time as they struggle with, assimilate, and radiate the Gospel in their lives.

Extraordinary Music

The Congregational Church of Boothbay Harbor found itself richly blessed by the presence of Eugenie O'Connell. Genie came back to the church as its organist and music director in September 2003. She brought with her not only a deep well of natural talent but also impressive training: the Westminster Choir College of Princeton, New Jersey; and University College in Cork, Ireland, where she received her bachelor's degree in music. For every service much thought went into the choice of music, working to ensure that its message, the message of the Bible, and the cutting edge of the sermon would form a harmonious whole. Genie stated that her goal for each service was "to provide a musical supplement to the message for the day with perhaps a side serving of humor or recognition of current events." Out of gratitude to God for her many gifts and years of service to the church, in 2010 the congregation honored Eugenie O'Connell, bestowing upon her the title, "Minister of Music."

Combined with the significant talent Genie brought to bear

on worship, she drew a magnificent choir—above average in both numbers and performance. The quality emerged from the innate musical talents of many church members and from the ability of Genie to raise the musicality of all of the members. And while "performance" is a word associated with the end result of practice, performance is never the purpose of music in worship. It is, rather, a vehicle to glorify God, to draw each person closer to the words and work of Jesus Christ, and to provide space for God's Spirit to move within and among the congregation. The quality of the music was so much the norm at the Boothbay church that persons who worshiped at the church regularly and who visited other churches looked forward to returning to Boothbay Harbor to hear outstanding and spiritually uplifting church music.

As the interim pastor, Rev. Foulger, herself a member of the choir, called attention to the need for a new hymnal. She suggested that *The New Century Hymnal*, promoted by the Conference, in some cases lost some of the poetry of the original hymns, and the *Pilgrim Hymnal* had left out many of the beloved hymns such as "Amazing Grace." Her advice to the music committee as the interim minister was that it should wait for the new minister, however, to pursue further a decision on a new hymnal. In 2005, the congregation approved purchase of a new hymnal entitled *Hymns of Truth and Light*, published by Sheridan Books with permission of the first Congregational Church of Houston, Texas. This hymnal retained some of the most beloved of the old hymns and brought together some great new hymns while being sensitive to inclusive language and incorporating hymns that lift up God's redeeming purpose. It also includes the "Covenant Hymn" written by Rev. Foulger.

Along with Sunday morning worship, music has been part of the fabric of the church. Frequent musical events occur there on a regular basis: Lincoln Arts concerts, organ concerts by masters such as John Weaver and Timothy Whistler, performances by the Boothbay Region Elementary School choruses, and Jazz Sunday, which attracted huge crowds to worship and inspired replication

Celebrating the Past...Preparing for the Future: 2003–2016 371

Covenant Hymn

S-5

1. In the presence of God, in the comp-'ny of friends,
we are bound in a cov-'nant of love.
And as chil-dren of God, ho-ly word for our light
we seek wis-dom with-in and a-bove.
With Christ our re-deem-er, God's spir-it, our guide,
God's strength gives us cour-age in faith to a-bide.
To live God's com-mands, seek-ing sym-bols of grace
we bap-tize, com-mune, and give thanks in this place.

2. U-nit-ed in faith, one in wor-ship and prayer
we at-tend to God's word ev-'ry day.
And we pro-mise to live as Christ Je-sus, in love
ev-er mind-ful of God's self-less way.
We pledge to watch o-ver each oth-er in kind,
to la-bor in faith, all our gifts to God bind,
to build up of liv-ing stones this sa-cred home,
a tem-ple of bles-sings, an o-pen love poem.

WORDS and MUSIC: Sarah M. Foulger, 2005   Used by permission of the Rev. Dr. Sarah M. Foulger

Covenant Hymn

as far away as Monroe, New York.

New to the church music program in 2014 was a magnificent twelve-member handbell choir. The choir was formed by church member and volunteer director Jamie Knobloch, who also arranged for the purchase of good used handbells at a great cost savings. The bells were paid for by funds bequeathed to the church by Captain Marion Dash, a talented musician and church leader who had participated in and supported the church music program and who had been instrumental in founding Lincoln Arts.

The Faithful and Active Ministry of the Laity

Clearly, the Boothbay church was doubly blessed in the early years of the twenty-first century with its pastor and organist. But there is more to the story. The church was also richly blessed through the ministry of a great office staff with Debi Wood as the church administrator, Deanne Tibbetts as the children's education director starting in 2008, and faithful lay leadership of the church in general. Protestants have recognized the importance of the laity since the Reformation. The United Church of Christ states in its constitution that every member is "called to participate in and extend the ministry of Jesus Christ by witnessing to the Gospel in church and society." [823]

The ministry of the laity had long been a natural part of the life of the church. Earlier chapters clearly demonstrate the importance of lay leadership from the time of Andrew McFarland, (John Murray's uncle), Andrew Reed (from whom Eugenie O'Connell is descended), and John Beath, all of whom traveled by boat to Boston in the colonial era to secure the services of Rev. John Murray; and from the vital role of Judge Kenniston, Henry Perkins and James Blenn Perkins, Sr. and Jr., in the church in the early 1900s and down to the present.

Rev. Foulger described the church as "a lively place blessed with bright and interesting people." The work of the laity was obvious and Rev. Foulger's style as pastor "encouraged this people who are engaged in the life of the community and who care deeply about the world."[824] When parishioners brought ideas to Rev. Foulger regarding a new ministry or form of outreach that could be useful in the church, they were supported and empowered by her to implement the idea with her blessing as long as it was consistent with the goals of the church. Much of the ministry of the laity can be seen in the work of its boards and organizations. Some amazing work was accomplished during this period. More will be said about the work of the laity in the discussion of the Sunday school, the deacons, and the trustees. Each year, during the annual meeting, Rev. Foulger presented "Living Stone" awards to those who had made a noteworthy contribution to the life of the church. The following examples of "Living Stone" awards offer a lovely glimpse into the power of the laity in the Congregational Church of Boothbay Harbor.

> 2003 Bill Ostermann, for taking and organizing photographs of all church members into a directory.
>
> Guy Ribble and Earle Smith, for countless hours of work improving the church facility.
>
> 2004 Theodore and Betty Repa, for starting a Sunday morning Adult Education program.
>
> Bill Harvey, for his generosity in keeping the church grounds mowed and shoveled.
>
> 2005 Kim Burnham, for her remarkable work with the Senior High Fellowship.
>
> Jackie Mundy and the deacons, for leading the effort to finish building Rev. Foulger's home in West Boothbay Harbor.
>
> 2006 Florence Harrold, for supplies gathered for the "Safe Passage" mission in Guatemala. These supplies were delivered by youth of the church who traveled on a mission trip.

2007 Debra Ramsey, for designing a curriculum and leading an exciting Vacation Bible School.

Denise Griffin, for the extra miles she went to keep the church running smoothly. while Rev. Foulger was away with her son at Dartmouth Hitchcock hospital.

2008 Elliott Barker, Maurice Landemare, and Barclay Shepard for their founding work as members of the "Woodchucks," a group of volunteers who harvest, cut, and split donations of hardwood and deliver wood to families in need who heat with wood.

2009 Marty Helman, for helping to eradicate polio in Nigeria through her work with Rotary.

Sally Barter, for leading an effort to procure a new home and furnishings for a local family in need.

2010 Tom Dewey, for his creative leadership in the church-wide Parable of the Talents challenge, in which church members fundraised using their unique talents and ideas.

2011 Carol Cragin and Susan Duckworth, for leading the Church World Service Health Kit campaign following a devastating earthquake in Japan.

Bob Hilscher and Peggy Pinkham, for the development of a Master Facilities Plan.

2012 Holly Stover, for her tireless grantwriting in the development of Boothbay Region Community Resources (BRCR) and for birthing the Community Navigator Program (part of BRCR).

Judy Eastwood, Dorothy Freeman, Linda Ludemann, Ron Ross, and Barclay Shepard, who bravely shared their stories at a marriage forum held at the church.

2013 Joan Rittall and her son, Scott, and Bruce and Enid Johnson, for their beautiful work on the community garden.

2014 Jamie Knobloch, for establishing a church bell choir and procuring a set of bells with funds bequeathed by Captain Marion Dash.

Sue Burge and Jen Orchard, for establishing the "Food for Thought" program to feel hungry children in the community.

2015 Jon Dunsford, Bob Hilscher, Alex Logan, Eric Marden, Peggy Pinkham, and the entire building committee for their unique contributions to renovating the church facility and bringing it up to code and into the twenty-first century.

Education

Christian education became a renewed priority in 2003, both at youth and at adult levels. In 2004, the nursery was greatly improved, classroom space expanded, and one of the classrooms was made handicap accessible. Music became an integral part of children's Christian education as both traditional hymns were learned and contemporary music introduced. Volunteers such as Jennifer Ziegra and Jill Syp continued to superintend the Sunday school but the days of church members being available to volunteer many hours each week to run the religious education program were in the past. In September 2008, Deanne Tibbetts was hired to fill the part-time position of children's education director. Deanne brought an undergraduate degree in elementary education from the University of Maine in Orono and master's degree in library science from Simmons College. For eight years, Deanne had home-schooled her own children. Under her leadership, the Sunday school blossomed with energy, creativity, compassion and intelligence. A walk through the Sunday school wing quickly revealed to the passerby the creativity of the leadership and the innovative ways in which the Bible can be taught. As stated in Rev. Foulger's 2013 pastor's report, "Our Sunday School children are bright, spunky, talented, and blessed with the leadership of Deanne Tibbetts and music help from Emily Mirabile."[825] Deanne reported that same year,

> During 2013 we welcomed 50 children from toddler to teenager to our Sunday School and youth programs. Our Sunday School kids hosted foster grandparents for a milk and cookies mixer, organized a Fiesta Fundraiser on behalf of Safe Passage in Guatemala, started a children's garden, made gifts for moms, went on an Easter Egg Hunt, performed a dramatic interpretation of the Christmas Story, had a youth service auction, and delivered a gift basket to the local fire department volunteers. [826]

In addition they raised over $200 for the Barbara Bush Children's Hospital and honored the church's veterans with a coffee hour in November 2014. Numerous volunteers, primarily parents, supported the children's education program.

With leadership from church members Kim Burnham, Barry and Lori Grinnell, Tim Pinkham, Tom Dewey, Paul Noah, and Carrie and Rodney Eason, the Junior High and Senior High youth groups engaged in a wide variety of activities and projects during this time period. Some of these many and diverse activities included concerts, skiing, skating, sledding, bowling and swimming, making soup for the sick, raising funds to help disaster relief efforts through a bottle drive, and decorating the biggest Christmas tree they could find each year. They also participated in Christmas caroling, hosting coffee hours and ice cream socials, cookie bakes, pie sales, and visiting St. Andrews assisted living facility and the Gregory Wing. They took trips to the Children's Hospital in Boston to deliver toys, brought clothing and funds to the Rockland Breakwater Shelters for teens, and went to the local animal shelter to walk dogs awaiting homes. They took two mission trips to Safe Passage, an educational mission in Guatemala started by the late Bowdoin College graduate Hanley Denning, and raised funds to participate in a weeklong Habitat for Humanity work project in New Mexico during the summer of 2015. The importance of the church to these youth is evident in the presence of college students like Ben Dewey who returned to worship whenever they had the opportunity.

In 2004, a dynamic Sunday morning adult education class was started by church members Betty and Ted Repa to view and discuss courses by college professors on such topics as comparative religion, the early church, and the formation of the New Testament. This class developed a loyal and lively following, which included both church members and nonmembers who were eager to stretch their minds and souls. Additional educational opportunities were initiated, including a self-led Tuesday morning book and meditation group, a Sunday evening Bible survey course taught by David Eastwood, as well as periodic book discussions and Lenten studies led by Sarah Foulger.

Leadership Directions and Outreach

The Trustees

The Trustees undertook herculean tasks in the period between 2003 and 2015 to improve the accessibility and efficient operation of the church and to bring the church facility into safety code compliance. During this time period, the trustees implemented numerous tasks beyond routine monitoring of the budget and addressing ongoing repairs to the historic facility. Under the leadership of head trustee, Elliott Barker, some of these tasks included creation of two handicap-accessible bathrooms, paving of the back parking lot, and installation of a sound system, a lift that stopped at all three levels of the church building, and a library. Under the leadership of Roger Severance, an investment committee was established to oversee the endowment and invested funds of the church. This proved to be an important and consequential way to manage church funds. Under the leadership of head trustee, Peggy Pinkham, additional land was secured and designated for parking on the corner of Townsend and Eastern Avenues. With leadership of "Building and Grounds" trustee, Dick Whittier, new controls were installed on the furnace to save ten percent in energy costs, and the church was insulated. With special gifts from church members such as Howie and Sally Barter, Sue Bogart, Peter and Jackie Mundy, and Dick and Jeanne Whittier, the sanctuary was improved through the installation of new carpet, addition of a cork floor in the choir loft, beautiful new pew cushions, construction of wooden steps and railings to the chancel area, and renovation of the vestry, the fellowship hall, and Sunday school rooms. During every renovation, Eric Marden, owner of Marden Builders, was a key leader. One of the monumental tasks of the trustees was to evaluate the persistent suggestion for a major church renovation and eventually, the need to appoint a special subcommittee to do much of that work, chaired by Bob Hilscher.

The trustees also tackled major policy issues. In 2005, work began on an endowment investment policy. On January 27, 2013, the trustees presented the policy to the congregation and it was adopted. The policy states:

> Care will be taken to avoid investing in companies whose major activities or practices are contrary to the Church's beliefs and goals, including: for example, tobacco and liquor companies, firearms manufacturers, and firms whose domestic or international labor or environmental practices are harmful to people or to the environment. As business criteria emerge to assess corporate social responsibility, the investment committee shall consider investing in such companies, provided they meet the other standards listed in this paragraph.[827]

A second policy statement adopted by the trustees was presented in 2007 and referred to as a "Safe Church Policy." The purpose of this policy related to abuse prevention and committed the church to maintaining an atmosphere free from all forms of discrimination, harassment, exploitation or intimidation."

During this era, the trustees also developed a code of conduct and reviewed and revised the church bylaws. In 2008, the trustees formed a subgroup to enhance the business operations of the church, create more effective checks and balances, and develop an operations manual. All of these policy statements were designed to improve and ensure the efficiency, transparency, and general character of the church. On January 25, 2015, an extensive revision of the bylaws was approved, aligning the church's procedures even more closely to Robert's Rules of Order and creating a position of church moderator to be elected annually. The first moderator to be elected to this position was Sally Smith.

Long Range Planning

The emerging vision of the church included a major renovation and expansion to meet the needs of a steadily growing congregation with high community usage through its outreach programs. The long range planning committee began in 2004 to clarify the congregation's hopes, dreams, and ideas about such renovations by holding "cottage" meetings in members' homes. In 2008, the committee again held a series of "cottage" meetings that identified specific facilities and spaces that needed to be moved, improved, or enlarged. Conclusions from the cottage meetings were presented and prioritized at a planning retreat held in the spring of 2010. Subsequently the trustees, in consultation with all other committees and groups that use the building, developed a master facility plan. On January 29, 2011, a first draft of the "The Master Facility Plan" was presented to the congregation. The draft attempted to incorporate the priorities that had been communicated by members of the church and its organizations. The ground-floor entrance of the church would be greatly improved and would allow guests to be greeted immediately upon entry. A new elevator and enlarged stairwell would make the entire church more accessible to everyone. The food pantry would increase by seventy-five percent. The upstairs office, vestry, kitchen, and small library would be transformed into a larger library with archival space and a multipurpose chapel area with choir preparation and music storage space and overflow capacity for larger services and events in the sanctuary. A new sacristy would ease the work of the deacons.

In January 2012, the congregation approved a motion to authorize the trustees to complete a study to determine the feasibility of raising funds to undertake such a building project. Church member and development specialist, Dorothy Freeman, conducted the study, interviewing key leaders in the congregation. At the January 2013 annual meeting, looking ahead to the potential renovation of the church, Bob Hilscher presented the authorized report from the Knickerbocker Group, an architectural, design and building company. This presentation was primarily informational. In July 2013, the results of the feasibility study were shared. On September 22, 2013, the congregation met and approved a capital campaign in the amount of $850,000 to pay for the revised renovation model.

Stewardship and Spiritual Growth
While the work of the long range planning committee and of the trustees is impressive, the outcome of the ensuing capital campaign was astounding. In a letter dated February 19, 2014, campaign co-chairs, Betty and Ted Repa, invited the congregation to participate in this adventure. Their letter perceptively and prophetically contained this sentence, "As God's living stones, we feel called to work together to make our space more accessible and functional in order to strengthen our ministries and service." And in the introduction to the booklet entitled "Faith Stories," to which many members contributed by sharing some of their own faith experiences, Betty and Ted remarked, "In nearly 250 years, any and all construction that has taken place in our family of faith has been accomplished using one primary building material—living stones, the living stones from which God builds and rebuilds a spiritual

home and center of hope in our community. You and I are now those living stones."

Clearly the congregation took to heart Betty and Ted's words and the constant framework Sarah Foulger created in her sermons and in worship. Based on the results of the feasibility study, the goal for the capital campaign had been reduced from over $1 million to $850,000. The aim was to come up with a realistic and feasible goal without having to borrow money or tap heavily into endowment funds. During the service on Campaign Sunday, April 6, 2014, individuals walked up to the front of the sanctuary and deposited a small stone they carried with them into a beautiful little stream of water that meandered artistically across the front of the chancel surrounded by flowers, the creative work of Ron Ross and Fred Kraeuter. Then, congregants placed their pledges in a designated stone vessel. While most people assumed the final number would be short of the goal since summer residents and others were not present, the outcome was truly surprising. After the service, church treasurer, Alex Logan, handed the report to Sarah Foulger. She exerted effort to control the emotion in her voice as she read the report. Pledges nearly reached the goal. It seemed to many that a miracle had happened on Townsend Avenue in Boothbay Harbor by the grace of God and the inspiring work of the Holy Spirit in the lives of this congregation. In a time when churches were closing because of lack of numbers and money, in a time when churches in general were having trouble meeting their budgets, and in a time when the average church was required to borrow at least some money or pull heavily from endowment funds or both to finance any major renovation project, the results of this campaign were a strong confirmation of members' commitment to the Boothbay church and its leadership.

As deacon Donald Duncan wrote in an article in the *Boothbay Register,* "When all was added up that day [in April 2014], it was announced that the total was nearly $830,000 with additional gifts on the horizon from within the church and from the wider community. Having reached their initial goal, they were now able to consider further improvements. As of April 2014, the total pledged was $949,323 from 101 donors."[828] By early February 2015, the pledged amount was $987,000.

The Deacons

The deacons of the Congregational Church of Boothbay Harbor continued to be a major support to the spiritual life and nurture of the congregation. Their broad responsibilities included religious education, music, outreach, membership, stewardship, and preparations for worship services. Their work focused on preparing the sanctuary for worship each week, developing ways to welcome visitors, and making audio-recordings available to shut-ins or others who may have missed a service. The deacons also provided "Thinking of You" care packages for college students and service people, helped the mission committee with an annual international workers' welcome (a social event at the church for international summer students working in the Boothbay region), and assisted the pastor with the monthly communion service at the Gregory Wing for seniors at St. Andrews Village. They also helped mentor the confirmation classes and assembled Church World Service emergency kits. Deacons assisted in raising funds for Safe Passage in Guatemala, promoted the work of Rebuilding Together (a locally strong organization that implements modest renovation and repair projects in the community), and responded to local, national and international emergencies.

In 2005, the deacons celebrated Sarah and Russ's thirtieth wedding anniversary, not with a splashy event, but through an extraordinary offer. The deacons, under Jackie Mundy's leadership in consultation with Ted Repa, Doris Burnham, and fellow deacons, responded to the crisis that faced Sarah and Russ after the contractor for their new home left the area without completing the job for which he had already been compensated. As an anniversary present to Sarah and Russ, the congregation provided hundreds of skilled and unskilled work hours to complete the construction of their house. It was a very emotional moment when the offer was delivered and accepted on Russ and Sarah's unfinished deck. This appeared to many to be one more instance of God's redemptive hand at work as the bond between Sarah and the congregation was enhanced. Later, when their son Noah became gravely ill with Burkitt's lymphoma, the caring congregation stepped in to assist Sarah personally and professionally. "The Reverend Bob Dent, an energetic retired Presbyterian minister who, with his wife, Judy, became involved in the life of the congregation, was a special help during this time. Rev. Dent rallied and trained a group of lay visitors to make pastoral calls, and Dent himself made many hospital calls."[829] The compassionate help offered on so many levels was a clear demonstration that there was something more at the Boothbay Harbor Congregational church than a minister and a congregation. This had become truly a church family.

For several years the deacons, with the encouragement of Rev. Foulger, worked to help the congregation move toward the adoption of a statement identifying the congregation as an "Open and Affirming" church.[830] While some congregations split apart over issues of inclusiveness, the Boothbay Harbor Congregational church traversed the waters of that discussion with understanding for one another and respectfulness toward persons of varying views. Then, in 2011, the deacons developed an historic "Open and Affirming Statement," which was adopted by a majority vote of the congregation. Discussions about same-sex marriage had been suggested by the deacons in the spring of 2004, and had taken place over the years. After much thought, work, and prayers, this statement was presented to the congregation:

> The Congregational Church of Boothbay Harbor, UCC, is an open and affirming community of faith, hope and love. We seek to embody a faith that transcends all differences, and we are committed to affirming every person as a unique and precious creation of God. With sadness, we acknowledge that the Christian Church has, throughout history, condemned and mistreated persons based on distinctions such as gender, race,

gender identity, gender expression and sexual orientation. We believe such actions are inconsistent with Jesus' call "to love one another" and his prayer that "they may all be one." By the grace of God, we joyfully and gratefully welcome all persons who wish to be a part of our community into the full life, leadership and ministry of the church."[831]

This statement was subsequently approved at the January 29, 2012 congregational meeting, with a general sense of accomplishment and enthusiasm. In her 2013 annual pastor's report, Rev. Foulger stated, "It is always a delight to officiate at the wedding of young couples who are steeped in hope, but it was also deeply satisfying to officiate at the weddings of those who had been together in loving committed relationships for many years and whose vows are now legally recognized by the great State of Maine."[832]

Each head deacon brought unique gifts and energy to the work of the diaconate and to the life of the church. Head deacon Jackie Mundy (2003–2005) brought organizational vigor, much-needed focus, and a resolute concern for hospitality to newcomers. Head deacon Laura Honey, who shared the responsibility with Jackie Mundy in 2004, brought to the job deep faith and attention to detail. Head deacon Lori Grinnell (2006) initiated a church brochure that became a useful tool in welcoming and encouraging visitors to consider becoming part of the congregation. Head deacon Denise Griffin (2007–2009) brought compassion and strength to the challenge of securing substitute pastoral care and leadership while Rev. Foulger was caring for her desperately ill son. Head deacon Sally Barter (2010–2012) enlivened the role with a contagious nurturing joy. Head deacon Pat Yetman (2013–2014) brought deep thoughtfulness and sensitivity to the ministry of the diaconate, as the Common English Bible was introduced to the congregation, replacing the Revised Standard Version, and as tissue and cough drop holders were created for each pew. Head deacon Carol Ostermann (2015–2016) brought a wealth of church experience and a practical kindheartedness evident to all. Other deacons made significant contributions. For instance, deacon Phyllis Van Siclen brought communion preparations to a new level, and deacon Donald Duncan pursued the "Open and Affirming" designation with determination, understanding, and patience.

Outreach

The outreach of the congregation is clearly seen in the work of the deacons, but is also evident in various projects that have been undertaken through the initiative of individuals and the work of the pastor, with support provided by the deacons and the congregation. Church mission committee member Holly Stover and Rev. Foulger successfully wrote a grant for $180,000 from the Doree Taylor Foundation for use toward the development of a community navigator program to oversee case management of local persons in need. The church assisted hundreds of persons with food, utility bills, medication, and even a generator for a person whose medical needs required the guarantee of electricity at all times. In addition, special offerings were received for hurricane victims, and more than 100 "Welcome to Maine" gift bags were distributed to evacuees from New Orleans who relocated temporarily to the State of Maine in 2005.

The Boothbay Region Food Pantry in particular has done an amazing job of helping families in need. It opened its doors in December 1985. Chester Johnson of Our Lady Queen of Peace Roman Catholic Church and the Rev. David Stinson of the Congregational Church of Boothbay Harbor had jointly approached other churches in the region earlier that year about the possibility of developing a communitywide program to alleviate hunger in the region. While small-scale attempts to address community needs had undoubtedly occurred before, church leaders agreed in 1985 that the most pressing need was for a food pantry. The pantry was originally housed in the Congregational church manse, but was relocated to the church's fellowship hall, where it has operated continuously since its inception. Directors and many other volunteers serve residents needing assistance in the four towns of the Boothbay peninsula: Edgecomb, Boothbay, Boothbay Harbor and Southport.[833]

Women

Throughout the history of the Congregational church in Boothbay, women have played a vital role. Women's groups looked beyond themselves to see the needs around them in the church and beyond and found ways to meet many of those needs. Fundraisers were a common tool for supporting the mission of the church. For decades, the church-sponsored dinner at the annual Fishermen's Festival in Boothbay Harbor was a widely anticipated event and successful fundraiser. With more women working and others aging and unable to help as they once did, membership in the Women's Fellowship declined, and in 2012 the group disbanded formally. Sarah Foulger noted this transition in her 2012 annual report: "When Women's Fellowship Groups were first formed in this congregation, there were numerous weekly-meeting "circles" named for women of the Bible. Over the course of many decades, meetings of circles shrank to two monthly fellowship meetings, a daytime group and an evening group. Then, about twenty-five years ago, these two groups combined to form one fellowship that met during the day."[834]

Over the course of those many years, women served many meals, prepared supplies for soldiers in the Civil War, offered support to families who needed a little extra help in the Christmas season, and encouraged numerous persons through Bible study, fellowship, visits, flowers, cards, phone calls, prayers and powerful words of faith, hope, and love. In addition, the mission of the church was enhanced by women whose efforts produced thousands of dollars over the years to various causes and for the church itself, assisting in the accomplishment of many improvement projects to the facility. Although a formal organization of women does not presently exist, many of those same functions continue to happen through the efforts of women working on their own or collaborating with others. Women's breakfasts and luncheons continue to take place. In addition, the participation of women on boards and committees of the church is particularly noteworthy.

Veterans

Over the decades since Vietnam, veterans have been at times ignored, abused, forgotten, and misunderstood as a group. Some churches have celebrated Veteran's Day with an awkward nod and bare mention in the prayers, straining against the pressure of denominational boards to press for peace in the world and to condemn violence. Other churches have given some recognition by inviting veterans to stand on Veterans Day during worship. Often the compassion of Jesus was present in worship when Rev. Foulger asked veterans to stand. One Veteran's Day she also asked veterans to give their name, rank, unit in which they served, and their place of service. The prayers that day embraced the veterans with appreciation and compassion and embraced the world with a deep longing for peace.

Many of the following were present that day to share their fascinating credentials: John Andrews, Jack Bauman, Joe Blake, Brian Blethen, Bill Burge, Doug Burnham, Rick Conant, Bob Conn, Rusty Court, Fleet Davies, Brandt Dylan, Peter Doelp, John Druce, Jim Dun, Donald Duncan, Mike Eastwood, York Fischer, Steve Francis, Frank Helman, John Hochstein, Ken Honey, Russell Jackson, Bruce Johnson, Maurice Landemare, Ralph (Cy) Seifert, Roger Severance, Barclay Shepard, Bob Shepard, Ed Thibault, Dick Thompson, Harold Van Siclen, John Waldman, Don Walker, Dick Whittier, and Lee Yereance. Individually and collectively their service was diverse and exceptional. Those men represent every branch of the U.S. Armed Services. Some from the Coast Guard served in protecting both the East coast and the West coast stationed from Nantucket to Alaska. There were Air Force officers who were pilots and trained other pilots in Florida and Texas, as well as those who served in logistics in Thailand during the Vietnam War. Among the Marines was a First Lieutenant based on Guadalcanal, who fought in Okinawa and was sent on a mission to China. Army personnel in attendance had served in Korea. Among those serving in the Navy were a veteran who was a medical doctor on a hospital ship and another who retired as a Lieutenant Commander having served in Harbor Defense in Iceland and other places. Another service person was a part of the Manhattan Project. Collectively, their stories were so moving and impressive that a whole book could well have been written about their experiences.

Conclusion

This book began with Rev. John Murray, a talented Presbyterian pastor who became a powerful voice for the American Revolution. It took continued persistence on the part of the Boothbay laity to get John Murray to accept the call to become the first installed pastor of the Boothbay church. And so, 250 years later the Congregational Church of Boothbay Harbor celebrated its most recent pastor, Rev. Dr. Sarah Foulger, a Presbyterian pastor who came to Boothbay trained in Scottish tradition similar to that of John Murray but at Princeton Theological Seminary, and who initially saw herself as accepting a call as interim minister to the church in Boothbay Harbor. But in both cases the will of the laity prevailed and secured the services and blessings of both for the Boothbay church and for the whole Boothbay community. In both cases, with the arrivals of both Murray and Foulger, numerous ripples began spreading out and reaching out to the world at large from the church, first from the Boothbay commons and later from the beautiful church with its striking tall steeple in the small town of Boothbay Harbor.

And so it seems fitting to conclude this chapter and this book with the words the Reverend Dr. Sarah Foulger spoke on October 19, 2014, at the service which celebrated her tenth anniversary as pastor of the church:

> Over the last ten years together, in this congregation, we've seen each other through births and deaths, through diseases and healings, through disappointments and celebrations. My greatest privilege of course, has been and continues to be

working with all of you, with an amazing congregation and extraordinary staff. I realize that no pastor can be all things to all people and no pastor connects with everyone but I love you so. I love you best of all.

I've met some of the most extraordinary people in this congregation and in this community, and my heart breaks in thinking about how many we've lost in our time together, how many have gone to join the great communion of saints. I love you all, each and every fascinating and blessed one of you. In looking back, the blessings of serving this congregation are beyond measure.

I'm not interested in looking back, however, as much as I am interested in looking forward. This is a challenging time in the life of the church—capital C and small c. I visited other churches this summer and as I drove to them, I saw where people were on Sunday mornings. I saw where the parking lots are overflowing between 9 and 11 AM on Sundays. People worship at Foster's Auction House and they worship at the Wiscasset Flea Market and they worship at Wal-Mart and they worship on the soccer fields and football fields. Churches have been recycled into restaurants and theaters and pool halls. This is an interesting time in the life of the church! I feel very privileged to be in a congregation that is, by all comparisons, thriving.

The next two years will be very exciting as we begin to celebrate in a variety of ways the 250 years of blessings which began when the young John Murray made his way from Northern Ireland to this beautiful corner of God's wildly wonderful world. I thank God and I thank you for the opportunity to serve and follow Jesus and listen for the whisperings of the sacred spirit in this place.

Lots of Love,
Sarah.[835]

ILLUSTRATION CREDITS

Photograph of Congregational Church of Boothbay Harbor, UCC, 2014, courtesy of Susan Goodrich.

The painting of Rev. John Murray is used with permission from the Museum of Old Newbury Collection, Newburyport, Massachusetts.

Article from the *Wiscasset Citizen,* (undated), describing Rev. Charles Cook's call to ministry at the Congregational Church of Boothbay.

Photograph of Rev. Nathaniel Chapman, courtesy of First Congregational Church of Camden, Maine.

Photograph of Rev. David Q. Cushman, from *The History of Ancient Sheepscot and Newcastle, Maine,* (Bath, ME: Upton, 1882).

Photograph, c. 1910, of Congregational Church of Boothbay and the 1768 Session House, now the Nicholas Knight house, courtesy of the Boothbay Region Historical Society.

Photograph of Rev. Samuel L. Gould, courtesy of Congregational Library and Archives.

Photograph of Congregational Church of Boothbay Harbor, Memorial Day, c.1880, courtesy of the Boothbay Region Historical Society.

Photograph of Charles McCobb, courtesy of the *Boothbay Register* archives.

Photograph of Rev. Leander S. Coan, *Granite Monthly*, 1898.

Photograph of Ezra B. Pike, c. 1873, courtesy of his great grandson, Hugh Edward Donaldson.

Photograph of Rev. Lewis D. Evans, courtesy of the First Congregational Church of Camden, Maine.

Photograph of Rev. Dr. Peter MacQueen, with permission from the University of Iowa.

Photograph of Rev. Dr. Walter H. Eastwood, courtesy of the *Boothbay Register* archives.

Photograph of Rev. Dr. Harry Emerson Fosdick, courtesy of *Time Magazine,* September 21, 1925.

Photograph of Rev. Charles S. Hartman, courtesy of the *Boothbay Register* archives.

Photograph of Rev. David Stinson, courtesy of Rev. Stinson.

Photograph of Rev. Peter Panagore, courtesy of Whitney Wright.

Photograph of Rev. Dr. Sarah M. Foulger, courtesy of Barbara Fischer Eldred.

Photograph of Rev. Dr. Foulger's Covenant Hymn, located in *Hymns of Truth and Light, The Congregational Church of Boothbay Harbor,* (Houston, TX: First Congregational Church of Houston, *1998),* courtesy of the author and composer.

ACKNOWLEDGMENTS

We, the authors, John Bauman, Robert Dent, Sarah Foulger, and Chip Griffin, are indebted to the following individuals and organizations for their thoughtful assistance with historical records, research, editing, proofing, technical assistance, and other support:

> The History Committee of the Congregational Church of Boothbay Harbor, which, in addition to the authors, has included Stan Bolster, Susan Duckworth, Judy Eastwood, Carol Ostermann, and Roger Severance;

> Doreen Dun, who poured hours of work into editing our chapters with enthusiasm and brilliance;

> Sue Goodrich, who provided long hours of technical assistance during the editing process;

> Faith Meyer and Sandra Leonard, who proofread the book with great care;

> Debi Wood, church administrator of the Congregational Church of Boothbay Harbor;

> Former ministers at our church, Peter Panagore and Joseph David Stinson, who were willing to be interviewed at length;

> Church members and others who were willing to share their recollections during the process of writing this book. Special thanks to Donna Closson and the late Jerry Closson, John Druce, Andy Holmes, Peter and Jackie Mundy, Leah Sample, Bob Shepard, Tom Tavenner, and Alice Thompson;

The patient spouses of the authors and editor, who put up with our long hours of perseverating on various historical matters—Barbara Bauman, Judith Dent, Denise Griffin, Russell Hoffman, and Jim Dun;

Jane Karker, President of Maine Authors Publishing, who guided us gently and effectively through the publishing process, Dan Karker, Editing Supervisor, and David Allen, Art Director;

Nick Noyce of the Maine Historical Society;

Local historian Barbara Rumsey, for many years the director of the Boothbay Region Historical Society and author of several books and many historical articles to which we refer in this book; and the administrator and volunteers of the society;

The Boothbay Region Historical Society, which holds archived church documents and artifacts; the *Boothbay Register,* the Maine Historical Society; the Maine State Genealogical Archives; the Newburyport Historical Society; the Massachusetts Archives; Drexel University, Philadelphia; and the Presbyterian Historical Society and Archives, Philadelphia.

ENDNOTES

CHAPTER 1

1 Bass, *A People's History of Christianity: The Other Side of the Story* (2009), pp. 10, 11, 13, and 17.

2 Zelinsky, Wilbur, *Cultural Geography of the United States* (1973, 1992 ed.), pp. 13-14. Zelinsky notes that this doctrine, which he coined in 1973, is "roughly analogous to the psychological principle of imprinting in very young animals. Whenever an empty territory undergoes settlement, or an earlier population is dislodged by invaders, the specific characteristics of the first group able to effect a viable, self-perpetuating society are of crucial significance for the later social and cultural geography of the area, no matter how tiny the initial band of settlers may have been. ...Thus, in terms of lasting impact, the activities of a few hundred, or even a few score, initial colonizers can mean much more for the cultural geography of a place than the contributions of tens of thousands of new immigrants a few generations later. The history of the northeastern United States clearly illustrates how indelibly the early colonial patterns have marked its cultural landscape."

3 Johnson, Paul, *A History of the American People* (1997), p. 71.

4 Blaikie, Alexander, *A History of Presbyterianism in New England, Its Introduction, Growth, Decay, Revival, and Present Mission*, pp. 87-88.

5 Rumsey, Barbara, *Colonial Boothbay*, p. 103. Rumsey notes that the only known early settlers a decade later in Townsend, now Boothbay, who were not Scots-Irish were two, Edmund Brown and his father-in-law, David Bryant, both from Sudbury, Massachusetts and of English descent, Brown being Boothbay's first murderer and Bryant his victim.

6 Webb, James, *Born Fighting* (2004), pp. 68, 73. King James I of England, also James VI of Scotland, planned and planted thousands of Calvinist Scots in

Catholic Northern Ireland. In 1600, less than two percent of Ireland was of English or Scottish descent; within a century that percentage rose to twenty-five percent, almost all of it in Ulster.

7 Fischer, David Hackett, *Albion's Seed* (1989), p. 786.

8 Fischer, pp. 813-815; Herman, Arthur, *How the Scots Invented the Modern World* (2001), pp. 15-18.

9 Reed, Elizabeth F., *History of the Congregational Church*.

10 Webb, p. 106. The recently deposed King James II had fled to Ireland, where his French and Irish Catholic commanders initiated a siege to force the Scots-Irish Presbyterians to either surrender or starve. From April 18 to July 28, 1689, the 30,000 residents and refugees and 7,500 officers and men besieged in Londonderry suffered terribly amidst bombs, sleep deprivation, famine, and sickness. These Scots-Irish lost thousands, mainly to sickness and starvation, but they refused to give up. Rather, they resolved to eat horse flesh, dogs, cats, rats, mice, and even the Irish and then one another, rather than surrender to any but their own Protestant King William and Queen Mary. Griffin, Patrick, *The People with No Name: Ireland's Ulster Scots, Scots-Irish*, and the *Creation of a British Atlantic World, 1689-1764* (2001), pp. 9-12.

11 Reed, Elizabeth F., *History of the Congregational Church*, August 8, 1948, Boothbay Region Historical Society records.

12 Webb, pp. 219-233.

13 Leyburn, James G., *The Scotch Irish: A Social History* (1962), pp. 280-281.

14 Leyburn, p. 245,

15 Fischer, pp. 27-33.

16 Leyburn, pp. 256-272.

17 Fischer, pp. 754-758.

18 Dobson, David, *Scottish Emigration to Colonial America, 1607-1785* (1994), p. 81.

19 Blaikie, pp. 49-50.

20 Johnson, pp. 88 and 108.

21 Blaikie, p. 49.

22 Blaikie, pp. 49-50. Recent scholarship shows that such warning out of Boston was not necessarily done with hostility, but rather "warning was the hinge in a distinctive, two-tiered welfare system," in which the province's taxpayers paid for the relief of needy strangers. Robert Love, Boston's most successful and long-tenured enforcer of warning immigrants, had been attacked and captured by Abenakis at Georgetown in 1722. Nevertheless, Cotton Mather appears to have recruited Scots-Irish to land in the city, depart to the wilderness, and then protect the urban Bostonians, just as Secretary of State James Logan, himself Scots-Irish, recruited Scots-Irish into and immediately out of peaceful Quaker Philadelphia to protect that city from the French and Indians. Dayton, Cornelia H. and Salinger, Sharon V., *Robert Love's Warnings: Searching for Strangers in Colonial Boston* (2014), pp. 4-5.

23 Blaikie, pp. 49-50.

24 Blaikie, p. 63.

25 Wheeler, George Augustus and Wheeler, Henry Warren, *History of Brunswick, Topsham, and Harpswell* (1878), p. 54; Penhallow, Samuel, *Penhallow's Indian Wars, or A History of the Wars of New-England with the Eastern Indians* (1726), pp. 85-88; also Pamela Crane archaeologist, with John Mann, leader of Maine's Ulster Scots, who located this site on land in Merrymeeting Bay owned by Brad McFadden, descendant of the McFaddens who were burned out of their homes by the Norridgewock Indians in 1722.

26 Fischer, p. 606.

27 Griffin, Patrick, p. 1.

28 Kershaw, Gordon E., *The Kennebeck Proprietors 1749–1775* (1975), p. 152.

29 Beath, John, deposition (1772) and recorded in Vol.9, Page 54B, Lincoln County Registry of Deeds.

30 Williamson, William D., *The History of the State of Maine; From the First Discovery, A.D. 1602, to the Separation, A.D. 1820, Inclusive* (1832), pp. 165–167.

31 Blaikie, p. 87.

32 Kershaw, p. 152.

33 Coleman, Emma Lewis, *New England Captives Carried to Canada* (1925), pp. 2-6.

34 Reed.

35 The first Indian war, known as King Philip's War after its Wampanoag leader, had begun in Massachusetts in 1675, but did not spread to Maine until 1676. There were only brief intervals of peace until 1749, with the Treaty of Falmouth. King William's War, the First Intercolonial War, raged from 1688 to 1697, a period that came to be known as the "Decade of Sorrows." A mere five years later, in 1702, the third Indian war, known as Queen Anne's War or Governor Dudley's War, and sometimes as the Second Intercolonial War, ravaged almost all border villages such as Deerfield and Haverhill in Massachusetts and Kittery in Maine. It ended in 1713 with an uneasy peace negotiated in the Treaty of Utrecht. After almost a decade of relative peace, the Three Years' War, also known under three more common names, Governor Dummer's War, Father Rale's War, and Lovewell's War, raged and included Abenaki raids down the Kennebec and Androscoggin rivers to Brunswick and Georgetown, across the Sheepscot River from Boothbay to the Boothbay region's wooded frontier from 1722–1726. Finally, in 1744–1748, there was the Third Intercolonial War, also known as King George's War, Shirley's War, Five Years' War, locally as the Old French and Indian War, and in Europe as the War of the Austrian Succession. Coleman, pp. 2-6.

36 Ghere, David L. and Morrison, Alvin H., "Searching for Justice on the Maine Frontiers," *American Indian Quarterly*, vol. 25, issue 3, pp. 378-399; also Griffin, Chip, *Heroes, Heretics, and Hellraisers In Our Colonial and Post-Revolutionary Midcoast* (Feb. 15, 2011), pp. 37-46.

37 Leyburn, pp. 54-56, 74.

38 Murray, John, *Bath-Kol* (1783), p. 31.

39 Bailyn, Bernard, *The Barbarous Years* (2012), p. 483.

40 Gaustad, Edwin and Schmidt, Leigh, *The Religious History of America* (2004), pp. 58-59.

41 Herman, Arthur, *How the Scots Invented the Modern World* (2001), pp. 237–238.

42 Herman, p. 238.

43 Gaustad and Schmidt, pp. 58-59.

44 Herman, p. 239.

45 Greene, p. 177.

46 Sarah Foulger website research of Newburyport church.

47 Greene, p. 177.

48 Taylor, Alan, *Liberty Men and Great Proprietors,* 1990), p, 212.

49 Gaustad and Schmidt, pp. 61-62.

50 Gaustad and Schmidt, pp. 83-84, 157–161; Beck, Robin L., *The History of the Boothbay Baptist Church, 1809–1909* (2009).

51 Greenleaf, *Ecclesiastical Sketches* (1921), p.264; thanks also to the research provided by Dr. Rev. Sarah Foulger.

52 Blaikie, pp, 87-88.

53 Blaikie, p. 88.

54 Blaikie, p. 37.

55 Johnston, John, *A History of Bristol and Bremen in the State of Maine, Including the Pemaquid Settlement* (1873), p. 286

56 Blaikie, p.88.

57 Wheeler, George Augustus and Henry Warren, *History of Brunswick, Topsham, & Harpswell, Maine* (1878), p. 802; see also Johnston, p. 393.

58 Blaikie, 1881), p. 88.

59 Blaikie, p. 88.

60 Blaikie, p. 96.

61 Wheeler, pp. 729-730.

62 Blaikie, pp. 110–111.

63 Blaikie, p. 137.

64 Blaikie, p. 111.

65 Greene, p. 177.

66 Blaikie, p. 126.

67 Rumsey, p. 131.

68 Sessional Records, pp. 214–215. The author was probably John Beath, the secretary of the church and likely writer of the session records in 1767.

69 Rumsey, p. 103.

70 Rumsey, pp. 126–127.

71 Rumsey, p. 138.

72 Brown, Edmund, deed from Brown to Murray, recorded in Vol. 8, Page 45B, Lincoln County Registry of Deeds.

73 Miller, William, deposition, Vol. 8, p.73, Lincoln County Registry of Deeds.

74 Greene, p. 139.

75 Rumsey, p. 187; Greene, pp. 142, 186.

76 Greene, p. 146.

77 Greene, p. 179; Foulger research, including timeline; Rumsey, *Colonial Boothbay*, p. 187; and Rumsey, "Out of Our Past, BRHS, Boothbay Center in the 1700s," *Boothbay Register* (2014)

78 Rumsey, Barbara, "Out of Our Past, BRHS, Boothbay Center in the 1700s" (2014).

79 Rumsey, *Colonial Boothbay*, p. 187; Sessional Records, p. 213.

80 Ferguson, Frank and McReynolds, Alister, *Robert Dinsmoor's Scotch-Irish Poems* (2012), pp. xviii-xix. ("Mools" and "moul" are examples of Scots words that matter and mean earth or mold, as a body moldering in the dust. Robert Dinsmoor of Londonderry, New Hampshire, was known as America's counterpart, the "Rustic Bard," to the Bard himself, Robert Burns. At 15, in 1772, Robert Dinsmoor wrote a poem about his pet dog "Skip," emphasizing the concept of equality with all God's creatures, "Their bodies maun gang to the mools, as weel as oors."

81 Greene, p, 189.

82 The Baptists in 1830 secured permission from the town to build a church, and in 1831 Boothbay's Baptists and Methodists combined and built their first church, the Union Church, at the north end of the Boothbay Common, occupied until 1856 when the new and current Baptist church was built. This Union Church was later sold to Robert Montgomery, who tore it down and rebuilt it in East Boothbay, where it was used as a store for many years, until J. H. Blair purchased and moved the building to the Harbor. The store was the source of the great fire in October 1886 that burned much of downtown Boothbay and was one cause of the separation of Boothbay Harbor from Boothbay three years later. Greene, pp. 195, pp. 316-331.

CHAPTER 2

83 Moore, Professor John, "John Murray and Presbyterianism in New England," in *The Church At Home and Abroad,* vol. 22 (Nov. 1897), pp. 368-371.

84 Moore, pp. 368-371.

85 Rumsey, Barbara, "Boothbay's 250th Anniversary, Part I," *Boothbay Register.*

86 Vermilye, p. 158.

87 Vermilye, p. 158.

88 Vermilye, p. 158.

89 Session Records, p. 216.

90 Blaikie, p,143.

91 Foulger, Sarah, Timeline: John Murray 1763–1764, based on her primary source research at the Presbyterian Historical Society in Philadelphia in 2013.

92 Foulger research.

93 Sessional Records, pp. 216–217.

94 Sessional Records, pp. 216–217.

95 Foulger research.

96 Vermilye, p. 157.

97 Blaikie, Alexander, *A History of Presbyterianism in New England: Its Introduction, Growth, Decay, Revival, and Present Mission* (1882), p. 180.

98 Foulger research.

99 Session Records, p. 249; Greene, pp. 141, 178–179.

100 Session Records, pp. 214–226.

101 Foulger research.

102 Foulger research, Synod minutes.

103 Vermilye, p. 158.

104 Vermilye, pp. 167–170; Session Records, pp. 230–231.

105 Elizabeth Reed notes in the Beath file of the Boothbay Region Historical Society.

106 McReynolds, a lifelong teacher and college principal in Northern Ireland, has opined that Beath may have been pronounced Booth in colonial times. McReynolds, Alistair, email communication to John Mann. Professor s is not certain.

107 Rumsey, Barbara, *Boothbay Region Historical Sketches, Volume II* (1999), "The Origin of the Name 'Boothbay,'" pp. 8–12.

108 Fischer, *Albion's Seed*, p. 640; Griffin, "Scots-Irish in Boothbay (June 9, 2009), pp. 12–15; and Rumsey, *Sketches II,* p. 11–12.

109 Vermilye, pp. 155–170.

110 Greene, p. 181.

111 Williamson, William D., *History of the State of Maine* (1832), vol. 2, p. 375

112 Greene, p. 181.

113 Ashby, p. 68; Wheeler, George Augustus and Henry Warren, *History of Brunswick, Topsham, & Harpswell, Maine* (1878), p. 365.

114 Rumsey, *Colonial Boothbay*, p. 185; sessional records, p. 348.

115 Patterson, William D., *The Probate Records of Lincoln County Maine, 1760 to 1800* (1895), pp, 43–44.

116 Patterson, pp, 43-44.

117 Sessional Records, pp. 287–288.

118 Sessional Records, pp. 311-312.

119 Rumsey, *Colonial Boothbay*, pp. 231–232.

120 Sessional Records, pp. 251–253.

121 Sessional Records, p. 205.

122 Sessional Records, p. 210.

123 Blaikie, p. 136.

124 Rumsey, *Colonial Boothbay*, p, 126.

125 Sessional Records, p. 205. Elizabeth Freeman Reed, a careful mid-twentieth century historian and descendant of many of these Townsend founders, stated unequivocally in her introductory notes to these Sessional Records that Robert Murray, an original Ruling Elder of the Presbyterian church here, was the father of Rev. John Murray. Thus, it appears that Francis B. Greene was in error when he admitted uncertainty and opined that Robert Murray was probably a brother of Rev. John Murray, on page 593 of his Boothbay history.

126 Sessional Records, pp. 213, 253.

127 Sessional Records, p. 324.

128 Sessional Records, p. 327.

129 Sessional Records, p. 232.

130 Sessional Records, pp. 232–233.

131 Sessional Records, p. 234.

132 Sessional Records, p. 309.

133 Sessional Records, p. 321.

134 Sessional Records, pp. 237–240.

135 Hatch, Louis C., *Maine A History* (1919), p. 785.

136 Sessional Records, pp,. 252–262.

137 Sessional Records, p. 262.

138 Rumsey, Barbara, "Boothbay's 250th Anniversary, Part 1" (2014) *Boothbay Register*.

139 Sessional Records, pp,. 213, 237–240, 261, 285, 308, 327-332.

140 Sessional Records, pp, 327-332.

141 Sessional Records, pp. 333-355.

142 Sessional Records, pp, 275–277.

143 Sessional Records, p. 320.

144 Sessional Records, pp. 261–262.

145 Sessional Records, pp. 313-314.

146 Sessional Records, p. 317.

147 Sessional Records, p. 322.

148 Sessional Records, pp. 262–265.

149 Sessional Records, p. 287.

150 Sessional Records, p. 308.

151 Sessional Records, pp. 318-319.

152 Sessional Records, pp. 313-314.

153 Sessional Records, pp. 321-322.

154 Sessional Records, p. 323.

155 Sessional Records, pp,. 323-327.

156 Sessional Records, pp. 272–273.

157 Sessional Records, pp. 275, 277–278.

158 Sessional Records, p. 274.

159 Sessional Records, pp. 309-310.

160 Sessional Records, pp. 312-313.

161 Sessional Records, pp, 320-321.

162 Sessional Records, pp. 324-325.

163 Sessional Records, p. 325.

164 McCobb file at the Boothbay Region Historical Society shows that Samuel and Mary McCobb were the parents of William (1740–1816), John (1744–1831), James (1746–1821), Jean (1748-after 1785), Frances (1750–1808), Mary (1753–1773), Samuel (1755–1832), David (1762–1805), and Beatrice (1764–1849) McCobb. John Auld was their brother-in-law, who married Mary McCobb in 1770, and two years later his brother, James Auld married her older sister, Frances; see also Greene, pp. 570-571.

165 Sessional Records, pp. 319, 327, 329.

166 Sessional Records, p. 319.

167 Sessional Records, pp. 322, 324.

168 Sessional Records, pp. 325-327.

169 Greene, pp. 374-375.

170 Sessional Records, p. 335.

171 Greene, p. 610.

172 Shaw, Patrick, *Digest of Cases Decided in the Courts of Session, Trends, and Judiciary*, pp. 445-446; see also http://www.scottishlegalcomplaints.com/glossary.

173 Vermilye, pp. 161–164.

174 Greene, pp. 217–218.

175 Taylor, Alan, *Liberty Men*, p. 14.

176 Johnson, p. 172.

177 Webb, pp. 160–161.

178 Greene, pp, 225–227; Reed, Elizabeth F., "History of the Congregational Church," Boothbay Region Historical Society records.

179 Leamon, James S., *Revolution Downeast* (1993), p. 85, from Dudley Saltonstall to Solomon Lovell, Aug. 13, 1779, Doc. Hist, Me., 16:461.

180 Reed (August 8, 1948).

181 Sessional Records, p. 205.

CHAPTER 3

182 Blaikie, p. 179; Miltimore, James, "A Sermon Preached in The Presbyterian Church in Newbury-Port," (April 7, 1793), p, 33.

183 Blaikie, p. 179.

184 Blaikie, pp. 179–180.

185 Blaikie, Alexander, *A History of Presbyterianism in New England: Its Introduction, Growth, Decay, Revival and Present Mission* (1881), p. 159.

186 Blaikie, p. 160.

187 Taylor, *Liberty Men*, p. 65.

188 Murray, *Bath-Kol*, pp. 76-78.

189 Blaikie, p. 272.

190 Vermilye, pp. 161–164.

191 Greeene, pp. 235–246 service lists; Boothbay Church Sessional Records from 1767–1779.

192 Greene, pp. 228–232.

193 Greene, p. 234.

194 Greene, pp. 224–225.

195 Hurd, Holly, K., "Roots in Ancient North Yarmouth" in *The Church at Walnut Hill: A History of the First Congregational Church*, United Church of Christ, North Yarmouth, Maine (2006), p. 3.

196 Greene, p. 188.

408   LIVELY STONES

197 Weston, Isaac, "Pastoral Relations No. V," in *Christian Mirror*, January 15, 1856, p. 1, (located by Elizabeth F. Reed at the Boston Public Library, provided by Barbara Rumsey at the Boothbay Region Historical Society, in F035 3668, Congo ministers 1856 profile).

198 Greene, p. 188.

199 Weston, Isaac, "Pastoral Relations No. V," in *Christian Mirror*, January 15, 1856, p. 1.

200 Kellogg, Elijah (Jr.), *Good Old Times* (1877), in Foreword by Professor Emeritus of History at the University of Southern Maine and State Historian, Robert M. York.

201 Weston. op. cit.

202 Weston. op. cit.

203 Ramsey, William M., 1 *Presbyterians in America: Church History 101*. Thanks to Robert Dent for furnishing this.

204 Gaustad and Schmidt, *The Religious History of America* (2002), p. 83.

205 Reed, Elizabeth Freeman, summary of Jonathan Gould's diary in Boothbay Region Historical Society.

206 Guild, R.A., Librarian of Brown University, in letter to William D. Patterson of Wiscasset, in Boothbay Region Historical Society (September 29, 1892).

207 Reed, Elizabeth Freeman, summary.

208 Greene, p. 188. This was probably 1790 and not 1789, Greene's understandable error based on Gould's erroneous writing of "January 1st 1790 for his 1791 journal, as clarified by Gould's titling of his diary, "A Diary for Ye Year 1791 and due perhaps also to the title page in Greene's time with someone else's handwriting of "Iary of Jonathan Gould, Pastor in Boothbay Maine 1790." Gould further clarified 1791, not 1790, as the year through his additions of the days of the week. Gould's title entry for January 1 as 1790 was mistaken, a mistake of writing the prior year made by most of us in early January of each year. See www.dayoftheweek.org, and the following: *January 1, 1790,* is the 1st day

of the year 1790 in the Gregorian calendar. There are 364 days remaining until the end of this year. The day of the week is *Friday.* January 1, 1791, is the 1st day of the year 1791 in the Gregorian calendar. There are 364 days remaining until the end of this year. The day of the week *Saturday, January 1, 1792,* is the 1st day of the year 1792 in the Gregorian calendar. There are 365 days remaining until the end of this year. The day of the week is *Sunday.*

209 Elizabeth Freeman Reed handwritten notes and typed memorandum at the Boothbay Region Historical Society.

210 Reed, Elizabeth Freeman, summary. I have had to rely exclusively on Bess Reed for Gould's 1790 diary, which in her era was in the hands of Mr. B. Packard, but Bess Reed received Gould's 1791 diary from William D. Patterson of Wiscasset. See Elizabeth Reed's typed memo in #1465 of F036 in the Boothbay Region Historical Society. And I have relied extensively on Bess Reed's better ability to decipher Gould's almost inscrutable handwriting, but I deserve this as my own handwriting is as bad or worse.

211 *Dictionary of National Biography: Doddridge, Philip;* www.ccel.org/cceh/archives/eee/doddridg.htm.

212 Reed, "Centennial Anniversary," p. 5a.

212a Sloane, Robert K., *The Courthouses of Maine* (1998), pp. 55-66.

213 Reed notes, page 72.

214 Gould, sermon, January 16, 1790, Boothbay, at BRHS.

215 Gould, sermon of April 9, 1790, in Boothbay.

216 Gould diary for 1790, p. 10, per Elizabeth Reed's notes.

217 Reed, p. 57, 58, or 97.

218 Rumsey, *Colonial Boothbay*, pp. 144–153, 115, 145,

219 Rumsey, pp. 145–153.

220 Linekin, Clark, in *Baxter Manuscripts*, vol. 15, pp. 250–251 (Sep., 1777).

410   LIVELY STONES

221 Wikipedia, Hatfields and McCoys, www.enwikipedia.org.

222 Reed, p. 63.

223 Sloane, pp. 62-63.

224 Greene, pp. 378, 390-393.

225 Sloane, pp. 67-68.

226 Johnston, John, *A History of Bristol and Bremen in the State of Maine, Including the Pemaquid Settlement* (1873), pp. 379-382.

227 Reed, "Centennial Anniversary," p. 5.

228 Reed, p.105.

229 Greene, p.188.

230 www.msn.com/?OCID=EIEHP+PC=UP50http://id.loc.gov/authorities/names/n84140490.html; Library of Congress website.

231 Greene, p. 188

232 Taylor, *Liberty Men*, p. 16; Vermilye, pp. 161–164.

233 Taylor, p. 17.

234 Taylor, pp. 1-3, 17.

235 Taylor, pp. 210–212.

236 Rumsey, *Colonial Boothbay*, p. 196.

237 Vermilye, pp. 163–164; Miltimore, pp. 35-36.

238 Murray, John, *Nehemiah* (1779), p. 17.

239 Murray, *Nehemiah*, p. 21.

240 Murray, *Nehemiah*, p. 25.

241 Murray, *Nehemiah*, p. 4.

242 Murray, *Nehemiah*, pp. 6-7.

243 Murray, *Nehemiah*, p. 9.

244 Murray, *Nehemiah*, p. 12.

245 Murray, *Nehemia*h, p. 54.

246 Murray, *Jerubbaal*, p. 5.

247 Murray, *Jerubbaal*, p. 54.

248 Murray, *Jerubbaal*, pp. 56-57.

249 Taylor, p. 16.

250 Murray, *Bath-Kol*, (1783), p. 2.

251 Murray, *Bath-Kol*, p. vii.

252 Murray, *Bath-Kol*, p. xi.

253 Murray, *Bath-Kol*, p. xii.

254 Murray, *Bath-Kol*, pp. 92-93.

255 Miltimore, John, "A Sermon Preached in The Presbyterian Church In Newbury-Port" (April 7, 1793), p. 32.

256 Hovey, Rev. Horace C., "John Murray, Pastor and Patriot" in *The Herald* and *Presbyterian*, in the Boothbay Region Historical Society, F035B.

257 Miltimore, pp. 36, 57-61.

258 Reed, Elizabeth F., Historical Address, August 8, 1848, on the Centennial Anniversary of the founding of the Second Congregational Church, or South Parish, at the Boothbay Region Historical Society.

259 Blaikie, p. 298.

260 Blaikie, p. 301.

261 Murray, Rev. John, codicil file F035B at the Boothbay Region Historical Society.

262 Burns, James MacGregor, *Fire and Light: How the Enlightenment Transformed the World* (2014), p.268.

263 Burns, p.268.

CHAPTER 4

264 Greene, Francis B., *History of Boothbay, Southport, and Boothbay Harbor, Maine, 1623–1905, with Family Genealogies* (1906), pp. 281–285, 287.

265 Greene, pp. 188–189; Elizabeth F. Reed notes and records of the Congregational church at the Boothbay Region Historical Society File F035.

266 Clark, p. 10.

267 Greene, pp. 188–189; Reed notes and records, BRHS, F035.

268 Weston, Isaac, "Pastoral Relations No. V," in *Christian Mirror*, January 15, 1856, p. 1, (located by Elizabeth F. Reed at the Boston Public Library provided by Barbara Rumsey at the Boothbay Region Historical Society, in F035 3668, Congo ministers 1856 profile).

269 Greene, p. 497-498.

270 Greene, pp. 188–189; Reed, Congregational Church records at the BRHS.

271 Greene, family histories at the end.

272 Greene, p. 498.

273 Bible Dictionary, "chambering" in King James English means adultery or fornication; "chambering" refers to a bed chamber, which is a bedroom, www.seekfind.net_bible_dictionary_define_chambering.

274 Reed, Congregational Church records, BRHS.

275 Reed, Congregational Church records, BRHS.

276 Greene, pp. 188–189.

277 Greene, pp. 188–189; Clark, Calvin Montague, *The History of Bangor Theological Seminary* (1916), pp. 18–19, 21, 23 27, and 357.

278 Greene, pp. 152–154, 252, 259, 261,340, and 453.

279 Greene, p. 189.

280 Owen, Katherine Chase, *Early Edgecomb, Maine* (1986), p. 25.

281 Weston.

282 Greene, p. 526.

283 Greene, p. 189.

284 Greene, p. 190.

285 Greene, p. 189.

286 Reed's notes, BRHS; see also Greene, pp. 189–190.

287 Reed's notes, BRHS.

288 Williamson, Joseph, *Bibliography of the State of Maine* (1896, reprinted 1985), vol. II, p. 609.

289 Greene, p. 190.

290 Greene, pp. 189–204.

291 Greene, pp. 592-593.

292 Greene, p. 498.

293 Greene, pp, 610-611.

294 Greene, pp. 498-499.

295 Greene, p. 621.

296 Greene, pp.150–151, 395.

297 Greene, pp. 550-551.

298 Greene, pp. 527-528.

299 Greene, pp. 279–287, 570.

300 McCobb file notes, Descendants of Samuel McCobb, p. 11, BRHS.

301 Greene, p. 499.

302 Greene, p. 499.

303 Greene, p. 517.

304 Greene, p. 500.

305 Greene, p. 517-518.

306 Greene, p. 554.

307 Gaustad and Schmidt, p. 193.

308 Beck, Robin L., *The History of the Baptist Church 1809—2009* (2009), p. 8.

309 Hatch, Louis Clinton, *Maine: A History* (1919), pp. 788-789.

310 Greene, pp. 192–194.

311 Greene, p. 190.

312 Beck, p. 8.

313 Greene, p. 194.

314 Greene, p. 194.

315 Beck, p. 15.

316 Beck, p. 10.

317 Beck, p. 14.

318 Greene, p. 195.

319 Levett, Christopher, "A Voyage into New England (1624), in *Forerunners and Competitors of the Pilgrims and Puritans*, (1912), vol. 2, pp. 618-619.

320 Greene, p. 310.

321 Greene, p. 197.

322 Greene, p. 195.

323 Greene, p. 195.

324 Greene, pp. 196–197.

325 Greene, p. 202.

326 Taylor, p. 301.

327 Hatch, p. 785.

328 Johnson, Paul, *A History of the American People* (1997), p. 205.

329 Blaikie, p. 298.

330 Johnson, pp. 296–297.

331 Gaustad and Schmidt, p. 139.

332 Gaustad and Schmidt, p. 140.

333 Gaustad and Schmidt, pp. 140–145.

334 Gaustad and Schmidt, p. 145.

335 Clark, *Bangor Theological Seminary*, pp. 10–12.

336 Gaustad and Schmidt, p. 132.

337 Johnson, p. 307.

338 Greene, pp. 247–248.

339 Taylor, Alan, *The Civil War of 1812* (2010), p. 6.

340 Taylor, *Civil War*, p. 117.

341 Taylor, *Civil War*, pp. 278–279.

416 LIVELY STONES

342 Rice, George Wharton, *The Shipping Days of Old Boothbay* (1938), pp, 34-35.

343 Rice, pp. 38-39.

344 Rice, pp. 50-52.

345 Greene, pp, 504-505; 522-523.

346 Rice, p. 52.

347 Rice, pp 52-54.

348 Taylor, *Liberty Men*, p. 214; Greene, p. 248.

349 Rice, pp. 54-55.

350 Greene, pp. 249–250.

351 Greene, pp,. 250–252.

352 Taylor, *Civil War*, p. 292.

353 Rice, pp. 55-56.

354 Longfellow, Henry Wadsworth, "My Lost Youth," in part: "I remember the sea-fight far away,/ How it thundered o'er the tide!/ And the dead captains, as they lay in their graves, o'erlooking the tranquil bay/Where they in battle died./ And the sound of that mournful song/ Goes through me with a thrill:/ A boy's will is the wind's will,/ And the thoughts of youth are long, long thoughts."

355 Greene, pp. 252–254.

356 Greene, p. 255.

357 Greene, pp.259–261.

358 Greene, p. 259.

359 McCobb papers, page 13, in BRHS.

360 Boothbay census in *Baxter Manuscripts, vol. 21*, p. 63.

361 Boothbay census (1810), copied by Elizabeth Reed, p. 2.

362 Goode, George Brown, *The Fisheries and the Fishing Industries of the United States: The Fishermen of the United States* (1881, 1882, 1887), vol.8, p. 71.

363 "Gazette Ship News," *Portland Gazette and Maine Advertiser*, (July 23, 1810), vol. 13, no. 15, p. 3.

364 Greene, p. 576.

365 Rice, George Wharton, *The Shipping Days of Old Boothbay* (1938), p. 268.

366 Greene, pp. 32-335.

367 Rice, p. 59.

368 Johnson, p. 284.

369 Johnson, p. 310.

370 Johnson, p. 284.

371 Johnson, p. 290.

372 Johnson, p. 317; Letter of Thomas Jefferson to John Holmes, April 22, 1820.

373 Crane, Elaine Forman, *Ebb Tide in New England: Women, Seaports, & Social Change 1630–1800* (1998), p. 108.

374 Fischer, David Hackett, *Albion's Seed: Four British Folkways in America* (1989), pp. 675-680.

375 Crane, p. 4.

376 Crane, p. 44.

377 Crane, p. 6.

378 Crane, p. 7.

379 Crane, p. 48.

418 LIVELY STONES

380 Crane, p. 40.

381 Crane, p. 51.

382 Crane, pp. 62-64.

383 Crane, p. 97.

384 Crane, p. 73.

385 Beck, p. 10; Greene, pp, 192–194.

386 Crane, p. 82.

387 Norton, Mary Beth, *In the Devil's Snare: The Salem Witchcraft Crisis of 1692* (2002), p. 304.

388 Crane, p. 89.

389 Crane, p. 89.

390 Crane, p. 86.

391 Crane, p. 242.

392 BRHS, F035.

393 Foulger, Sarah, in Chapter 5 of this work, was the person who unearthed, analyzed, and reconstructed this amazing story of Charles L. Cook, the dismal failure of church leadership then, and ongoing lessons for all of us today.

CHAPTER 5

394 In the 1830s, there were both great energy and excitement in "winning" the West" and deep pain within Native American communities who were "removed" either through genocide or by forcing them into portions of land no one else wanted. During 1838, the forced removal of 15,000–17,000 Cherokee Indians from Georgia on the "Trail of Tears" resulted in an estimated 4,000-8,000 deaths. Whole European-American communities moved west, not only fledgling groups such as the Mormons, but also established Congregational

communities, which left locations in New England and Ohio and, following the Oregon Trail, planted new churches on the Northwest Coast.

395 Francis Greene, *History of Southport, Boothbay, and Boothbay Harbor*, p. 363. Couplet attributed to an old Bristol fisherman.

396 *Boothbay Region Historical Sketches*, Vol. 2, Barbara Rumsey, editor.

397 "Mr. Charles L. Cook was called August 10, 1830, ordained October 6, and for irregularities dismissed and deposed November 5, 1832." *History of Boothbay, Southport and Boothbay Harbor*, p. 190.

398 From the centennial sermon delivered by Rev. Leander S. Coan to the congregation in Boothbay on September 23, 1866.

399 "Irregularities" is the word used by Francis Greene to describe Cook's sexual malfeasance.

400 *The American Quarterly.* Vol. 12, p. 259. Publication conducted by B.B. Edwards and W. Cogswell, 1841.

401 As published in the *Boothbay Register*, January 26, 1989, p. 19.

402 As recorded in an 1827 newspaper article. Special thanks to Susan Simeone who located several nineteenth century news articles regarding Cook.

403 *History of the First Baptist Church, Hanson, Massachusetts, 150th anniversary, 1812–1962.* Written and compiled from church records by Antone Slaney.

404 History relayed by Debbi Bailey, Office Manager, First Baptist Church, who reviewed archived church records.

405 From the "Trial (Before the Municipal Court) of Charles L. Cook, Late Preacher of the Gospel of the Orthodox and Restorationist Denominations," 1835.

406 As reported in the *Newburyport Herald*, 1830.

407 According to a Wikipedia article on the "Back to Africa" movement, *The American Colonization Society*, founded in 1816 by Charles Fenton Mercer, was made up of two groups: on the one hand, "philanthropists, clergy, and

abolitionists who wanted to free African slaves and their descendants and provide them with the opportunity to return to Africa. The other group was the slave owners who feared free people of color and wanted to expel them from America." The movement to create a free Liberia was also started by Mercer. According to the *Encyclopedia of Georgia History and Culture*, "as early as 1820, black Americans had begun to return to their ancestral homeland through the auspices of the American Colonization Society, and by 1847, the American Colonization Society founded Liberia and designated it as the land to be colonized by all black people returning from the United States of America." By the decline of the Back to Africa Movement, the American Colonization Society had migrated over 13,000 blacks back to Africa.

408 Minutes of the Congregational Church of Boothbay.

409 Minutes of the General Conference of Maine, 1834.

410 From an account of the proceedings of the church council by Lincoln County Attorney, S.D. Parker, as inserted into the Boston trial notes of 1835.

411 Proceedings of the church council, S.D. Parker.

412 Proceedings of the church council, S.D. Parker.

413 Sophia and Charles had at least one child, and the use of the word "family" may indicate that, by the time of the Ecclesiastical Council, this child had been born.

414 Cecil Adams: "In the 1800s, Onanism and masturbation were tied to homosexuality." *Psychology Today,* September 29, 2010: "Noted 19th century physician and early sex research pioneer Richard von Krafft Ebing linked masturbation to homosexuality."

415 From the "Trial (Before the Municipal Court) of Charles L. Cook, Late Preacher of the Gospel of the Orthodox and Restorationist Denominations," 1835.

416 Minutes of the General Conference of Maine, reported: "By an unanimous vote the council dismissed him from his pastoral relation without the usual recommendations and advised him to devote himself to some secular calling.

ENDNOTES 421

Finding his character gone and himself cut off from the Christian ministry in our churches he joined himself about two months afterwards to a Universalist Association in Boston and is now a preacher of that denomination."

417 Misidentified as Watertown, New Hampshire, in some news accounts.

418 The claim of service in a Methodist church remains unsubstantiated.

419 "Trial (Before the Municipal Court) of Charles L. Cook, Late Preacher of the Gospel of the Orthodox and Restorationist Denominations."

420 The *Independent Messenger* began publication in 1831 and lasted until 1839. Susan Simeone, archive researcher.

421 "Trial (Before the Municipal Court) of Charles L. Cook, Late Preacher of the Gospel of the Orthodox and Restorationist Denominations."

422 ibid.

423 31 Minutes of the General Conference of Maine, beginning in 1828.

424 Minutes of the General Conference of Maine.

425 Robert T. Handy, *A Christian America*, (Oxford University Press, 1971), p. 29.

426 Minutes of the Annual Meetings of the General Conference of Maine, 1835–1846.

427 Thomas Jefferson's "Letter to the Danbury Baptist Association," 1802.

428 "The Brigham Young University Law Review," November 15, 2004, p. 1394.

429 Robert T. Handy, *A Christian America*, p. 37.

430 Peck, Thomas Bellows, *The Bellows Crest*, 1898.

431 Obituary published in the annals of Andover Theological Seminary.

432 Records of Dartmouth College.

433 Andover Theological Seminary, *Necrology*, Second Printed Series, 1890–1900.

434 Minutes of the General Conference of the Congregational Church, 1834–1835.

435 Blake, Mortimer, *A History of the Town of Franklin, Mass. from its settlement to the completion of its first century, March 2, 1878*; with genealogical notices of its earliest families, sketches of its professional men, and a report of the centennial celebration.

436 *A History of the Town of Franklin*, Massachusetts.

437 From a letter of personal remembrances of the General Conference of Maine written by Rev. E.F. Cutter and printed as part of the minutes of the Annual Meeting of the General Conference of Maine, Volume 46.

438 General Conference of Maine, *Necrology Report,* 1858.

439 General Conference of Maine, *Necrology Report,* 1872.

440 Cole, Arlene, *Biographical Sketch of Cushman*, for the Newcastle Historical Society.

441 The Maine Underground Railroad Association lists Boothbay as a possible stop along the Underground Railroad.

442 Fifty-four forty referred to the latitude line that marked the northern boundary of Oregon.

443 Minutes of the General Conference of the Congregational Church, 1899 indicate that Tobey left Boothbay in 1847. Greene reports his departure in 1848.

444 Minutes of the Lincoln Association of the Maine Conference, Congregational Church.

445 *Collections of the Maine Historical Society*, Volume III, 1853.

CHAPTER 6

446 Theodore Thornton Munger, *Horace Bushnell, Preacher and Theologian* (Boston and New York: Houghton, Mifflin, & Co.), 1899.

447 *From History of Boothbay, Southport, and Boothbay Harbor* by Francis Byron Greene: "In the 1837 report of the state geologist Doctor Jackson, he says speaking of Boothbay, 'This place is one of the most frequented Harbors on the eastern coast of the State and is a favorite resort for invalids.'"

448 Elizabeth Reed, *Historical Address*, August 2, 1948. Address given to commemorate the 100th anniversary of the "South Parish" or "Second Congregational Church" founded in 1848 in the Harbor area of Boothbay, two miles south of the original church.

449 *Obituary Record of the Graduates of Bowdoin College and the Medical School*, 1892.

450 *Necrology Report of the General Conference of Maine*, 1861.

451 *The Congregational Quarterly*, Volume 19, p. 321, *Necrology Report*.

452 "Minutes of the General Conference of Maine."

453 *The Congregational Quarterly*, 1877.

454 Minutes of the South Parish, April 4, 1861.

455 Elizabeth Reed spells this name 'Duckendorf.'

456 1850 Minutes of the South Parish church, as transcribed by Elizabeth Reed in the twentieth century.

457 Church minutes, 1848, transcribed by Elizabeth Reed in the twentieth century.

458 "Minutes of the General Conference of Maine," 1850–1852, Bangor Theological Seminary Records.

459 *History of Boothbay, Southport, and Boothbay Harbor*, p. 383.

460 "Minutes of the General Conference of Maine."

461 *History of the Presbyterian Church in the State of Illinois* by Augustus Theodore Norton.

462 *History of the Presbyterian Church in the State of Illinois.*

463 Tougaloo College is still associated with the Congregational Church, now the United Church of Christ.

464 In the 1980 Federal Census, Deering identified himself as a Presbyterian minister. The census taker misspelled his name 'Dearing.'

465 *The Congregational Quarterly*, Volume 6.

466 Minutes of the South Parish of Boothbay, September 12, 1856.

467 Minutes of the South Parish of Boothbay, September 12, 1856.

468 *Forbes and Forbush Genealogy: The Descendants of Daniel Forbush* by Frederick Clifton Pierce, p. 131.

469 Charles was lost off Prince Edward Island when the *C. G. Matthews* wrecked. See: *Descendants of James and William Adams* by Andrew Napoleon Adams, 1894. (Tuttle Company, Printers). *The Sailor's Magazine*, Vols. 24 and 25 pinpoints the cause of the wreck as a gale.

470 *History of Bowdoin College* by Nehemiah Cleaveland (Boston: J.R. Osgood & Co.), 1882.

471 "The Twelfth General Catalogue of the Psi Upsilon Fraternity," p. 373.

472 *History of Boothbay, Southport, and Boothbay Harbor* by Francis Byron Greene, p. 424.

473 *Bowdoin Daily Sun*: "Whispering Pines: Bowdoin at Gettysburg," July 2, 2013.

474 "Bowdoin Daily Sun" "Whispering Pines: Bowdoin at Gettysburg," July 2, 2013.

475 *History of Boothbay, Southport, and Boothbay Harbor*, p. 570.

476 *Boothbay Register,* Monday, December 9, 2013, online edition.

477 Four uncles on their father's side; two on their mother's.

478 The unusual gravestone was recovered in 2011 and researched by Rick Helin, a member of the California Pioneers. The stone was originally placed in a Masonic graveyard in Vallejo, CA but was found sitting in a warehouse belonging to the Art Department of a large junior college. McCobb's name was carved on one side (misspelled as Abiel), Plummer's name on the other.

479 Perhaps if you are the last in your family line, the impulse to be remembered is stronger than usual.

480 Notes of Elizabeth Reed.

481 The story is told that Abial bequeathed $500 to the church in exchange for a memorial plaque to be placed in the church in his name. There is no known evidence to support this story. Abial McCobb, in fact, bequeathed everything he owned to the South Parish, and there is no evidence that he requested the plaque.

482 Article located on the "Maine Memory" website:www.mainememory.net, a project of the Maine Historical Society

483 *A History of the Cobb Family* by Philip L. Cobb, 1907.

484 Minutes of the General Conference of Maine.

485 Rendering of Leander S. Coan by J. N. McClintock from *Granite Monthly*, Volume 4.

486 J.N. McClintock, *Granite Monthly*, Volume 4, 1880.

487 *History of Boothbay, Southport, and Boothbay Harbor* by Francis Byron Greene, p. 190.

488 *A Century in the Life of an Old New England Church* by Leander S. Coan.

489 Minutes of the Annual Meeting of the General Conference of the Congregational Churches in Maine, 1868.

490 Listed as serving both churches in *The Congregational Quarterly*, vol.15, 1872.

491 Minutes of the Annual Meeting of the General Conference of the Congregational Churches in Maine, p.483.

CHAPTER 7

492 The dispensationalist movement was started by John Nelson Darby and promulgated through the Scofield Reference Bible.

493 Strong, William E., *The Story of the American Board,* (Pilgrim Press, 1910).

494 Dr. Shepard was widely known as an excellent eye surgeon. He is also recognized for his attempts at dissuading the Turks from deporting the Armenians and was an eyewitness to the Armenian genocide.

495 Bulgaria became the primary mission field of the Clarke family, including Sarah Foulger's great and great-great grandfathers, James Cummings Clarke and James Franklin Clarke. James Cummings Clarke was an eyewitness to the Armenian genocide and left copious notes and letters describing atrocities committed by the Turks.

496 *History of Boothbay, Boothbay Harbor, and Southport* by Francis Byron Greene, (First Copyright 1906, Picton Press), p. 373.

497 After 1900, the steamboat trade began to decline, and by the 1930s it was nearly gone.

498 Bangor Theological Seminary Historical Catalogue, 1816–1916.

499 Also known as "Jenkyn," the Welsh spelling of this surname.

500 According to the Maine Irish Heritage Trail organization, "The area at the end of Main Street in South Portland was known as Ligonia and was home to many generations of Irish families. It was probably named for Lygonia, an early land patent in southern Maine. The area was home to several successful businesses at one time, including the Portland Rolling Mills, the Cumberland Bone Company, the Portland Kerosene Oil Company Works, and the Atwood Lead Company. These companies employed many Irish and Welsh immigrants." For more information, visit: www.maineirishheritagetrail.org.

501 Original list of pew purchasers rests in the church archives.

502 Elizabeth Reed's unpublished "Historical Address," 1948. Church archives.

503 "Articles of Faith and Covenant," adopted by the Second Congregational Church, Boothbay Harbor, revised and published in 1881.

504 Emerson commanded some of the best-known vessels, including the *Eliza McNeil*, a ship made famous for carrying supplies from San Francisco to Pitcairn Island in 1874. Matthew, Frederick C., *American Merchant Ships, 1850–1900*, Volume 1, p.100 ff.

505 *History of Boothbay, Boothbay Harbor, and Southport* by Francis Byron Greene, (copyright 1999, Picton Press), p. 617.

506 1900, as reported in the *Bath Independent*.

507 *Who's Who at Mountain View* by Barbara F. Dyer (Camden Printing, Inc. 2010).

508 For the complete poem, see *Who's Who at Mountain View* by Barbara F. Dyer (Camden Printing, Inc. 2010).

509 The Francis Greene date was corrected by Barbara Rumsey *in Boothbay Region Historical Sketches*, Volume 2.

510 Francis Greene recounts the division of Boothbay in sad detail in Chapter XVIII of *History of Boothbay, Boothbay Harbor, and Southport* (Rockland: Picton Press, copyright 1906).

CHAPTER 8

511 Shared by Chip Griffin. Special thanks to Judy Eastwood and to co-authors Chip Griffin and John F. Bauman for material they shared about these decades.

512 http://en.wikipedia.org/wiki/Chicago_race_riot_of_1919

513 First Principles Series Report #12 on on-line journal, *Political Thought*.
    July 18, 2007 *The Progressive Movement and the Transformation of American Politics* by Thomas G. West and William A. Schambra. See http://www.heritage.org/research/reports/2007/07/the-progressive-movement-and-the-transformation-of-american-politics

514 Sweet, William Warre, *The Story of Religion In America*. Harper and Brothers, 1950, pp. 357-359

515 Gaustad, Edwin and Schmidt, Leigh. *The Religious History of America,* Harper Collins, 2002, p. 231.

516 Sweet, p.372f.

517 Sweet, p. 373.

518 Sweet, p. 53.

519 Gaustad and Schmidt. p. 279.

520 Sweet, p. 348.

521 Sweet, P. 349.

522 Research based on notes from J.F.Bauman on Congregational church history, January 16, 2009.

523 Sweet, p. 345.

524 *Boothbay Register,* (hereinafter BR*)* May 27, 1911, p. 2.

525 Sweet, p. 351.

526 Sweet, p. 389.

527 Sweet, p. 351.

528 Gaustad and Schmidt, p. 266.

529 BR, August 29, 1914, p.3.

530 BR, February 17, 1914, p. 3: *Congregational Notes.*

531 Conforti book.

532 BR, June 4, 1915, p. 4.

533 Much of this material gathered by John F. Bauman.

534 http://www.thefreelibrary.com/Harry+Emerson+Fosdick's+role+in+the+war+and+pacifist+movements.-a0155475841

535 Greene, Francis, *History of Boothbay, Southport, Boothbay Harbor, Maine 1623–1905 With Family Genealogies.* Loring, Short & Harmon, 1906. P. 208

536 Rev. Dr. Thomas De Witt Talmage (7 January 1832–12 April 1902) was preacher, clergyman and divine in the United States who held pastorates in the Reformed Church in America and in the Presbyterian Church. He was one of the most prominent religious leaders in the United States during the mid- to late-nineteenth century, equaled as a pulpit orator perhaps only by Henry Ward Beecher. He also preached to crowds in England. During the 1860s and 1870s,Talmage was a well-known reformer in New York City and was often involved in crusades against vice and crime.

During the last years of his life, Dr. Talmage ceased preaching and devoted himself to editing, writing, and lecturing. At different periods he was editor of the *Christian at Work* (1873–1876), New York; the *Advance* (1877–1879), Chicago; *Frank Leslie›s Sunday Magazine* (1879–1889), New York; and the *Christian Herald* (1890–1902), New York. For years his sermons were published regularly in more than 3,000 journals, through which he was said to reach 25 million readers. http://en.wikipedia.org/wiki/Thomas_De_Witt_Talmage

537 BR, Saturday, June 15, 1912.

538 BR, August 29,1908, p. 3.

539 BR, September 19, 2008, p.3.

540 BR, March 19, 1910 p.3.

541 BR, December 24, 1910.

542 BR, January 7, 1911.

543 BR, November 14, 1914.

544 BR, November 14, 1914.

545 BR, Congregational Notes. August 15, 1914, p. 3.

546 BR. April 14, 1919.

547 BR, June 11, 1911.

548 BR, June 10, 1917.

549 BR. January 21, 1917.

CHAPTER 9

550 Gaustad, Edwin and Schmidt, Leigh. *The Religious History of America*. Harper Collins, 2002, p.255.

551 Gaustad and Schmidt, p. 267.

552 Gaustad and Schmidt, p. 267.

553 See http://en.wikipedia.org/wiki/William_Ernest_Hocking.

554 See http://www.ask.com/wiki/Social_Gospel?o=2801&qsrc=999&ad=doubleDown&an=apn&ap=ask.com.

555 See http://www.who2.com/bio/jane-addams.

556 See http://en.wikipedia.org/wiki/Ku_Klux_Klan_in_Maine.

557 See http://www.gilderlehrman.org/history-by-era/roaring-twenties/essays/f-scott-fitzgerald-and-age-excess.

558 Griffin, Chip, *I'm Different: A Biography of Ethelyn Pinkham Giles of Boothbay Harbor and Southport*, Boothbay Harbor, ME, 1999, p. 36.

559 Griffin III, Carl R. (Chip), *Coming Of Age On Damariscove Island, Maine*. Northeast Folklore, Orono, Maine. 1980.

560 Records of the Congregational Parish, Boothbay Harbor, ME. 1893–1929, p.78.

561 Records of the Congregational Parish, Boothbay Harbor, ME. 1893–1929, p 81.

562 *Boothbay Register* (BR), March 19, 1920, p. 2.

563 http://en.wikipedia.org/wiki/The_Economic_Consequences_of_the_Peace.

564 BR, December 3, 1920, p.1.

565 BR, March 19, 1920 p. 2.

566 BR, October 10, 1921.

567 BR, Nov. 11, 1921, p. 1.

568 BR, February 4, 1921, p. 1.

569 Records of the Congregational Parish, Boothbay Harbor, ME, 1893–1929, p.787.

570 BR, May 27, 1921, p. 1.

571 Records of the Congregational Parish, Boothbay harbor, ME, 1893–1929, p.82.

572 The Weymouth House was built in 1848 on Oak Street, was razed in 1925 and replaced by the Village Inn, another hotel, where the Boothbay Harbor Post office is today.

573 BR, January 11, 1924, p. 1 (lead headline).

574 Author's notes from co-author Chip Griffin.

575 BR, January 11, 1924, p.4.

576 BR, September 5, 1924, p.1.

577 Dorrien, Gary J., *Soul In Society: The Making And Renewal of Social Christianity*. Augsburg Press, 1995, Minneapolis, MN

578 *Evangelical Dictionary of Theology*, Baker Reference Library, p. 463.

579 BR, August 8, 1924,p. 1.

580 BR, July 1924.

581 BR, August 15, 1924.

582 BR January 2, 1925, p.2.

583 Records of the Congregational Parish, Boothbay Harbor, ME, 1893–1929, p.90.

584 BR, June 19, 1925.

585 Notes provided by co-author John F. Bauman.

586 BR, December 23, 1925, p. 8.

587 http://en.wikipedia.org/wiki/Young_People%27s_Society_of_Christian_Endeavour

588 Records of the Congregational Parish, Boothbay Harbor, ME, 1893–1929, p. 105.

589 BR, July 26, 1928.

590 BR, August 27, 1926, p. 1.

591 Records of the Congregational Parish, Boothbay Harbor, ME, 1893–1929, p.116.

592 Fannie Perkins was the wife of James Blenn Perkins, well-known lawyer, active civic leader and Congregational church member for a half century. Their son, James Blenn Perkins, Jr., was also very active for roughly 50 years as town moderator and as a Congregational church leader. Vice Admiral James Blenn Perkins III is an Annapolis graduate and brother of Boothbay Harbor resident Tom Perkins, whose family currently lives adjacent to the Congregational church building. The first two Perkins were shakers and movers, often serving the community behind the scenes. Vice Admiral Perkins had an outstanding naval career.

593 Oct. 24, 1928: H.S. Perkins Clerk, announced a gift to the church of $1,000 from M.K.H. Richards. It was stipulated that the money be used whenever the fund of the church required. At a special meeting of the parish on Nov. 14, 1928, it was voted that a special page in the records of the church be set aside

in grateful acknowledgement of the generous gift of Mr. Richards and that a copy be published in the *Boothbay Register*.

594 BR, January 10, 1930, p.1.

595 BR, November 14, 1930.

596 BR, December 19, 1930, p.1.

597 Remarkable decision since daylight savings time was first introduced in 1918 and 1919. It was repealed in 1919 following a Congressional override of President Wilson's veto. Daylight savings time became a local option and was continued in a few states, such as Massachusetts and Rhode Island, and in some cities, such as New York, Philadelphia, and Chicago. (http://www.webexhibits.org/daylightsaving/e.html). It became standard during part of World War II and then was on again and off again during various presidencies.

598 BR, May 8, 1931.

599 Bauman, John F., *Gateway to Vacationland: The Making of Portland, ME,* University of Massachusetts Press, 2012. Pp. 159 f.

600 Bauman, p. 166.

601 http://www.pbs.org/wgbh/americanexperience/features/timeline/worlds.

602 BR, March 20, 1931.

603 BR, June 12, 1931.

604 BR, March 20, 1931, p. 2.

605 BR, August 12, 1932, p. 1.

606 BR, July 1, 1932, p. 1.

607 http://www.pbs.org/wgbh/americanexperience/features/timeline/worlds.

608 "The Theological Declaration of Barmen" taken from: *The Church's Confession Under Hitler* by Arthur C. Cochrane. Philadelphia: Westminster Press, 1962, pp. 237–242.

609 T. F. Torrance, *Karl Barth: An Introduction to His Early Theology, 1910–1931*, p. 9.

610 http://en.wikipedia.org/wiki/Karl_Barth.

611 Philosophy of Buber.htm

612 As quoted from *The Children of Light and the Children of Darkness*—(1944):http://en.wikipedia.org/wiki/Reinhold_Niebuhr.

613 (http://en.wikipedia.org/wiki/Paul_Tillich).

614 BR, February 23, 1934, p. 1.

615 BR, May 10, 1935, p. 1.

616 BR, November 2, 1934 p. 1.

617 BR, November 9, 1934, p. 1.

618 Author's correspondence with John F. Bauman.

619 BR, May 10, 1935, p. 1.

620 BR, July 22, 1938, p. 1.

621 BR, September 30, 1938 p.1.

622 http://www.dontow.com/2009/04/japans-biological-and-chemical-warfare-in-china-wwii.

623 BR, January 13, 1939.

624 BR, March 3, 1939.

625 BR, November 18, 1938.

626 BR, February 22, 1939.

627 BR, Friday, December 20, 1940.

CHAPTER 10

628 For general histories of the postwar era, see Lizabeth Cohen, *A Consumers' Republic: The Politics of Mass Consumption in Postwar America* (New York: Knopf, 2003); David Halberstam, *The Fifties* (New York: Villard Books, 1993); Fred Inglis, *The Cruel Peace: Everyday Life in the Cold War* (New York: Basic Books, 1983); Stephanie Coontz, *The Way We Really Were: American Families and the Nostalgia Trap* (New York: Basic Books, 1992); William Oneil, *Coming Apart: An Informal History of America in the 1960s* (Chicago: Quadrangle, 1971).

629 Minutes of the Boothbay Harbor Church business committee [hereinafter BCM], January 11, 1943, found in Boothbay Harbor Congregational church archives [hereinafter BHCCA]. On minister's salary, see BCM, March 2, 1942 and April 4, 1942; on new families as potential members, see BCM, January 11, 1943.

630 On Fosdick, Hodgdon and Spencer checks, see BCM, November 1, 1942.

631 On cold winters, see *Boothbay Register* [hereinafter *BR*], January 1, 1943:1; on vestry project see BCM, January, 11, 1943; on "buckling vestry floor," BCM, April 4, 1942 and April 20, 1942, where committee voted to raised Gray's salary by $100 a year.

632 On Gray stating he may be called into military, see BCM, April 20, 1942; on "recalling" Gray and increasing salary, see BCM, January 11, 1943; February 1, 1943; and March 1, 1943; on union services see BCM, February 15, 1943 and "Proposed Plan for a Series of Union Services," in BCM, March 1, 1943; see also *BR*, March 12, 1943.

633 "James B. Perkins, 66, Dies After Outstanding Career," *BR*, January 15, 1948:1.

634 See, "Report of Annual Meeting, in BCM, January 5, 1942; on Congregational Guild, see Minutes of Congregational Guild Meeting, January 22, 1942, in BHCCA [hereinafter CGM; see also Minutes of Meetings, February 19, 1942; March 19, 1942; on Samples' minesweeper trials and sandwich sales, January 7, 1943; on "Cootie," February 18, 1943, in CGM.

635 On Congregational Guild fundraising activities during World War II, see CGM, January 22, 1942, March 19, 1942, November 2, 1942; February 4, 1943, March 18, 1943.

636 On Gray's departure, *BR,* April 7, 1944; on "Installation of Rev. Aubrey Hastings, see Rodney W. Roundy, Congregational Church Conference of Maine, et. al., to Mrs. Benjamin Rand, October 25, 1944; and Roundy to James Blenn Perkins, November 6, 1944, both found in Box 2, Folder 1940-52, BHCCA.

637 See "Yearly Summaries of Activities, 1944–1945," in CGM.

638 On fire, annual meeting and election of officers, see BR, January 12, 1945:1.

639 Financial Report of Dorcas Guild, in Minutes of Annual Meeting of Congregational Church of Boothbay Harbor, January 8, 1945.

640 See CGM, November 1, 1945; BR, January 4, 1946; BCM, January 1946.

641 On postwar culture, Cohen, *Consumers' Republic,* pp. 118, 153–157; Loren Baritz, *The Good Life: The Meaning of Success for the American Middle Class* (New York: Harper and Row, 1989).

642 Halberstam, *The Fifties,* pp. 277–280, 472, 485, 489

643 Edwin Gaustad and Leigh Schmidt, *The Religious History of America, revised edn.* (New York: Harper One, 2002), pp. 318-319; for Niebuhr quote on religious revival as one of "emotion, not religion per se" See Baritz, *The Good Life,* p. 223. On Billy Graham, see Grant Wheeler, *America's Pastor: Billy Graham and the Shaping of a Nation* (Cambridge: Harvard University Press, 2014).

644 Gaustad and Schmidt, *Religious History of America,* p. 341.

645 U.S. Bureau of the Census, 1900, 1920, 1930, 1940, 1950, 1960, 1970; Clifford, *The Boothbay Harbor Region, 1906–1960,* pp. 275-348.

646 Clifford, *Boothbay Harbor Region,* pp. 263–264; BR, December 22, 1950; July 6, 1951, February 8, 1952, and July 2, 1954.

647 For Whitnall biography, see his obituary in BR, May 21, 1948.

648 See Whitnall's" Minister's Report for 1945," c. January 1946, found in Box 2, folder, 1945–1948, BHCCR; on Portland, World War II, and "Girl Problem," see John F. Bauman, *Gateway to Vacationland: The Making of Portland, Maine* (Amherst: University of Massachusetts Press, 2012); see also James Gilbert, *A Cycle of Outrage: America's Reaction to the Juvenile Delinquent in the 1950s* (New York: Oxford, 1986).

649 See Whitnall's Minister's Report, January 1945.

650 For Whitnall quote, see BR, August 9, 1946.

651 BR, March 7, 1947:7; and June 13, 1947.

652 BR, January 10, 1947; see, "Superintendent's Report of Church School for 1945," mimeographed, c. January 1945, found in Box 2, folder 1945-48, BHCCR; on poor health, see BR, March 29, 1946:8.

653 Congo Guild records, 1945–1948; Blenn Perkins' death, BR, January 16, 1948; on Whitnall's death, BR, May 21, 1948:1.

654 On Campbell see BR, September 3, 1948:1.

655 BR, September 3, 1948; program "One Hundredth Anniversary: Congregational Church, Boothbay Harbor, *Maine, 1848–1948,*" in possession of the author.

656 See Perkins obituary, BR, January 19, 1995.

657 See Congregational Guild Minutes, January 8, 1948, and February 5, 1948.

658 The author of this chapter was born and raised in the Evangelical and Reformed Church and was age ten in 1948. He attended church with his parents "religiously;" his uncle, who died in 1945, had been a minister in the E&R church. He recalls nary a word being spoken about the "Merger" in his Tabor Evangelical Reformed Church far from Boothbay Harbor, in Philadelphia, Pennsylvania.

659 See Gaustad and Schmidt, *Religious History of America*, p. 393; David K. Ford, chair of the Committee of Fifteen, "A Letter Missive to all Congregational

Churches," forwarding "Joint Statement adopted in Cleveland, November 10, 1948;" and also in favor of the merger, pamphlet, Raymond Calkins, *An Open Letter Regarding the Proposed Union with the Evangelical and Reformed Church* (Cambridge, Massachusetts, self-published, 1949), found in Merger File, BHCCR.

660 See "Whence This Merger?" in *ANTIMERGER*, Number 1, Volume 1 (Chicago: Antimerger Committee, November 1948). Hallowell and Bangor were centers of antimerger fervor, see pamphlet, Professor Marion J. Bradshaw, *I, Respectfully Reply to Dr. Merrill* (December 21, 1948); pamphlet, Bradshaw, *Shall We Vote in the Dark, undated*). Chicago was one of the centers of antimerger activity, see Malcolm K. Burton, *Legal Grounds for Repudiating Oberlin Action on Merger*, August 20, 1948; all in Merger File, BHCCR.

661 See handwritten, annotated list of "Members of the Congregational Church," c. 1948, found in Box 2, BHCCR; U.S. Bureau of the Census, *Sixteenth Census of the U.S: Census Tract Data, Boothbay Harbor, 1940* (Washington, D.C.: GPO, 1940). The 1940 manuscript or enumerated (detailed demographic data) census is the last one available for researchers.

662 On Search, see Rev. Horace Holton to Mrs. Benjamin Rand, April 12, 1949; Wilbur Bull to Rand, May 17, 1949; and Gledhill to Rand, June 8, 1949, all in Box 2, BHCCR.

663 On Korean War, David Halberstam, *The Coldest Winter: America and the Korean War* (New York: Hyperion, 2007).

664 On 1950s shipbuilding contracts, BR, December 22, 1950, January 18, 1952, July 2, 1954, June 24, 1955.

665 On Fishing Industry, BR, February 24, 1950; "Hope for Shoe Factory," BR, October 19, 1951; "Region Must Raise $35,000 Before Shoe Factory Opens," BR, January 1, 1951; "Drop Shoe Factory Project," BR, June 13, 1952.

666 On high school, see Clifford, *Boothbay Harbor Region,* pp. 275–279; BR, March 30, 1950; April 6, 1951; November 8, 1954; on Route 1, BR, January 4, 1952; on early summer settlements and tourism, Bauman, *Gateway to Vacationland,* 72, 90-95; Sidney Baldwin, *Casting off from Boothbay Harbor* (Booth-

bay Harbor: Boothbay Harbor Press, 1948); for new shops, BR, June 22, 1951, July 3, 1953. On tuna tournament and Rupert Neily's festival, see BR, July 27, 1951, January 25, 1952, and August 21, 1953.

667 Gledhill's sermons, BR, June 30, 1950, July 16, 1950, February 25, 1952, February 8, 1953. For sample of summer preaching, see Robbins, BR, July 17, 1952; Gilkey, BR, August 13, 1951; and Baldwin, BR, August 20, 1951.

668 John Howard Stevens and John Calvin Stevens II to James Blenn Perkins, July 17, 1953 submitting "schemes B, C, and D." On January 3, 1955 at Congregational meeting church voted to adopt budget and voted "to raise sum not to exceed $20,000 to build an addition to vestry and equip same." See BCM, Box 1, BHCCR.

669 February 3, 1954, Rev. Edward L. Manning accepts call to church at $3,600, see Box 2, BCM, February 3, 1954; Manning had been guest preacher January, 24, 1954, see BR, January 22, 1954.

670 Neil Sheehan, *A Bright and Shining Lie: John Paul Vann and America in Vietnam* (New York: Random House, 1988); see also, Allen J. Matusow, *The Unraveling of America: A History of Liberalism in the 1960s* (New York: Harper and Row, 1984).

671 Taylor Branch, *Parting the Waters: America in the King Years, 1954-1963* (New York: Simon and Schuster, 1988), passim.

672 BR, January 22, 1955 and August 2, 1954.

673 On movie "Carousel," see BR, July 8, 1955 and August 26, 1955; on House of Logan, BR, May 20 1955.

674 Business Committee (Norman Hodgdon, George Vaughn, Mrs. Clarence Dodge, Mrs. Caroline Kendrick, Mrs. Edward Dunton, Mrs. Robert Walbridge, Mrs. Mabel Rand, Miss Irene Fowle, Rev. Edward Manning, to members and friends of the Congregational Church, July 10, 1954, in BCM, Box 2, BHCCR.

675 For new vestry, see "Minute Book, Building Committee for New Vestry." See minutes of building committee, January 4, 1955, January 10, 1955, January 25, 1955, April 11, 1955, April 25, 1955, August 20, 1955, September 9, 1955,

440   LIVELY STONES

and November 29, 1955, in Box 1, BHCCR.

676 BR, October 17, 1954; January 23, 1955; February 20, 1955.

677 On Welty's first sermon, see BR, February 4, 1956, and February 14, 1956; on fishing, Clifford, *Boothbay Harbor Region,* p. 324; on labor issues and Samples' final two minesweepers, see BR, March 29, 1956, and April 4, 1956.

678 On Hodgdon's naval contract and its shift to pleasure craft, see BR, February 13, 1958; on sloop, BR, July 17, 1958, and March 29, 1959.

679 On high school, BR, February 12, 1954 and January 12, 1956; for Baldwin quote, BR, July 17, 1958.

680 BR, March 6, 1958.

681 BR, May 12, 1956 [Welty's first sermon], May 19, 1956; June 3, 1956; January 27, 1957; February 3, 1957; May 19, 1957, September 8, 1957. For summer preachers, Robbins, BR, July 8, 1956; Lenhart, August 26, 1956; Shepard, July 14, 1957.

682 "Report of the Uniting General Synod," July 12, 1957, p. 22, found in www.ucc.org-US/short-course/the-united-church-of-christ-html.

683 On church officers, see BR, January 9, 1958.

684 On Hill-Burton Act (1946), see Rosemary Stevens, *In Sickness and in Wealth: American Hospitals in the Twentieth Century* (Baltimore: Johns Hopkins, 1999); on St. Andrews Hospital, BR, March 17, 1960 and May 19, 1960; also Clifford, *Boothbay Harbor Region*, pp. 283–285; and BR, May 5, 1960.

685 BR, November 14, 1960.

686 On fluorine in water, BR, February 15, 1962; polio vaccine, BR, March 28, 1963; on sewage problem, BR, April 26, 1962, February 7, 1963; Rachael Carson's *Silent Spring,* BR, October 4, 1962.

687 *Stephen I. Engel v. William J. Vitale,* 370, U.S. 421 (1962);

688 Ivan Welty on "Prayer Ruling," in BR, July 5, 1962.

689 The *Boothbay Register* on August 9 carried huge picture of JFK, and the Strand movie theater displayed a sign " Mr. President Welcome to Boothbay Harbor, " see BR, August 9, 1962; also "2500, On Land and Sea, Greet JFK As He Arrives For Sunday Services," in BR, August 18, 1962.

690 BR, August 16, 1962; November 28, 1963.

691 On vote to join UCC, see BCM, May 1, 1961.

692 On securities, see BCM, May 1, 1961, December 4, 1961; on Welty staying as long as he wishes, BCM, December 31, 1961; on Welty sermon topics, *BR*, January 28, 1961; October 26, 1961,

693 On Alexander Tener and Tener Gift of Land, see BR, September 14, 1961; BCM, February 1, 1965.

CHAPTER 11

694 On the 1960s, see William L. O'Neill, *Coming Apart: An Informal History of America in the 1960s* (New York: Quadrangle, 1971); David A. Hollinger, "After Cloven Tongues of Fire: Ecumenical Protestantism and the Modern Encounter with Diversity," *Journal of American History* (June 2011): 21-47; Harvey Cox, *The Secular City: Secularization and Urbanization in Theological Perspective* (New York: 1965); on Nixon, Ford, and Carter, see Eric Foner, *Give me Liberty! An American History, Vol. 2* (New York: W.W. Norton, 2006); Douglas Brinkley, *Gerald R. Ford* (New York: New York Times Books, 2007); Peter G. Bourne, *Jimmy Carter: A Comprehensive History from Plains to Postpresidency* (New York: Scribners, 1997).

695 See Record of the Ordination of Richard B. Balmforth, January 22, 1967, found in Records of the Boothbay Harbor Congregational church, January 11, 1967-May 14, 1979, in Box 2, Boothbay Harbor Congregational Church Archives [hereinafter BHCCA]; see also, church business committee records, [hereinafter BCR], June 1, 1965, BHCCA; and also, "Rev. Richard B. Balmforth to be Ordained Sunday," in *Boothbay Register* [hereinafter *BR*], February 2, 1967.

696 Chip Griffin, personal interview with Jerry and Donna Closson, Boothbay Harbor, Maine, March 19, 2011; Chip Griffin, personal interview with Leah Sample, Boothbay Harbor Maine, February 19, 2011, March 12, 2011, and April 10, 2011.

697 "Special Meeting—An Ecclesiastical Council of the Lincoln Association of the United Church of Christ to Examine Rev. Richard B. Balmforth (Called to the pastorate of this church June 7, 1965) now candidate for ordination as a minister of the Congregational Church of Boothbay Harbor in the United Church of Christ," January 22, 1967, found in Congregational Church of Boothbay Harbor, business committee minutes, January 22, 1967.

698 "From the Pastor's Desk: the Cosmic Day," in BR, July 24, 1969.

699 "Pastor's Report, Annual Church Meeting, January 13, 1969," Box 2, Congregational Church Annual Reports, 1966–1969, BHCCA.

700 For quote, see minutes of the business committee, March 8, 1966, BCM.

701 Jerry and Donna Closson interview with Chip Griffin; on Tener gift, Letter from Judge Alexander Tener to Mr. Tilton, September 14, 1965, in BCR; on Etta Brewer, see Arthur Beaulieu to James Blenn Perkins, Jr. November 17, 1967, Box 2, File 13, Church Financial Reports, 1966–1973, BHCCA.

702 Interview John F. Bauman and Rev. Sarah Foulger with Andrew Holmes in minister's study, Boothbay Harbor Congregational Church, January 8, 2015.

703 Records of Congregational Church of Boothbay Harbor Real Estate Holdings from Law Offices of Franklin A. Poe, Road End File, in BHCCA; on furnishings, see Church Financial Reports, 1966–1973, Box 2, File 3, BHCCA.

704 On Pierce Marine dockage controversy, see Balmforth to Mr. Lloyd Whitney, chair of business committee, September 30, 1970, BCR; and Francis and Mildred Pierce to Board of Trustees, Boothbay Harbor Congregational Church, January 27, 1970, and Willard Van Allen to Pierce Marine, February 3, 1970 all in Box Two, BCR, 1970–1972, BHCCA.

705 Griffin interviews with Sample and Closson.

706 On "derogation" and "criticism," see minutes of church business committee, May 6, 1968; and on the church not being "involved in community and national affairs," see Marge Creaser to business committee, November 27, 1970, both in Box 2, BCM.

707 See "Boothbay Harbor Congregational Church Financial Statement for December 31, 1967;" Box 2, folder 13, Church Financial Reports, 1966–1975, BHCCA; on "no longer a rich church," see "Financial Report of Boothbay Harbor Congregational Church, Calendar Year 1971, Box 2, BCM.

708 Balmforth to Lloyd Whitney, July 30, 1970, Box 2, BCM; Lloyd Whitney, chair of business committee to "To Whom it May Concern," undated, Box 2, BCM; "Rev. and Mrs. Balmforth to Leave Pastorate Here," BR, October 29, 1970.

709 On pulpit committee and choice of David Laney as interim pastor, see Church Financial Reports, 1966–1973, Box 2, Folder 13, BCM; pulpit committee submitted to the business committee, March 7, 1971, a long and detailed letter explaining exactly how they conducted their search for a new minister and justifying their selection of Bruce Riegel, see report of search committee to business committee, March 7, 1971, Box 2, business committee records, 1971, BCM.

710 Report of search committee to business committee, March 7, 1971.

711 Business committee minutes, March 9, 1971, BCM.

712 Business committee minutes, October 18, 1971, BCM.

713 Business committee minutes, December 27, 1971; January 17, 1972; February 18, 1972.

714 Riegel purchased his own mooring. On March 7, 1972, the business committee voted to buy the mooring from Mr. Riegel "at a value not to exceed $50 with payment delayed until May or June if possible." Business committee minutes, March 7, 1972, BCM.

715 Pastor's Report, Annual Church Meeting, January 11, 1972, Box 2, Church Business Records, 1970–1972; "Rev. Bruce Riegel Resigns-Plans to Leave Ministry," BR, March 23, 1972. On Jung, see Wikipedia.org/wiki/Carl Jung.

716 "Financial Report of Boothbay Harbor Congregational Church, Calendar Year 1971, Box 2, business committee records, January 1972. August 26, 1972, Box 2, pastor search committee Records, 1972.

717 Sumner Fairbanks to William MacCormick, August 26, 1972, Box 2, search committee, BHCCA.

718 William MacCormick to Rev. Arthur Rice in Roxbury, MA. August 12, 1972, in search committee files, Box 2, BHCCA.

719 Willim A. Thompson, to Rev. William R. Booth (notifying Thompson of Hartman's inclination to leave the large Greensburg church for a smaller church like Boothbay Harbor), July 25, 1972, Box 2, search committee records.

720 Charles S. Hartman to MacCormick, September 2, 1972, in Box 2, search committee records, 1972, BHCCA.

721 William A. MacCormick to "Dear Friends," September 19, 1972, Box 2, search committee records, 1972, BHCCA.

722 Harlow Russell to "the members of the Boothbay Harbor Congregational Church," October 1, 1972, in Box 2, search committee records, 1972; on Harlow Russell, see "Harlow Russell to Observe 100th Birthday," BR, March 18, 1976.

723 Search committee report, September 14, 1972, Box 3, Folder 4, BHCCA.

724 Résumé or "Ministerial Record" of Charles S. Hartman, September 1970, submitted to search committee in letter of Charles Hartman to William M. Thompson, August 2, 1972, found in Box 2, search committee records, 1972.

725 On Nixon, Ford, and Carter, see Foner, *Give Me Liberty!*; Brinkley, *Gerald R. Ford*; and Bourne, *Jimmy Carter: A Comprehensive Biography*.

726 Chip Griffin, "An Open Letter to Area Residents," BR, November 2, 1972; Mary Brewer, "A Landmark Year," BR, January 3, 1974.

727 "Senator Muskie Meets with Fishermen to Discuss Lab Closing Here Saturday," BR, March 22, 1973; "Hodgdon Bros. Boatyard Unaffected by Sale," BR, March 18, 1976; brochure on "Boothbay Harbor Region," included in packet sent to Hartman, see Box 2, search committee records, 1972.

728 "Pastor's Report for the Year 1972," in Box 2, File 13, "Warrant for Annual Meeting," January 8, 1973, BRCCA.

729 "'Meals on Wheels' Project Begins Service Here in Region on Monday," June 21, 1973; "Boothbay Harbor Congregational Church," BR, September 2, 1976.

730 Business committee minutes, October 9, 1973.

731 On CETA, see State of Maine Executive Department Office of Manpower to County Municipal Unit, Stephen Bennett, Director of Title II, CETA, October 22, 1974, including typed notes of Hartman's proposal, in Box 2 Envelope 7, CETA Proposal, BHCCA; also on CETA, see "CETA to Continue But Exact Amount Not Yet Known," BR, April 29, 1976. See also business committee minutes, January 26, 1975, and March 11, 1975, both in BCM.

732 On Black Colleges and Achievement Fund, see "Minister's Report for 1974," Box 2, Folder F13; on "Liberty Tree," see photograph in BR, July 18, 1976; on Cloutier and elderly housing, see "Zoning Board Grants Variance to Elderly Housing Project," BR, January 8, 1976.

733 See Hartman "Minister's Reports for 1973 and 1974" and "Minister's Report for 1977," all in Box 3, File 4; on trip to New York, see "Report of Young People" in Annual Report for 1974

734 Business committee minutes, December 8, 1970, July 27, 1976, BCM.

735 On purchase of Cutts property, see Church Bulletin, August 21, 1977; "Congregation Votes to Purchase Cutts Property at Congregational Meeting August 14th," BHCCA.

736 Harold Wood to business committee, May 6, 1978, Box 2, File 12; Hartman to Balmforth, April 27, 1978, and Balmforth to Hartman, May 3, 1978, both in Box 2, File 10.

737 Closson interview with Chip Griffin

738 Report of the interim minister at annual meeting of Congregational church, January 28, 1979, Box 3, Folder 4.

739 Patti Jo Barter to Karl Phillippi, January 12, 1979, in Box 2, Folder 2.

740 Robert Dallek, *Ronald Reagan: The Politics of Symbolism* (Cambridge: Harvard University Press, 1984), pp. 63-64; Gary Wills, *Reagan's America* (New York: Penguin, 1988); "Ronald Reagan," http://wikipedia.org.

741 BR, May 1980 and December1981; see also, business committee to "Members and Friends of Boothbay Harbor Congregational Church, May 20, 1981, and August 11, 1981, Box 3, Folder 17, Building Repair Fund, BHCCA.

742 On Cutts house, see Minutes of Congregational church meeting, June 21, 1981, Box 3, Folder 17, Building Repair Fund

743 Karen Chandler Leatherbee, RN, to Rev. Karl Phillippi, September 25, 1979, and Phillippi to Leatherbee November 29, 1979, Box 3, File 9; on Menninger, see BR, January 1981; Karl Menninger, *Whatever Became of Sin* (New York: Bantam, 1988).

744 BR, July-Aug, 1980.

745 Chip Griffin interviews with Leah Sample and the Clossons; on Phillippi resignation, see Phillippi to business committee, September 29, 1981, in Box 3, Folder 20. On Karl Phillippi as Noah and on brown bag lunches, see personal communication, Sarah Foulger to author, August 11, 2015.

746 *U.S. Navy Biography*, Rear Admiral Joseph David Stinson, forwarded as part of email: Rev. Dr. Joseph David Stinson to author, September 17, 2014. The email also included a record of Rev. Stinson's ministerial career, including highlights of his ministry at the Boothbay Harbor Congregational church.

747 Email, Stinson to author, September 9, 2014; *Boothbay Harbinger: The Newsletter of the Congregational Church*. The *Boothbay Harbinger* was published and mailed out to the congregation monthly. Hereinafter the name will be shortened to *Harbinger* and month without volume or number. It can be found in the BHCCA] July and August, 1983; BR, July 11, 1982 and August 15, 1982.

748 *Harbinger,* August 1982, September 1982, January 1983.

749 *Harbinger,* April 1983; also BR, July 24, 1984.

750 John F. Bauman and the Rev. Dr. Sarah Foulger, personal interview with Andrew Holmes, January 8, 2015; see also Andrew Holmes to the Rev. Peter Panagore, undated, Box 4, BHCCR.

751 *Harbinger,* February, 1983, March 1983, August 1983, September 1983, August 1984, May 1985; BR, October 3, 1985.

752 *Harbinger,* March 1984, December 1984, October 1985.

753 BR, June 17, 1985

754 *Harbinger,* March 1984, August 1984; Andrew Holmes, chair of business committee to Stinson, February 2, 1984, Box 7, business committee minutes; minutes of business committee, December 12, 1984, Box 5, BHCCA; *Harbinger,* February 1984.

CHAPTER 12

755 Joseph David Stinson, "What's to be Done About A Herod?" A Sermon Preached by Rev. Stinson, Congregational Church of Boothbay Harbor on the First Sunday After Christmas, 1990, Box 8, Newsletter Current File, BHCCA.

756 See, Eric Foner, *Give me Liberty! An American History, Vol. 2* (New York: W.W. Norton, 2006).

757 U.S. Census 1980, 1990, 2000; *Boothbay Registers* for years 1980–2000.

758 On NORCs, see *Leading Age; 2014 Boothbay Comprehensive Plan,* See demographic data in Appendix to plan.

759 On "Coastal Maine-Four Season Vacationland,"), see BR, October 13, 1988; on change, See "25 Years Brings Many Changes in Waterfront," in BR, March 19, 1987. The article pointed out that the old Pierce and Hartung lumber yard was now the Boothbay Harbor Inn and that the Polychoke boat builders had become the Rocktide Inn; and also BR, October 13, 1988.

760 On Cowan, see "Publisher Howard S. Cowan Dies at 72," BR, January 29, 1987; see the Windjammer Days edition of BR, July 9, 1987; on February 19,

1987 Marylouise Cowan, his widow, assumed publisher duties, see BR, February 19, 1987.

761 On Bigelow's Charles Yentsch testifying about the need for a "major overhaul of solid waste disposal," see BR, September 17, 1987; on zoning and growth controls, see "Boothbay Takes a Cautious Look Ahead," BR, December 3, 1987, and "Many Changes in Waterfront," BR, March 19, 1987.

762 BR, August 6, 1987.

763 Business committee minutes [hereinafter BCM], December 12, 1985, Box 8, BHCCA. The business committee in 1986 included Charles Gillespie, Jack Hanselman, Andrew Holmes, David Parkhurst, and Robert Campbell; for statistics on the church's growth, see United Church of Christ Board for Homeland Missions, "United Church of Christ Trend Reports, Eleven Year Church Profile Based on Data Reported in UCC Yearbooks," for Boothbay Harbor, ME Congregational, in Box 8, BHCCA.

764 "Annual Report of the Council, 1986," found in BCM, January 18, 1987, in Box 18, BHCCA; personal interview, John F. Bauman and Sarah Foulger with Andrew Holmes, Boothbay Harbor, January 8, 2015.

765 "Annual Report of the Council, 1986," In BCM, January 18, 1987.

766 "Annual Report of the Council, 1986," in BCM, January 18, 1987.

767 On Church Council and launch of planning, including Kidd's draft of church renovations, see BCM, July 21, 1986; and August, 18, 1986. Box 8, BHCCA.

768 See " Pastor's Report, Annual Meeting Reports for 1986," found in BCM, January 18, 1987, Box 8, BHCCA.

769 Faith for the Future File, Otis A. Maxfield, Chair of Faith for the Future Campaign, to George McEvoy, December 12, 1989. On "timid little thing" see Andrew Holmes to John F. Bauman, January 11, 2015.

770 Faith for the Future File, Maxfield to McEvoy, June 15, 1990; BCM, July 16, 1990, August 3, 1990.

771 BCM September 6, 1990.

772 BCM, September 17, 1990.

773 BR, September 6, 1990; BCM, April 16, 1990, August 3, 1990, September 17, 1990.

774 BCM, April 16, 1990.

775 BCM, August 20, 1990; September 17, 1990.

776 BCM, December 10, 1990.

777 BCM, Minutes of Annual Meeting, January 27, 1992.

778 BCM, Minutes of Annual Meeting, January 27, 1992; Faith for the Future File, "Dig Deeper Campaign," April 1991; Otis A. Maxfield to Members of the Congregation, undated c. September 1991.

779 Annual Report for 1992 (January 1993). In January 1993 Martha Campbell stepped down as church treasurer. Her replacement was Melodee Burnham.

780 On Svendsen, see BR, February, 25, 1993, July 22, 1993, September 2, 1993; On Luccock, see July 22, 1993; on Panagore's arrival, BR, November 4, 1993.

781 See "United Church of Christ," in Wikipedia.org/wiki.unitedchurch-of-christ.

782 See "To All Members," from Robert Shepard, Senior Deacon, "SUBJECT: Our UCC Connection and Our Mission Giving: A Response to the Report and Charge of Long Range Planning Committee, January 1996," found in Diaconate File, Box 4, BHCCA

783 "Profile of the Congregational Church of Boothbay Harbor, United Church of Christ: Prepared in October 1992 in connection with the search for a new pastor, c. October 1992, in search committee File, Box 4, BHCCA.

784 Church Council and search committee minutes, July 1993, Box 4; personal interview, author with Peter Panagore, Boothbay Harbor, December 9, 2014.

785 Personal Interview, author with Peter Panagore, Boothbay Harbor, December 9, 2014.

786 Peter Panagore, "Ministerial Profile, Part I: Personal History" and "Ministerial Profile: Part II: Statement on Ministry," February 29, 1992, in search committee File, Box 4; personal interview, John F. Bauman and Sarah Foulger with Andrew Homes, January 8, 2015.

787 Church Council, Annual Report for 1994 (January 1995), in Box 4.

788 Andrew Holmes to Peter Panagore, undated, (c. 1995), in Box 4.

789 Panagore, "Ministerial Profile," February 29, 1992; Council Minutes, April 19, 1995; Diaconate Minutes; on being computer savvy, see Council Minutes, June 21, 1995.1

790 Personal interview, author with Peter Panagore, Boothbay Harbor, December 9, 2014.

791 BCM, "Bond Committee Report, January 31, 1994; BCM, February 1, 1994; February 16, 1994.

792 Long Range Planning Committee Minutes, October 20, 1994, Box 4; BCM, October 18, 1994; October 31, 1994; Diaconate Minutes, October 11, 1994.

793 BCM, February 5, 1995; Minutes of Special Business Committee Meeting, February 26, 1995; Long Range Planning Committee Minutes, "February 2, 1995, all in Box 5, BHCCA.

794 Minutes of Church Council, September 20, 1995, on "Proposed Bylaws Revision;" Minutes of Church Council, October 18, 1995, on $6,000 shortfall.

795 BCM, January 16, 1996; BCM, May 21, 1996; at the June 18, 1996 meeting it was announced that Debi Babcock had become the new church secretary.

796 BCM, January 16, 1996; Long Range Planning Committee Minutes, April 4, 1996.

797 Board of Trustees Records, Report of Annual Meeting, January 1997; Board of Trustees Records, Audrey Curtis to Board of Trustees, "Estimated Financial Condition as of 3/23/97;" on sale of parsonage, Board of Trustees Minutes, June 18, 1996, that stated that Tindall and Callahan had been selected to represent the church in the sale of the parsonage at an asking price of

$369,000; on May 19, 1997, sale to Lloyds, see Franklin A. Poe (church lawyer) to Robert Memory, senior trustee, March 25, 1997. On proceeds, see Board of Trustees Minutes, June 22, 1997.

798 Minutes of the Board of Trustees, January 21, 1997.

799 Board of Trustees Minutes, March 17, 1998

800 Board of Trustees Minutes, June 16, 1998.

801 Personal interview, John F. Bauman with Peter Panagore, December 9, 2014, Boothbay Harbor; "Melodee Burnham Pleads Guilty of Theft," BR, November 4, 1999, p.1.

802 "Melodee Burnham Pleads Guilty," BR, November 4, 1999.

803 Minutes of Special Meeting of the Trustees, December 7, 1999; Ralph Prall, "To the Deacons." November 8, 1999. On civil suits, see Thomas Leahy of First Federal to Franklin Poe, December 2, 1999, Box 4.

804 Susan E. Bogart, secretary to the board of trustees, "Statement of Congregational Church of Boothbay Harbor to be read at Sentencing Hearing," in Board of Trustees Minutes, December 7, 1999, Box 4.

805 Burnham Pleads Guilty of Theft," in BR, November 4, 1999, p.1.

806 Personal interview, John F. Bauman with Peter Panagore, December 9, 2014.

CHAPTER 13

807 John B. Cobb, Jr., *Theology in the Twenty-First Century. 1991*

808 Cobb. *Theology*, p.19.

809 http://en.wikipedia.org/wiki/Neo-orthodoxy:- Neo-orthodoxy, in Europe also known as a theology of crisis and dialectical theology, is an approach to theology in Protestantism developed in the aftermath of the First World War(1914–18). It is characterized as a reaction against doctrines of nineteenth

century liberal theology, particularly the Social Gospel as a human solution to all of humanity's problems and a reevaluation of the teachings of the Reformation.

810 The Rev. Dr. John Phillip Newell is based in Edinburgh, Scotland. He has been the Warden of Iona Abbey in the Western Isles of Scotland, and is now Companion Theologian for the American Spirituality Center of Casa del Sol at Ghost Ranch in the high desert of New Mexico where he and his wife spend their summers.

811 Celtic Christianity had its roots especially across Britain, Ireland and Scotland. There "a religion immersed in the natural world arose at some unknown point in history when the glaciers had left and people found their way once again to these northern reaches of sea and land. Central to Celtic thought was the close relationship between the "other world," the divine; and the land and the waters where springs, rivers and hills were inhabited by spirits. The sea, ever near, influenced everything. …The Wesleyan movement beginning with John and Charles Wesley in 1700s. Great Britain picked up some of the Celtic Christian strands of belief and practice. In particular, the hymns of Charles Wesley present Celtic influence in their attention to the cosmic creation, the world sky-sea-wind-cloud-sun, human passions, vivid descriptive words/concepts and the orderly daily life. This was in contrast to the Reformation from the continent with its fierce presentation of the Written Word as of elemental importance over and above all natural life. Awareness and celebration of nature was an alien thought to some Christian leaders in early times. However, many Christians found the natural world to be evidence of the mind of God. And a growing number of Christians in the twentieth century were discovering again what their Celtic ancestors knew well: the handiwork of the creator is a cause for thanksgiving and a school of learning." (See http://www.christianitysite. com/Celticchristianity.htm)

812 Marcus Borg was a historian and theologian who died in 2015. For "a generation he helped popularize intense debates about the historical Jesus and the veracity and meaning of the New Testament." Fredrick Schmidt, Jr., professor of spiritual formation at Garrett-Evangelical Theological Seminary, counted Borg as a "cherished friend." "Marcus Borg, born in Fergus Falls, MN, shaped the conversation about Jesus, the church and scripture in powerful ways,"

Schmidt wrote. "I came to different conclusions about a number of issues but Marc was always incisive, tenacious, thoughtful and unfailingly gracious." Once Borg wrote, "Imagine that Christianity is about loving God. Imagine that it's not about the self and its concerns, about what's in it for me, whether that be a blessed afterlife or prosperity in this life." (See *The Christian Century*, February 18, 2015. p. 15.)

813 Progressive Christianity…is characterized by a willingness to question tradition, acceptance of human diversity, a strong emphasis on social justice and care for the poor and the oppressed, and environmental stewardship of the earth. Progressive Christians have a deep belief in the centrality of the instruction to "love one another" (John 15:17) within the teaching of Jesus Christ. This leads to a focus on promoting values such as compassion, justice, mercy, tolerance, often through political activism. (See http://en.wikipedia.org/wiki/Progressive_Christianity)

814 These words are from the installation questions listed in the Presbyterian Church, USA's Book of Order.

815 Report of the search committee, 2004.

816 Sarah Foulger, sermon delivered on October 19, 2014.

817 Pastor's annual report for 2011.

818 Jackie and Pete Mundy, "Living Stones."

819 Chip Griffin, Living Stones."

820 Ted Repa, "Living Stones."

821 Russ Hoffman, "Living Stones."

822 Romans 8:28.

823 Barbara Brown Zikmund, *Theology and Identity: Traditions, Movement, and Polity in the United Church of Christ*, (New York: Pilgrim Press, 1990.)

824 Pastor's annual report for 2008.

825 Pastor's annual report, January 27, 2013.

826 Deanne Tibbetts' 2013 annual Sunday School report.

827 Roger Severance, "Annual Report for the Trustees," January, 2005.

828 Donald Duncan, "Rejoicing at the Congregational Church" *Boothbay Register*, May 2, 2014.

829 These sentences included by Dent when Foulger agreed to permit her picture to be included in the chapter.

830 "Open and Affirming" is the designation given to churches that have voted to be intentionally welcoming of all persons, regardless of age, gender, race, or sexual orientation.

831 "Annual Report of the Diaconate," January 2011-December 2011.

832 Foulger, Sarah, "Annual Report for the year 2013."

833 Information supplied courtesy of Fleet Davies.

834 Pastor's "Annual Report for 2012."

835 Foulger, Sarah. remarks made at the tenth anniversary of Rev. Dr. Foulger's service as the called pastor of the Congregational Church of Boothbay Harbor, October 19, 2014.

INDEX

Abenaki 235

Abbott, Mrs. Paul 279

Abolition 10, 126, 130, 141, 146-147

Adams,
    Jonathan viii, 95, 150, 159-160, 182
    Samuel 30, 45, 54-55, 117, 150, 160, 257

Adams Pond 117, 189

Addams, Jane 225

adultery 48, 51, 54, 86, 92, 101, 120, 122

African-American 6, 226, 298, 323

agrarian 59, 66, 80-81, 84-85

Albee, Obadiah 20

alcohol 103-105, 122-123, 128, 130, 134, 147, 180, 210
    alcoholism 9, 14, 148, 174, 176, 225

American Bible Society 110, 160, 224

American Colonization Society 130

American Legion 246, 257
    Charles E. Sherman Post 246

American Revolution 7-9, 23, 45, 58-59, 61, 66, 69, 72, 80-83, 85, 108-109, 114, 119, 257, 388

Anderson, Andrew 154, 183

Andover Theological Seminary 137-138, 271

Andrews,
    John 154, 387
    Martha 154
    Susan S. 154
    Appomattox 168

Arab Spring 357

Armistice service 257

Army 58, 68, 153, 162-165, 176, 180, 193, 219-220, 234, 260, 299-300, 323, 387
    Army of the Potomac 165

Arthur, President Chester A. 183

Articles of Faith & Covenant 154

Auld,
    Edwin 154
    Elup 157
    Daniel 154
    Eliza G. 154

Eunice F. 154
Frances M. 154
Jacob 116-117, 154, 158
James 56, 154, 157
John 56-57, 154-155, 159
Mary Ann 154

Awakening 7, 9, 22-24, 26, 40, 47-48, 67, 69, 81, 89, 106, 109-111, 125, 139, 146, 321
    Great Awakening 7, 9, 22-24, 26, 40, 69, 81, 89, 106, 109-111, 125, 139, 146, 321
    Second Great Awakening 7, 9, 89, 106, 109-111, 125, 146

Ball, Samuel 20

Balltown 23, 80-81

Balmforth, Rev. Richard B. ix, 299

Bangor Theological Seminary 3, 7, 94, 138-139, 151, 156-157, 160-163, 170, 173, 181-182, 187, 258-259, 281, 300, 330

baptism(s) 53-54, 80, 103

Baptist 23-24, 70, 75, 79, 81, 89, 97, 102, 106-108, 120-122, 126, 129, 133, 152, 176, 206, 235, 239, 243, 282, 286

Barker, Elliott 374, 377

Barter,
    Edward 141
    Isaac 141
    Sally 374, 378, 384
    William 141

Barth, Karl 196, 226, 251, 253-254

Bassett, Elton K. ix, 248

Bath 6, 92, 109, 117, 140, 158, 168, 179-180, 243, 266, 270, 273, 336, 342, 359, 391

Bath-Kol 85

Bayville 173, 178, 180

Baxter, Benjamin 133-134

Beale, Charles H. 239, 252

Beath,
    James T. 154-155, 159, 183
    Jeremiah 76, 96, 99, 104-105
    John 28-31, 34-35, 37, 39-40, 44-45, 47, 55, 57-58, 92, 98-99, 117, 372
    Mary 154-155
    Walter 14-15, 39

Beecher,
    Henry Ward 7
    Lyman 109, 130, 237
    Lyman Beecher Lecture 237

Beecher's Bibles 161

Belfast 40, 87-88, 156

Bible 21, 85-86, 106, 110, 160, 176, 181, 185, 194, 224, 237, 239-240, 244-246, 249, 251, 254, 261, 263, 320, 358, 360, 369, 374, 376-377, 384, 386
    Bible survey course 377

Bigelow Laboratory for Ocean Sciences 329, 365

Blake, Laura 308

Blake, Wilder 267, 291-292

Blair,
    Benjamin 154-155, 183
    Elizabeth Fullerton 188
    John 183, 185
    Margaret Fullerton 154-155

Blossom, Alden 173, 183

Bogart, Susan 345, 350-352

Booth, John Wilkes 168

Boothbay Common 30-31, 46, 91, 107, 328, 342

Boothbay Region High School 305, 312

Borg, Marcus 358

Boston University 359

Bowers, Sarah 51, 122

Boyd,
    Alexander 27
    Samuel 183
    Thomas 154, 173

Bradford, Walter P. ix, 209, 220, 227

Brewer, Mary 312

Briggs, Charles A. 195

Bristol 13-15, 19, 24-25, 40, 48, 51, 57, 59, 76, 80, 105, 126, 138, 149, 187, 220, 227, 359

Brown,
    Antoinette 147
    Edmund 28-29, 75

Brunner, Emil 254

Brunswick 18, 24-26, 41, 138, 285, 307, 359

Bryant, David 28, 75

Bulfinch, John J. 162

Burnham, Kim 363, 373, 376

Bushnell, Horace 7, 146

Buber, Martin 254

Burge, Sue 375

Burnham, Melodee 337, 345-346, 348-349, 351-352

by-laws 198, 228, 231, 258, 347-348, 360, 379

Calvin, John 20, 286, 321

Camden 65, 138, 188, 199, 205, 210, 359, 391-392

Campbell,
    Archie 267
    Mary 154

Canada 89, 112, 118, 167, 210, 225, 300, 304

Capital Campaign 92, 367, 380-381

care packages 382

Carousel (movie) 295

Carlisle, Charles 173, 183

Carter, John H. 183

Castine 58

Church, Catholic 198, 246, 293, 317, 385
    Roman, Our Lady Queen of Peace 246, 293, 385

census 125, 168, 197, 275, 282-283

centennial 97, 127, 172, 278-279

Chamberlain, Joshua 165, 182

Chancellorsville 164, 173

Children's Hospital in Boston 376

choir(s) 203, 249, 258, 260-262

Christian Endeavor Society 244, 256

Christian realism 254

Christmas 177, 216, 232, 248-249, 260, 262, 271, 278, 326, 328, 376, 386

Christian Mirror, The 130

Church World Service 321, 374, 382

Civil War 4, 6, 10, 30, 89, 91, 94, 112-114, 125, 146-148, 157-158, 162-168, 171-174, 178-179, 182-183, 187, 193, 212, 216, 314, 346, 386

Chicago race riots 194, 226

Clifford, Harold 256, 258, 285

Climo, Leslie 314

Closson, Donna 307, 393

Clough, Hannah Antoinette 150

Cobb, John B., Jr. 355

Cold Harbor 164-165, 173

Collier, Sir George 59-60

colonization 20, 125, 130, 142

Comprehensive Employment Training Act (CETA) 313

Conkling, Nathaniel W. 218

commerce 5, 84, 89, 107, 119, 126, 146, 148, 178, 285, 312, 316, 328-329

Commission Creed, 1883 178

Common English Bible 384

communion 17, 21-22, 48-51, 53, 93-94, 99, 106, 130, 172, 260, 382, 385, 389

Cook,
    Charles viii, 124, 127-129, 132-133, 135-137, 141-142, 148, 152, 172, 391
    Sophia 131, 133

cotton 17, 167

Coulombe, Paul 365

covenant 3, 11, 41-42, 91-93, 100, 121, 128, 154, 185, 291, 331, 365, 370-371, 392
    Covenant Hymn 370-371, 392

Cowan, Howard S. 329

Cox, Harvey 299

Cox, B.T. 180

Cragin, Carol 374

Damariscove 49, 115, 191

Dartmouth 110, 136, 151, 359, 374

Darwin, Charles 145, 176

Darwinism 193

Dash, Marion 372, 375

Davis, Israel 45, 48, 128

deaconesses 182, 188

Declaration on the Unity of the Church 176

Deer Isle, Maine 343

Department of Marine Resources 312

Depression, Great 10, 223, 227, 247, 249-250, 257, 265, 268, 272, 285, 296, 357

Dewey, John 193

disestablishment 90, 111, 135

dismissal 37, 51, 97, 134, 136, 152, 156, 255

dismissed 26, 38, 50, 116, 122, 127, 133, 135, 140, 150, 255

dispensationalism 176

doctrine 13, 23, 45-46, 69, 86, 106-107, 177, 224, 253

Dolloff, Addie 270, 279

Dolloff, Warren 183

domestic abuse 14

Dorcas Guild 221-222, 230, 235, 241, 261-262

Doree Taylor Foundation 385

Dow, Neal 147

Duckworth, Susan 374, 393

Dunbar, David 18, 25

Dunbar Homes 266

Duncan, Donald 381, 385, 387

Dunlap, Robert 26

Dunsford, Jon 375

earthquake 55, 356, 374

Easter 177-178, 241, 243, 259, 269, 271, 338, 376

Eastwood,
    David 377
    Judy 375, 393

Eddy, Mary Baker 176

Edinburgh 33, 36, 195-196

education 15, 39, 42, 126, 129-130, 134-136, 143, 171, 173, 177, 182, 187, 192-193, 210, 224, 229, 248, 252, 256, 261, 274, 282, 287, 322, 360, 367-368, 372-373, 375-377, 382

Christian education 182, 322, 375

Edwards, Jonathan viii, 22-24, 160, 321

Emerson, John 103, 185

embezzlement 8, 11, 350, 352, 354

Enlightenment, The 88

Enterprise 115, 142, 224-225, 308, 342

existentialism 176

Faith for the Future vii, 11, 325, 330-338, 342, 345-346, 353

Fairbanks, Sumner C. 307

Farnham, Weston 235, 247, 267

Federal Council of Churches 196-197, 201

Federal Housing Administration 267, 273

Finney, Charles Grandisson 7, 125

Fire 20, 116, 189, 201, 212, 232, 269, 272, 287, 290-291, 376

fish
- fish oil 10, 179
- fishing 5-6, 67, 74-75, 115, 126, 141, 147, 157, 161, 175, 178-179, 198, 266-267, 275-276, 283-285, 289, 295, 312, 327, 342
- mackerel 141, 161, 179
- menhaden 141, 179
- pogy, porgy 179

Fisher,
Charles 95, 155, 166
William H. 184

Fishermen's Festival 180, 329, 386

Fishermen's Wharf 291-292

Fitzgerald, F. Scott 226

Fletcher, Elliott B. 108

Ford, President Gerald 298, 311

fornication 48-49, 51-53, 86, 92, 101, 103, 122

Fosdick, Rev. Dr. Harry Emerson 5, 8-10, 192, 237-239, 205-206, 225, 252, 268, 279, 274-275, 279, 286, 309, 392

Fotos, George 334, 339

Foulger, Sarah iii, ix, 4, 6, 8-9, 125, 145, 175, 355, 358-359, 361-363, 377, 381, 386, 388, 392-393

Fredericksburg 165, 199

Freeman, Dorothy 375, 380

Freeman, Ned 345

French-Canadian 226

Fukuyama, Francis 325

Fuller,
John 101-102
Rachel 101-103

Fullerton, Ebeneezer 152

fundamentalism 9-10, 245

Gaewski, David 361-362

Gamage, Gleason 288

Garfield, President James A. 183

General Court 22, 34, 39, 43-44, 60-61, 67, 74, 85, 103, 106-107

Georgetown 18, 24-27, 49, 92, 317

Gettysburg 126, 164-166, 173

Gilded Age 193

Giles, Ethelyn 240

Gilman, Tristram 67

Gledhill, Rev. George ix, 283

Globalization 224, 274

Glusker, David 353

Goodrich, Sarah 359

Goudy & Stevens 4, 6, 266, 276, 284, 287, 329

Gould,
    Samuel Lamson viii, 149

Gove, John 154

Graham, Billy 10, 274, 357

Great Proprietors 7, 67, 80-81, 85, 108

Greene, Francis 23, 44, 66, 68, 118, 142, 163, 166, 178

Graham, Marjorie 319

Great Awakening 7, 9, 22-24, 26, 40, 69, 81, 89, 106, 109-111, 125, 139, 146, 321

Greene, Francis B. 44

Gregory, Dr. Philip 284, 292

Gregory Wing 376, 382

Griffin, Denise 374, 384, 394

Grinnell, Lori 376, 384

Grover, John 116

Guild, Congregational 262, 270, 279-280

Habitat for Humanity 377

Hamlin, Hannibal 162

Hanselman, Jack 332-333, 34

Harrington 19, 40, 47-49, 101

Harris,
    Bud 345
    Joseph 141
    Louis Lincoln ix, 247
    Martha J. 154
    Paul 155

Harrold, Florence 373

Hartman, Rev. Charles S. ix, 307, 392

Harbinger 320

Harvey, Bill 373

Hastings, Rev. Aubrey ix, 271

Helman, Marty 374[*]

Herrinden, Hezekiah 48, 52-53

Hilscher, Bob 374-375, 378, 380

Hilton, Sarah 131

Hitler, Adolf 250, 252, 255

Hocking, William E. 224

Hodgdon,
> Archer W. 242, 268
> Stephen G. 141
> Thomas 141
> Norman Jr. 267

Hodgdon Yachts 329, 365

Hodgkins, Ezekiel 173

Hoffman,
> Russell 359, 394

Hofstra University 359

Hogg, Robert 52

Holmes, Andrew 321, 330, 345, 353

Holmes, Louise 348

Holton,
> Mary 154, 161
> Willard 154-155
> William 154, 161

homosexual 129

Hooper, Henry Northey 153

hospitality 179, 384

Huff, Fred 187

Hull, George H. ix, 209, 212-214

Hull House 225

Hussy, Norris 187

Hyde, Frank B. 209-210

Hymns of Truth and Light 370, 392

New Century Hymnal 370

Pilgrim Hymnal 370

ice 6, 141, 147, 178, 344, 364, 376

incorporation 34, 61, 106-107, 247

Independent Messenger 133

Ingraham, John 101

Ireland 5, 14-18, 25-27, 33-37, 39-42, 52, 64, 76, 92, 145, 369, 389

Irish immigrants 226

ISIS 357

Isle of Springs 178

James, William ix, 16, 57, 193, 279, 282

Jameson, Daniel 342

Jazz Sunday 370

Jefferson 5, 9, 23-24, 80-81, 111-112, 114, 119, 135, 211, 340

Jefferson, President Thomas 112

Jerubaal 84

Johnson,
> Bruce 387
> Enid 375
> Hildy 338, 345

Johnson, President Lyndon Baines 297

Jones, William 76

Jung, Carl 307

Junior Guild 222, 235

Kashmir 356

Katrina 356

Kierkegaard, Soren 10, 176

Kellogg, Elijah viii, 68

Kendrick,
    Albert 188
    Charles 173, 188
    Daniel 132

Kennebec Company 19

Kennedy,
    James 53, 122
    Phoebe 53, 122

Kenniston,
    Antoinette 182, 188
    David 96-97, 106
    Eliza 182
    George, Judge 182
    William 75

Kidd, Robert 332-333, 353

Kincaid, Earl 334

King, Martin Luther 287, 299

Kirschbaum, William ix, 241

Knight,
    Charles 154
    Mary Ann 154
    Nathaniel 113
    Nicholas 30, 45, 101, 105, 391

Knobloch, Jamie 372, 375

Knox, John 9, 20-22, 33, 321

Klan, Ku Klux 191, 226

Landemare, Maurice 363, 374, 387

Lanham Emergency Housing Act 266

Leavitt,
    William viii, 152, 163, 169-170
    Fredrick 216

legal 37, 44, 82, 120, 131, 135, 153, 163, 198, 240, 316

Leishman,
    Deacon John 90, 94
    Jane 93
    John 29, 90, 92, 94, 99, 102

Lewis, Grace 270

libertarian 13-15

liberty 14, 49, 52, 66, 72, 80, 82-84, 88, 100, 140, 147, 170, 175, 212, 236, 265, 286, 315

lighting 200, 244

Lincoln Arts 370, 372

Lincoln Association 91, 134, 140, 159, 162, 182, 187, 259, 271, 362

Lincoln County Ministerial Association 246

Linekin,
    Clark 73
    Joseph 73

Lenhart, James 8, 286, 291, 319-320

Lewis,
    Giles 182
    Sinclair 194, 232
    Susan Wells 182

Liquor 11, 50, 93, 97, 103-104, 378

lobster 29, 87, 101, 266, 283-284, 288-289, 295-296, 303

Logan, Alex 375, 381

Long Range Planning 379-380

Love,
    James 157
    John, Jr. 154
    Susan 154, 157

Ludemann, Linda 375

Luther, Martin 20, 287, 299, 321

Maddocks, Millicent 241, 247, 258

Maine tourism 250

Maine Conference of Congregational Churches 161-162

Manning, Rev. Edward ix, 286

Marden, Eric 375, 378

Markon Club for boys 244

Marty, Martin E. 299

Massachusetts 3, 7, 18-19, 22-24, 26, 28, 33-34, 39-40, 43-44, 58, 60-61, 63-64, 67, 69, 74, 81, 85, 88-89, 92, 103, 106-108, 112, 114, 118, 120, 123, 128-129, 133, 135, 137-138, 151, 157, 160, 164, 171-172, 181, 220, 233, 276, 280, 283, 295, 302, 317, 320, 343, 391, 394

Master Facility Plan 379

Mather, Cotton 17

McClintock, John 103, 114, 155

McCobb,
    Abial 166, 187-188
    Charles 4, 164-166, 392
    Charles S. 164-166
    James 56-57, 183
    Jane 94, 154
    John 57, 92, 94, 98-99, 102, 113, 118
    Leonard 174, 183
    Mary 92-93
    Paul 154
    Rachel 92, 94
    Samuel 29, 56, 165, 359
    Squire William 104
    William 48, 73, 90-92, 98-99, 102-104, 112-113, 117, 183

McCormick,
    Austin 203-204, 229
    Donald ix, 203, 209

McCormick Associates 336

McEvoy, George 316, 335-336

McEvoy, Dorothy 313

McFarland,
    Andrew 34, 37-38, 57, 98, 372
    Ephraim 45
    John 29, 58, 117, 372
    John Murray 58, 117, 372

James 29
Margery S. 154

McKown, Stella 270

Meals on Wheels 313, 315, 318, 321

medicine 50, 149, 166, 177, 227, 359

Merger (of Congregational and Evangelical & Reformed churches) 9, 16, 18, 22, 130, 147, 171, 177, 180, 182, 194, 224-226, 228, 245, 249, 255-256, 273, 280, 299, 304, 358

Merrill, Henry viii, 139

Merry, Newell 174

Memorial Day 153, 180, 231, 236, 252, 286, 391

Menwarment Hotel Orchestra 213

Methodist Church, Boothbay Harbor 5-6, 220, 268, 271-272, 275, 281-283, 294, 300-301, 305, 311, 317, 319-320, 339

Middlebury 150

Miller, William 29

Minister of Music 368-369

Mirabile, Emily 376

mission,
home mission 151, 156, 160, 323
missionary 94, 125-126, 140, 143, 158-161, 177, 195-196, 202-203, 224, 228, 291, 315, 321, 341

American Board of Missions 137

American Missionary Association 158

American Missionary Society 125, 143

Mitchell, Daniel 26

moderator 45, 50, 52, 57, 76, 90, 124, 132, 186, 188, 216, 379

Modernism 9-10, 207, 245, 274

Monhegan 115, 154, 199, 309

Montieth, Rev. Charles 316

Montgomery,
Jane 94
Robert 73, 119
Sarah 73, 119

Moody, Dwight 176, 195

Moore, William 30, 45, 55

Moore, Willis 219

Moravian College 305

Mundy, Jackie 358, 362, 373, 378, 382, 384, 393

Mundy, Peter 332, 353, 363, 367

Murray, John viii, 3-5, 8, 21, 27-30, 33-38, 40-43, 45-47, 49-50, 55-61, 63-68, 71-72, 80-88, 90, 95, 98, 105, 108-109, 117, 124, 128-129, 150, 246, 310, 321, 346, 355, 359, 364, 367, 372, 388-389, 391

Murray, Robert 42, 45-47, 54-55

Murray, Susannah 82

Music 125, 145, 176, 181, 186-188, 196, 202, 213, 218, 221-222, 228, 257-258, 269, 279, 321, 330, 334, 359, 366-370, 372, 375-376, 380, 382

Muskie, Senator Edmund 312

National Education Week 256

Navy 162-163, 269, 284, 290, 320, 388

Nazism 10

Nehemiah 45, 82

Neo-Orthodox 226, 254

Newburyport 23, 28, 30, 33, 39, 41, 43, 59, 61, 63-68, 80, 82-84, 86, 128-129, 133, 394

Newcastle 24, 26-27, 49, 92, 113, 140, 162, 307, 391

Newbegin,
    David 154
    Mary 154

Niebuhr, Reinhold 10, 254-255, 259, 274, 280, 321

Nietzsche, Frederich 176

Nixon, President Richard M. 311

Northern Ireland 5, 14-15, 17, 25-27, 33, 36, 39-40, 42, 64, 76, 92, 389

Obama, Barack 357

Oberlin Declaration 176

Ocean Point 178-179, 266, 285, 342, 347

O'Connell, Eugenie 368-369, 372

Onanism 131-132

Open and Affirming 383, 385

Orchard, Jen 375

Oregon Trail 125

Ostermann, Bill 373

Ottoman 177

Panagore, Rev. Peter 353, 392

Pacifism 192, 206, 208, 254

Pageant of Pilgrims 231

parsonage 28-31, 68, 90-91, 94-95, 99, 101, 181, 185-187, 200, 203, 222, 232, 236-237, 241-242, 246, 261-262, 289, 295-296, 302-303, 310, 316-318, 331-334, 336-338, 342-343, 346-349

Parkhurst, Caroline 319

Parkhurst, David 306

Peale, Norman Vincent 275

Perkins, Rev. Jack 340

Perkins,
    James Blenn, Sr. 243, 270, 279, 372
    Henry 241, 372

Pettingill, Arthur G. viii, 209

pew(s) 165

INDEX 467

Phillips Academy 123, 137

Pierce Marine 303

Pierce, Elizabeth 50, 122

piety 23, 41, 85, 128, 165, 216

Pinkham,
    Benjamin E. 187
    Judy 313, 316
    Peggy 362, 363, 374, 375, 378
    Mary J. 154
    Nathaniel, Jr. 154

Pinneo, Annie E. 202

pipe organ 180, 188-189, 199, 231

Pisgah 29-31, 49, 81-82, 90, 95

Plan of Union 150

Plummer, Ambrose 167

Poe, Franklin 339, 351

polity 9-10, 177, 231, 281

Pope 176
    Pope Francis 358

Porter, L.D. 242

Post, Stanley ix, 209, 215-217, 219

Postmodern Era 355

poverty 67, 111, 126, 176, 225, 297-298, 322, 332

Pownalborough 40, 44, 47, 49, 66, 71, 75, 79, 140

Predestination 20, 23, 106, 178

Prall, Irena 349, 351

Presbytery of Northern New England 360

Mid-Coast Presbyterian Church 359

Princeton 15, 37, 69, 219, 233, 236, 299, 359, 369, 388
    Princeton Theological Seminary 359, 388

Progressive movement 194

Protestant Establishment 299

Puritan(s) 13

Pythian Opera House 213

Quimby, Llewellyn 75

Ramsey, Debra 374

Rand, Benjamin 270, 272, 278-279

Rand, Mabel 247, 260, 270

Rauschenbusch, Walter 9, 196, 225

Reagan, President Ronald 298

Reawakening 40-42, 47, 58, 61

Rebellion, The 108, 163, 172, 274

Rebuilding Together 382

Recession, Great 357

Reed,
    Andrew 34, 37-38, 42, 57-58, 81, 98-99, 117, 188, 372
    Elizabeth 14, 44, 61, 70-71, 77, 87, 96, 101, 105, 148,

468   LIVELY STONES

152, 154, 162, 164, 186, 188, 279
George   116, 141, 154-155, 159
Isaac   155
Jane   48, 52, 122
Margery   98-99, 117
Martha   50, 122, 154
Paul   60, 78, 98, 117
Paul Captain   60, 98
Samuel Miller   154
Sarah   33, 81, 101, 117, 154
Reed, Walter S.   345

Reformation,   9, 20, 54, 85, 105, 121, 321, 372
    Scottish Reformation   9, 20

Regiment
    Maine
        5th   173
        6th   173
        28th   174
    Massachusetts
        38th   164

Reichert, Courtney   359

renovation   378-382

Repa, Ted   367, 377, 380, 382

Revival
    Revivalism   7, 9, 22, 89, 106, 110, 117, 126, 134-135, 146, 161
    Revivalist   3, 6, 22-23, 40, 61, 109-110, 126, 137, 140

Revolution   7-9, 23, 45, 58-59, 61, 65-66, 69, 72, 80-83, 85, 96, 108-109, 114, 118-119, 125, 135, 145, 196, 226, 257, 304, 356, 388

resignation   156, 186, 238, 241, 246, 269, 284, 286, 295, 304, 306, 311, 339, 342, 352
    resigned   160, 183, 187-188, 245, 257, 298, 304, 358

Revere, Paul   153

Ribble, Guy   373

Rice, Otis   174

Richards, Keyes   183

Rittall, Joan   375

Roads End Parsonage   310, 343

Rockland Breakwater Shelters for teens   376

Rockefeller, John D.   198

Rogers   19, 288

Root, Elihu   208

Rowe, Alberta Poole   191, 227

Ross, Ron   375, 381

rum   9, 90, 113

Rumsey, Barbara   40, 81, 126, 166, 394

Russian Revolution   226

Rutherford Island   25

Rutherford, Robert   25

Sabbath School   147, 182, 202, 211

Safe Church Policy   378

INDEX 469

Safe Passage 76, 373, 376-377, 382

Sample, Leah 300, 308, 313, 363, 393

Sample's Shipyard 6, 8, 10, 265-266, 282, 285, 287

St. Andrews Village 382

Salvation Army 176, 220, 299-300

Sawyer, John viii, 3, 90-91, 94, 103

Sargent,
    Caroline F. 154
    Charles 154-155, 158, 164
    Eliza 154
    Mary 100
    Stephen 154, 164
    Weld 164-165, 180

Sawyer, John viii, 3, 90-91, 94, 103

Scagliotti Associates 333

Schleiermacher, Friederich 176, 225

Scopes trial 240-241

Scotland 7, 14-15, 20-22, 27, 33, 233, 358

Scots-Irish 3, 5, 7, 9, 13-20, 22, 25, 28, 33, 40-41, 59-60, 68-70, 72-75, 80, 83, 88, 90-92, 106, 108, 119, 165-166, 235, 359

school
    public 136, 152, 186, 257
    school board 152, 155, 274, 293, 312

sea, lost at 148, 150, 157, 161, 180

secession 112, 163

Seguin 115

Second Congregational viii-ix, 4, 128, 137, 150, 152, 179, 181-184, 269, 279, 323

Sermons 67, 72, 76, 78, 95, 121, 134, 142-143, 148, 207, 211, 215-216, 219, 225, 228, 235-237, 241, 244, 249, 251, 255, 259-260, 286, 289, 291, 300, 306, 309, 321, 343-345, 353, 366-367, 381

Sessional Records 44-45, 47, 49, 53, 122

Session House 30, 45-47, 54-55, 82, 149, 391

Sessions, Joseph Washburn viii, 137

seventh commandment 105-106

Sheepscot 19, 26-27, 40, 49, 78, 87, 140, 391

Shepard, Barclay 177, 363, 374-375, 387

Shepard, Robert 177, 341

Sherman, Charles E. 204-205, 246

ship
    clipper 142
    schooner 73, 113
    ships 27, 66, 76, 115, 142, 196, 204, 266, 283

470 LIVELY STONES

shipbuilding 5-6, 10, 117, 126, 147, 168, 178, 223, 231, 266, 268, 273, 275-276, 282-285, 287-289, 327, 365
shipyard 4, 155, 164, 266, 268, 271, 276-277, 290

Singer, Faithful 49

slavery 4, 83, 111, 119, 126, 134-135, 140-141, 143, 146-148, 161-162, 170, 174
    slave 89, 114, 125, 236
    anti-slavery 5, 9-10, 89, 143

Smith,
    Earle 373
    Stevens 141

Smuggling 112-113

Social Gospel 9-10, 196, 207, 225-226, 357

social justice 13, 225, 301

social networking 357

soldiers 163, 165, 168, 207, 241, 257, 297, 303, 386

Sommers, Dr. Otto 342

South Congregational 6, 126, 320

Spanish influenza 227

Speer, Robert E. 224, 228

Spencer, Frank 268

Sproul,
    Robert 174

Spurgeon, Charles 176

Squirrel Island 173, 178-179, 205, 285

stewardship 179, 260, 361, 380, 382

Stinson, Rev. Joseph David ix, 128, 319

Stover, Holly 374, 385

Stowe, Harriet Beecher 109, 148, 161

Sunday, Billy 10

Sunday School 110, 147, 182, 190, 211, 214, 218, 229, 232, 241, 245, 249, 262-263, 269, 271-272, 278, 286, 288, 291, 296, 314, 320-321, 330-332, 336-337, 339, 353, 360, 373, 375-376, 378

Southern District Convention of Lincoln County Sunday Schools 218

Svendson, Rev. Charles 340

Talmadge, Frank Dewitt 210

Taylor, Harold 333, 335-336, 339, 353

temperance 9, 97, 130, 140, 146-147, 171, 180, 216
    anti-temperance 180

Tennent, Gilbert 36

Tennent, William 37

theology 9, 20, 23, 27, 70, 108, 136, 146, 158, 176, 196, 206, 225-226, 237, 240, 253-255, 263,

274-275, 279, 300, 310, 318-320, 355, 357, 359
    Liberation Theology 226

Thompson, Alice 338, 393

Thorp, Lewis 96

Tillich, Paul 10, 253-255

Tibbetts,
    Benjamin 80
    Deanne 372, 375-376

Tobey, William viii, 141-142

Topsham 24, 49, 359, 364

tourism vii, 6, 10, 147, 175, 178-180, 223, 250, 266, 275-276, 283, 285, 287-290, 312, 327, 337, 342, 366

Townsend 5, 9, 18-20, 23, 25-29, 33-34, 39-40, 42-43, 45, 58-59, 73, 77, 90, 92, 107, 113, 115, 128, 148, 152, 174, 204, 221, 262, 328, 333, 364, 378, 381

Turkey 177, 202, 234, 291, 315, 341

Turner, Nat 125

Union 17, 49, 110, 112, 119, 140, 142, 148, 150-151, 153, 157, 162-163, 166-167, 171, 180, 183, 201, 205-206, 211, 214, 219, 233-234, 236, 243, 245, 248-249, 255, 259, 272-273, 280, 286, 291, 326

Union Theological Seminary 206, 233, 255

U.S. Christian Commission 157, 162

Vacation Bible School 244, 249, 374

Vacationland 6, 249, 286, 312, 328, 366

Van Siclen, Phyllis 385

Veterans 7, 174, 179-180, 190, 267, 276, 376, 387

violence 14, 143, 194, 326, 387

Volstead Act 226

Voluntarism 9, 135-136

Walbridge, Robert 291, 322

Wales 7, 182, 187

Waldoboro 48-49, 162, 173

Walpole 19, 40, 47-49, 136

war(s) 4, 89, 112, 118, 193, 206-207, 220, 271, 276, 297
    Iraq 326, 356
    post-war 10, 266, 272-275, 282, 295-296, 299
    Korean Conflict 10
    Mexican War 236
    Vietnam 287, 290, 297-298, 311, 322-323, 387
    War of 1812 9, 89, 112-114, 116-117
    World War I 6, 10, 114, 192, 196, 204-206, 226, 228, 230, 278
    World War II 6, 8, 10, 265-266, 269, 274, 276-277, 280, 282, 285-287, 295-296, 327

Weaver, John 370

Weld,
    Charles E. 157
    Luther 154-155, 157

Welty, Rev. Ivan ix, 289, 292

Westminster Choir College 369

Westminster Confession of Faith 21, 42, 86

Weston, Isaac viii, 67, 91, 95, 97, 135, 172

Weymouth,
    Elizabeth Fullerton 154
    James R. 157
    John W. 153-155, 159

White, Moses 174, 183, 185, 188

Whitefield 23-24, 26, 40, 49, 80-81, 86-87

Whitefield, George 23, 26, 40, 81

Whittier,
    Dick 378, 387
    Jeanne 378

Wiley,
    Elizabeth 101
    Mary 99

Windjammer Days 329

Winnegance 19

Wiscasset
    Wiscasset Congregational Church 234, 259
    Wiscasset Citizen, The 129, 391

Williams 68, 126, 164

Wilson,
    Mary J. 154
    Parker 154-155
    Woodrow 194

Winslow, William J. 185, 187

women('s) 9, 119-121, 123, 146-148, 174, 187, 221-222, 230, 271, 318, 386
    Guild 221-222, 230, 235, 241, 261-262, 269-270, 279-280, 291
    Women's Fellowship 386
    Women's Rights 9, 146

Woodruff 180, 214

Woodward, George H. ix, 235, 237

Wright, Frank Lloyd 194

Wylie, Sewall 141

Yale 136, 237, 240, 299, 310, 320-321, 343, 345

Yarmouth 67, 181

Yetman, Pat 384

Young, Brigham 141

APPENDIX A

Modern Era: Late nineteenth to early twentieth century to about the 1950s in some fields, longer in theology:	Postmodern Era: 1950s in some fields (1990s to the present in theology):
• Exclusivist absolutism or debilitating relativisms, sometimes leading to nihilism • Eurocentric • Elitist, heavily pitched to academic communities • Colonizing, as with early foreign missions • Otherness of God (often far removed) patriarchal orientation • Dualisms of God and world, spirit and matter, human and natural, soul and body, leading to greater rigidity in social issues, such as homophobia.	• Openness to the values in other traditions, to inter-religious dialogue, and to positive reconstruction • More globalcentric • Grassroots theology as in liberation theology in Latin American-based communities • Focused on building up the human community, the natural world, and appreciation of other cultures • Immanence of God—God even suffers with us • Inclusive orientation, learning from the feminist movement • Moving toward a new wholeness enabling dialogues about science and religion, greater care for the natural world, sexuality as a gift from God to be used in the service of God and neighbor.

JOHN F. BAUMAN, Ph.D., is professor emeritus of California University of Pennsylvania and a visiting research professor at the University of Southern Maine. He is past president of the Pennsylvania Historical Association and of the Society for City and Regional Planning History, and a member of the board of trustees of the Retirement Housing Foundation. He has authored numerous scholarly articles and co-authored seven books, including, most recently, *Gateway to Vacationland: The Making of Portland, Maine* (2012).

ROBERT W. DENT is a graduate of both Princeton and McCormick theological seminaries. Ordained in 1966 by the Presbytery of New Brunswick, NJ, he served churches in McConnellsburg and Chambersburg, Pennsylvania, and in the First Presbyterian Church of Monroe, New York, of which he is now pastor emeritus. While in Chambersburg he was also part-time chaplain at Wilson College. Married to Judy Pollock in 1964, they have two children, Douglas and Janice. Rev. Dent and Judy love living in Maine in their retirement.

The Reverend Dr. SARAH M. FOULGER is a minister in the United Church of Christ. She was ordained by the Presbyterian Church (USA) in 1979 and has served congregations in Delaware, Virginia, and Maine. Sarah is the author of three works of fiction: *Yards of Purple*, *No Revenge So Complete*, and *O'er All the Weary World*, but prefers reading nonfiction, especially theology, mysticism, and history. Sarah and her husband, Russ, live in Boothbay Harbor, have two grown sons, and are enjoying being grandparents. In the summer, she wishes she had more time for kayaking; in the winter, more time for snow-shoeing and cross-country skiing.

CHIP GRIFFIN grew up in Boothbay Harbor, where he developed a zest for history from his seventh grade teacher, Terry Leighton, and majored in history at college. For the past thirty-five years an attorney with offices in Boothbay Harbor, Chip has authored two local history books, *Coming of Age on Damariscove Island, Maine* (1980) and a biography of Ethelyn Giles, *I'm Different* (2002), and has researched and written many articles on place-based history and its relevance today.

Editor DOREEN C. DUN is a former grants administrator and writing consultant at the Ford Foundation in New York.